Spider in a Tree

Spider in a Tree

a novel

Susan Stinson

Small Beer Press
Easthampton, MA

An earlier version of Chapter 4 appeared as "Spider and Fly" in the Volume 9, Number 1, Winter 2011
issue of *Early American Studies: An Interdisciplinary Journal*.

Thanks to *The Common Magazine*, *Necessary Fiction*, and *Frequencies: a collaborative genealogy of spirituality*,
where excerpts from the novel have also appeared.

Small Beer Press
150 Pleasant Street #306
Easthampton, MA 01027
www.smallbeerpress.com
www.weightlessbooks.com
info@smallbeerpress.com

Distributed to the trade by Consortium.

Library of Congress Cataloging-in-Publication Data

Stinson, Susan, 1960-
  Spider in a Tree : a novel / Susan Stinson.
      pages cm
Summary: "In his famous sermon "Sinners in the Hands of an Angry God," Jonathan Edwards compared a person dangling a spider over a hearth to God holding a sinner over the fires of hell. Here,
spiders and insects preach back. No voice drowns out all others: Leah, a young West African woman
enslaved in the Edwards household; Edwards's young cousins Joseph and Elisha, whose father kills
himself in fear for his soul; and Sarah, Edwards' wife, who is visited by ecstasy. Ordinary grace, human failings, and extraordinary convictions combine in unexpected ways to animate this New England
tale"-- Provided by publisher.
  ISBN 978-1-61873-069-5 (pbk.) -- ISBN 978-1-61873-070-1 (ebook)
  1. Edwards, Jonathan, 1703-1758--Fiction. 2. Preachers--Fiction. 3. Massachusetts--History--Co-
lonial period, ca. 1600-1775--Fiction. 4. Northampton (Mass.)--History--Fiction. 5. Biographical
fiction. 6. Historical fiction. I. Title.
  PS3569.T535S75 2013
  813'.54--dc23
                              2013028893

First edition   1 2 3 4 5 6 7 8 9

Text set in Centaur.
Printed on 50# Natures Natural 30% PCR Recycled Paper by the Maple Press in York, Pennsylvania.
Cover illustration © 2013 by Elisabeth Alba (albaillustration.com).

To Sally Bellerose—who was alarmed when I started this book and immersed in the sublime when I was first ready to send it out—in honor of twenty years of love, work, and company as writers.

To Lynne Gerber for deep work, strong love, gorgeous willingness, and witness.

So deep were their prejudices, that their heat was maintained; nothing would quiet 'em till they could see the town clear of root and branch, name and remnant.

Jonathan Edwards to Joseph Hawley
November 18, 1754, Stockbridge, Massachusetts

Prologue

In Northampton, where, long after his time, daughter Mary would
worship on a chair outside the sanctuary so she wouldn't have to
join the congregation (she took a boat across the river to Hadley
for communion), they say that the Reverend Mr. Edwards wrote his
sermons in a tree. He would climb the big elm in front of his house by
boards nailed to the trunk and dangle his long, skinny legs off a limb.

People peered up at him through leaves that sifted light, which, he
had taught them, was akin to sifting God. Even in the tree, he was aloof
and somber, but passersby craned their necks to enjoy the spectacle of
him in his Geneva collar and second-best wig, writing furiously against
a smooth place worn clean of bark. His inkpot was wedged in a knot,
and when his elbow jostled branches, great arches of leaves shook.

Jonathan Edwards ate from pewter plates, not wooden trenchers,
which did not go unnoticed in the town. He was useless with an auger,
and his wife was better than he was on one end of a two-man saw,
but most people who passed by the house on King Street had felt his
sermons hammering at their souls. A yeoman like Mr. Root, driving by
in his wagon, might think of a pumpkin gone soft on the ground after
a frost and imagine reaching through the wet skin for a fistful of seedy
pulp to fling at his minister (perched so oddly and conspicuously on the
limb) as at a criminal in the pillory. He might have the thought, but he
would know it to be Satan whispering in his ear. He would tip his hat
and drive on. Others, more docile or reverent, would stop and reach up
to give Mr. Edwards plums, cups of chocolate, and prayer bids written

on scraps for him to read aloud from the pulpit. He would lower a bucket on a rope to receive the gifts, but came down for those in need of counsel. They would retire to his study, another place where he wrote long days and into the night.

One breezy day, he was working in the tree, writing in a booklet made from scrap paper. He was only half conscious of reading fragments of old prayer bids on the backs as he turned the pages.

> *Thos Wells and his Wife Desire Thanks may be given to God In the Congregation for his Goodness to her in Childbed in making her the Living Mother of a Living Child.*

As he dipped his quill into the inkpot, a red ant reached the knee buckle of one leg of his breeches. Mr. Edwards brushed it away.

> *The widow Southwill Being Sik of a Feavour desires the Prayers of the Congregation.*

A translucent yellow spider with light brown stripes rushed up the broadcloth of Mr. Edwards's shirt as if he were a peak to be conquered. As it neared his collar, he took up his pages and knocked it away.

The spider landed on the ground, where it balled up and became almost invisible, a tuft of earth in the grass. After a time, it climbed the underside of one blade to the very tip and froze there, vibrating in the faint breeze. Mr. Edwards was looking in the other direction, upwards, as verses from Genesis rose in his mind. Suddenly, the spider lifted its abdomen and spun off to come toward him again, crossing a scraped root to begin to climb the tree.

> *Mr. Lyman and his wife desire Prayers for their negro tht is dangriusly sick.*

It moved very quickly over the lichen-covered bark to a mossy cleft strung with strands of web, flecks of seed pods, and small wings. It stopped on a tiny shelf of bark, went flat, then headed farther up into the folds, crevasses, and smooth places where the tree had been skinned by fire.

The spider skimmed higher, passing the preacher without attracting his notice. It jumped and crossed a gap of sky left by broken limbs, leaving a thread behind it. Still looking up, Mr. Edwards witnessed a darting and tugging in the air.

Samu Wright & his wife Desire the prayers of this Congregation that god wood sanktifie his Holy & aflicting hand To them in Taking a way of thire Son Samu Wright by Death Thay Desir prayers that god wood fit and prepare them for thire grate and last Change.

Mr. Edwards looked down at the blank side of the next page and began filling it again, unhearing and intent on his struggle to bring shadows into language while the spider preached a silent sermon from the web in the tree:

Whatever your God would say of me, I am not damned. I did not turn to salt. Maybe that's because you never looked back to crack me into tiny crystals like Lot's wife. It's all dissolving in water, salt water, the blue part of the world's eye, the planet looking back at God, who blinks.

You need me more than you've ever admitted. I'm still with you. I didn't perish. I didn't burn, although God dangled me over the fiery pit as you knew he would. He dangled me over the fire, but you observed spiders carefully, once. Didn't you know that I would sail out of his hand as if taking great pleasure in the motion of my escape, spinning out trails behind me lighter than air might be? I am a hunter, and I ate as I went. God was disappointed, of course, but he wasn't the least bit surprised.

No birds or bats ate me, no toads, frogs, no reptiles of any kind, no tree limbs cracked and smashed me, no near stone fell. You were right: at the end of my life I was swept on an insistent, crowded current of air with all of the other insects to the sky above the sea. We came disguised in clouds, and we fell, I fell. You were right about all that, too. I fell into the water; light, brittle bodies dimpled the surfaces of waves all around me. I was washed over, lost my breath and disintegrated, but I didn't die. God wasn't chasing me; he was busy burning sticks, watching the tips heat and color, wondering how long he dared to let the flame go before he ground it out in his box of sand. I entered the deeps as something very heavy and very small. I sank without reason, I sank with abandon, I went down, losing everything but motion, gravity, density— my ability, still, to fall. I had no legs by then, no chance of swimming, no dream of correcting the course, no course at all. I was low, far under the roots and depths of everything I knew. Lost to God, although, of course, he could have found me if he hadn't been still playing in the fire, tilting dripping candles over his hand to see if it would burn. I was falling, and he was waving his fingers in the air to cool, slipping perfect wax impressions from the tips.

What happened then was that I tried to take a breath. No lungs. I landed.

I fell, but I didn't burn.

Slowly, Mr. Edwards became aware of a sound like many fingers rubbing together. He looked up at the rustling dome of leaves and saw meaning in it. Wind was a shadow of spirit. The world was as full of images of divine things as a language was full of words, but he found spiders hard to read. They were sagacious and hard-working, taking flights on glistening strings, but would devour each other like devils after the day of judgment if they were trapped and shut up without any flies.

He took a note on the shape of the web. A dense scattering of gnats rose around him like spray from the great rippling waves of branches.

Chapter I
June 1731
Newport to Northampton

The girl saw a tall, gaunt man look up from a slice of raisin pie (she had baked it, perfecting her hand with cold water crust) when she walked into Captain Perkins's parlor with Phyllis close behind her. She could see that he was the one doing the buying. Phyllis put a hand on the small of her back to position her near the table where the men sat. The girl stared at the oozing, dark-flecked pie from which the buyer had spooned a tiny bite.

"Mr. Edwards, this is Venus." Captain Perkins spoke smoothly. "I kept her as the pick of the lot when I unloaded most of the cargo in the Caribbean on my last voyage. I got a shipment of very good allspice, as well."

"Impressive," murmured someone.

The girl held her hands clasped and her back straight, but her legs were trembling. Phyllis kept a hand on her back. She had said that there would be others in the room, come to witness the sale over pie and rum punch. The girl barely took them in.

She raised her eyes and found Mr. Edwards looking at her face. She felt locked out of her own mind, both numbed and spinning, but she held his gaze. This was improper, but he kept looking himself, steadily, into her eyes. He was, perhaps, twice as old as she was, so still young. He had on a black coat with a beaver hat resting on his knee. She could see that he was a stranger, and his collar marked him as a preacher. Whatever else he might be, as a person to exchange glances with, he was uncommonly intense.

Captain Perkins spoke up from his chair. "She's a dutiful girl. And she's already had the small pox."

Phyllis made a tiny sound, using breath as speech, so the girl dropped her eyes. A servant in this house, herself a slave, Phyllis was the one who had braided her hair beneath her headscarf, an act which had left the girl shaking with grief because the touch was so different from her mother's. She was grateful to Phyllis, who had been kind in teaching her better English and all the proprieties in the months since Captain Perkins had led her away from the holding pens at the docks with her hands tied in front of her.

The captain had put the girl up for auction at the Granary near the docks soon after his ship had arrived home in Newport. She had stood stock still, as had been clear that she must, for an old farmer, but had made a serious break in deportment by grimacing with her jaw clenched when he tried to pry open her mouth. The auction master had lashed her ankles with his quirt, hard enough to burn but not mark. She had stilled everything in her and opened her mouth so the old man could examine her teeth. He had leaned close, with his smell of sweat and tobacco, running his finger around her teeth. She could do nothing but swallow her gagging. She had felt her true self leave to hide in a clean, prickly heap of palm leaves waiting to be sliced and split into strings of raffia behind her mother's house. The moment sometimes came back to her later, his sour finger pulling slickly under her tongue the way she'd seen Saul open the mouth of a new horse to check its age by its teeth. Not every time it rose in her, but often, even after she was awakened, she would imagine giving a bite that took that old man's finger off. As she thought of this, leaning over the wash pot or kneading bread, she would wonder whether she actually did have the strength to bite clean through bone, and how quickly she could turn her head to spit the raw stub out of her mouth, or if she might have to swallow his blood, and what they might cut from her as punishment afterwards. In the story of the finger as she told it to herself, the focus was the crack and pull of that one hard, fierce bite.

But she had not done it. The old man had pulled his hand out, wiped it on a kerchief stiff with stains that he stuffed back into his waistcoat before he said, "No."

That had been the first attempt at selling her. Phyllis had told the girl that Captain Perkins had gotten only offers far below his asking price of eighty pounds. This meant nothing but ugliness to her, but Phyllis had said, "It is useful, at times, to know your price."

The girl had done well in the months of her training. Phyllis had been through it with many others before. The girl no longer jumped every time she heard hooves and carriage wheels pass on the stone street. She didn't even blink at the sight of a cast iron pot. She knew how to dress a turtle or a calf's head for the table, knew that meat pies required a hotter oven than fruit, and bruised the crookneck squash well when she made a pudding. She knew how to brew spruce beer, which the captain swore by against scurvy, and she could manage to smooth shirts and aprons with the box irons without being a danger with their coals. Her mind strained meaning from the things said to her, and she spoke English that could be easily understood. There was a ferment of loss and confusion working in her, but there was nothing to do but let it stand, for all that she was blood, memory, spirit, and skin, not a cask full of watery hops and molasses.

Now, as Captain Perkins listed her skills to Mr. Edwards, she tried to empty herself. She thought of the story from home of the spider who tied the lion to a tree with its own hair. That story had made her laugh and roll her eyes when her father told it to her. It hurt, coming back at this moment. Her dry mouth suddenly filled with spit. She swallowed, waited.

Mr. Edwards stood up to look at her more closely. She thought she saw a break in his certainty, some sense of discomfort, a blankness. He reached and picked a bit of dough out of her hair. She could do nothing. A window in the parlor was open, and a fly had begun circling the piece of pie on his plate. He stepped back from her and waved his hand at the fly.

Captain Perkins said, "She's from the Grain Coast, you know. Best slaves there are. I could take her down to Sullivan's Island and get 100 pounds for her on the spot."

One of his friends lit a pipe covered with scrimshaw. She knew that kind of carving from the sailors on the slave ship, but the conversation was gibberish. "No doubt about it. I'd take her to Charleston myself if I weren't distracted by marauding Papists."

The men laughed, except Mr. Edwards, who addressed her. "Do you know your catechism? What must you do?"

She didn't understand the first part of the question, but thought he must be talking religion. The second part was obvious. "Obey. Work hard."

Mr. Edwards nodded, but seemed to be waiting for something else. She only knew what scripture she had heard listening at the back of Trinity Church of a Sunday, but thought to offer some of that which, as had been made clear when Phyllis elbowed her ribs, she was to say aloud with all the others. "Let the people say, 'amen.'"

Phyllis became a bit more stiff behind her. Captain Perkins put down his pie. "Perhaps you know, I'm an Anglican." He spoke soothingly to Mr. Edwards. "She hasn't learned that a phrase from our prayer book might not be a proper thing to say to a Congregationalist clergyman like yourself."

Mr. Edwards nodded again, then spoke to the girl. "You must learn the catechism for Negroes. To the question I asked you, you should respond, 'I must love God, and pray to him, and keep the Lord's day. I must love all men and never quarrel nor be drunk nor be unchaste nor steal, nor tell a lie, nor be discontent with my condition.'"

Eyes down, she said, "I will be happy to learn."

The previous Saturday, Captain Perkins, red-faced and cheery from Election Day celebrations, had given Phyllis a pig to take to the balloting for the black election held under a huge tree. She killed a black chicken she had fed all winter, too. The girl, curdling with fear about the future, had been allowed to go.

"It's a mixed thing," Phyllis told her. "The town fathers make the black governor give punishments and do their dirty work. They laugh at us. But, you know, it is our day and our man. And it's a better party than they have."

The two of them had helped urge men to line up behind Quashi, who had led a procession through the woods to a clearing after he won. He was so strong, people said that he could flip a bull to the ground by the ring in its nose. They had all drunk punch, eaten cake, and roasted the pork.

Drums and fiddles had been brought out, small bells and a rattling squash that had reminded the girl of the *shegureh* her mother and aunts played at home. She had gasped at the sight of it, then started to weep, saying their names.

"Hush now, child. Hush, *do.*" Phyllis had pulled her into a ring of women to dance. Stomping her feet as if she meant to crack the dirt, she had felt her fear and grief loosen enough to let her scream and laugh when masked figures wearing costumes of torn army uniforms and swathes of gold sea grass had come leaping out of the woods.

Now Mr. Edwards said, "I'll take her."

She took a step back from him, nearly losing her balance. Phyllis put up a hand to steady her, and, leaning forward, gave a low hum that buzzed in the girl's ear.

She was still numb as she walked behind Mr. Edwards and his cartful of purchases down Griffen to Thames Street and the harbor. They didn't go to the Granary or the slave pen at Honeymoon Wharf, but she felt panicked as they boarded a small ship. Mr. Edwards looked at her standing rigid and silent, and said, "You go below and keep watch on my things." He did not say "my other things." Before he turned away, he added, "It's not far to New Haven. This is not a long voyage." Was he thinking of the slave ship? She could think of little else.

She sat below on a crate of candles, sucking a piece of hard cheese that Phyllis had slipped her. Sooner or later, the new master would arrange for her to be fed, but from the bony look of him, there was no telling when that might be.

Memories were slopping around inside her like stinking refuse from the necessary buckets in the hold of that demon slave ship. Captain Perkins had kept her up on the deck for much of the voyage, tied or under the sharp eye of the boatswain to be sure that she didn't get through the netting to throw herself over the side. She had not tried to do so, but it had been clear that the captain thought she might. He had given her the name Venus, whipped her himself when she refused to eat and spoke to her often to teach her English words. With an eye to her value and his soul, he had kept her from further abuse, but she had not been spared long stretches in the hold chained in the fetid heat with many other ill and dying people who had been, like herself, considered cargo.

She swallowed a bit of Phyllis's cheese, then raised her feet to the wooden edge of the crate when she saw rats scurrying in the passage. She wrapped the rest of the cheese in a bit of cloth and slipped it back into the pocket Phyllis had made her to wear beneath her clothes. She kept it tied around her waist with a thin, soft, plaited rope. The captain might have objected, had he known. The girl had a broken shell and a paper of pins in her pocket, along with the rag Phyllis had given her in preparation for her monthlies, which had not yet come. Phyllis had said that it was a matter of decency that a young girl—a new slave so far from her mother—not leave her tutelage without at least a pocket and a rag of her own.

The girl, who missed Phyllis already, could hear men singing a rude tavern catch about cats night-walking and yowling. She kept out of sight behind the stacks of barrels. It was dark around her, rocking and damp. Trying to drown out the drunkards, she worked silently on a song of her own about going to a river in the morning. She thought of her mother bending low to pound cassava roots in the yard. She remembered the wetness on her face as the gray river flung itself against great flat rocks in breaks of spray that hit the air with intricate, dissipating fierceness. She thought of the sound Phyllis had made in her ear at the moment of the sale. She took it as a kind of goodbye, much more than she had gotten when she had been stuffed in a sack and snatched from the yard of her mother's house. It came back to her there in the hold of the ship, a low hum that seemed to rise from inside her, or else from far away.

The next day, Mr. Edwards rode ahead of the hired cart carrying the girl and the rest of the goods he had picked up on his journey. The cart mule was slow, and the driver knit as he drove, making mittens and stockings to sell in towns he passed through. He had said nothing to the girl and only good day to Mr. Edwards, but would suddenly cry out, hawking his goods, whenever new people were in earshot. Mr. Edwards found this annoying.

He brought his horse too near the clanking wheels of the cart so that he could look at the girl closely again. In New Haven, where they had spent the night, his elegant mother-in-law had looked her up and down, then pronounced her serviceable. Now, Mr. Edwards watched for the flash of a soul in her eyes, which were the color of oak gall. Some claimed that there was no such thing as a soul in an African slave.

As the girl looked back at him, he felt some discomfort, almost as if some part of his agile mind were deprived of motion, despite the fact that he, the girl, the driver, and the animals were all jolting along the road. In the stoppered space within him, though, all solidity had ceased, and there was neither white nor black, neither blue nor brown, bright nor shaded, pellucid nor opaque; no noise or sound, neither heat nor cold, neither fluid nor wet nor dry, hard nor soft, nor figure, nor magnitude, nor proportion, nor body, nor spirit. It was a place of nothingness, for all that what he was doing was perfectly ordinary and nothingness was impossible in a world of necessary, eternal, infinite, and omnipresent being.

She looked away, to the trees along the road. The horse was skittish about the cart, so he dropped his eyes and moved on ahead, but skilled at such concourse with people in his congregation, he was sure. A soul.

He thought of the book of Job, chapter thirty-two, verse thirteen. He wanted to look it up when he got home, but believed that the point it raised was that God might justly do by a man as that man did by his own servant. If Mr. Edwards were to despise the right cause of his maidservant when she came to plead with him or stood before him to be judged, what then would he do when he came himself to stand before God and be judged? Mr. Edwards was God's servant as the girl was his, and much more inferior to God than she was to him.

He hit a boggy patch of road and attended to the horse while she chose her footing, then stopped to watch the cart come safely through. He tried to remember her name. Was it Nancy? That seemed right, but he wasn't certain. It had, he thought, been spoken, and it had also possibly been mentioned in the letter from his mother suggesting that he enquire in Newport after Captain Perkins. She had heard from a member of his father's congregation who had recently traveled there that there would be a good house servant for sale, suitable for the country and nicely younger than her prospective mistress, fresh and ready to train to her liking.

Mr. Edwards had contacted the Reverend Mr. Clap at the Congregational church in Newport. Mr. Clap had been amiable in his confirmation of the availability and suitability of the young slave, and had extended an invitation for the Northampton minister to stay with him should he travel to Newport, which Mr. Edwards had been happy to accept.

They had enjoyed each other's conversation on matters of theology the night before the purchase. Mr. Clap had described the tumult which had overtaken his church when the flock had become so stiff-necked and contentious as to split when he had refused to administer the Lord's Supper to them because they had been unable or unwilling to testify to individual encounters with grace.

Mr. Edwards, who, like his grandfather before him, did not require members of his own thriving congregation to make professions of their experiences of godliness, had been sympathetic. He had tapped his pipe against the table, and said, "Surely, Mr. Clap, you have enough trials here in a seaport full of heretic Quakers, Jews, and Arminians, without dissension in your flock."

Mr. Clap shook his head and passed the tobacco, murmuring with rueful composure, "I did manage to keep half the congregation."

The cart cleared the bog. As they rode on, Mr. Edwards tried to think about scripture that could bolster the application of a sermon he was to give in Boston, but he couldn't keep his mind on his argument. Instead, he was overtaken with memories of other times in his life spent traveling in this part of the country, on a horse borrowed from his father in East Windsor or rattling in a dusty cart between Wethersfield and New Haven. Mostly, he thought of courting his wife.

Sarah had been thirteen when she first caught his eye. Younger surely, than the slave now traveling behind him in the cart, but not by much. She had been seventeen and he twenty-three when they married. He had come to know her in New Haven when he had been an impassioned student of theology at Yale. Her father, the late Reverend Mr. James Pierpont, had been one of the ten ministers who had piled their books together on a table to found the college. Young Mr. Edwards, voracious reader that he was, had felt hidden pleasure whenever he opened a book and found Sarah's father's inscription. It was as if in turning the pages of the big old books, he had been bringing his fingers nearer to her engendering spirit, and so nearer to every part of her. He had gotten along well with her brother, too, who had been first in his class, based on sheer social status. Mr. Edwards had been the top scholar.

He had been surrounded by other young men, some of them boisterous in drinking too much hard cider and pounding on each other's doors late at night. He had worked in the buttery, tending to the meals of his classmates, bossing around his younger cousin, and avoiding the excruciating chatter at meals. His cousin had been so negligent in the task of drawing pots of cider that Mr. Edwards had wept with frustration in the cellar among the cider barrels more than once. He had resolved to enter more into conversation, but, as he was also determined not to gossip and to keep the talk as often as possible to the great, saving things of religion, he had little success. When the other students had organized a protest against their meager meals of bread and milk, Mr. Edwards, who never cared much what he ate, wrote his father to reassure him that he wasn't taking part. He was very lonely.

His solace had been losing himself in Latin with Augustine and Calvin, or loosening up in English with Caryl's exposition with practical observations on the book of Job. He had studied logic, philosophy, and the natural sciences. He had read the Bible as the source of God's words and laws, and it had submerged him in language that got into his eyes, beat down his neck like blood, and articulated muscles in his fingers to move his quill. He possessed the beauty of focused attention, which his teachers loved, but he felt alien to those less ardent about the things of religion.

One morning he had been walking in an early mist that obscured the shapes of the trees. When he came to a meadow, he gasped as the mist opened before the approach of a very young woman whose face was starkly illuminated against the shrouded air. At first, mesmerized, he had noted nothing except for damp skin, eyebrows like moth wings, and that she looked away without seeing him, singing as she walked across the field, leading a horse. The buckskin snorted against the chill, and she lifted her hand to rub its chin. The outlines of their figures had been muffled, almost ghostly, but her face was as detailed and specific as the manuscript copy in a familiar hand of a passage he loved. He read her face as a sacred text, both before and after he recognized her as young Miss Pierpont. The horse, too, had been approaching the perfection of its creaturely nature in the way it walked behind and then beside her with quick steps muted by grass.

As he stood at the edge of the woods, listening to her singing without being able to make out the words, she had seen him. She made a wry face and he stepped backwards into the trees, embarrassed to be caught gawking. She took a swig from the water skin she wore slung across her shoulder, then raised her hand to greet him. She clucked to her horse and strode toward him while he gathered himself to approach her as well.

She called out, "Good morning, Mr. Edwards. Would you like an oatcake?"

He silently revised the terms of a self-imposed fast, and said, "Yes, thank you, Miss Pierpont."

What he remembered wasn't his surprise that she had known his name, or the oatcake she had taken from her saddlebag and broken in half to share with him, or the dryness that had filled his mouth and slowed his tongue after he had eaten it, since he himself had been without water and could in no way consider presuming to ask for a sip from her skin. What he remembered was listening, transfixed, from a distance, to the wordless sweetness of her voice.

Now, four years wed, he knew things about her that he never would have thought to imagine: that she could be haughty; that she had strong preferences among other ministers; and that she kept her beauty mark in a silver box when it was not on her cheek. He loved her more than he did his own bones. Their little girls ate her oatcakes, drenched in milk, with a spoon. The thought of them made him shake the reins to hurry his horse. He was eager to be home.

When he and the girl finally arrived in Hartford, Mr. Edwards arranged to have his things loaded onto a barge. In the course of transferring the goods, he looked over his receipt for the girl. He had paid the full eighty pounds. It was more than half a year's wages, but a fine household slave was worth it. The receipt gave the girl's age as fourteen and her name as Venus. Although both classical and common, it was heathen. This, he felt, would not do. In scripture, God had much regard for the names of persons, which might signify remarkable things concerning them. Mr. Edwards resolved to give the matter of naming his servant some attention.

After the cart driver tipped his cap and went off to barter his socks and mittens for a cartful of goods for the return trip, Mr. Edwards glanced at the girl standing quietly behind him, then lifted the pillion he had retrieved from the cart and put it over the rump of his horse. He mounted, rode over to a raised pallet on the dock and said, "Get on."

He had to show her how, but, once instructed, she rode the rest of the trip behind him, her legs hanging modestly to one side of the horse as if she were his wife or one of his daughters. He could smell her: mostly sweat from the long journey, with hints of allspice and spermaceti from the ship's hold, then a tang of pomade from his own wig. He could tell that she had never been on a horse before, but she hung on.

They stopped for the night in East Windsor, where Mr. Edwards bumped foreheads with his father leaning over the Bible in the study before dinner. Both of them had great red knots on their faces at the table, which slowed their tongues not at all, until his mother bade them stop talking to eat. The sisters gave messages for Sarah about the fit of the dresses they'd been making for the little girls, slipping in a few theological opinions of their own. The whole family traipsed out into the orchard after the meal, tripping over fallen apples and observing the fireflies until time for evening prayer. Usually, they would have read after supper, but father and son had headaches, and the pleasure of the visit was too much to be contained within the house. The slaves took care of the kitchen. Two of the sisters retired to the parlor so that Mr. Edwards could sleep in his childhood bed. The girl had a blanket in the attic.

They travelled along the Connecticut River all the next day. As they rode down the slope to the ferry on the Hadley side very late in the afternoon, Mr. Edwards felt the girl lose her struggle for erectness and jostle against his back. He approved of her effort; she had not once complained of the tailbone of the horse, which he knew, himself, could be jutting and sharp, even when cushioned by a pillion. As she slumped, he was reminded of how young she was. He hadn't spoken to her for hours, but knew that she had been watching the soft lines of the mountains in the distance, her whole body behind him turned that way more than she turned to the river or to the promise of wheat, corn and flax in the stretches of open fields, still boggy from spring floods.

It was rich land, and, although he knew that the fields had first been cleared by the Nonotuck and others (some of whom, redeemed as Christians, still farmed and fished there), Mr. Edwards felt his people, his grandfather's people, had been called to this part of the valley by God. There was a dip in the mountain range that to Mr. Edwards looked like a dent where God's thumb, no, better, his presence, had pressed on the earth, was pressing still, smoothing out the ground and raising the waters. The river was dark, while the new leaves on the trees were translucent in the low sun.

The ferryman came from his gray shack, waving a small bone by way of greeting. Duck or dove, perhaps; he had been interrupted at his dinner by the sound of hooves on the road. He tossed the bone into the river, then ambled over to his barge.

The girl was upright again, on guard against a stranger. Mr. Edwards, stranger and master to her that he felt himself to be, was touched by the momentary lapse (now over) in her intense apprehension, which they had both been travelling with for these past two days. He didn't choose to be aware of this, but he was on the same horse with her, so he was. He raised his arm and pointed at the opposite shore, with its thick fringe of trees, stirring more than the surface of the water. Noxious smells, not yet warmed to summer fullness, drifted on the breeze.

"Northampton," he said. He did not turn, but felt that she did, attention pulled from the mountains and the ferryman to the far bank.

"Two pence a person," yelled the ferryman. Most would remember the fare to the place they lived, but Mr. Edwards never did. "Six pence for the horse."

They crossed on the flat barge, the ferryman pushing with his pole while his son helped pull them across by grabbing a rope tied across the river. The river was high from spring floods, and they rode low in the water. The girl held the horse. Mr. Edwards stood at the front—he could hardly think of it as prow—tilted back ever so slightly on his thin hips, enjoying, with a proprietary air, the open river after so many miles of narrow road hemmed in by trees. The water was holding color from the day's last light.

"One hand on your hat, Mr. Edwards," the ferryman called out. His own was tied on with a leather strap.

Mr. Edwards, who was not wearing his best, nodded at the man, but didn't touch his hat. As he turned back to raise his own eyes to the hills, he caught a glimpse of the girl's face. She was watching the water, after all, covertly, with an unreadable intensity that reminded him of his duty to her as his servant.

"Elwell Island," he said as they passed that heavily wooded shard of land in the middle of the river.

"Yes, sir." She spoke over the evening cicadas beginning to thrum; the splash of the pole in the river; the water rustling limbs long down, caught on a rock; the current clapping against the sand and rock of the bank.

There was always a smell of piss at the river's edge. Mr. Edwards wondered why men, if not their beasts, didn't send their streams into the river and save others the stench, but, of course, he knew it was part of a great odor from the tannery, mills, swamps, and the dung heaps in the road. The horse gave a sigh as he climbed back on, and the ferryman lifted the girl up behind him.

"Thank you," she said as he walked back to his boat.

Mr. Edwards felt a shift in her seating as the pillion she was sitting on slid halfway off the horse's rump. "Not far now," he said in his dry, sure way. Then, "You will know this as Bridge Street."

"Yes, sir," she said. She was more rigid than ever behind him.

Without turning to glance at her, he caught a question that she did not ask. "It's not the big river. Nothing but boats cross that. You will see."

They were passing a few houses with much space between them, all of them bare clapboard seasoned brown and gray. Every house lot had a low wooden fence to contain the household animals at night, although the Proprietors—the town's founders, their descendants, and those, such as Mr. Edwards, they chose to include—let their sheep and cattle graze the common meadows during the day, watched by boys who brought them home to their owners at night.

Mr. Edwards nodded vaguely toward the east and said, "The meadows are over there, bounded by a curve in the Connecticut." He started telling her the names of roads and sections of land: Young Rainbow. Old Rainbow. King's Bottom. Webbs Hollow. Bark Wigwam. Great Swamp.

The sun was setting behind the burying grounds as they passed. They were riding along the edge of the old palisades that the Proprietors had forted themselves in with when they had founded the town nearly eighty years ago, but Mr. Edwards did not see any need to mention this to the girl. There were few on the road, nothing like Newport, with its harbor bristling with ships and its markets full of goods, but the stench was growing stronger. The girl didn't speak, but he had no expectation that she would.

"Here is Pudding Lane," he said. "The Hawleys, who are kin to me, live at the south end of the road." He guided the horse onto a small bridge over the murky stream that crossed Bridge Street, fed by freshets coming from the two directions on the other side, and joining to follow along Pudding Lane. "Market Street to the west. We're on Main Street now that we're over the bridge."

They rode up a hill to the center of town. Mr. Edwards pulled up at a wide crossroads, with a well and the small school. The smell was denser than ever, acrid enough to make them both cough as he pointed up the hill to a large, squat, square building with a cupola, showing its age. "The meeting house," said Mr. Edwards. He paused this time, waiting for her response.

She waited, too, but finally said, "Amen?" She lifted herself up and hitched the pillion more securely beneath her.

He said, "Amen." Any moment could be a prayer. They turned to the right. He said, "Our road. King Street. Not named for the monarch, but for one Mr. King."

On the lot adjacent to the meeting house, men and boys were working this close to dark, dumping barrels full of fluid over hides in a great pit and riding horses ankle deep in tanbark over another. He pulled a handkerchief from his sleeve. "They must have opened the pits while I was gone. It's a good thing that they're curing with lime instead of sour milk. The fall slaughtering smells much worse."

She groaned a little, and he shifted to look at her. Most towns built tanneries downstream, well away from the center. Northampton had not, nor did they show any signs of moving it as the town grew. "You will become accustomed to it."

He did not bother to point toward the brickyard, but started humming to himself as they passed a few more houses, then pulled up at his own: large and, unlike the others, painted white. White paint was expensive and hard to get, but Sarah had managed to secure some through her New Haven connections. She said that it protected the wood, although some of townspeople had indicated to him that she was putting on airs. He could imagine little that mattered less to him than his congregation's opinion of the color of his house.

As he got off the horse, she hurried into the yard, passing beneath their cherry trees in late bloom. She came close enough to him that her skirt brushed the tops of his boots as she reached up to touch the purplish spot on his forehead where the bump from the collision with his father had been. He bowed awkwardly so that she could look at it.

"A comfrey poultice for that bruise," she said.

"As you say." Pulling two leaves from a flourishing elm, he presented one to Sally, three, who rolled it up like a precious scroll, and tucked the other into little Jerusha's bolster. "My girls."

The girls laughed, and Sarah did, too, before she took Jerusha's leaf so that she wouldn't chew it. She stepped back then and looked at the girl, who was holding both the reins and the pillion, looking tired enough to go to sleep where she stood. She didn't seem frightened to Mr. Edwards, but Sarah said, "You must not be afraid. Take the horse to the barn, just there, you can see it. Give it some grain and water, wash the sweat from its body. There's a bucket near the door. You know how to do that, do you not?"

The girl, hugging the pillion, said, "Yes, Madame."

Mr. Edwards's interest in mundane details was fading. He started toward his study, but, once Sarah had told the girl her first work, he heard her ask her name. He answered for her. "It's supposed to be Venus," he said from the doorway, doffing his hat, "but we will not have that."

The girl did not look at him. Soon enough, Sarah told her that she could go. She touched Mr. Edwards on the sleeve, and said, "We might get on inside before mosquitoes come out."

She had an eel pasty waiting with elderberry wine and a raisin tart. Jerusha nursed before they ate. Sally offered him a taste of her tart. The girl helped set out the supper, then Sarah sent her with her meal to the shed out back where she would be sleeping. After they ate, Sarah rang a bell to call the girl back for washing up, and then motioned her to follow the family into the parlor for prayers.

Sarah nodded as the girl stood uncertainly in the doorway, letting her know that this was a suitable place for her to stay. The family drew their chairs together. Mr. Edwards gave them Genesis chapter twenty, with Jacob working in the fields for seven years to earn a wife. Here, Mr. Edwards looked at Sarah as she delicately traced a small gather in her waistband with one finger. He read how Jacob chose to serve seven years more to get the beautiful Rachel, whom he had been promised and truly loved. First, though, he had to marry her undesirable older sister, Leah, who had been forced upon him. Jacob was blessed with heaps of sons, from Leah, from maidservants, and finally, most gloriously, from Rachel.

When Mr. Edwards finished reading, he asked little Sally who in the story was most loved. She said "God" right away, because that was never wrong, then said "Mama," and finally "Rachel," because this was teaching, and she had to get the answer right. When she tried to lean against her mother, Sarah placed her gently back in her chair.

Her father wasn't finished with questions. "And if we were to choose a good name for our servant, what name from the scripture would you choose?"

Sally thought hard and started to say Rachel again, but turned her head to look at the girl, who seemed to be having trouble with her stomach. The child turned back to him and said, "Leah."

"Good," said Mr. Edwards, nodding first at Sally—who nodded back at him with lucid attention—and then at the very still young woman holding her hands clasped against her belly just inside his parlor door. "That is who she shall be."

That night beside Sarah, Mr. Edwards dreamed of the swamp where, as a boy, he had built a booth for secret prayer. Surrounded by ferns, trout lilies, purple trillium, marsh marigolds, beaver, possum, and newts, he followed the subtle migrations of leaf-filtered light into a patch of skunk cabbage that attracted insects with a reek like foul meat. He lay on the wet ground, working on his Greek and watching birds and squirrels being charmed into the mouth of a snake like sinners being charmed by the devil, and so destroyed.

Chapter 2
May – June 1735

Four years later, on a warm spring Sabbath, Leah stood at the back of the meeting house gallery, holding the baby with three-year-old Esther asleep on the bench beside her, singing a psalm. Below her, the congregation was fervent and harmonious, raising the song in four parts. The people's frenzy hadn't started with the singing this morning, but she knew it would come, as it had almost every Sabbath and lecture day for the past six months. They were all waiting for it.

Shifting his daughter against her shoulder, Leah looked down at Mr. Edwards, who was singing with his head arched back, muscles straining in his neck. He wasn't loud, but his urgency drew out the music. Hummers and mumblers sang more cleanly joined with his voice.

Leah's hip pressed against that of her friend Bathsheba, who was using the sound of the singing to cover the crack as she squeezed two walnuts together. Bathsheba was in servitude in the home of Sheriff Pomeroy. All of the female slaves and servants sat in the gallery; many children did, too. Sally and Jerusha Edwards, young as they were, had been honored with seats downstairs near the front. Saul, the other slave in the Edwards household, was out of sight to Leah at his place by the door, but she knew that he would not even be moving his lips.

As the baby sucked on one of her fingers, Leah sang out. Bathsheba nudged her, offering nutmeats in their broken shells. Leah shook her head with a look at Sarah Edwards, who stood before a bench perpendicular to the wall that anchored the pulpit, half facing the people. She sang with vigor, the gold wires in her ears glinting in the dim light.

Bathsheba leaned closer to Leah, and, through a mouthful of walnuts, started messing with the words of the psalm. Leah, staring straight ahead as little Esther reached up from the bench to take hold of her skirt, caught something about who got the fat and who did the work. She gave her friend a sideways glance and got a little louder with the proper verse.

Yea blessed shall that man be called, that takes thy children young:
To dash their bones against hard stones, which lie the streets among.

Esther stopped playing with her skirt and went to asleep again, curled against the planked wall of the meeting house. Leah gave the baby a soothing little jog in her arms as she sat down. The violence of the verse spoke to her more than it scared her. It was a harsh world. Bathsheba swallowed her walnuts.

Mr. Edwards had his Bible open on the pulpit before him, one finger pressed hard against the small pile of notes resting in the crack of the book. He read the doctrine in a thin, whispery voice.

But to him that worketh not but believeth in him that justifieth the ungodly his faith is counted for righteousness. Romans 4, verse 5.

He began to speak of an opinion he opposed: the belief that obedience to the commands and laws of God was justification of a person as a true Christian, fit for life on this earth and in the world to come. As she listened to his arguments——which he built in meticulous lists that were shot through with heat like an iron screen before a fire— Leah watched him breathe, not from his chest, but from deep in his skinny gut. His robe rose and fell. His use of logic plucked at her mind, joining together edges of thought that had never touched. She often felt this during his sermons, and when he didn't preach, she craved it like food on a fast day.

The baby made a sound, so Leah began to rock as she listened. She traced the hem of the swaddling cloth, checking that her stitches were still tight. Mr. Edwards expanded on the phrase *he that worketh not.* She understood him to be saying that faith was godly in a way that work could never be, that faith was like blood running in the body, blood without which there could not be acts of the hands, or none that were in any way good.

A faint moaning started. Mr. Edwards didn't falter, and Sarah, swaying a little, had her lips pressed closed. Leah could see only some of the faces on the main floor, but, underneath the sermon, sounds of distress were coming from all around her, from people in the gallery as well as from their betters below. Excitement rippled through her. The baby's eyes were open, and Esther sat up. Bathsheba was silent, but she had put away her pocket of walnuts.

Mr. Edwards stood tall and still, regarding his people intently, and spoke of an act of the soul directly toward God.

Faith is that in us by which this union is accomplished and 'tis only upon that account we are justified by it and not on account of the goodness or loveliness of faith.

Leah relaxed into the strictness of his thought. She felt his words as exhalations of the room's common lungs, rising above the smells of old milk, damp wool, tobacco, and manure. She knew that he must smell it, too. They were all in a close body together.

In a prominent seat, Joseph Hawley hung his head. He crossed his arms tightly across his chest as his shoulders started to shake. His wife, Rebekah, leaned forward to look at him from the women's side of the aisle. She was Jonathan Edwards's aunt and usually quite forceful, but now she seemed parched and worried. In the children's section, their son Joseph groaned loudly, ignoring rapid jabs in his ribs from his younger brother, Elisha, who was trying to make him laugh instead. Sheriff Pomeroy, a stern man of seventy, began weeping with his mouth open. Seth Pomeroy, his nephew, panted as if he were at his anvil. Bathsheba let her empty hands rise and fall.

God treats man as a reasonable creature capable of act and choice and therefore judges it meet that in order to the establishing of a relation or union between Christ and the sinner there should be the mutual act of each, that each should receive the other.

The moaning got louder, swelling from all parts of the meeting house in concert with Mr. Edwards's dry voice, which, in heightened discourse, crumbled the ordinary world. It was not any one thing he said.

It was, as everyone knew, the outpouring of spirit from the unusually near presence of God. Bathsheba, who had been born in Northampton, said she'd never seen anything like it.

Now, all around them, people forgot themselves. An old woman drew her lips awry, as if convulsed. Mr. Hawley collapsed with his chin on the knee of the man beside him. Some rows behind them, a young man fell from the bench headfirst, his coat tenting over him lining side out, his neighbors arching away from his flailing boots, until he got his feet underneath him and popped up again, standing in the tight space between benches to pray with his eyes closed and the hem of his coat folded up to his waist. There was a gasp from those around him, but it was swallowed up by the general clamor, and the sermon went on.

On the women's side, Mrs. Hutchinson slipped a handkerchief to her invalid daughter Abigail, who coughed violently into it, then raised sticky hands, wrists turning and fingers rippling in elegant articulations of the air above her head. Nobody, not even the sick, wanted to miss meeting.

Leah felt spasms of mind and spasms of want. The twitchiness of some people's bodies under awakening did not shake her, but what Mr. Edwards was preaching did. Exercises of sin and corruption were intermingled with the holy acts of the godly. Mr. Edwards had said this, and she knew it was true. She felt malefaction and defilement in her own *works*. He was still saying that word, over and over. She was haunted by work and sin every day of her life. She sinned. God knew, she worked. Mr. Edwards, who had sweat dripping from under his wig, was so possessed by work as to shut himself in the study, write until dawn, and then (like Jesus, who had been up very early when he rose from the grave), he would climb the elm in the morning to write more. He wanted her work so much it seemed that work was all he wished her life to be. That and this. She bent to one side, then the other, giving the baby a swooping ride in her arms. There were other things that she wanted for herself, but, just now, she felt blasted clean by the agony in so many faces below her as they readied to become vessels for joy. People were writhing on their benches because they knew, as she did with a certainty born of hard service, that they sinned.

She felt Sarah's eyes upon her, and sat up straight. Bathsheba was watching her, too. Little Esther was clasping and unclasping her hands. The baby's grave expression quivered as if she were deciding whether to laugh, cry, or drop back to sleep.

God don't accept anything at our hands till he has accepted our persons.

She felt Bathsheba grip her elbow beneath the baby's head (sleep it was). Leah followed her friend's gaze to three young English women sitting a few benches in front of them in the gallery, leaning against each other. Some of the most carnal frolickers in the town, they had recently been welcomed into the church. A month ago, all three had fainted as they had been talking about the things of religion at the town well. They had been hauled down King Street to the minister's house in the back of a cart loaded with potatoes. While they revived and testified, Leah had scraped enough potatoes to feed the resulting crowd. They were from poor families, without even the right to use the common for grazing sheep, but lately had been bold enough to speak at women's prayer meetings.

The one in the plum-colored gown went rigid on the bench. Leah could see her dress darkening with sweat between her shoulder blades. As the woman rolled off her friends' laps, Bathsheba glanced sideways at Leah and whispered, "Us, too?"

Could they join the church? Could any slave? Not just make what they would of prayers from the worst benches, but be taken into the covenant? Leah didn't know. It had never happened, but, then, she had never seen the sheriff cry in public before this awakening.

She gazed down at Sarah Edwards, who looked away, as if she felt a little vulnerable with so many eyes passing over her to get to her husband. Leah had heard from the children, bragging as if about a foot race, that Sarah had felt stirrings of the spirit when she was only five years old. Sally, who was seven, tended to look a little worried for her own soul as she boasted about it, but Jerusha, just turned five, puffed up with as much pride as if they were talking about herself.

As Mr. Edwards preached and people yielded up their dignity to God, Sarah shaded her eyes with her hand, looking into the gallery seats.

Leah hugged the swaddled baby, then mouthed the word "sleeping." As Sarah gave a nearly imperceptible nod, Leah answered Bathsheba. "I will ask."

On the following Saturday morning, Sarah Edwards pushed a strand of hair out of her face and looked at the web she needed. It stretched across the upper left corner of her kitchen door. There were a couple of dark lumps she took to be captured gnats, but no sign of the large spider she had seen there before. Feeling skittish, she reached out a finger to pull a single filament near where it touched the wood of the door frame. It resisted her touch, but when she pulled a second thread, the whole web curled up to the top of the door, almost out of reach. Bits of debris flew out of it, and a tiny spider, trailing new thread, landed on her arm. She gasped and took a step back. Just then, Leah came down the hall, carrying bedding, trailed by Sally and Jerusha with pillows. The girls stopped and gaped at their mother, who composed herself and, waving a bit of flannel, motioned them through the door. "Go on. Quickly. I'm gathering web and don't need anyone getting bit." She glanced at her own arm, but the spider was nowhere to be seen.

Leah looked at Sarah's flushed face, and thought, "Not the right moment to ask her. Not now. Not yet." It had been a chorus in her head every time she had seen Sarah alone since the Sabbath. She had been thinking constantly about what it might mean to be a member of the church. Women didn't vote in decisions facing the congregation, but perhaps Saul might. Hoisting the bedding higher to keep it from dragging the floor, she crossed into the kitchen and out the back door to the yard. Sally followed, moving swiftly and holding the pillow over her head against the possibility of falling spiders. Jerusha dawdled as much as she dared, looking back over her shoulder at her mother, the flannel, and the open air where a web had been that morning. She wanted to ask questions, but she and her pillow bumped into a chair.

"Mind where you're going," Sarah said, a little pleased that her work so fascinated her second daughter. Perhaps Jerusha had inclinations toward healing. The girl blushed and followed the others out the back.

Sarah took a deep breath, then stood on her toes to run her flannel along the ridge of the door frame, gathering web. She got more dust and milkweed than she wanted, but found corners where the web was concentrated, thick and spongy. She was stretching to get as much as she could when her husband came out of his study into the hall. He had been writing most of the night and into the morning. His mind was swallowed up with trying to give a good account of the revival which had the town in its grips, but the sight of Sarah on tiptoe framed by the doorway with web in her hair was enough to make him come toward her.

"I think I'm starting to get it," he said. "Mr. Colman in Boston will receive nothing from me but what is undeniable. That's the only way that learned men will believe that three hundred people in our town of two hundred families have been saved."

Sarah, who had heard him fret about this same problem dozens of times, finished her own work. She folded the flannel into a soft packet with the web inside. "You must give this to Uncle Hawley when you see him. He is in the grips of melancholia. Rebekah's concerned."

Her husband regarded her, blinking. The only thing more important than spreading the word about how his people had come to see more of God was the state of any one soul under his care. He rubbed his eyes. "He has many signs of being under awakening. Suffering with the knowledge of his sinful nature is one of them."

She tied the packet with a bit of string and offered it to him. "Tell Rebekah it should give him some relief. I will gather some to take to poor Abigail Hutchinson, too."

"Aunt Rebekah does worry," he said, soberly. "She has spoken to me, as well." He didn't take the packet. "I'm going to pray in the woods."

As Sarah shook her head with exasperation, she was already pulling a straight pin from the hem of her sleeve to pin the flannel to his coat, so he couldn't possibly forget it. As she leaned close, he lifted his hand and offered his finger to the tiny spider wandering the strands of her hair. It climbed on, and he held it before him.

Sarah, scalp crawling, stared at her husband. He was regarding the spider almost tenderly, turning his finger as it tried to roam, with a look of affection like that of a boy scratching the nose of his first horse. He was dear to her, but so strange. "Out of my kitchen, sir," she said. "And kindly rid us of the spider. People will be filling up the house again before you're back."

He put on his hat with the other hand and carried the spider on his finger to the door. "I'll finish the letter about the revival tonight."

"Good," she said, reaching for the broom. "Don't forget to give Uncle Hawley the web."

Mr. Edwards nodded absently and stepped into the yard. Leah and the girls were beating bedding with sticks, raising clouds of dust to thicken the diffuse morning light. When she saw her father, Jerusha dropped the pillow that she had been walloping and hurried to greet him. "Is that a spider on your finger?"

He bent down to her as, in the near distance, her sister picked up the fallen pillow and began whacking it against her own. "When I was a young man, I spent many hours trapping spiders on bushes and shaking them on sticks."

Jerusha stood, chubby and erect, gazing at the spider crouched on his knuckle. "Why?"

He brought his finger closer to her face, just under her nose. "To know more intimately the wisdom of the Creator by observing how he provided for the necessities of his creatures. And also for their recreation."

She stayed very still, watching the spider through her lashes as the breeze lifted strands of her hair, which her father felt might be, like the thread the spider draws out through its bottle tail, lighter than air. He pulled his finger away from her face and let it hover above the stump they used for chopping wood. Both of them watched closely as the spider cast a shining line and floated to the stump. "Back to your duties," he said to Jerusha, who was gazing at him as if he had just revealed more brilliance than was contained in all of the Royal Society's *Philosophical Transactions*, where he had yet to be published. He turned to the barn to saddle his horse. "That pillow is not your sister's burden, but yours."

"They shall lie down alike in the dust and the worms shall cover them."

Sarah was reading from the book of Job to gaunt young Abigail Hutchinson in her bed when her mother came in with an apple baked so soft that it puddled in the bowl, skin brown and loose, with Sarah's cobweb stuffed inside. Abigail, who had had an awakening, listened with palpable intensity.

Abigail was suffering from an illness seated in her throat, which had swollen inward and filled up the pipe so that she could swallow almost nothing. When Sarah had arrived, her chamber had been crowded with neighbors asking if she were prepared to die and marveling at the composure of her answers.

Sarah had sent them away, and now Mrs. Hutchinson watched as Sarah sat on the bed, mashing the apple in the bowl with the back of the spoon and clearing away bits of skin with the edge. She took a scant spoonful and held it to Abigail's cracked lips.

"Must I eat?" murmured Abigail. "I want to pray."

"Eat," said Sarah and Mrs. Hutchinson, both at the same time. "Then pray," added Sarah.

Spider web baked in apple was known to be good for ague, chills or fever, but as soon as Abigail had some in her mouth, she started retching and choking. She kicked off the blanket and struggled to swallow. Mrs. Hutchinson took her hand and watched her closely. Sarah reached to help the young woman sit up just as she lost her fight to take food into her body. Wet apple with strings of web sprayed from her mouth and nostrils as she gasped for breath.

Sarah had a handkerchief. She wiped Abigail's face soberly and tenderly before she saw to her own bodice and apron. Mrs. Hutchinson, well-practiced at this duty, brought towels and a basin of water warmed on the hearth. Sarah stayed with Abigail until the girl had enough composure to meet her eyes again, then she took up the spoon and offered it to her, empty. Abigail sucked on a bit of apple that had dried on the edge.

Mrs. Hutchinson stood and said, "Thank you, Mrs. Edwards. She needs to rest now." Her tone was sharp and protective. Abigail added, "Thank Mr. Edwards for coming, too. My spirit was much moved."

Sarah tied her horse to a tree on the way home, then got mud on her petticoat as she washed her face in the river. She suspected that Mrs. Hutchinson thought she had done her daughter harm. Abigail had not been able to get down enough web for it to be of any help, but Sarah was sure—or, at least, she hoped, and wished to seem sure, because her position demanded it—that the attempt had not worsened the girl's suffering. She had done what she could.

Uncle Hawley sought him out in his study in the late afternoon. Mr. Edwards had forgotten all about the web still pinned to his coat, but as he reached out to brush away a fly that had settled in a stiff curl of his uncle's wig, he found himself thinking of spiders. He let his hand rest on the wig for a moment, touching powdered horsehair in an attempt to reach the man. "You have seen how a spider thrown in the midst of a fire exerts no strength to oppose the heat, or to fly from it, but immediately stretches forth itself and yields; and the fire takes possession of it at once."

Uncle Joseph Hawley pushed back his wig and ran his hand over his shaved head. "I am filthy and corrupt to the core. There is no way for me to be saved."

Worried that he had made a bad choice to speak of burning, Mr. Edwards answered quickly and clearly. "Trust in God."

Uncle Hawley turned suddenly and flicked his fingers at the fly buzzing behind him on the chair, muttering, "I am nothing but a dung hill." He had been saying such things for two hours as they prayed together in the study. His voice seemed more stricken, somehow, with his wig knocked askew.

Such a state was pious and necessary, perhaps, to prepare the heart to receive the Spirit, but, having been alerted by Sarah, it did make

Mr. Edwards anxious. He drew his chair closer and tried again. "Your convictions of guilt and misery are hopeful signs."

Uncle Hawley had gone back to scratching his head in an awkward, detached way, as if his hand were not his own. "I am a hard-hearted, senseless, sottish creature sleeping on the brink of hell."

Mr. Edwards knew from Aunt Rebekah that Uncle Hawley had, in fact, slept very little for something like two months. His suffering was especially worrisome since melancholy was a distemper that the Hawley family was prone to. The preacher touched the older man's shoulder. He spoke haltingly. "Sir, you need to rest."

Uncle Hawley closed his eyes and took a breath that sounded painful in his lungs.

Mr. Edwards looked at him for a moment, taking in the strain in his face and the way he slumped in the chair. He resisted the impulse to straighten the man's wig. Uncle Hawley had been kind to him when he had first arrived in Northampton nine years ago, and Aunt Rebekah was constantly sending the boys from their house on Pudding Lane to bring Sarah one of her four meal cheeses. Mr. Edwards felt another jab of worry as he thought of the boys, who worked with their father at the family store. Joseph was eleven and Elisha nearly three years younger. He wished that he could spare the boys' father this suffering, but knew that this was a Godly man following a well-marked path to redemption. He saw that he had left a faint handprint of powder from Uncle Hawley's wig on the shoulder of his coat. Trying to brush it off with dusty fingers would only make it worse. Aunt Rebekah would not be pleased.

Empty, he told himself. Disobediently, his mind turned toward the account of the revival he had been working on for Mr. Colman, well-known cleric and publisher. Ambition stirred in his heart, but, equally strong, came a memory of standing beside one of Uncle Hawley's gentle oxen, holding Joseph, barely old enough to wear breeches, on its back, while Uncle Hawley laughed from the porch of the store and Rebekah held on to Elisha—who had been yelling that he wanted to ride, too—for dear life. Then, like the unearned gift it was, there rose inside Mr. Edwards the words God used to announce himself to Moses in the bush. He said them aloud, that his uncle might hear. "I am that I am; I am."

Uncle Hawley dropped his head and moaned. His wig didn't fall, but held crookedly to his scalp.

Mr. Edwards looked at the wig and the fly circling it again. Perhaps horsehair smelled like home to a fly. He bent in his chair so that he was close to his uncle's slack, red face, close enough to notice that the bristles in his ears had gone gray. "Courage, uncle." He wanted to tell him to sit up straight and look his sins in the face, to think of his wife and children and shoulder his life's load with a little decent gratitude, as becomes a well-loved and well-fed man. He wanted to tell him to have some dignity and see to his wig, but Mr. Edwards knew that the temptation to say that came from Satan. A soul had to be prostrate and humbled to prepare it for grace. Uncle Hawley was still, not shaking, his face crumpled up with what looked like the most abject pain, but which might have been a physical manifestation of the holy spirit thickening and dispersing inside him.

Mr. Edwards offered the encouragement he could. "God may sanctify your suffering by saving more souls than your own. Your boys can see that there is no duty more important than doing his will."

Uncle Hawley was pressing the backs of his hands through his breeches into his thighs. His wig had fallen off onto the floor. The fly had been joined by another to trouble the room, but when a series of loud steps passed in the hall, Uncle Hawley raised his naked head and the flies dispersed.

"I must go home," he said, standing up. "Rebekah is waiting for me."

Mr. Edwards sat in his chair and looked up at his uncle, wondering if he should try again to warn him about the fires of hell or quote more scripture. He felt drained by the persistence of his uncle's despair, which had drawn all of their talk back to it in great buzzing loops. As Uncle Hawley began tapping his foot with something of his old impatience, Mr. Edwards stood, too. "No one but God can be certain, but I see signs of grace in you," he said.

Uncle Hawley didn't reply, but Mr. Edwards felt his own spirit lightened by the fact that his uncle stooped down to retrieve his wig and position it (somewhat askew) on his head before he opened the door and they stood together in the hall, blinking in the noise that rose from the rest of the house. For months now, people had been coming every day and some nights, seeking counsel.

There was singing coming from the parlor, but Rebekah Hawley must have been listening intently for the sound of the study door, because she came rustling into the hallway from the kitchen, carrying a sauce boat in one hand. She was not a woman who could wait in a working kitchen without putting a hand in, and she had had enough of the parlor. She took a good look at her husband, eyes red from crying and his wig in his hand, and said, "This way, my dear. Kitchen door."

Rebekah, who was not prone to the use of endearments, reminded Mr. Edwards so much of his mother as she nodded gravely at him and drew her husband into the warm room, which smelled of roasting chicken. There were probably others under religious convictions crying in the parlor, but Uncle Hawley was deep in difficulties, and Rebekah was protective of him. She handed Leah the gravy boat, gently situated the wig on his head once again, then rid his coat of powder with a few brisk sweeps of a kitchen towel.

As she stepped back, Uncle Hawley roused himself to take up her shawl from the back of a chair and hold it open for her. She looked startled but pleased as he wrapped her more tightly than the mildness of the day demanded.

"Mind the fritters," she said to Leah, who was basting the chicken with a brass skimmer.

Leah said, "Madame." She had found that saying a title aloud was received as well as "yes," but it saved something in her, too. She was, in fact, already minding the fritters, the chicken, and chopping the last of last year's parsnips, as well. She also needed to get the rest of the household cups from the parlor to be washed before the Saturday evening sun went down, and, in Mr. Edwards's household if not everywhere in Northampton, the prohibition on work began.

As if drawn by her thoughts, a group of little girls stalked and toddled into the room, carrying cups, except for Esther, who could yet barely carry herself. Sarah came in behind them, holding baby Mary, but it was the child of a neighbor, Phoebe Bartlett, who rushed up to Mr. Edwards and hugged his legs. "Oh, my minister," she said rapturously, coffee dregs slopping out of her cup. Phoebe was four. Sally, Jerusha, and even Esther, fist in mouth, stared at her, affronted. Mr. Edwards patted her head a bit shyly. He had never felt so well-liked.

"Mr. and Mrs. Bartlett need to talk with you about Phoebe before they go," Sarah said to her husband, handing the baby to Leah, who had put down the shovel and was standing between the overexcited little girls and the hearth. "She's been praying constantly in her closet, and may be in a regenerate state." Phoebe looked modestly at the drops of coffee on the floor. Aunt Rebekah noticed that Uncle Hawley, whose face had shown so little feeling for so long, was regarding the child with a look full of rank envy.

Mr. Edwards, utterly wrung out, took Phoebe's cup. She let go of his knees and didn't look up. Seeing that they had nothing more to say to each other at the moment, Sarah stepped forward. "Go outside, now, girls. The eggs need to be gathered before dark, and the animals need to be fed. Listen to Sally, she knows what to do."

The little girls were out the door before she finished speaking. Aunt Rebekah and Uncle Hawley were moving more slowly, so Sarah unpinned the flannel from her husband's coat and handed it to Aunt Rebekah. "A poultice at the temples," she murmured. "Or feed it to him with strawberries soaked in Madeira. Sure to aid digestion and revive the spirits."

Aunt Rebekah nodded her thanks without asking any questions, slipped the flannel up her sleeve, took her husband's arm, and said, "Come." As they opened the back door, Sarah caught a glimpse of their boys sword fighting with rake handles under the cherry trees in the yard while the little girls chased chickens, cheering the eggs.

Mr. Edwards went back to work on his letter to Mr. Colman about the revival without finishing his dinner. If he tried to make it all the way through the meal, he feared he might fall asleep. He prayed at the table, questioned Sally on the names of the branches of the river that ran out of Eden, and gave Jerusha an easy one about how long Jonah was in the belly of the great fish, while little Esther fed half her biscuit to the baby. He drained his cider, ate a biscuit himself, and came away. Sarah sighed as he got up from the table, then slipped another biscuit into his hand. He did not refuse it.

In his study, he set the biscuit on a piece of paper. It was an old shopping list for a trip to Boston: cheese, lute strings, chocolate, and Chambers' *Cyclopedia*, which he had searched for in vain. He usually folded such scraps into booklets and wrote on the backs, but now he brought a stack of clean foolscap to the center of his desk. He ached to continue the story, but he was hungry. The smells of ham and biscuits were distracting him. He found it hard to believe that he could be tempted by dinner at the moment when, after such a long day, he finally had the chance to get the spirit that had been flooding the lives of his people down on paper for publication, but he was. Putting his hands flat on the desk, he meditated on the verse from Jeremiah that he had recited as grace at the table: *Then the Lord put forth his hand, and touched my mouth. And the Lord said unto me, Behold, I have put my words in thy mouth.*

He took a quill, sharpened the end where it had split, and put it down again. He felt as if he were breathing swamp air thick with the sin of enjoying his own righteousness. He gritted his teeth to stop them from chattering with the excitement of the wildfire of conversion among his people, and, especially, of sending the story to the Reverend Mr. Colman. (That famous name rang like a bell, and he kept pulling the rope.) He willed himself to act in humility, for the glory of religion, and tried to bring himself back to the task at hand. He thought of Uncle Hawley, too distraught to maintain control of his own wig. This was a harrowing thought, but Mr. Edwards was, still, so hungry. He thought he could eat sheets of paper with nothing to wash them down but his own copious spit, and then speak books. His mouth was full of desires.

He broke off a piece of biscuit. He wanted his flesh and mind to quiet so that he could write. He thought of Jerusha's radiance as the spider let go its thread. He meant to eat slowly, but swallowed before he could stop himself. He took another bite, waited for it to melt on his tongue, then pressed it against the roof of his mouth, eking honey from it. It was subtle and sweet. He thought of Sarah's hands shaping the dough. That it had actually been Leah did not occur to him. He thought of Abigail Hutchinson's swollen throat and sure faith. As he swallowed, his hunger abated, and he felt that the act had been sanctified. The natural world was filled with grace so that eating a biscuit was not a carnal indulgence, but as good as a prayer. It was a rare state, but these were unusual times.

He dipped his quill in the ink and lost himself in his faithful narrative of the surprising work of God in Northampton. He knew himself best as a writer. There was a rhythm to writing that he thought might be tied to the breath, and so, of course, to the soul. Certainly, yes, this was felt in the curl and press of the fingers on a quill, in the way an arm slid along a page, how a sleeve might pick up ink, might smear the words of the careless. Certain ministers—Mr. Edwards was one of them, and the late Solomon Stoddard had been even more so—could write so small as to get the full hours of a sermon onto one or two sides of a most diminutive page. The whole town could be held still by the rise and lean of inked letters, to wait for God in his house.

To write a letter was to reach for another person in a private, circumspect way. A letter that might be published was still allowed a certain personal expression, a feeling of casual discourse, not to say intimacy, that was rarely approached in a sermon. A letter writer could feel the pull of a true correspondent from the other end of the world. There was that itch, that opening of feeling in privacy, the recalcitrant pleasures of pressing meaning into a surface, of letting a silent version of one's voice spill recklessly across the page, or in tracing the minutest inflections of beloved matters in careful sentences, composed and reflected upon, then copied again. And then, bravely, uncertainly, irrevocably, sent.

He finished the letter. After he signed and sealed it, he touched one fingertip to a spot on the desk that was sticky with honey, then, like one of his daughters forgetting her manners at the table, put the finger into his mouth.

In the shed behind the house, Leah spoke from her pallet with the slow syllables of exhaustion. She slept on the floor, with Saul overhead in the loft. They talked through gaps in the thin boards. "Did you listen to the prayers in the parlor, or were you sleeping then, too?"

He was silent long enough to make her think that he wouldn't answer. Sometimes, if he was too tired or disliked the question, he didn't. He was older than she was, but she had been with the family longer. He had worked in Barbados until his hip gave out, then had been shipped to the smaller New England market to bring a new price. When she had first seen him two years before, limping into the yard behind Mr. Edwards's horse wearing a tow shirt, checked trousers, and a red cap, she had been wary about the stranger she would have to share her quarters with. He had barely spoken, even once they were alone.

Bathsheba had seen him in the road, and had come that first night with basswood to make a poultice for his hip. Bathsheba, who had never been so far out of the confines of Northampton as to cross the river into Hadley, liked to get a look at anyone newly arrived in town.

After Bathsheba had made Saul the poultice and been thanked for it, she and Leah watched to be sure he could manage the ladder to the loft. Then the two women had gone outside to stand talking at a spot near the elm where they were visible to neither house nor road. They could hear the stream that ran along the other side of King Street gurgling and slapping its banks. It was good to be upstream from the tanning yard, and upwind, that night, as well. Leaning against the tree, Leah had said, "If he groans and snores all night, I will never rest again."

Bathsheba, leaning, too, had smoothed her tucked-up skirts against her opulent belly. "Maybe you won't want to."

Leah had turned and slapped the tree not far from her friend's head. Bathsheba had jumped and they both laughed, but Leah had meant it when she said, "I ask you not to talk that way."

Bathsheba had made no promises, but settled back against the tree as if she planned to stay all night, and, changing the subject, said, "Listen to that," as a catbird ran through demented versions of a whole woods' worth of songs.

When Leah had gone back inside, Saul had, in fact, been snoring, but over time she found that she usually fell asleep before he did, and so was not disturbed. They shared meals, and she came to appreciate his company. Bathsheba kept a speculative eye on them. They looked at each other, not with desire, but with a partial, pressing sense of recognition that had its own commitments.

She had given up on a response to her question about prayer and started to drift off, when she heard a rustling in the loft, and he said, "I floated."

Saul stood beside her near the doorway during family prayers, and now she pictured him floating as he listened, turning very slowly like a spoke of a wheel until his feet were in the air and his head over the fire. She asked him, "Why was that?"

He sighed, and she knew that she would have to let him sleep soon. He said, "I've got no use for God."

Leah caught her breath. She thought every day about reaping the promises. It was in her like anger, shrouded, hot and deep. It was scripture: *whosoever exalteth himself shall be abased.* That was one of the promises not everybody seemed to hear. She had been thinking to raise the idea to him of joining the church, and to ask his advice about how to approach Sarah about it, unless he thought it best to try Mr. Edwards himself. Now there seemed to be no point to starting that conversation. She sank into the sound of both of them breathing, then told him, "Fair enough." Which was as good as good-night.

No work was to be done the next day because it was the Sabbath, not even the making of beds, but young Joseph Hawley awoke to the rasp of his father grinding a knife. *He's forgotten*, the boy thought. *His mind has wandered that far.*

Joseph fell back to sleep and dreamed of following the birch bark torches at night to go with his brother Elisha and hunt eels in the river. As they jabbed at the water, a sharp sound broke his sleep.

Joseph, who had moved upstairs to the attic at the approach of spring, put on his clothes for the cold trip to the privy. He climbed down the stairs and walked quietly past Elisha on his cot in the kitchen. Sometimes they slept up there together, but lately Elisha had wanted to stay closer to their mother and father. The fire had been kindled, so he knew that his mother had already gone out to feed the cows. Only chores essential to sustaining life were not sins on Sunday. The grinding had stopped, but the door to the parlor, where his parents slept in their fine bed, was open. When he glanced in, he saw his father gasping on the floor, his chest wet, his eyes glazed, and his mouth leaking blood. In the instant before Joseph screamed for Mama and pulled off his shirt to try and stop the blood, he knew that his father was after the answer to the question of whether he was truly, finally, saved.

Mr. Edwards sat beside the woodshed on the scarred stump the family used to chop wood. There was no sign of Jerusha's spider. He held the pages of his sermon against his knees in the cold morning wind, but he already knew it well—text, doctrine and application—so that all he needed to do to prepare was to open himself like a hunk of ash wood before the strikes of the Lord.

A black bug so tiny that he thought at first it was a comma crawled across the sermon. It sat still for a moment while he stared at its wispy legs and then vanished so quickly that he was unable say whether it flew or jumped. Suddenly, he heard a rustling in the thickets of seedlings that were trying to bring the woods back to take over the garden. He thought it was an old porcupine that he had seen pounding through the woods on the way to its stony hill riddled with dens, indifferent to the amount of noise it might make, dragging its bristling tail. But porcupines were slow, and whatever this was, it was approaching fast.

He had just formed the idea—dogs—when his young Hawley cousins astonished him by breaking through the thicket. Joseph's half-tucked shirt had a dark stain rising from the hem and Elisha had on only his woolens and shoes under an overlarge cloak now covered with brambles.

They pelted into the yard at such speed that Joseph was already hard up against the stump, pulling Mr. Edwards's coat, gasping, "Please, oh, please."

Elisha, a little behind, ran into the axe handle and knocked the blade from where it had been lodged in the stump. As it thudded to the ground, the preacher rose, and Joseph, giving a moan too deep to come from the throat of a boy, let go of his coat to snatch at his brother and keep him from falling.

Mr. Edwards slipped the sermon into the pocket of his coat and put a hand on each of their shoulders. "Kinsmen," he said, thinking to shore them up with this honorific as they wavered back in forth in front of him, unable to return to speech. "Boys. It is the Sabbath. Why are you in my garden?"

Joseph looked at him desperately, then gave his brother a shove toward the house, where Jerusha had just emerged through the back door with scraps for the chickens. Elisha broke away and staggered a few steps in that direction, then started crying in the middle of the dusty yard. Jerusha, always tenderhearted, dropped the crusts and came to him.

Joseph moved close to Mr. Edwards again, twisting his mouth before he spoke softly, as if to keep the words from his brother. "It's my father. He's cut his throat. My mother says to come."

Mr. Edwards reached for the boy and pulled him close, overwhelmed by the impulse to protect him. In that first stunned moment, he thought of web folded into a bit of flannel. Sarah's web had not worked. He thought of God, then of his own father, and then his mother, whose sister Rebekah was now asking him to come. "Does he live?"

The boy gave a look of such wretchedness that Mr. Edwards was sorry to made him speak at all. "Yes."

Mr. Edwards didn't ask him anything else, but held on to him and called out to his daughter, "Jerusha! Take Elisha into the house and tell Saul to get over to the doctor's and fetch him to Mr. Hawley's. Tell him to take your mother's horse."

Jerusha, five years old to Elisha's eight, already had her arm around the boy's waist and was leading him toward the kitchen door and her mother's sure help.

It calmed Mr. Edwards to witness Jerusha's tenderness. Her example brought him back to his own duty to young Joseph, who still waited before him, white-lipped and swaying. Mr. Edwards had no son, and here was this boy, as in the book of Daniel, a child in whom there was no blemish, standing there to do his duty under a blow that would have knocked many of his elders to the ground.

Mr. Edwards pushed gently on Joseph's shoulders so that the boy sat on the stump, dropping as if the wind had been knocked out of him. Looking down at the boy half collapsed on the stump, Mr. Edwards remembered Uncle Hawley's frantic agonies in the study, his obliviousness to reassurance. Also, the happy look on the man's face one morning many years ago when he had sauntered down from the porch of his house, climbed onto his ox, and Mr. Edwards had put little Joseph before him on the animal's back. The thought of it wrenched Mr. Edwards's heart and made his gut burn.

The boy was swaying, not keeping perfectly still. He didn't look at the preacher, but down at the axe in the dirt, or at nothing but the dirt itself.

"Joseph," Mr. Edwards said, "son." As if the boy were his own.

The child rocked a little harder, grinding fists into the rough edge of the stump. Mr. Edwards squatted down and took Joseph's hands to keep them from splinters. He held them in silence for a long time. Both of them were sick with grief, but if they had already lost the father, Mr. Edwards was ready to fight to save the son. "Satan is raging among us, Joseph, and he got a grasp on your father in his weakened state. Whether he lives or dies, you must remember the sight of him as he was this morning." His voice trembled, but he said what had to be said. "Think of the fragile state of your own soul."

The boy looked at him with a sudden red-eyed stare, then threw his arms around the preacher as if he were already behind him on a horse, clinging for dear life to the cloth of Mr. Edwards's coat as they rode back to Pudding Lane and his father's house. Mr. Edwards spoke no more, but held him, too, as Leah ran with Saul toward the barn and Sarah called from the doorway.

A swarm of mayflies encompassed Joseph and Mr. Edwards in a great cloud of witnesses, animate sparks certain to bite, rising and falling so thick in the air that it was impossible to tell which direction they had come from first.

Mr. Edwards loosened his coat to cover them both, and took the boy to the barn to fetch the horse.

Days later, after the town fast and the coroner's inquest, before Mr. Edwards finally gave his letter to Benjamin Colman to a merchant who had business in Boston, he broke open the seal and, making the fate of his uncle part of the story of the revival, added a postscript:

> Since I wrote the foregoing letter, there has happened a thing of a very awful nature in the town; my uncle Hawley, the last Sabbath day morning, laid violent hands on himself, and put an end to his life, by cutting his own throat.

Chapter 3
July 18, 1735

The day that Elisha Hawley turned nine years old, six weeks after his father's death, his mother made apple flummey seasoned with cinnamon and ginger for breakfast and let him have the last of the bacon with pea soup for supper. She made doughnuts, despite the heat, and let him lead the evening prayer, even though his older brother, Joseph, mouthed a silent *gobble gobble gobble* as Elisha stammered over the verse. Life was rising as loss burrowed in. Elisha wanted to snicker at Joseph, or weep with relief that his brother was trying to be funny, but he swallowed all that and sounded out the scripture more loudly, even *abomination*, which he didn't know how to say. Rebekah fixed her eyes on Joseph as Elisha mangled the vowels, then gave them each half a doughnut and a sip of cider before bed.

Rebekah had scrubbed the blood stain from the floor of the parlor with sand the boys had hauled in buckets from the Mill River, which emptied into the Connecticut. She had the bed moved to one of the chambers above stairs. She hired a boatman to arrange for deliveries to the store from seaports like Lyme, New Haven, and New London by way of the big river. She bartered with the Hunts for time from their man Joab to cut firewood for winter and work in the fields. She never wept within the curtains of the bed, at least not so that Elisha could hear. She had written a prayer bid requesting that God sanctify the mighty blow of his rod at the loss of her husband to the saving of her soul, adding that her sons desired the same. The Reverend Mr. Edwards had read it aloud in a trembling voice to silence in the congregation.

Eben Pomeroy, who was Elisha's brother Joe's age, said that the revival was over. He did not say to Elisha and Joe that their father had killed it, for he was a friend, but Elisha knew that he thought this was true.

Joe, Elisha, and Eben, plus Joab and the rest of the Pudding Lane Pomeroys (Seth and Ebenezer, father of Eben, and their other sons, were neighbors, not like the Elm Street Pomeroys, headed by Seth and Ebenezer's father, Sheriff Pomeroy, who lived next to Seth's blacksmith shop) had helped Rebekah attach a buttery to the north side of the house. She had made enough pudding that day that their lane could have been named for her, instead of the shoemaker's wife from some years back who, Elisha had heard, fed her husband's apprentices nothing but pudding. Rebekah made a deal with Mrs. Mary Pomeroy and Mrs. Hunt to combine a share of the milk from their cows, so that she had enough to make cheese.

She spent hours straining milk, skimming cream, and scalding the milk pails. The tasks were urgent and her absorption complete. It was too hot that summer to keep butter long, but her four-meal cheeses sold well, and sometimes she added sage or garlic or dill. Her clothes carried the faintly sour smell of whey. She turned the ripening cheeses twice a day, without fail, polishing them with butter and red annatto. Rubbing them in the small, cool room, she wept. Elisha tried to keep far from the house when his mother turned the cheese.

On the night of his birthday, after Joseph had climbed the steep stairs to the attic, Elisha could hear his mother snoring, the sound muffled by the hangings, but familiar, deep and sad. He remembered sleeping in the trundle bed under his parents' bedstead in the parlor, before he had grown too big to fit in it and they had sent him to the cot in the kitchen. The trundle had been comforting, close and dark with a soft edge of light from the banked fire flickering under the bed curtains. His father had kicked and turned above him while his mother had breathed in stuttering rasps. The motions of their bodies had seemed as inescapable as the movement of the heavens, dust and feathers drifting from their bedding to make his nose itch as he had lain enclosed and content in the dark.

Lying sleepless in bed was something everyone said had helped bring his father to his death. Elisha knew that the coroner's inquest had judged him to have been delirious. He had heard Mr. Edwards say that his father had been past a capacity of receiving advice or being reasoned with, that there had been the urgent, harsh voice of a demon in his ear, as insistent and repetitive as the call of a crow, saying, "Do it, do it now, now, NOW."

Elisha wished that Mr. Edwards would shut up about his father, and about everything else, too. He started breathing hard, drawn into sleep, fighting the night terrors that had been coming ever since his father's death. He heard the sound of his father grinding the knife. Had he heard it that night? He couldn't be sure. He heard it now—steel on stone, or teeth gnashing themselves down to nubs—then saw his father gasping and bleeding on the parlor floor. He woke with his fist in his mouth, biting down. He hadn't broken the skin, but it was covered with spit. He wiped it dry on the bedclothes, then got up and pulled on his clothes.

He slipped out the kitchen door. He didn't take a lantern, and Rebekah wouldn't let him touch the gun. He had a new knife from Joseph, made out of a hammered nail and sharpened on the whetstone in the barn until it shone. It gave him confidence. Awake, he was a bold boy.

He took a back path to the Mill River, which he knew well enough to walk easily in the starry dark. The Mill was not like the Connecticut, where men might be lingering at the tavern near the ferry crossing even past the bell for nine o'clock curfew. (If they were from Hadley, they would have to pay double to cross by ferry at night, but some brought their own canoes, and others were free with their pence.) Elisha stayed well clear of Licking Water, the watering spot on South Street where people brought their livestock and which was sometimes patrolled by the night watch. He avoided Pleasant Street, too, but followed a path he knew across Venturer's Field toward the river.

He tripped over a root and stumbled over a few stones, but mostly he was quiet and careful as he walked. He had grown up on the story of his mother's brother, Colonel John Stoddard, who had leapt from a second-story window when the Abenaki raided Deerfield, and ran barefoot across the snow all the way to Hatfield for help, which arrived much too late.

Elisha admired Colonel Stoddard, who had let him hold his gold watch at the meal after his father's funeral. A watch like that had never been seen in Northampton, and the colonel had been trying to be kind, even if he had muttered something about mortal life and time that had reminded Elisha of the verse for the letter Y in his old primer, the one about youth illustrated with a skeleton. Elisha very much respected his uncle, military hero that he was, but he had sometimes wondered if it might have been braver to use the stairs and put up a fight while the slave woman and the baby were killed. He couldn't imagine fighting raiders barefoot, though, and had no doubt that the colonel would have risked a battle-axe to the head if he had bent down to buckle his shoes. This didn't seem to bother anyone except Elisha. The flauntish way his daughters dressed occasioned more talk. Elisha thought that the key to the colonel's situation would have been tall boots, easy to pull on and suitable for snow, if worse came to worst. Better than that would have been a horse, but, in his uncle's place, Elisha would have settled for boots.

Elisha wasn't worried about Indians. He knew plenty of Abenaki like Mary Stockbridge, who was friendly enough, if overly inclined to mess with his hair. He did have a plan in case he encountered wolves or bears. If he heard wolves nearby, he would climb a tree. If he heard thrashing like a bear or a moose, he would hide.

Elisha was nine tonight, thrice three, and Christ had been thirty three when he died to human life. Joseph had brought that up, trying to lend a tone of solemnity and provide moral direction, as he was prone to do when he wasn't making fun of his brother, but Elisha ignored him. Joseph didn't know as much about what was right as he thought he did.

At the fast day after his father's death, Mr. Edwards had said that God had spit in the face of the people in the town. Their faces. His face. Elisha, who had been numbly sucking on a piece of hard cheese that his brother had slipped him, bit it in two when he heard that. Mrs. Edwards had looked at him then, and he thought that she might have seen him chewing, breaking the fast, but all she had done was gaze at him. He had not known if she was condemning him, but feared that she might do so in a public way. He had not swallowed until she looked away.

After the fast, Mrs. Edwards had sent Leah to their house with a basket full of bread and chess pie. They had plenty of food. Elisha had drawn himself up in their doorway and had made Leah leave before his mother saw the basket. "Eat it in the woods," he had commanded, doing his best imitation of his father in his own high, young voice. "Nobody will know."

She had looked at him silently, but had taken the basket away.

It made him angry. Mr. Edwards hadn't said anything about spit when Abigail Hutchinson died two weeks ago; then, Elisha had seen only sadness. All of the saving, praying, and meeting in this God-addled town had left it dripping with God's spittle while his father's soul fled barefoot into a field of cold devils. Eben Pomeroy had told him that devils were drawn to revivals and other great works of God, so as to do fiercer battle with the Lord. There did not seem to be much that Elisha could do about that, but, half consumed with anger and night terrors every night in his cot, he wanted to prepare in more practical ways than prayer against the dangers of the world. He wasn't sure how to do it, but had decided to start with the thick, quavering dark.

Looking up at the stars with the vague intention of using them to fix his own location and stay out of the swamps. Elisha thought again about the darkness of the trundle. He felt much less frightened now in crossing the field—where he had worked grazing common herds of sheep and cattle before returning them to their owners at dusk—than he did every night in his cot. If he had still been sleeping beneath his parents' bed, he might have been able to grab his father's ankles in time to fight off the devils by reciting Psalms, some of which he would have remembered right all the way through, if he had to, he was sure. At the very least, he had the Lord's Prayer and the recitations from his primer that his teacher, Dr. Mather, who also treated the sick, had drummed into his head. He whispered some now. "A. In Adam's fall, We sinned all. B. Thy Life to mend, This Book attend. C. The Cat doth play, And after slay. D. The Dog will bite, A Thief at Night."

Elisha reminded himself to watch out for the Pomeroys' hunting dogs, who might not know him if they couldn't see him. They were supposed to be penned, but Eben could be sloppy with a latch, and, on other nights, Elisha had heard them run loose. Now, he could hear the river. The sound of it running made him feel, for the first time since he had left the house, a little frightened.

He came to a bit of firm, clear ground, downstream from where the Pleasant Street freshet entered the river, and not yet into the muck of Lyman's Swamp. He didn't give a thought to anything people might have dumped in the river from the tannery or the mills. The water would have borne any ill humours away. He felt for bare dirt, then sat down to take off his shoes and stockings. Poison ivy grew at spots along the bank, and he didn't want to sit in a patch. He had been at the river at night to hunt eels with Joseph and Eben Pomeroy, but they had brought torches and dogs. As his lone state struck him, he got a flash in the dark of his father struggling on the parlor floor, then felt a sudden sting of pain. Mosquitoes were biting his feet.

Slapping away bugs and fear, he unbuckled his breeches, stepped out of them, and pulled his long shirt off over his head. Pale, harried by bites, and determined to test his own mettle, he moved to the edge of the bank and slid slowly into the water.

The cold was a shock on such a hot night, and he wondered if he were being leeched of vital humours as he caught a few thrashing breaths. He grabbed hold of a root in the side of a bank and tried to wriggle like an eel to stay afloat. He found himself on his back, waving one hand in the water as if it were a fin, his legs hanging loosely, bent at the knee. He hovered there, suspended, a husk of a body held and jostled by the river. He wanted more than anything to let go of the root and float with the current as far as the river might go. If he made it all the way to the Connecticut, that might be very far, indeed.

It was the thought of getting home after the drift that held him back. Mosquitoes were still circling his head. He shook it violently, but the one settled in his hair didn't budge. He couldn't face the prospect of a walk naked to the mosquitoes, stumbling through poison ivy, nettles, and rocks, trying to find his clothes again in the dark. He cast a more fully empathetic thought toward Colonel Stoddard in the fields

Susan Stinson

of snow, then held his breath and let his face go under to clear off the mosquitoes.

Elisha never rested in the water, but clung to his slippery root for a good length of time, working his free arm to stay afloat. He let himself think about the things that might be near him in the river, the shad that could be wavering past his legs with their cold eyes and active little mouths. Joseph had caught a snapping turtle in the Mill River that bit through a branch as thick as Elisha's neck. The eels had their own jaws and slithering ways, and he could hear a constant, hushed crackling in the trees and grasses that might hide anything, of this earth or beyond, coming to the water to drink or feed.

He flipped on his stomach and held the root with both hands. For a moment, he thought he felt it writhing, and wondered if serpents lived in the bank. Still, he didn't let go.

He was good and scared now of whatever might be in the water, but he was also full of fight. He drew his knees in toward his chest and kicked one leg out behind him again and again, like a donkey breaking a fence or a dog scratching the air in the middle of a terrible dream. His heel broke the surface in loud, foolish splashes. Elisha's grandfather Hawley had been gored by an ox, his father had cut himself out of his body, but Elisha had left his own knife on the bank. He wanted to be braver and tougher than either of them, but when a small, dark shape flew low above him, he panicked and pulled hard on the root, scrabbling with his naked feet and grabbing the lip of grass and dirt to haul himself back onto the prickly bank.

By the third time the shape passed above him, he knew it was a bat, not a ghost. It flew swift and close to eat the swarming insects that had been dipping into him as if he were a river of their own. He grabbed his shirt and pulled it over his head, his heart pounding with the strange pleasures of leaving the river, of having gone into it, of having gone out in the night, of breaking curfew despite laws and hard preaching. His mother was a widow. He was one of two fatherless sons, but he was determined to ready himself for an unexpectedly happy life.

He lay back in the grass, waving his feet in the air to dry them before he put his stockings on. The stars clustered and thickened above him, every crease of darkness pinched and leaking light. His shirt was long enough to cover most of his legs, and he swatted his long stockings in the air as a tribute to the mosquitoes. He felt sanctified, as the prayer bids always asked. He was thudding with it. He kept seeing stars rush a ways and then go out above him. He knew he should be remarking their number and location in case they might be portents, but all he did was let his feet drop to the ground in time with one thick, bright, distant fall.

He had almost forgotten himself enough to begin to drift to sleep when he heard a strange slapping on the water. He lay still among the grasses, thinking. Bear. Fishing. Am I hidden? Hide.

The sound was quiet and rhythmic, distinct above the river's current, unmistakably approaching from upstream. He hoped it was a beaver or some other creature of the river that could do him no harm on firm ground. Moving slowly, he drew on his stockings and breeches, fastening the garters, and located his shoes. He had tucked his knife inside them, since Joseph hadn't given him a sheath. Now he took it in his hands and crawled to the edge of the water.

At first he saw nothing but the river, which took shape from its smell and the sound of lapping as much as from any glints of light. He knew where it was and how it went and so found suggestions of its edges even in the moonless dark. The mysterious slapping became another shape of sound. He trembled as he began to see the lines of a garment in the water, and soon he could catch the motion of a swimmer's dark, reaching arms.

Elisha knew that devils roamed both the earth and the waters, hunting human souls, and that the ground itself might bleed where a murderer walked. He suspected that his father's death had been violence enough to excite monsters and marvels, although possibly not this far from the house. He endured the hungry mosquitoes covering his neck without moving or flinching. When a prayer started to rise, it didn't come from him.

The swimmer in the river was chanting in a woman's voice, reciting the Lord's Prayer and the Apostle's Creed.

Elisha couldn't have been more astonished if his knife had started to preach in his hand. Would a devil pray? He dropped the knife and gripped the dirt, caught with the wild fear that the figure in the river was his mother, chasing him with prayers. The voice that was not at all his mother's was very near him, saying what he thought was a Psalm.

"Deliver me, oh my God, out of the hand of the wicked, out of the hand of the unrighteous and cruel man."

He heard her pass him, then stop and clamber out onto the bank. He held himself low and still as he heard her strike a flint, and stared through the flash as the Edwardses' servant Leah stood on the riverbank in her wet shift, cupping her hand over a lit pine knot as she reached into a hollow and brought out a hidden pair of shoes. Was she a witch? He had heard old stories about witches and water, but he had seen her swimming the same as him, only farther and better. Maybe she was a runaway. There were ads about escaped slaves in the Boston paper all the time. If he had been standing, he might have stepped forward, but he stayed on his belly in the dirt.

She never saw him as she put on her shoes, doused the light, and began to walk back toward town, murmuring the Ten Commandments as if she were a pious white mother seated in a parlor with a child to teach upon her lap. She didn't follow the stream that would lead between Pleasant and Pudding into the center of town, and then fork up King Street. Like him, she chose the dark path through the meadows. Still, walking to town was not running away. He watched her go.

A small bug with a hard carapace and threadlike legs crawled the length of Elisha's arm, indifferent to swimmers and prayers. It followed his shoulders to the loose neck of his shirt, skirted the feeding mosquitoes with its solemn, methodical pace to take a meditative position, shining back aslant, in the hidden, scaly region behind Elisha's unwashed ear. It clung there, vertical to the ground, and preached as the boy waited unhearing until he thought he was alone in the night:

You killed a mosquito when it was sluggish and sated with your blood, then washed the stain in the river without ever knowing it was there. You want a life of adventure? Dip yourself in the wet from the fresh crushed belly of a mosquito.

Mourning is crisp enough to eat like a leaf. Let the birds have the berries and chew where you are, boy. I who thought to leave my hungers now do little but gnaw. It's a short life, and anything that walks in sap has understood the adhesions of sweetness.

Elisha groped for his own shoes, then began his own walk home, the bug still clinging to his head.

I won't lay eggs to split and wriggle in your ear. I'm wishing vigor to you and the larvae, both. Insect wishes whir and crack under everything. I might have kissed you that morning and left my breastbone whole, but I was so intent on carving the world into an eternal meal that I had nothing to offer you, then.

I'm riding you so lightly. My feet taste your skin. I won't get greedy and scuttle. You might feel me, and that's not a thing I can afford to want. Still, I'll crawl a little higher, into the fine streets and bridges of your hair. A mosquito will keep biting under water, even as it drowns. Am I saved? Are you? You smell of the river.

When he got back to the house on Pudding Lane, Elisha paused, sobbing now, before the kitchen door. He scratched his head, fingers brushing against the bug, which opened its armored back in buzzing flight.

Chapter 4
August 1735

As Mr. Edwards rode through the meadows on the outskirts of town, he raised his eyes to the soft, green rise of Mount Tom. A few crows rose from the dust in front of him. Two took up perches on a pair of dead trees. As he watched them, it came to him that ravens fed on rotted carcasses just as devils fed on the souls of the wicked. Since Uncle Hawley's death, which had been dominating his mind and troubling his sleep for nearly three months, he'd heard of other suicide attempts and unexpected fits of melancholia. Devils had descended on Hampshire County and stomped out the revival. Satan raged against God's close presence and used the vilest means to stop the awakening from spreading, but he could not stamp out the great good that the awakening had done. Still, the Northampton congregation had become stolid and indifferent. Last night in his study, Sarah had shocked him by saying she felt he was in the danger of succumbing to melancholia himself. Now, as his horse stepped alertly, ears up and forward, Mr. Edwards took up that possibility by letting his mind spin out the question of how true grace was to be distinguished from the experience of devils.

The devil was once holy, but when he fell, he became perfectly wicked. And if those qualities and experiences which the devils are the subjects of had nothing of the nature of holiness in them, then they could be no certain signs that persons who have them are holy or gracious. Devils clearly believed in the one holy, sin-hating God, so that in itself was no evidence of grace. Mr. Edwards began ticking off all of the things that damned men and devils would experience on judgment day, which therefore could be no sure sign of grace. Applying logic to dread revived him.

As he rode Pleasant along a cornfield, the crows suddenly left the stalks in a dense flock, troubled away from their thieving by an onslaught of boys. The boys, mostly Roots and Pomeroys by the looks of them, came hurtling fast from the direction of the river, pelting the air with fists full of stones. As Mr. Edwards saw the Hawley boys running through the corn, he felt his heart clutch as if they were once again hurtling into his yard to cry out that their father had cut his throat.

Most of boys stopped running when they saw Mr. Edwards, who had to work to control his mind and his horse, but Elisha, the smallest, hurled another rock at the circling flock. The boy stumbled to the ground and came up screeching, holding a crow's body high in the air. Mr. Edwards, who had seen nothing fall from the sky, was in some doubt as to the cause of the crow's death, but there was no doubting the boy's pride as he claimed his prize. There were so many crows in the fields that summer that the town had put a bounty on their corpses.

Elisha, still brandishing the body of the crow, led the rest of the boys away from the road. Most touched their hats to acknowledge their minister, but Elisha did not glance his way. He seemed much more frantic than he had been before his father had died. His older brother, Joseph, was lagging behind. He stopped and waved at Mr. Edwards, disturbing the crows, which seemed inclined to settle back on the corn in the wake of the other boys, who were dropping abruptly out of sight in the stalks, stooping, no doubt, to gather more stones with which to earn their shillings. Joseph, standing alone, waved again and called out something impossible to hear. Mr. Edwards couldn't face turning his horse to walk through the corn to speak to the boy, just then, so, belly twinging with guilt, he raised his hat, then clicked his tongue to urge the horse into a canter, away from the cultivated places to the woods.

The woods were swarming with mosquitoes, so he found a clearing where he could kneel in the sun. All around him, grasses spiked off into seed heads, gold and dry. Berries turned white behind small flowers. His knees crushed low leaves that smelled of lemon. Green shimmered everywhere, but instead of resuming his analysis of devils or marking the resemblance between the shining field and a virtuous soul, he knelt there, clutching his gut, fighting despair.

Until Uncle Hawley died, the people had been with him. Now, he could barely keep them awake. Perhaps if Mr. Colman in Boston published his account of the revival, it might stir people's souls again, but, as yet, there had been no word.

All around the clearing, leaves were shushing as if their surfaces were mouths. Some loosened and dropped as, even in August, they do. Crows flapped by, first one, then three together, making their percussive, conversational cries. Mr. Edwards felt another clutch of worry for the Hawley boys; for Elisha, who seemed to think that he could knock every bird from the sky, and especially for Joseph, who looked so lost as he stood waving in the field, and was so quick when questioned about matters such as where the Israelites had pitched their tents when the Philistines gathered their armies at Aphek.

Christ expressly used ravens as types of the devil in the parable of the sower and the seeds. Perhaps he could add this to a sermon, directed to Joseph, to all the boys, who were spending so much time hunting crows in the fields. Mr. Edwards received the thought as a gift. He fumbled in his great coat, but he had no paper, quill, or ink. Denied the comfort of making notes, he felt a spasm of putrefaction in his nether parts. The charcoal he had been taking in his porridge seemed to do him no good. He was not approaching prayer, and bugs had followed him into the sun.

The crack and thud of a tree coming down made him realize that he had been hearing the sound of an axe. Glancing over toward the next rise, he saw Bernard Bartlett and two of his sons working their wood lot. It occurred to Mr. Edwards that he might set his man Saul to work chopping wood, too, if Sarah could spare him from the fields. Although they were often slow about it, the townspeople supplied the Edwards family with wood as part of his living as their minister. If Saul did some chopping, as well, Mr. Edwards would have enough to spare that he could send a cartful to the Hawleys to season for winter. It was a small thing after such a terrible loss.

Crows cawed above him. He thought that they, hunted themselves, might be harrying an owl, as they often drew together in daylight to do. Mr. Edwards suddenly remembered the story of his great aunt, who had killed her own seventeen-year-old son in his bed, and that of his great uncle, her brother, who had killed yet another of his sisters in front of the hearth. Both had used axes. Mr. Edwards's grandmother was sister to them both.

The stories had been half whispered to him by a boy his age— Joseph Hawley's age now—who had been the family's slave. Once or twice, hard trouble had been referred to indirectly, with evasive walls of praise, when Mr. Edwards's father had spoken about his own father, who had married into that family. Now he pictured the murder before the hearth with a terrible freshness fed by the image of Uncle Hawley bleeding to death in his own parlor. Both deaths had been witnessed by children.

He shivered in the sun, thinking of Joseph holding on to his coat in that parlor. The boy had stayed close behind him as if they were still on the horse. His mother had to take him by the shoulders and lead him bodily into the kitchen to give Mr. Edwards room to kneel. Remembering the stillness of Joseph's face as he had been pulled from the room, Mr. Edwards thought again of his own father. Timothy Edwards's mother had been pregnant with another man's child when she had married his father. Later, she had threatened to cut her husband's throat, sister of two murderers that she was. It had all come out in the divorce proceedings. Timothy Edwards, their eldest boy, had given testimony against his mother. Mr. Edwards hated the thought of this public ravaging, although he knew it had been right. He felt panicked, as if the hoarse calls of the birds had separated from their throats and wrapped his own. The children had been taken from the woman, and if anyone knew what became of her, he had never been told.

He slapped a mosquito that had settled on his eyelid. The slights of mortal suffering were soon over for a bug. He knelt, bitten and swatting, thinking again of Joseph, so like himself as a boy, stopped in the field. When human life was too much for a man to bear, what could be asked of boys? Convulsed by a shudder of nausea, Mr. Edwards lost all thought.

Bernard Bartlett looked up from his chopping to see Mr. Edwards on his hands and knees, vomiting bile black as charcoal all over the ground. Mr. Bartlett dropped his axe and rushed through the woods, his sons running behind him. They lifted Mr. Edwards onto his horse to lead him home, calling the boys in from their hunting in the cornfield to walk alongside ready to catch him, should the need arise. Joseph felt hysterical at the sight of Mr. Edwards slumped helplessly on his horse, but he marshaled his courage and kept close as he walked so that his shoulder braced his minister's knee. Elisha, by turns running ahead and falling behind, was equally serious, although of less actual help.

Later, in the tavern, Bernard Bartlett told the whole bar that when Mr. Edwards fell sick, he had given a raucous cry like that of a crow.

"Devils are everywhere in these parts these days," he added. No one declared him in the wrong.

Sarah put her husband, who often suffered disturbances of the stomach, to bed. When she joined him after the children were asleep, she felt heat and misery along the whole sweaty length of him. She lay awake much of the night, trying to think what might help heal her husband's grief, which would also ease her own. Mr. Edwards seemed much restored in the morning. Sarah, who didn't trust his abrupt equanimity, wanted him to rest in bed badly enough to consider giving him a double dose of anise and rhubarb to further trouble his bowels, but knew her duty and did not do it.

Late in the morning, Sarah sat on a stool stringing beans as Mr. Edwards paced back and forth in front of her in the hot kitchen, reading a draft of his sermon. "But this very much spoils the beauty of the public worship to see men to and fro in the assembly sleeping in the time of public service. 'Tis a very disagreeable and unlovely sight and will tend very much to the prejudice of religion amongst us, and especially to be a stumbling block to the unconverted." He lowered the manuscript. "Honestly, do they not know that I can see them snoring? They have returned to their sins like a dog to its vomit."

Sarah snapped a bean in two, "That reminds me, did you inhale your birch smoke this morning? I mixed charcoal in with your oats, but it might not be enough."

Mr. Edwards (who, had, in fact, forgotten) did not relish being reminded that he was suffering from a bad case of griping in the guts. "That's hardly the point, Sarah," he said, his belly rumbling unpleasantly, just as Mrs. Clapp, carrying a dish covered with a cotton napkin, knocked at the kitchen door.

"Leek stew," she announced, pushing a mound of beans aside to set the dish on the table. "Good for what ails you. Have a bowl, sir." Mr. Edwards, not poised in the best of times, was hit by a wave of nauseous cramps. He half bowed, quoting scripture on his way out the door. "No thank you, Madame."

Sarah was on her feet, resisting the urge to glare at her husband's back in favor of gesturing Mrs. Clapp toward the seat of honor at the head of the table. The last thing they needed was for a member of the church to take offense when she was attempting a kindness. "What beautiful leeks, and so early, too."

Mrs. Clapp took a seat, looking thoughtfully after Mr. Edwards as he rushed toward the jakes. "What ails your husband?"

Sarah was trying her best, but she did not like the woman's tone. She put down the leeks and quoted the Bible. "His mind is entertained with meat to eat that others know not of."

In May in the grip of the awakening, Mrs. Clapp might have burst into tears and begun to praise God at the sound of a Bible verse. Now, though, she rolled her eyes.

"Comfrey tea and a poultice for his belly."

Sarah gathered herself and controlled her temper. She didn't know how much of the conversation with her husband Mrs. Clapp had overheard, but decided to count her blessings not to be discussing dogs and vomit as they pertained to the congregation. She took a small breath, then spoke sweetly. "Shall we sample a bit of your soup?"

Late that afternoon, Sarah found herself—irritable from worry, Mrs. Clapp, and lack of sleep—chasing her chickens. Too foolish to come in out of the rain, they were splashing across the yard on their splayed, scaly feet. Finally, one forgot to run and started pecking the muddy ground, so she grabbed it and tossed it squawking into the henhouse.

"I should leave you out all night to feed the foxes," she yelled at a particularly agile hen with a leaf caught in its wattle, which darted past Sarah's sodden skirts into the barn.

She stomped in after it to find Saul stacking hay with a steady rhythm, ignoring the hen, which was settling down on loose hay with satisfied little clucks. The sight of its sudden contentment made Sarah feel wild, but she could hardly scream at a chicken in front of a servant, so she turned to him. "That's not all the hay, is it?"

He stopped stacking. "No, Madame, it's all cut, but we had to leave some in the field. The rain."

Sarah usually made an effort to give her directives in a mild, reasonable way, but now she was furious. "You should have finished. I find that slothful." She tried to wring the anger out of her voice, but it was no use. Feeling polluted herself, she said, "Saul, you must conquer the pollutions that are so strong in your people."

Saul did not answer, but simply looked at her, letting her see every bit of hard weather in his face. Christians had the duty to point out each other's sins and errors, but he knew he had no leave to speak of hers. All she had given him to work with that day was a team of borrowed oxen and Timothy and Simeon Root, a pair of sly cousins who had staked out a tiny corner of the field in which to do their cocky, slovenly, lackadaisical work. They had fled at the first sign of rain, and still she had stopped Saul in his stacking—hungry, dirty, and wet—to speak of his people in a way that would never cause any good work to be done in the field or in the soul. The insult burned in places where he had thought all feeling was gone. He didn't speak or nod, but turned back to his work until Sarah, ashamed for reasons that were obscure to her, gathered the hen and left the barn. Then he spit on the hay-covered ground.

He didn't speak of this, or of much of anything, to Leah for two nights. On the third, Leah swept out the kitchen hearth, went to the back-house, and sat down to shell beans. Saul was already up in his loft, but, tired as he was, he climbed down the ladder, sat across from her on a stump chair padded with a folded blanket, and said, "Mrs. Edwards was mad about the wet hay."

Leah looked at him. "There's always something to be mad about."

The expression on his face made her think that he might be about to curse or cry, so she got up to fetch the stone jug. She poured spruce beer into a wooden cup that he had scraped and carved over many nights until it was smooth to the lips and decorated with faces that were all round eyes and deep lines for each nose. She poured beer into her own carved cup and sat back down before the purple-specked beans and their split, shed skins. She waited a long time for him to talk. He drank and said nothing, until finally he shook his head again, swallowed big, then made a bow in her direction and got up from the stump to climb the ladder to his loft to go to sleep.

The next morning, Leah cleaned a pig's foot for pie while Sarah kneaded the bread. Thinking of Saul's raw silence, she said, "Madame, may I speak to you?"

Sarah was finding her dough a bit flat. Still, she and Mr. Edwards had both slept soundly the night before, so she pushed into the loaf and said pleasantly, "Yes, Leah, what is it?"

Leah scraped the hoof and risked her question. "I feel an urge in my heart to join the church." Not a question, after all. She kept working the hoof.

Sarah looked down. The only sounds in the kitchen were the spitting fire, the thump of her hand in the dough, and the rasp of

Leah's knife. She thought that her servant's intensity about the task with the pig's foot seemed almost like criticism, and as she gazed through her lashes at Leah's moving hands, she did not fight the recognition that she deserved it. Neither did she articulate why, not to God, and not to herself, but she punched the dough and considered her duty. Finally she said, "Undertake to study the Bible. I will tell the girls to help you. And I will talk with Mr. Edwards."

"Thank you, Madame." Leah had learned the alphabet in the household of her first enslaver, but she never used it, and had largely forgotten. She had a gift, though, for remembering passages of scripture. She had the sixty-ninth psalm with its waters and deep mire pounding in her head, and had come today ready to recite it. Instead, she put her full weight behind the knife. Madame had not said yes, but this was an opening.

In the afternoon, Leah took some eggs to the Pomeroys and helped her friend Bathsheba lug the washtub into the yard as she reported on her conversation with Sarah. "So, what we have to do now is apply ourselves to the study of religion."

"Well, now that most of them have left off crying in the Edwardses' parlor every night, there should be room for us to take it up." She laid more wood under the tub.

Leah shook her head at her friend's hard tone. She knew it was earned, but it would not help them in the study of religion, which she intended to do in earnest.

Bathsheba poured another bucket of water in and said, "It has got to be at least as profitable an employment as beating dirt from bed linen with a stick."

In the morning, Leah went to the barn to milk. She sat beside the brown cow with the speck of white on the right side of its nose, rubbing the udders to bring down the milk. When the animal swung its head to look at her, Leah leaned forward and waved flies away from the corners of its eyes with her cheek pressed against its loud, warm belly. She felt strangely moved by the gurgles, the circling flies, the slowness of the milk, the emptiness of the pail, the calmness of the eyes, the darkness of the barn, and the glints of light on the dust that rose in a stately haze from the scattered hay and grain in the raked-over mud to the weathered crossbeams above the wooden ladder to the loft. She wanted to sleep, but she wanted more to climb. She rose, and, stepping around the empty bucket, went up the ladder hand over hand into the hayloft. The cow raised its head to watch, and the flies, disturbed from their sojourns on mounds of dung, swarmed more thickly into the slant of light.

Ignoring the rustling in corners and the lowing of the cows below, Leah dropped on her back in the fresh-stacked hay while the flies settled into stillness in cracks and flat places on the rough plank walls. She took off her shoes and let her bare feet rest on the scattered pads of loose hay on the weathered boards. There were spiders in the corners, gnats shaking the webs. Moths gnawed and flew above the cribs full of oats and corn. Leah smelled the sharp, smothering, awakening smell of hay, then she felt a Bible verse pulse through her as if she had taken into her body a ball of light the size of a fist.

I have digged and drunk water; and with the soles of my feet have I dried up all the rivers of the besieged places.

Still on her back, Leah remembered that her mother had taught her never to put her feet on a chair, and never to do another person the disrespect of pointing her soles toward them. Her feet had power. She kicked hay aside and began to stomp, reckless of noise and the shaking of the boards. Straw scratched against her legs and caught on her hem, but she didn't stop. She beat the floor of the hay loft with the soles of her feet until the blood in her veins slowed to a seep.

If any do thirst, let them come to me.

A voice seemed to rise from the cracks between the boards. Stilling her feet, she heard a rustling below her, as if something, maybe a rat, were coming through the hay. She sat up, but could find nothing, until a brush on her forearm made her look down to see the shine of a spider's abdomen dragging across her rolled-up sleeve and disappearing around her elbow. Feeling skittish, she lifted her arm but could not see the back of it. There was no tickle of legs through the fabric of her sleeve. She didn't want to try to kill it, for hadn't she heard scripture and been thinking of her mother, both things to mark a moment apart from ordinary life? Besides, attacked, the spider might bite, so instead of slapping, she brought her arm near her face, pursed her lips, and blew.

The spider, the color of tar and old honey, rounded the top of her arm. It stopped there, raising bristled front legs. Leah blew directly at it, and just as she was fighting the idea of it crawling across the edge of her mouth onto her teeth, it crouched and jumped to where her skirt folded over her lap.

Leah, losing sight of it, took a breath. "Trickster," she whispered. As she relaxed, the spider appeared again, climbing her dress, coming upside down over a breast, heading toward the skin of her neck.

Leah took up a handful of straw and knocked the spider to the floor of the loft, but it righted itself and jumped onto the straw in her hand. She flung the straw away. The spider landed under the small heap, but climbed out and crouched. She blocked its jump with one of her shoes, coaxed the spider onto the sole, then shook it off into a crack between the boards of the loft. It might have fallen, but, instead, dangled high above the bucket and the cow looking up from below.

Leah put her shoes on and watched as the spider, still in the crack, walked the thin edge of board, coming toward her. She did not know what it wanted, could never know. This, in itself, was revelation. Her feet and legs prickled with how much she couldn't know. She shivered, then sat utterly still, praising, thanking and fearing God while the spider came with inhuman persistence along the board. Finally, she bent over the crack and hummed into it. She made the sound, which was almost a whistle, with parted lips. The spider dropped from the loft, throwing a strand of web that glistened like a piece of her own hair.

Leah came down the ladder, filled with God and suddenly thirsty. The cow gave her more than enough milk to fill the bucket and also to fill the tin cup which hung on a nail for anyone needing to drink. Leah gulped it down, frothy and warm, keeping her eye out for the spider, but it had gone to a secret place, or else was hiding in plain sight as a dappled spot on the hay that littered the ground.

Saul was spreading a stack of damp hay to dry in the field when he saw Leah coming across the pasture. She was carrying a packet of food and a bucket of water, and she had her hair tied in a white cambric cloth. The hem of her skirt was tucked up in her waistband so that the bottom edge made a scallop moving cleanly above the ground. She had a beautiful motion, as if she carried the promise of fall's wheat rippling through her as she strode forward, bringing a meal, watching him.

The sun was high, so they went to eat in the shade of a maple. They sat among its roots at the edge of the common woodlot, which was the only place for those without a lot of their own to get wood for ten miles around. All the wood rights had recently been voted to revert to the proprietors—the founding families of the town and their designees—in ten years' time. What could be owned, what should be shared, and who decided were questions that Saul muscled around in his head most every working day, which was every day except for the Sabbath, fast days, and thanksgivings, when sometimes he prayed about them, too. Saul prayed like he worked, not with belief or hope, but with a percussive strength that the gods of this valley demanded of him. He and Leah thanked the Lord before they ate their pig's foot and bread.

Leah dipped the cup into the bucket, took a drink, and then said, "Something happened over the milking this morning."

Saul wiped his hands on the grass and sat back to listen.

As she told him about the spider and the verses of scripture she had heard, wind was blowing in the maple leaves, which crackled like fat in a skillet. Saul looked to the hay, which was stirring. Leah knew she had to tell him. "I want to join the church."

He didn't even shake his head, but as she suffered his silence, she felt that he was standing before her as he did during prayers in the parlor, worshipping nothing. A verse of scripture came to her, and she said it aloud, although whether it was a warning for him or her, she could not tell: "How much she hath glorified herself and lived deliciously, so much torment and sorrow give her: for she saith in her heart, I sit a queen, and am no widow, and shall see no sorrow."

Saul closed his eyes as she spoke. When she finished, he opened them slowly, then stood, knees stiff and back aching. The wind had calmed. He gave her his hand, and she took it and rose. He picked up the half-empty bucket, then began to walk to his work. He didn't have anything to say about her vision. Leah was disappointed but not surprised. As she caught up to him, he was looking back at a dragonfly darting among midges at the edge of the woods. It made her hope. Leah had learned from listening to Mr. Edwards that inclining toward beauty was a sign of a soul receiving and embracing the savior that devils and the damned never see.

Saul shifted the bucket in his hand. "I need to learn how to stay up in water. Will you teach me?"

She blinked, but did not hesitate. "Yes."

That night she made him turn his clothes inside out to discourage ghosts, then led the way to the Mill River, silently saying prayers to appease the bears and bobcats, as well as the sleeping people of Northampton and their fiercely jealous God. She kicked in the water and called aloud to the father with his hallowed name.

Saul thrashed as she gave him instruction in swimming. After he made it back to the bank, he watched intently, as, neck deep in the river, she found her footing and drank.

The next afternoon, still in a heightened state, Leah cleaned the study. The cut hay in the field was not yet dry, so Saul was out harvesting corn. Madame was husking with her daughters and neighbors on stumps and chairs set in the yard. Leah finished her sweeping and approached Mr. Edwards's reading table, where books were gathering dust.

There were no windows in the study, but Leah could hear the girls and women speaking and laughing over the sounds of ripping husks and scraping cobs. As she touched the big, leather-bound Bible, she thought of the pleasures of corn husking: opening the corn, the silk and mess of it, the pearly kernels full of sweetness. She could, she knew, join that work, and would go when summoned to bring cakes and drinks out to the ladies gathered in the sunlight, surrounded by the dance of gnats slowed and made fewer by the season's cooling air.

She let the Bible's pages drop as lightly as husks to wherever they opened naturally. The scripture was printed in the center of each page, surrounded by ruled paper covered with Mr. Edwards's handwriting. She thought to try to recognize the letters, or maybe even words, without any knowledge or context, nothing read aloud to leave a path of sound from which to trace their shapes. When the book fell open, though, she found that the words, printed and handwritten, weren't speaking at all, but had settled into a backdrop for a dead fly. It was a portent, like the spider.

She tried to read it, thicker than paper, flattened and still. The small head was all red eyes, which were divided into facets like jewels cut for a ring. One leg was stretched out straight—jointed, twiggy, and delicate; the other was in the familiar crouch, pulled up close to the soft, lint-gray body which had leaked yellow at the shoulder and out the back. There was only one antenna.

Leah was bent low over the table, her hands framing the page, but now she stood up straight, no longer touching the open book, looking down at the fly from her full height. What she saw was a small, dead body with big red eyes. It was a nuisance, a letter written in skewed wings that said that she might die sooner than she thought, that she too might be caught in the thoughtless closure of a book. Anything that lived in the sky might look down or not, might see Leah or not, might wait until she had died to play with her bones, or might have other business with greater beings than her and never open the world to this page at all, if the world were a book. If the world were a wind, everything would buzz. If the world were a fly, people might speckle its wings or gather on dung in hopes of the coming of vast, rubbing legs or the damp paths of the young or the glories of being swallowed into one urgent day of god-swatted life.

Leah was still reading the fly against silk strands of words when Mr. Edwards opened the door behind her, letting in afternoon light.

"Lawful heart!" Leah swung around to face him. She had been hoping to find him, but now she was nervous.

"Ah, yes, Leah, I am glad you are here." He approached her curiously. He followed the teachings of his grandfather Stoddard, minister in Northampton for sixty years before him, and, so, unlike many churches outside their valley, did not require that a new member give a spoken profession of an experience of grace before the congregation in order to join. Still, bearing witness to accounts of such experiences, no matter how humble, was one of his most sacred and sustaining duties. It was especially dear to him now that he had had to use the pulpit to condemn sleeping in church, advocating that good Christians jog the slumberer's arm, and that no persons so jabbed should take offense. Sarah felt that the sermon had not been well received. He very much wanted to hear what his slave had to say. "Mrs. Edwards advises me that I should question you about your faith."

Leah grasped the broom more firmly to remind herself that she had been cleaning, and both of them looked down at his Bible open on the reading table, the fly dead on the scrawl of notes. For several moments, they gazed at it together in silence.

Finally, he said, "You can't read, can you? I have been neglectful. The girls must teach you."

Leah wanted to tell him about reading the fly, and how the spider had made her tremble yesterday morning in the barn. She wanted to talk about how she had trusted in God as the boards of the hayloft had groaned aloud under her feet, and try to explain how the touch of the spider skittering on her skin had felt like reading each of her names, known and secret, in the language in which it had been given, in the book of life. She wanted to tell him, and he was looking at her openly, eagerly, thirsty himself for signs of grace come to end this dying time in Northampton.

She was about to speak when little Jerusha knocked on the door frame. When her father turned to beckon her in, she came close enough to Leah to brush against her skirts. "Mama said that she would have you go and fetch more corn with the hand cart."

Corn. Leah nodded, and Mr. Edwards walked to his desk, glancing at the pile of papers there. Jerusha noticed the fly and (the image of her efficient mother) pulled a handkerchief from her sleeve which she used to knock it to the floor. The body lodged against the bristles of the broom with other such dust. Then, five-year-old that she was, Jerusha squatted down to look more closely. "If it were still alive, we could capture it under that bowl and name it Zacharias."

"Tell your mother that Leah will be there soon," Mr. Edwards said. "I need to ask her about sin and divine love."

The possessiveness of the child, the casual claiming, made Leah glad that she had not spoken. By the time they finished in the study, Mr. Edwards believed that Leah was under genuine religious convictions, confirming what she felt so deeply herself, but she said nothing to him about the dead fly or the spider in the hayloft. She did not feel required to give them up as testimony. As much as a creature living or dead could belong to anyone but God, they were hers.

Chapter 5
December 1735 – January 1736

As the months passed, the town settled back into ordinary life. There was more time to be social as work slowed in winter. On a militia training day in December, when men filled Stebbins's tavern down by the ferry after their drills, Elisha sat near the door, teasing the cat with a cork attached to a string and earning a few shillings by keeping his eye on the horses tied out front, especially Bernard Bartlett's old swayback, which sometimes chewed fences. He was to be paid for looking after the horses, but spent as much time surreptitiously watching Bernard Bartlett himself, who, at the center of a rowdy table drinking flip, was the loudest man in the place.

Joseph was off studying in the Edwardses' parlor, which he did so often that Elisha, flicking the cork at the cat's nose, suspected his brother of wishing to live there. While most of the town was falling away from religion, Joseph was digging deeper in. Both boys worked at the mill, the family store, and in the fields as needed, edging away from their mother, although they worried about her constantly. Elisha had overheard Mrs. Root outside the store saying that his mother had gone so sour with grief that she was surprised that it didn't taint the milk. He always searched for a little mold or cracking in a cheese to sell her after that, but she or, more often, her comely daughter Martha, still came back for more.

He wouldn't have said that Rebekah had soured, but she had become bigger and louder since their father had died. She had given Joseph his books. Virgil. Cicero's *Oratio*, a volume on military discipline, which had belonged to his grandfather, who had practiced law.

"Before he was *gored!*" Elisha would yell to make Joseph stop bragging about his library. It never worked. Elisha was short and, according to Joseph, puny, although the younger boy already had a chest very like an ox, and, like their mother, was loud and stout. One afternoon when Joseph pressed the puny business after citing *The Rules of Pleading* once too often, Elisha charged with his head down and stiff-armed his older brother right in the stomach. "Gored!"

Joseph fell over and, for once, shut up.

As much as Joseph was obsessed with the subject of their grandfather's practice of law, he had confided in Elisha that he wanted to go to Yale to study divinity. He rattled off the things he needed to know to be accepted. "The Four Evangelists in Greek. Latin, Hebrew, rhetoric, logic, math, and oratory. And a good word from Mr. Edwards might help."

Elisha hated that Joseph was so enthralled with Mr. Edwards. He no sooner would have set himself up to study in that house full of girls and preachers than he would have gone back to wearing a gown. Even during the awakening, the tavern had been almost as crowded of an evening as the minister's house. He couldn't think of anyone except Joseph and a few other mealy-faced scholars who relished dawdling in the Edwardses' parlor now.

Bernard Bartlett and the men at his table gave a great shout as Mr. Stebbins took the iron from the fire and thrust it into a flip mug to burn the rum. They were red-faced and arguing about why their town should go to the expense of building both a new meeting house and a courthouse when just a meeting house had been fine until now. Bernard Bartlett waved his stick and bellowed, "Just wait, they'll be setting women from the fine families, your Stoddards and your Dwights, they'll be putting them front and center in the best pews nestled up to their husbands, while good men are thrust to the back. It's indecent. I won't stand for it."

His sons were sprawled on benches on either side of him. The taller one cocked one eyebrow, looking up at his father towering over him, red-faced and swaying, and said mildly, "Won't come to that, Father. There will be a seating committee."

Bernard Bartlett snorted, then shouted, "That's them! That'll be those in the front. It's always the same."

Elisha, whose father had sat on a bench front and center, felt embarrassed but invisible, young and nondescript as he was. Not everyone in the room was listening to Bernard Bartlett, but the ones that were just nodded, laughed or shrugged. Mr. Stebbins, the innkeeper, started scrambling eggs in a long-handled pan over the fire, which Elisha had seen him do before when he wanted to sober up a messy drunk. Not even the most pious families balked at drinking, but a taverner was required to keep good rule.

Elisha was fretting that Mr. Stebbins, who sometimes turned him into a serving boy, would have him bring the eggs rather than slipping them discreetly onto the Bartletts' table himself. It was a tricky thing, not just because Bernard Bartlett might be offended—or recognize a Hawley if he thrust a plate under his nose—but also because Mr. Stebbins had no desire to feed eggs to the entire house.

Elisha rolled the string around the cork and kicked it across the floor for the lazy cat, who fixed it with her eyes, but didn't move. He was just pulling on his coat to slip out the door on the pretext of tending the horses when Bernard Bartlett erupted in a furious roar. "It's the devil, I tell you. He's listening to the devil, not to God."

This was a serious oath, actionable in court. Every other conversation stopped as people waited to hear if he would say a name.

Bartlett's sons had both risen. One was trying to get his father's attention by jostling his shoulder; the other raised a hand to his own mouth, as if stopping speech. Bernard Bartlett fixed his eyes on this one and cried, "Oh, not say it, not say it, then you're in league with the devil, too. Didn't we see Mr. Edwards in the woods on his hands and knees like a beast, emitting matter as black as his heart?"

Mr. Edwards. The minister. It was the worst case. Struggling with his sons, who were trying to restrain him, Bartlett railed on. "Hasn't he roiled up all kinds of demons and haunts and bad airs? He's speaking the word of the Devil, not of God, and that boy has got the worst of it." He shook a thick finger in Elisha's direction.

The boy stopped in his tracks, no longer edging toward the door, and leaned with deliberate casualness on the back of a chair like an experienced sport, reaching to the floor to send the cork spinning, since the cat had finally bestirred herself to knock it about. He felt calm and strangely warm. Bartlett was pointing at him, babbling and cursing their minister in a drunken way because his father had killed himself. Elisha did not give a straw about the devil when there was such a braying ass right there in the flesh. His guts were burning, but he would be damned before he would react. He might blame Mr. Edwards in his own heart, but this public raving made him feel as if he were being stripped of his skin. He wished for Joseph. He wished for his mother.

Mr. Stebbins pulled the pan from the fire, calling, "I'll not have such talk against Mr. Edwards in my establishment. If you knew what was good for you, which you don't, you'd hasten to the parsonage right now and ask pardon of Mr. Edwards after you prayed for God to forgive your sins. Or face the consequences."

That got through to Bernard Bartlett, who blinked and said, "Beg pardon." His boys let go of his coat.

Elisha sat down and picked up the cat, which was rubbing his legs. He stroked her with profound concentration, ignoring the dig of claws as she kneaded his arm. People stopped looking at him and went back to their drinking, some of them muttering to each other. It was blasphemy to say that they'd been listening to the word of the devil from their preacher. Mr. Stebbins brought the eggs to the table himself, setting the plates down in front of the Bartletts with a stern look and a few low words. Elisha kept his eyes on the rumpled black hair of the purring cat as Bernard Bartlett and his sons ate quickly, finished their flip, then stood and came toward the door. Elisha didn't take the coin that Mr. Bartlett waved in his face, but grabbed the man's chapped hand and pressed the cat's cork in his palm, instead. Elisha whispered into the back of the cat's neck. "To plug that great, gawping, ignorant mouth of yours."

The men didn't make out what he said, and neither did they ask. Perhaps Elisha's thoughts were visible on his face, though, because Bernard Bartlett opened his mouth to speak, then closed it again and staggered out with his sons into the winter night, the cork string straggling from his fingers. The cat stared after it as if ready to pounce, but did not stir from Elisha's lap.

"Stay out of the tavern," said Joseph when Elisha told him what had happened. They were raking dung from Pudding Lane in front of the house. "That way you don't have to listen to drunks."

Elisha, who had been feeling queasy at the smell of pipe smoke and burnt rum ever since Bernard Bartlett had waved a finger at him, gave no ground. "Listening to you is worse." Then he dropped his rake and jerked Joseph by his knees into the dirt.

They wrestled in the empty road until Joseph, going for Elisha's belly with his elbow, accidently bashed his eye. It swelled shut. Joseph made a compress for it out of one of his detachable cuffs and some week-old snow. Rebekah, who had been in the buttery in the grip of one of her bad spells, seemed not to notice. They had raked their marks from the dust after the fight.

Elisha never held a grudge. He was actually relieved that Joseph hadn't tried to make a theological point, for once. Joseph held grudges, but never toward Elisha. He loved the capacity for forgiveness in his brother and mourned the lack in himself. They didn't speak of their father. They tried not to speak of Bernard Bartlett, either, until it became impossible to avoid the subject of what had happened in the tavern with anyone in town.

On the day of Bernard Bartlett's flogging, Joseph and Elisha rode into the center of Northampton on their father's favorite horse. There was new snow on the icy, rutted road, which gave the big old bay good footing, and they let Eben Pomeroy swing up behind Elisha when he hallooed from the side of Pudding Lane. His family had taken their wagon, but he had been allowed to walk rather than squeeze in with the rest.

Rebekah Hawley had stayed to mind the store. "I've spent enough afternoons with ghouls and gawkers to last me a lifetime," she had said, handing each of her boys a packet of boiled potatoes and bacon, in case they got hungry. She didn't have to say that the gawkers would be with her all day, buying nails and saws and telling every flogging story they knew, since everyone in Hampshire County saved up their errands for a trip to town when court was in session.

Mr. Sheldon didn't ring the bell to bring people in to witness the punishment, but many did come, since it was winter, with the snow deep enough for sleighs. It wasn't a hanging, with a procession of judges and ministers riding in the cart to murmur in the condemned ears, making, other mutterers said, as fine a target for a ruined pear as any poor lout headed for the pillory. Those about to die gave speeches from the gallows, unless they could be reasonably predicted to blaspheme or spout heresy. Bernard Bartlett, even chastened, was a person much inclined to talk, but a flogging didn't merit a speech by the criminal.

Eben, whose grandfather was the high sheriff, had been hearing great billows of stories around his uncle Seth's anvil in the blacksmith shop up the hill on Elm Street for days, and he managed to tell most of them to Elisha and Joseph on their short, slow ride to Pudding Lane to town. He swung his hat at a branch laden with snow, and said, "It could have been worse. My grandfather says that a law on the books provided for blasphemy to be punished by having the tongue bored through, the nose slit, the forehead branded, and being whipped in every town in the colony, for a first offense."

Elisha, who got snow down his collar when Eben hit the branch, reached back to grab the other boy's arm, which was still waving the hat. "You don't know what you're talking about," he said, although he suspected that Eben did. He had been greatly relieved not to be called in to testify before the court against Bernard Bartlett, although everyone knew he had been at the tavern that night. "Slandering Mr. Edwards was what he did."

"Stop that," said Joseph, swatting his brother without turning around. "You two want to spook the horse?" The bay was old and calm, very accustomed to having boys on his back, but he had been flattening his ears, a sure sign of annoyance. Joseph had gone to the meeting house for the trial. He had been fascinated by the proceedings, and by the court in general, especially by the lawyers with their tie-back wigs and roomy voices. Joseph had been there when Bernard Bartlett, looking haggard and scrubbed, had been condemned to be lashed on the town common. As the sentence had been read out, Joseph saw Mrs. Bartlett hold firm, but the tallest of the Bartlett boys had begun to cry.

Eben stopped swinging his hat at the trees, put it back on his head, and talked faster. "I know a lot. Did you ever hear about Goody Parsons? Used to live right there on Bridge Street a long time ago before she was run out of town by Bridgmans and Bartletts calling her a witch. My grandfather remembers when Betty Negro was whipped ten lashes on her bare back for striking her grandson and saying that his grandmother was a killer and his mother was half a witch."

"That's got nothing to do with this." Elisha reached up with his bare hand and knocked snow off a branch onto Eben's head, who, much shielded by his hat, brushed it off with a good-natured laugh, although the bay snorted and gave an awkward hop. Elisha laughed, too, but he didn't want to hear any more stories. He half expected the flogging to change something or heal something about his father's death. He had said this to his mother, who had answered flatly, "It won't."

Joseph turned the bay off Pudding Lane and onto Bridge Street, which was too crowded with horses, carts and people walking toward the common for the boys to shake down any more snow. They had to wait a long time to cross the bridge, but although he wanted the bay to jump the frozen stream, he knew that the idea was too idiotic to try in front of all these people. They finally pushed in front of Martha and Simeon Root, who were on foot with their cousin Timothy. He brought the bay to a halt at the back of the crowd, closer to the well and the schoolhouse than to the spot next to the stocks in front of the meeting house, where the floggings took place. They were late, and had no sooner arrived than they heard the wagon with the prisoner coming up Pleasant Street from the jail. Mr. Pomeroy drove the wagon, looking neither left nor right, and boys who were strangers to Elisha and Joseph, probably in town from Hartford or Sunderland or Westfield for the session of the court, ran along beside it, throwing rotten squash, calling Bernard Bartlett Old Saucepot and accusing him of blubbering as he sat in the wagon holding on to its edge. He did look to Elisha as if he had been crying and might cry more, but he had long been a red-faced man.

Mr. Root, sworn in as constable and assigned to do the flogging, walked behind the wagon, beating a steady pace on a drum. The snow had been cleared from the main section of road through heavy use, but the ground was rough and frozen. Walking was treacherous. Among sailors, a drummer often did the flogging for the discipline and skill of his arm, but Mr. Root had no claims on either count, although he farmed, of course, and was more than strong enough. He looked at the crowd and hunched his back.

Eben whispered in Elisha's ear. "Timothy Root told me that his dad didn't want to do the whipping. Said Mr. Edwards should do it, with his precious slandered name. I told him he should know better than to repeat that. He said that all his dad could talk about was aiming the whip for the shoulders, not organs or the spine."

Elisha bent his neck as Joseph was leaning back to listen. Their heads touched. They left them together for a moment. Eben looked at the brims of their hats tilting awkwardly, then, as the boys started to draw apart, he rather gently knocked their heads together again.

Sarah Edwards rarely attended punishments, which she hated for the suffering of the punished and the avidness of the crowds, but she stood at the front next to her husband, holding baby Mary and surrounded by the rest of their girls. She could barely stand to speak, but she wished blessings on everyone who approached her. When she noticed Mrs. Lyman looking offended at her terseness, she worked to express herself more warmly. The skins would be covered and soaking in their vats of lime at the tannery, but there was still a faint smell. Mr. Edwards spoke gravely with townspeople, as well. Leah, just behind them, had one hand on Jerusha's shoulder to keep the child from sliding her feet back and forth on the ice without regard for balance or decorum.

The wagon pulled up to the pillory, and the rude boys, out of things to hurl, stepped back into the crowd. Mr. Pomeroy climbed down from the front of the wagon and, spotting Eben on the back of the old bay, motioned him over to hold the horse. Eben touched his hat respectfully and did as he was told.

They all listened to the old Reverend Mr. William Williams, husband to another daughter of the great Solomon Stoddard, like Rebekah and Mr. Edwards's mother. Mr. Williams had been brought in from Hatfield to let Mr. Edwards keep his peace in this matter that concerned him directly.

As he listened to Mr. Williams's exhortations to duty, Joseph started scratching a tuft of thick winter hair midway down the slope of the bay's nose. The horse shifted his ears in appreciation. Joseph glanced over his shoulder to confirm that Elisha was giving the rump a quiet scratch, too. It was the witness of his brother's inattention, not the experience of his own, that made him admonish himself to attend to the prayer. He turned his glance at Elisha into a stern look, but, as Mr. Williams droned on, he found his eyes drawn to Mr. Edwards, instead. They often were.

Joseph searched out the kinship with his mother in the minister's long jaw (his hands were once again scratching the horse, who snorted). He wondered why, when he was so giving in to his corruption as to let his mind wander from Mr. Williams, that he listened to everything Mr. Edwards said in sermon or prayer. He couldn't escape the words if he wanted to. Part of that might have been because there was the blood between them, his mother's, and in the other way, his father's. Joseph's mind flinched away from the memory, then arched back to his undeniable sense of their connection. He knew, because he had heard him preach it, that Mr. Edwards thought of his father's suicide as God's punishment of the town for its people's sins. He had heard others before Bernard Bartlett come close to saying that the wave of suicides were the devil's punishment of the whole valley for the awakening. Now Joseph, who knew that grace was worth any suffering, wondered if his cousin ever thought of his father's death, as he did, as punishment for himself.

How Bernard Bartlett must be suffering. He was kneeling in the wagon with squash still on his face, and the prayer was interminable. To prepare for the flogging, Mr. Edwards had sat with his young scholars in the parlor and spoken about the struggles he had had before his own awakening. Rubbing the family jaw, he had said that he had long been unable to see the justness of the ways sinners suffered in hell. Joseph, who had nightmares about being tormented with red-hot pinchers beside his dead father, had sat forward, listening intently, looking at the floor.

"Father," said Mr. Edwards. "I talked about it with my father in the orchard, then went walking on alone. The beauty and rightness of God's sovereignty over every being, every instant, and every action came over me. I could love and glory in the strength of God's mighty hand in punishment as I loved the strength of God's voice in thunder, which had always made me desperately afraid."

Joseph had listened in the parlor with his own desperation, digging his fingernails into his palms, and now, on the horse with his fidgety brother, it was Mr. Edwards's voice he heard again, not the other preacher droning on. "Bernard Bartlett's pain at the flogging, as great as it might seem, is but a fraction of what he will suffer for eternity if he doesn't repent and repudiate his crime. To repent is no guarantee of heaven, but failing to do so will certainly trap him in hell."

Sarah, who had watched her husband rip down the bed curtains in fury the night he learned of Bartlett's public taunting, had shut the door to the kitchen when she heard him lecturing the boys about it. Scrubbing skin and lumps from a turnip, she had said to Jerusha, "God's punishment and a flogging might be two different things."

Now Mr. Root helped Bernard Bartlett, who had repented and confessed, from the wagon, keeping an eye on the stranger boys. He helped him off with his coat, waistcoat, and shirt, then bent him down and fastened him into the pillory.

When the first lash fell, Elisha wished he had the reins to ride away. Since he was behind Joseph, he slid off the far side of the bay and leaned his head against the horse's belly, blocking the beating from sight. The horse smelled intensely of leather drenched with sweat. Elisha had seen floggings before and would, impassively, watch them again, but on this one January day, he only listened, thinking shoulders, just the shoulders, over and over. Bernard Bartlett gave a groan after the fifth hit, and then his guttural sounds didn't stop, but rose and fell in a terrible rhythm with the whip. His sons and their mother stood in a stiff row. Joseph could see them counting the lashes. He noticed pious little Phoebe Bartlett, whom he usually thought of as a bit prissy, watching the flogging of her uncle with terror-struck eyes. Joseph reached down to pat the bay's neck, then rubbed Elisha's shoulder.

Leah watched, too, not crying, not praying, but self-protective and vigilant, very clear on which direction she would turn if she had to get out of the crowd in a hurry, less clear on how to shake free of the Edwards children or how she could live in the woods. She knew there was no immediate danger, not to her, not to Saul (who was safe at home), not even to those children, whose lives she tended even as she fled them in her head. She had been reading the Bible every evening in the main house with the Edwards girls, Sally waving the hornbook in front of her and ordering her to recite the alphabet long after Leah had passed her by in command of the letters. The scripture had been yielding up guidance and meaning, but the harsh ways of serving in Northampton had also taught her a refrain that fell in cuts inside her as Bernard Bartlett's back welted up and started to bleed. "Not me. Not Saul. Please, not me."

Sarah, as a discipline, looked straight at her own revulsion, trying to imagine herself under the lash. She failed in picturing herself bent to the public pillory. The closest she could get was the memory of stinging, tight-lipped smiles from certain women of the congregation, who seemed to despise her for her pride in her husband, her fine house full of children, and her surfeit of joy. Other women, and sometimes the same ones in moments of desperation, brought stories to a preacher's wife, and so she could, instead, picture being beaten by her husband with a horsewhip. He would not do this, she knew, but she could imagine that he might. The test she set for herself as she stood watching the flogging was to find a place of total submission to God's sovereign will, if that fate should be what he chose for her. Holding Mary, looking down at her children's shaken faces, she found herself unable to submit. She prayed for greater humility for herself, for Bernard Bartlett, and, so urgently, for her husband, whose face had gone dead white as the blows fell. Joseph saw his lips move, and whispered to himself what he thought his cousin said: "Thunder. Love the thunder."

Elisha held on to Joseph's boot, until Joseph wriggled his stocking foot free for fear of being pulled off the horse.

The fifteenth lash bit into Bernard Bartlett's back, and then the flogging stopped. Bernard Bartlett was half fallen in the pillory, his back welted and striped with dripping cuts. Mr. Root, winded and stricken, lowered the whip, resting his hands on his knees. Joseph noticed Eben's hands shaking on the reins of the wagon horse, then felt his own body shaking, as well. Elisha raised his face from the bay's warm side and, staring away from the pillory, saw tough young Timothy Root's shoulders heaving, crying for his father because he had to give the whipping. He was comforted from both sides by his cousins Simeon and Martha. Dr. Mather stepped forward to rub salt in Bernard Bartlett's wounds, which caused the man to scream. Leah picked up Esther, who held tightly on to her neck. As Sarah turned to lead her children away, Bernard Bartlett's wife approached with rum and blankets. The sons carried their father's clothes. One of them dropped a bandage, and Mr. Edwards leapt forward with surprising swiftness to catch it before it landed on the trampled snow.

That night, Leah and Saul, who had stayed in the barn sharpening tools during the flogging, blew out the candles, pushed back the chairs, and danced. They sang a song that Saul taught her, more softly than it called for but loud enough to matter, and moved in thumping steps across the uneven plank floor. Outside, squirrel nests were thick and easy to pick out in the stripped limbs of the trees. Inside, Leah and Saul sang themselves into a full circle of people, calling to the clouds to come see how a redbird flies and making calls like slurred whistles until Leah's mind flapped and her body dropped.

Chapter 6
March 1737

Leah put a hand on Jerusha's cape to keep it from flying off as they walked past the burying ground on the way to meeting. In truth, the burying ground was not directly on the way, but Jerusha had heard of an improving sight to be seen there, which she proposed to meditate on before the sermon. Sarah, who believed that Jerusha had a true spiritual gift, allowed her to leave the house early with Leah, so that she might see.

The girl lifted her arms for a moment as if taking to the air, then stopped, with a smile at Leah, to tie her cape more securely at the neck. It was a warm, windy day in March, but the winter had been so severe that more than half of the grain sown in the county had been killed, and in places nearby, multitudes of cattle had died of hunger and cold. Brown grass was visible in hollows where snow was slowly melting around the headstones. As Jerusha had heard, one big maple had blown down completely. The huge knot of displaced roots had brought up enough earth to dig a crater in the ground. A gravestone was fallen beneath the tree, but, although Leah stood with Jerusha staring into the hole, they saw no remains. "It's scary," Jerusha said. "The way of all flesh."

Leah started her own prayer for the tree, the emptiness beneath, and the dead buried in the surrounding ground.

Behind them, she heard Bernard Bartlett, who held his shoulders stiffly more than a year after the flogging, tell his family that it was a work of Satan when the earth opened up and relinquished its hold on a tree. He was still a man with big opinions. Jerusha cast worried looks over her shoulder as Bernard Bartlett's wife said that she had heard of a town where it once rained wheat, and couldn't they use some of that? Jerusha whispered prayers until Leah gave her a comforting pat on her shoulder, took her by the hand, and hurried on. They could not be late.

Elisha had also persuaded Joseph and Rebekah to take a quick walk to the burying ground before meeting to see the upside-down tree. Rebekah was willing, as she found it a comfort to visit her husband there. Elisha was sad to see that it was this maple. It was a tree he knew. The first time he had noticed it, nearly two years ago, he had been visiting his father's new grave with Rebekah. A small snapped limb wedged in the crotch of a much larger branch had caught his eye. He had tried to knock it down with a rock, but it was stuck fast. His mother had turned from the mound of bare earth and told him to stop. After Rebekah had left off coming to the grave so often, he looked for it during every burial, waiting for the broken limb to fall. It was a shock to lose the whole tree.

When they got to the meeting house, Leah sent Jerusha to the front to be with her sisters among the first of the children. The elder Edwards girls now looked after the younger ones at meeting. Humming a little to herself, Leah climbed the stairs to her seat at the back of the gallery. Bathsheba scooted over to make room on the crowded bench. The people's heat rose, as always, from below.

All winter, Leah had worshipped as a member of the church. She and Bathsheba—along with four other slaves and Mary and Phoebe Stockbridge, who were Mahicans awakened during the revival—had been admitted to full communion. It had caused little stir in the congregation and made a warmth in her heart even as cold numbed her cheeks. There were no more disturbances during the sermon, but there was a fiery calm within her as she worshipped. She and Bathsheba had been sitting up straight for months to keep away from the ice on the wall behind them, which had formed slowly as seepage from the roof rotted splintering wood. The ice had frozen in drips and ripples as if the wall had waves. Now, it was melting.

Leah wished she could see Saul on his bench near the door. Sooner or later, most likely, he would do the cold, dirty work to seal the leaks and sop up the water. Work was moving forward on the new meeting house, but, as yet, they were still using the old one. Bathsheba stayed far away from the wall, but, this morning, Leah reached back and got one of her palms wet, thinking of how Phyllis in Newport had coddled a black feathered hen all winter, then, come spring, looking solemn and distant, had cut off its head to help feed the people gathered for the festival at the black election. The memory made Leah want to have a dance in the woods. It was still much too wet and sloppy for that.

This past summer, with the help of Sally and Jerusha, Leah, who had been reading almost every night for more than a year, had learned to write. The back side of every receipt, note, and prayer bid that entered the household was fodder for Mr. Edwards's sermons and notebooks, and Leah read the piles of them in his study, gathering language for how much things cost and what people wanted of God. Sometimes she slipped a bit of paper into her sleeve or the gathered top of her stocking, where it crackled just a little when she walked. At night she covered the scraps with letters and words, then she would burn them. Often, she worked on her name: *Leah*. It had seemed strange and angular when she first saw it, but she practiced it. She wanted to be able to make her mark with one of her names.

One muggy night in late August, Leah had thought to ask Saul if he liked the name Leah, but instead had called up to his loft to say, "Will you call me Mariama?" It was the name her mother and father had given her.

He had rolled from his pallet of cotton stuffed with straw and put his eye to a generous gap in the floorboards. "I will," he had murmured, and when he said the name aloud, it caught and pulled her, hard.

Leah had considered asking Mr. Edwards if she could join the church as Leah Mariama, but found that she did not want to give her second name to him. It was not a name for the meeting house, but for her and Saul, for the shell in her pocket, the family who had lost her and the river in the night. It was good, though, to have "Leah" written in the book of the church.

Mr. Edwards climbed the stairs to the high pulpit, his stomach rumbling as it often did. He was more aware than anyone might have guessed of the people looking up at him from the benches and down from the gallery. Out of the corner of his eye, he saw Leah and Bathsheba sitting on the edge of their bench. Bernard Bartlett was sitting forward, too. He always did, and Mr. Edwards let his own gaze linger on the man for a moment, imagining a back full of scars still painful when pressed, a year after the flogging. The thought of it brought Mr. Edwards a tangle of feelings—empathy, grief, satisfaction, dimming anger, sadness, loss, calm. He welcomed the fervid mess in his heart, willing it to drop away from Mr. Bartlett and open up to all of the people here. Every week he started the climb to the pulpit feeling stifled and clenched, trying to make a wholeness, trying already in his mind to pull scripture through the book and through himself into the building, which couldn't hold it, and into the community, which almost could. The people were there: yearning; varied; pregnant; sleeping, which enraged him; baffled, which exhausted him; owned; blessed; gurgling; adamant; wigged; and rough-clad. He wanted to be far away from them, riding through the woods on Mount Tom, but, even more than that, he wanted to join together with them for the glory of God. They had been quiet in worship for years now. He wanted to believe that, for most of them, it was the quiet of ordinary grace, more powerful by far than special moments of revelation, but he had some reason for doubt. He sought Sarah's eyes to keep from retreating into an internal chill far away from the stickiness of their gathered souls. She was ready for him, fully there in her gaze. It helped.

That winter, Mr. Colman in Boston had printed a condensed version of his letter about the Northampton revival as an appendix to a book of sermons entitled *The Duty and Interest of a People, among Whom Religion Has been Planted, to Continue Stedfast and Sincere in the Profession and Practice of It, from Generation to Generation. With Directions for Such as Are Concerned to Obtain True Repentance and Conversion to God.* The author was William Williams, Mr. Edwards's aged uncle. Now he had learned that famous clerics wanted to publish a version of the letter in London. When Sarah, who knew his ambitions, had sought him out in the woods to bring him the news, he had broken through the crust of ice to throw snow in the air, which she had knocked away with her elbows, both of them laughing. But by the time he was riding home with her, breaking frozen twigs with the brim of his hat, he had felt uneasy, because it seemed that many of his people, whom he had written about as models of piety, had become careless and indifferent to God.

Now, he stood in the pulpit and stared straight out at the congregation. Rebekah Hawley, exhausted, refrained from slumping in her front pew, as did Saul, struggling to stay awake on his bench near the door. Joseph sat up straight beside Elisha, who had his coattails bunched up behind him to make a little cushion so that he could slouch more comfortably. Timothy Root mimed popping a blemish for the amusement of his cousin Simeon, while Simeon's sister Martha, watching from the women's side of the aisle, rolled her eyes. Sarah, baby on her lap, was turned toward the pulpit, but he noticed that now she was keeping one eye on the Roots, too.

The attention of these people, imperfect as it was, brought Mr. Edwards closer to God. It wasn't the only way this happened, but he knew that it was one of them. There was no point in preaching unless their faces were toward him. He craved connection with their tangled hearts and the halting ways that they brought their experiences of grace into language. Strangely, he needed them. He laid down the text of his sermon.

Behold, ye despisers, and wonder, and perish.

There was a terrifying noise like a clap of thunder, so startling on such a warm day. Leah was looking at Mr. Edwards's face as the gallery gave way. She lost sight of him as she slid sideways, away from Bathsheba, who was screaming.

Mr. Edwards stared in horror as the gallery sank in the middle. Before he could react, there was another great wrenching crack as it broke and fell—people, benches, timber, and all—upon the heads of those seated below. The building was being ripped apart by the heavings of frost and thaw. He took his hand from the Bible and ran down from the pulpit into the screaming.

As the crash came, Joseph grabbed Elisha and went under the bench. They huddled there together, not crying, not screaming, ready to fight their way through another disaster, if they could. Elisha closed his eyes, his face right up against Joseph's waistcoat, and breathed together with his brother in their shared conviction that, at any moment, they might, like their father, suddenly die.

Mr. Edwards cradled his two-year-old, Mary, who was bruised and crying. Jerusha, beside her, clutched a hunk of timber, saying, over and over, "I tried to catch it. It knocked her down. I tried to stop it."

Mr. Edwards crouched down to Jerusha. "Put that down and help me hold her." Jerusha reached up and wrapped her arms around Mary, which let him hold on to both of them at once until Sarah pulled at his robe to say, "I'll take them. I've got them."

He couldn't hear her speak, but knew what she wanted to do. She had the baby in her arms, with Sally and Esther holding on to her skirts. She let Jerusha, who was nearly seven, carry Mary as she helped her daughters pick their way to the door. Mr. Edwards watched them reach it, then hurried to join the men heaving timber to free the people groaning beneath.

When Sarah got the children outside, she gave the baby to Sally, the oldest, and examined Mary. A bruise, she thought, just a bruise, please God. It was coming in a terrible purple down Mary's arm and shoulder, but she could lift her arm and waggle her fingers without grimaces or sharp cries. Sarah sent Jerusha running for the satchel of herbs and bandages she kept ready for doctoring at home, and told Sally to walk to the house with Esther and the baby, taking it slow and putting everyone in bed to wait until she got there. Sally was shaking but clearheaded. She took Esther's hand and set off down King Street. Then, keeping Mary with her, Sarah went back into the meeting house to do what she could.

Joseph and Elisha heard their mother shout as she started to fight her way back to them. Joseph pulled his brother out from beneath the bench as roughly as he had shoved him down and hoisted him in the air. Elisha kicked and struggled free as Joseph yelled, "Mother! Do not worry! We are not harmed!"

She saw but did not hear him because the meeting house was filled with shrieks of terror and cries of pain. Saul—together with Roots, Bartletts, and other men at the back—was up and tearing at the heavy timbers that had buried those who had fallen, along with the women and children from the middle aisle who had been seated beneath them. Everyone who was free to move quickly joined them.

Leah heard the thuds as they threw the heavy wood aside. She could hear Bathsheba crying, but all she could see of her was the cloth of her skirt trapped under a beam. She moved her hand to touch the cloth, but could not yet speak. Cries and voices were coming from all around her, so it was the direction of the light and the thudding sounds that let her know which way was up. She felt sickened and strangely unsurprised. She could move her arms but not her legs, and that was all she knew before she saw Saul heave a broken bench behind him through a new opening in the debris. It was a little like peering up from the hold of a ship. Leah saw Bathsheba's skirt rip as someone pulled her free, then she was able to call out to Saul. He came, with others behind him, lifting her away from the wreckage to whisper her secret name and carry her out the door.

Outside the meeting house, Elisha slipped away from Joseph and Rebekah, who had let go of him to help Martha Root staunch the bleeding from a cut on her head. Sick of being manhandled and God-handled, Elisha ran for the burying ground, where he could be alone except for the fleas hopping on old snow. He slipped on the edge of the hole made by the roots of the downed tree, then walked the trunk like a bridge to get through the tangle of limbs and grab the wedged branch, which had fallen without stirring from its place. It came away easily in his grasp, dropping lichen and bark. Like his mother and father before him, Elisha had never been given a toy. Now, ignoring the cries in the distance, he waved his stick in the air, then raised it to his shoulder and sighted down it like a gun. He kept it resting against his shoulder as he ran back to find Joseph and his mother, still in front of the wrecked meeting house, where his mother, howling, had just noticed that he was gone.

Chapter 7
March 1737 – January 1740

The thaw that brought the gallery down kept coming on, swelling the river with shad and snow melt. Wagons bogged down in the deep mud of the roads. It rained every day with dark insistence, the sky keeping to an unrelenting gray that weighed on the air as the fields of snow dissolved into muck, unburied old ham bones, flecks of eggshells, and broken crockery. Few hens were laying as the weather changed, but most would be broody soon.

People limped up the hill carrying crates and bushel baskets to sit on in the unfinished new meeting house (among other things, it lacked a spire) to keep a day of thanksgiving for their preservation. As she prayed, Sarah could smell onions on her hands from slicing them to hold to the feet of parishioners with infected wounds. Although neither she nor the boys were hurt, Rebekah and her family stayed home. Ever since her husband died, she had hated a fast day, and she was not moved to praise. The people there were huddled, damp and nervous, barely mumbling the hymns.

Mr. Edwards chose to emphasize the positive in an account he sent to Mr. Colman to be published in a Boston newspaper:

> But so mysteriously and wonderfully did it come to pass, that every life was preserved; and though many were greatly bruised, and their flesh torn, yet there is not, as I can understand, one bone broken, or so much as put out of joint, among them all.

Sarah paused when she read this in their chamber one evening. She had been visiting the injured with Madeira, snake skins, herbs, and bandages. She helped people write prayer bids and sang with those longing for ease. Now she nudged her husband, who was rinsing ink from his hands in a bucket. "There are injuries that are serious yet."

He stood up, shaking his fingers in the air to dry them. "Not one death. Not one bone. You and Dr. Mather both have said it."

Sarah put the paper aside. "Still."

As he bent to blow out the candle, he looked across at her, stubborn and sure. "Still."

Leah's legs were bruised from the tops of her feet to the top of her thighs. She had a gash in her belly that Sarah had carefully cleaned of splinters, and one knee was swollen and throbbing, unable to take her weight.

Saul made her a crutch from a limb of the downed tree in the cemetery, not waiting for the proprietors and the town council to meet to parcel out the wood. He went out at night for the limb, and brought home a bucket full of graveyard dirt, which he gave to Bathsheba for her cures. He kept a few spoonfuls for Leah, but they didn't want to store the dirt in the cabin. It was too hard to control what spirits it might attract.

The girls brought wool for padding and an old stocking that Sally had reshaped into a kind of bag, to be stuffed with the wool and tied to the crutch. Leah hobbled about her work, and was mentioned in the family prayers with a warmth that surprised her, but her knee became so tender that she could barely endure the brush of her petticoat against it, let alone hold Lucy in her lap.

Dr. Mather was too busy with the injuries of others to attend to a slave who could still do some work. Sarah asked Leah every day about her pain, and tied a rattlesnake skin around the puffy, discolored flesh of the affected knee.

Saul tried to store snow to use to cool Leah's injury, but soon all he had was water leaking from a barrel in a corner of the barn, good for hogs to drink, but useless for her knee. He watched her face when she stood, waiting nearby her to offer his arm. He found reasons to come to the house and carry wood and buckets for her. Sometimes the girls made extra efforts, too, but they were inattentive and these efforts sporadic.

When the roads were passable, Saul sought Sarah's permission to go to the swamps. He walked to Wolf Pit swamp, which made a shallow marshy pond between Elm Street and Broughton's brook, where he removed shoes and stockings and waded into the cold, green-skimmed water almost to his knees. As the slippery mud he had raised settled around him, he could see the dim shapes of small fish darting in the water. Clusters of frog eggs floated on the surface, which a hungry man might gather for their jelly, but Saul stood stock-still.

He waited, shivering a little, with the calm intensity any hunting could bring. It was too early for mosquitoes, too early even for mayflies, so, above the water, he was undisturbed. He began to feel things brush against his legs, sticks or leaves floating in the water. Or fish drawn to the heat and salt of his skin. Watching, he saw other quick, sinuous shapes, felt a touch, a muted tingling. He gritted his teeth and waited longer, but not too long, before he waded slowly out onto the uncertain bank with small, dark leeches dangling from his bleeding legs. He filled a tied-off pig's bladder with pond water then stood watching the leeches feed as they stretched and thickened with his blood. He waited, watching them closely, until they were sated and dropped off. Then he caught them in the bladder and held the top shut tight against the wriggling until the next one was ready to fall.

He was very careful to check his legs for any still feeding before he bandaged the bites and put his stockings on. Still holding his catch and still bleeding, he sat down on a stump and ate a piece of salt pork that he had brought with him. He was cold, drained and tired, and knew that he would be bleeding for hours, but that Leah should get relief for her knee.

They had to wait for the leeches to get hungry again, but once they were shrunken and active, Bathsheba came at night to apply them to Leah's knee. She kept an eye on the leeches until they latched on, and checked back every few minutes to be sure that none of them were wandering over Leah's skin.

Bathsheba had a bruised face and a sore back. She also had stories of everyone's injuries and rumors about what it meant to have the meeting house gallery fall. Someone had told her about a place called Blackfriars in London, where the gallery fell and papists died while secretly praying to the pope. And she'd heard about another church stuffed full for a Puritan funeral, where the beams began to crack but, by God's grace and preference for those who practiced true religion, held firm.

Leah barely listened, but watched the leeches, which had stopped their writhing after the bite. She felt the pull of the viscous, muscular bodies, and could see her knee shrink as they swelled. When they were full and slackened their bites, Bathsheba plucked them from wherever they fell and threw them in the fire.

Saul did not watch Bathsheba apply the leeches, which would have been indecent, but he watched Leah's face ease as the weeks went by.

Leah's knee never stopped aching, but she climbed into the gallery of the new meeting house with dogged concentration. She liked to get there early so that she could take her time. She was changed since the fall: more cautious and much slower to dance.

Leah was always waiting for another awakening, but, in the meantime, she and Bathsheba kept track of the squabbles about seating in the new meeting house. Saul said that they should just go ahead and place wagers if they were that interested in bear-baiting and cockfighting, but he shut up quick when she asked what he knew about such things. Some of the prominent townspeople had ended up clustered comfortably together in private family boxes, while others had stuck or been stuck with men's and women's benches, receding in significance toward the door. The seating committee, which did not invite the participation of Mr. Edwards, had let wealth erase age and contributions to the community as the criterion on which it placed people. On the Sabbath after the congregation first took their new seats in the meeting house, Mr. Edwards had reminded those who were pleased to be seated high that, soon enough, they would be dead and not interested in the stature of their seats, but Leah couldn't see that the reminder had had much effect on the contentiousness and preening.

Bathsheba and Leah nudged each other as ladies and gentlemen of the town passed in the aisle and established themselves on benches. Bathsheba gave Leah the elbow when she spotted the young rapscallion, Timothy Root, sticking out a stocking-clad leg to try and trip Seth Pomeroy, who dodged it with a kick as he strode to the front.

One hot day in August, Sarah's beauty mark fell off while she was offering water from a bucket she was lugging home from the well to some tired-looking boys who were emptying clay from molds to dry on the ground before firing in the brickyard next to the tannery. Sweat from her face melted the paste, and the beauty mark slid off her chin and dropped into the bucket. The boys, who had been lining up politely to drink, laughed, and she saw men look up from cutting clay to grin at her. She felt foolish to mind the laughter of children and laborers, but noted that people always seemed to choose moments when she was trying to be kind to find her foolish. She fished her beauty mark out with her finger and passed the bucket to the boys. They drank so much that she had to go back to the well.

That afternoon, determined to do her duty, Sarah got on her knees outside the door of her husband's study and scrubbed the floor while he was at work inside. Leah, who had relinquished the job with some amusement, kept the children busy boiling lye and hunting eggs in the yard.

Mr. Edwards had barely spoken to Sarah all day. She was fighting tears as she dipped her rag in dirty water and went at the floor. She heard more criticism and gossip than she could stomach; much more, always, than her aloof husband. She spent many more hours than he did in sick rooms and parlors (which were, in most homes, one and the same) and understood more about how shaken the community was by the fall of the gallery. She wanted to quote his sermons back to her husband and remind him that while holy visions were a great gift, they were less great than the ordinary way God came alive in a human heart.

She imagined being free of all of it, walking in a field with salt air blowing in from the harbor and no dirt as her duty ever any more. The children could come with her, with help from Leah. They could sail away on a ship of children every morning, and she would wave to them from the shore, then wave them home again at nightfall, and they would all eat clams and berries and never pray at all.

This was sin, she knew, the blandishments of an impure heart. She faltered at her scrubbing, and then went at it harder, grinding devils into slivers. Cleaning was only sometimes a prayer, but she had chosen this position before the study door. The water spilled through her fingers and the wide planks of the floor swelled and eased apart until she seemed to be floating in a sea of solace with each knee on a board and the bucket bobbing before her.

Sarah kept to her work. The boards heaved, but she reached out to the bucket for balance. Duty unleashed feeling and meaning, all that she could hold. The floor solidified. She wrung out her rag over the bucket, finished with cleaning, then rested on her knees for a moment. The door of the study opened. Her husband looked at her as she knelt there, red-faced and grimy, then he bent down to help her to her feet. Willing again, she stood and walked with him into the study.

They sat in chairs opposite each other drawn close together, as was their habit. She touched the buckle below his knee. He looked at her with an attentive expression.

She didn't tell him that she had been angry. Instead, she planted her feet and said, "I know that expenses are tight, but I think we should pay Joseph Hawley's tuition at Yale."

Taken aback, he glanced down at his desk. He had not been thinking of the Hawley boys at all, but as she waited, he felt an obscure relief. He nodded, and said, "Secretly."

It was a fine September morning when Joseph left for Yale. Elisha was thirteen in the fall of 1739. At thirteen, Mr. Edwards had been serving cider to upperclassmen with the proper deference and rectitude, while inventing a private language to record his strategic plans for shaking the known world. At thirteen, Sarah had been singing to herself in the New Haven fields. At thirteen, Leah had been learning to be a slave in Newport. Phyllis had braided her hair Sunday afternoons on rocks near the sea.

Rebekah had braided Elisha's hair that morning with a quick smooth and tug before milking. It was just one thick tail down the back, and he could have done it himself like Joseph did, but he liked the swift, tidy reassurance of her hands.

Joseph, who was to continue his studies to become a minister, wandered into the room as his mother was tying back his brother's hair. He said, "Did you hear that the Hampshire Association of Ministers took the position that one cause of the throat distemper that has been ravaging us is that God is displeased because parents are too indulgent?"

Rebekah and Elisha just looked at him, then Rebekah got up and said, "Praise God that both my boys are comely and healthy." She straightened Joseph's collar and got on with her work. Joseph and Elisha did the milking together while Rebekah packed johnnycake, cheese, and salt pork in a bundle so big that she had to pack it again in two bundles so that Elisha could help Joseph carry it down to the river.

Joseph and Elisha walked to the woods with an axe as if to work rather than to say goodbye in private, although the only one who saw them was Rebekah, who was not fooled. It had been cold early in the season, and walking on the fallen leaves was like walking on light. Joseph stood on a stump as if he were already a preacher in a pulpit and mock-lectured Elisha about vice, Godliness, and hard labor. Elisha leaned against another tree, laughing and loving his brother, who had never known how to be funny. Then he raised the axe and rushed the stump as if to hack it out from beneath Joseph's feet. He made chips fly with two dangerous swings, but Joseph simply stood on the stump in his thick travel boots and refused to yield an inch. "Little brother," he said, "be careful."

Elisha swung again and planted the axe next to Joseph's foot. He had strong arms for a boy his age. He let go of the handle, which stayed tilted in the air, as if seized by a ghost. "I'll miss you," he said, bumping Joseph with his shoulder to knock him off the stump. "Write to me."

Rebekah stood in Pudding Lane and looked her oldest boy in the eye before he got on his horse. He reached out his hand and rested it on her shoulder, neither pulling her to him nor holding her off. When the rector of the college had sent word that Joseph's education had been paid for, she had suspected Mr. Edwards, but decided not to ask questions about the source. She hadn't wanted to tell Joseph, but feared that Rector Clap might mention that he had a benefactor, so she had said as much to him herself. He had been grateful, but, like her, made no enquiries.

She had lost a tooth in July, and now pursed her lips in a density of wrinkles that almost scared him. He thought that she might speak of his father, but instead she thrust her parcel at his chest. "Bread," she said, beckoning his brother to pick up the other one. "Cheese."

She wanted to grab him by the hair to keep him from going, wanted to knock him over with her heaviest wheel of cheese, sit next to him on the ground, and stuff his gullet, to overwhelm him with sustenance so that he wouldn't have to get on that tall horse and ride off to immerse himself in the company of scholars and tutors, boys and men. She wanted him to flee everything and run back into the woods, to keep running until his shoes wore off and he was barefoot as a babe, to be the child he was, and never have to grapple with questions of livelihood, rank, or salvation. She was proud that he was going, and she wished that he would not go.

He was looking down, waiting, she could see, for her to dismiss him. She touched the brim of his hat as if to correct its angle, and said, "You'll be hungry. God bless."

Missing Joseph, Elisha befriended a barn cat and named it Sister. It was skinny and wary, but he had noticed it as a kitten, and it came when he called.

Rebekah was still at least half in mourning, although she did her work in the store and was silent in the buttery, with no great cries wracking the house. Elisha had moved up to Joseph's cold space in the attic, where he heard chewing and rustling. It had always been there, he supposed, and worse each winter when all the rats and field mice came into the house, but it had been distant, far up. Now, sleeping with the grain as he was, he was in the midst of the gnawing.

He taught Sister to drink whey from a gourd and persuaded his mother that the cat would not yawl or menace the cheese if she were allowed to live in the attic. Sister stalked among the grain barrels and brought him bodies of mice while he praised her fierceness softly so as not to wake his mother sleeping below. The rustling and gnawing lessened, but, of course, it never stopped.

Joseph was hungry at Yale, almost all the time. Bread and milk, milk and pie, salt pork and bread. The meals were scant, but the company was good. He relished meeting scholars whose family he didn't know from places he had never been. The whole college, with sleeping chambers for sixty-six students, was one unpainted clapboard building on a corner of the New Haven green. The chapel and the dining hall were the same room. He bore up well under his burden of serving the upper-classmen: fetching them cider, polishing their boots, and trudging into town to buy them ink, which they lacked facilities to make for themselves. It grated, but he was well-liked, and got off lightly. He joined a few rum-inspired rampages through the town, cursing and once jumping into a pen with some agitated geese. One night he parted from his fellows at three in the morning only to hear them pounding on the tutor's door, demanding a word. He liked his tutor, Phineas Lyman, and had no wish to risk expulsion by rousting him out in the night. He particularly did not wish to have to give an account of himself to Mr. Edwards and his mother if he were sent home in disgrace. The fact that he could see the Pierpont house across the green, shaded by elms and full of Mrs. Edwards's near relations, every time he stepped out of the hall, kept that possibility close at hand.

He moderated his ways and took solace for the resulting loss of companionship by walking the wharf. New Haven wasn't bigger than Northampton, but Joseph loved to watch the sloops, schooners and brigs sail in and out of the harbor. Their expansive, rippling sails and flags reminded him that, if he were far from home, at least he was reaping experience. The tidy green, on the other hand, with the First Church so close to the Hall that he had more than once to prevent a drunken scholar from stumbling into its doors instead of into the college, made him anxious with displaced familiarity. He very much missed his mother, Elisha, and all his people.

His other escape was the library, which, though rich in books, was simply another room in the Hall. One afternoon, feeling homesick and out of patience with logic and Latin, he stopped thumbing through a five-year-old bound set of *Tatler* and sought out Mr. Edwards's book about the revival in Northampton. Mr. Edwards had mentioned bringing a copy of the British edition to Yale. The title page raised his emotions into an agitation of yearning, pride, and dread, which he tried to ignore.

A Faithful Narrative of the Surprizing Work of God in the Conversion of many hundred souls in Northampton, and the neighboring Towns and Villages of New-Hampshire in New England. In a LETTER to the Rev^d. Dr. Benjamin Colman of Boston. Written by the Rev^d. Mr. Edwards, Minister of Northampton.

He liked seeing the phrase "many hundred Souls in Northampton," but it was irritating that the town was misrepresented as being located in New Hampshire rather than being accurately described as being in Hampshire County, Massachusetts. Mr. Edwards had expressly told him that he had written to both Benjamin Colman in Boston and Dr. Watts and Dr. Guyse in London twice before publication to correct this error, but evidently they couldn't be bothered with such specifics of wilderness geography. In this copy, though, *New* had been crossed out and "County of" had been added by hand. Joseph recognized Mr. Edwards's writing. Both the shapes of the letters and the insistence on making corrections long after others might have given up sang to him of his minister, and so of home.

"They have it wrong in London and we are right at Yale," Joseph thought, feeling sinfully puffed up, even as he stifled his excitement over the names of Dr. Watts and Dr. Guyse, so much larger than Mr. Edwards's own. It would have taken a saint of a greater magnitude than Joseph not to linger over the bottom of the page: Printed for John Oswald, at the *Rose and Crown*, in the *Poultry*, near *Stocks-Market. London.* He was practically there, smelling chicken and fishing out a shilling for a stitched copy of the book.

He opened the volume and read with a renewed quiver of guilt about how the young people in his town had left off their frolicking. He had been awakened himself during the revival. Reading about it gripped him with a terrible ache. He knew the farm houses in Pascommuck where the first five or six had been savingly wrought upon. He knew the loose persons who had found piety and those who had lost it again. He remembered the scoffing by people from South Hadley, Suffield, Hatfield, and Green River in Deerfield, until their towns had caught fire as well.

Just reading the lists of familiar place names on a printed page was a pleasure to him, as lonely for home as he was, but, even as he read, "This Town never was so full of Love, nor so full of Joy, nor so full of distress as it has Lately been," his heart was pounding with what must come next. He skimmed over the pious, modest, bashful death of Abigail Hutchinson, and Phoebe Bartlett's four-year-old raptures, more and more uneasy in spirit. It was very strange to have the awakening in Northampton so alive on the page when it had died so abruptly in the place itself when his father died.

He put the book down on the table, and thought of the many delightful drinks a body could make with buttered rum. He found himself thinking of all the birds to be spied in Western Massachusetts in early June, how his father had taught him to recognize loons, bitterns, flycatchers, warblers, eagles, and sparrows. He thought of how he had heard that tithing men used to whack worshippers with knobbed sticks if they slumbered in church.

He tried to resume his reading, and, as he did, a pale, crablike insect scuttled along his arm, long pinchers dragging. He noticed it when it stopped on his wrist and leaned back on its abdomen, pinchers in the air. Joseph brushed it off his hand and onto the book, where it crawled upside down into the long, delicate tunneled arch that had been made as one page had begun to rise from another, pulled but not fully persuaded by the weight of the spine.

Joseph peered down that paper tunnel and saw the bug's dark head and squarish translucent fangs as it started toward him again over more corrections in his distinguished cousin's hand. He stood, walked away from the table and out of the library, not killing the insect, not closing the book.

He sat through the rest of his classes that day like a sleeper in church, fighting the devil in his own ear who would have traded hundreds of souls from Northampton to North London to ease the certainty that one driven soul dear to him was blotted out, forever lost.

Chapter 8
June 1740 – October 1740

Saul and Leah started bundling. They didn't do it openly, in the manner of some English families, with the visiting suitor and the daughter of the house sewn with only their heads free into cambric sleeping sacks by the young woman's mother, indulgence and watchfulness tightening every stitch. Saul and Leah were not visitors, and they were not under the care and protection of their parents. No matter what was said about ethical slavery among the sentimental, an owner was neither mother nor father.

Leah and Saul practiced bundling alone and in secret.

One night when it was very late and the main house was dark, Leah climbed the ladder to Saul's loft. Should they be caught, it might have been easier to explain why Saul was downstairs rather than why Leah was up, but she chose when to join him, so it was she who climbed. Also, she wanted that, wanted to feel her nightshirt brush against the wood as she used the strength in her arms to balance out her weak leg. She liked that she had to make a physical effort to bring herself to him. She knew that he understood the worth of that kind of work, even when it was only a woman with a stiff leg climbing a ladder. He saw the gift in it.

He didn't hide the bundling board, but kept it in a stack with other wood against the wall in one corner of the loft. When he heard her coming, he lifted it from the stack and slid it into place on his mattress stuffed with straw. It was a clean board cut from one of the trees so big that by law they were to be saved for the use of the King of England, but the King was very far from the Hampshire County woods, and so pantries and back rooms of buildings up and down the valley were built from wide planks. The bundling board was wide but also thick, so that it would rest solidly on the mattress. Saul pulled the blanket over the board and lay still beside it for the time it took Leah to make her way over the top of the ladder. Bent beneath the low rafters, she eased under the blanket on the other side of the board.

Saul had his mattress lined up east to west so as not to sleep crossways with the world. They turned their faces to each other, the rough cut end of the bundling board just under their chins, smoothed and muffled by the blanket. She greeted him formally, saying his name. He greeted her, too, as Mariama. His hands were open on his own thighs, and his eyes gathered everything they could from the nearness of her face in the fingers of light from gaps between the slats of the wall.

Pressing against the board between them, they breathed together, lips not touching at first, but then the breath opened their mouths. The sound of breath passing from one to another was like a wind troubling the woods. Air blew out the edges of their lips and the corners of their mouths, and pulled back in again to keep the two of them caught and resting in the same lung-married, life-bound, board-edged rhythm until they dizzied and had to gulp separate air.

Leah had chosen this, first hinted and then flat-out asked for it not long after it became clear to her that, because of her knee, she had become slow to dance. She swam, still, with strength and pleasure, but stroking hard through a traveling river did not bring her any closer to touching Saul. Now she pulled her arms inside her nightshirt, and, shielded by the linen, pressed her palms hard against the board. Her breasts pressed, too, against the backs of her hands. She had wanted the restraint (and so he had agreed to it), wanted this covert custom of the culture that was claiming her, wanted to be righteous and also to know her desire, wanted no children, ever, to be born in shame. She felt that there was virtue and protection in staying on the other side of the board.

Oh, she could smell him. She could eat his breath. She looked at him above the edge of the board, which he was against, too. She could make out the shape of his arm, the textures of his face. She kept breathing back at him, her breath in his throat, his in hers.

Her hands were in fists against the board. Their feet met beneath it. His toe found a hole in her stocking, small opening of skin on skin. There was a catch in her breath.

Like a board nailed behind the pulpit by a skillful builder, the one tilting between them on the mattress amplified everything so that each one's breath and hushed voice echoed deep in the other. She wanted him wildly. He was desire, was love, was distance, so perilously close to grace. He forgot the distinction between wanting and getting, forgot everything except the dissipation of one more amplified breath.

They never crossed the board, but kissed and whispered until they felt approached by morning.

The next day was unseasonably hot for June. Leah stood among other women in the chamber attending to Sarah, who had been brought to bed with what would be, God willing, her sixth child. Saul had driven the wagon to the hills to take the Edwards children berrying, all except Jerusha, who had been allowed to stay home. The little girl, just turned ten, was in the kitchen tending an unhelpful fire under the supervision of elderly Mrs. Clapp, who burst into wavering snatches of hymns in an attempt to drown out the worst of Sarah's screams. Jerusha, boiling hot and choking back tears, wished that she had left in the wagon with Saul.

Listening helplessly from his study, Mr. Edwards found himself unable to complete a sentence. He finally gave up trying to write and rested his head in his hands. He didn't want to abandon Sarah and flee to the elm, so he took out a copy he had made of a letter he had written months ago. It was to George Whitefield, a young minister who had been preaching in England to crowds so huge that they had to take to the fields. Local ministers had been reading letters about Mr. Whitefield from their pulpits to stir up excitement about his coming tour of New

England. Listening to Sarah in travail, Mr. Edwards dug a hole in his desk with a penknife and read his own letter to Mr. Whitefield again.

> *I have a great desire, if it may be the will of God, that such a blessing as attends your person and labors may descend on this town, and may enter mine own house, and that I may receive it in my own soul.*

In the birthing room, Leah moved forward with a clean towel to replace a bloody one, then stepped back to her place by the door. Mrs. Dwight and Prudence Stoddard were holding Sarah by her arms on the birthing stool, while the midwife knelt between her legs and Mrs. Hawley held on from behind. Dr. Mather had come and gone, and Leah stood ready to fetch him if he were needed, but, in an ordinary way, this was a business for women.

With them, but in his room apart, Mr. Edwards read on:

> *Indeed I am fearful whether you will not be disappointed in New England, and will have less success here than in other places: we who have dwelt in a land that has been distinguished with light, and have long enjoyed the gospel, and have been glutted with it, and have despised it, are I fear more hardened than most of those places where you have preached hitherto.*

Mrs. Stoddard beckoned Leah over to take a turn supporting her mistress on the stool. Leah breathed in rhythm with Sarah. Did everything in this world come down to breathing and pushing? Sarah let her head loll back against Rebekah Hawley's belly and made a guttural sound. Leah crouched as she helped the midwife rub Sarah with hog's grease to ease the new baby girl into the sweet, sinning, sweat-salted world.

Rebekah Hawley cut the umbilical cord with care. Leaving it too long would make a girl immodest, and if she let it touch the ground, the child might never be able to hold her pee. Leah swaddled the baby tightly and brought warm wool from a living sheep to press at the site of the mother's pain.

Mr. Edwards lifted his head and dropped his penknife when he heard his new daughter begin to wail. He ran to the kitchen to find Jerusha huddled under the table as if she were half her age, singing faintly with Mrs. Clapp. He bent down and held out his hand. In her scramble to take it, she bumped her head. As they walked down the hall together, he smoothed her hair away from the hurt place. He felt glutted with love for his family, but as soon as they entered the chamber where Sarah and the baby had both quieted in sleep, he knew he had room for much more. He drew up a chair beside the bed and let Jerusha get a peek at her red-faced little sister before he sent her to the parlor to help Leah serve groaning cake to the exhausted women.

On the day Mr. Whitefield was finally due to arrive in Northampton, the baby was already sitting up in the kitchen, eating mashed peas with her mother while Mr. Edwards climbed the elm. It was a Friday afternoon in October with a sky full of clouds too bright to look at because the sun was beating in back of them, sensed but not seen. Mr. Edwards went higher than usual and stayed on the side of the tree facing the house, trying to escape notice from the masses of people streaming down the road on their way to the river to watch for Mr. Whitefield. So much for fears that the English preacher would have less success in Northampton than in other places. Mr. Edwards had never seen so many people on the road, but he himself had to climb.

The big tree had already lost most of its leaves. There were piles of them on the ground, damp and supple, almost translucent, veined like skin. A few had been left on the limbs. He watched as one shook, then dropped. Below him, Sheriff Pomeroy—whom Mr. Edwards had lately observed sleeping in church, gurgling with his mouth gawping open and no one taking up the Christian duty to jab him in the ribs—had paused to call a blessing to a wagon driver hauling a load of deer skins. His voice cracked as he commended the driver to God, as if he would faint in the road in front of his fellows, struck once again by his sins. Nothing like that had happened in Northampton for years. The driver was a Root, less moved by the fervor around him than Mr. Edwards would have wished. He touched his hat in a reserved way, clicking his tongue at his team of oxen, which seemed oblivious to the crowd of half-grown boys scrambling behind the wagon. Nobody looked up at Mr. Edwards at all.

Ever since Mr. Whitefield had arrived in Boston, the papers had been full of accounts of his powers. He preached without notes, his hands stretching out over each congregation to work the air. Women fainted from sheer mellifluence when he said the word, "Mesopotamia." The ruder newspapers called him Dr. Squintum because he had one crossed eye, but most found that this added to the intensity of his preaching. He had gathered a crowd of twenty thousand people on the Boston Common for his final sermon there, more than had ever gathered anywhere for anything in all of the colonies, even counting hangings. The governor himself, sobbing in his coach, had followed Mr. Whitefield as far west as Worcester.

Mr. Edwards squeezed one eye shut, muttered, "Mesopotamia," then stuck a blank scrap of paper to the bark with a pin. That felt satisfying, so he pulled another scrap from his pocket and did it again.

Jerusha came from the house and ran to the tree, calling, "Father! Mr. Whitefield is on the ferry. He sent a messenger ahead."

A leaf dropped past her upturned face in a spin. "Yes," he said, shifting on the limb, which shook loose more leaves. "I'll come."

He slid down the trunk, long arms wrapped around the tree, tattering the notes pinned to the bark as he passed. Jerusha was brushing bark from his coat when the crowd parted as a pocked, squinting man who could only be Mr. Whitefield came riding in on a dusty horse, standing up in his stirrups and shouting, "Come, come to Christ! Two o'clock at the meeting house!" in a voice so strong that half of the people straggling behind him could have stayed at home and still have been able to hear.

Mr. Edwards, who had planning on five o'clock for the meeting, sent Jerusha to alert her mother, which proved unnecessary; Sarah had heard the voice and was already putting the baby on a cushion in a basket so she could set ham and more peas on the table. They would have so little time to eat. With a scrap of paper clinging to his Geneva collar, bits of leaves in his wig, and his other daughters hard on his heels, he stepped forward to welcome Mr. Whitefield, who cried out, "Mr. Edwards! Brother! I admire your *Faithful Narrative!*" so loudly that his horse gave a pitch to gasps from the crowd. Mr. Whitefield, well-accustomed to spooking the livestock, gamely kept his seat, but his host had a headache for the rest of the afternoon.

Mr. Whitefield preached in the parlor that evening after meeting, and to the children in the morning. He preached in the late morning in Hatfield, then back in Northampton in the afternoon. He filled the Northampton meeting house twice on the Sabbath.

At the second Sabbath sermon, he swung his arms and cast his voice out so strongly that it seemed to shake the back wall of the gallery, which was already over packed with people. Leah felt the wall shake and remembered her injuries just long enough to offer them up to God as he moved again in the people of Northampton under Mr. Whitefield's voice. Timothy Root and the other boys started stomping from their benches to the rhythms of the preaching. Mr. Whitefield, swinging his arms, embraced the noise and sent it back to them drenched in meaning. Seth Pomeroy beat on the back of the bench in front of him with his great fists. Mrs. Clapp pounded her walking stick. Bathsheba stomped like a boy.

Mr. Edwards thought about the fact that Mr. Whitefield had read his story of the earlier awakening here in the *Faithful Narrative* across the ocean. The scenes of grace from that turbulent encounter with light was part of what had brought him so far to bring people in Northampton and across the colonies past their former heights in encounters with an extraordinary presence of God. He listened to Mrs. Hutchinson scream as if in travail with her Abigail again, and thought how word, voice, cry, and howl could answer and echo in ways no human might understand.

Rebekah cried throughout that sermon. Elisha watched her weeping in silence amidst outbursts of repentance from the fractious, backsliding people around them. He had heard her cry many times, but this was the first time he had seen it. Rebekah felt herself to be held apart, bitter and not redeemed by her tears. It was not a feeling she would describe to her son, who, with a vague feeling of enacting a betrayal, joined in stomping with the other half-grown boys.

Mr. Edwards saw four of his daughters gasping in what looked to be the first grip of awakening. Jerusha was bent double in her seat. Everywhere in the meeting house, people were giving up cries of anguish and replenishment such as he had not heard since the day before Uncle Hawley killed himself. Sarah, close beside him as she had been for so long, was vibrating like a tuning fork. It was when she gripped his hand that, with a great welling of tears and relief, Mr. Edwards himself let go.

Saul spent his evening with a lantern in the barn, currying the horses. Leah had been unable to persuade him to respect the Sabbath and join her in the doorway of the parlor for more preaching, although he had heard the sermons.

It was cold enough in the barn that he could see the breath of the horses as they snuffled and snorted, leaning against each other in affection or aggression, trying to get the best place at the feeding trough. Leah came to find him with a cup of chocolate as frothy and spicy sweet as any to be had in the parlor. She sat on a bale of hay near where he stood currying the bay. "Mr. Whitefield was singing new hymns before the fire in the parlor, and the shadow of his arms looked just like wings."

Saul gave the horse a pat and picked up a nail to clean hair from the comb. "Shadow and what really is are two different things." Leah felt frustrated with him, so stubborn in the cold, so unwilling to make the jump to pleasures not of this earth. "You know that you're not to work today. Twenty thousand in Boston turned to glory, but the one of you would rather sleep in the horse barn than listen to a famous preacher here for just a few nights."

Saul added the hair to a bagful that hung from a nail, waiting to be scalded and put to use. "There's no few nights about it, not for us, living here. You know that's the truth. I'm expected to go with them on their preaching trip in the morning. The horses have to be ready."

Leah kicked her heels back against the hay. "The fact that neither of us ever picked where we should live doesn't mean that we can't take the good we find here. Because we've got the bad, like it or not."

Saul smelled of horses as he sat down beside her and said, "Believe me, Mariama, I'm staying as close as I can get to the good."

It was cold, wet, and windy when Saul and Mr. Edwards rode away with Mr. Whitefield on Monday. They all had johnnycake and slabs of cold ham from Sarah in their satchels. Mr. Whitefield had bowed like a courtier and kissed her hand when she handed it to him. Sarah, in high spirits, did a moment of pantomime as an impressed lady making a show of offering him her other hand before she lifted her chin, drew both hands behind her back and gave him a blessing.

Mr. Whitefield murmured to Mr. Edwards as they were mounting their horses, "I pray that God might soon provide me with such a spiritually-gifted helpmate as you have, sir."

Saul, holding their horses before getting on his own, knew that Mr. Edwards had no idea what to say to a thing like that. He didn't even try. He and Mr. Whitefield did not seem easy in conversation in general, but, then, with Mr. Edwards, few were. Mr. Edwards forgot to tie his satchel and lost his cake to muddy King Street when they were barely out of the yard. Saul got his feet wet getting down to retrieve it, and they didn't dry out for days.

When they arrived at the bank on their horses, the ferryman, who had a rude shelter on both sides of the river, stood in the doorway of his dry hut, pointing at the waves. "I would not try to cross for anyone else today, Mr. Edwards. Mr. Whitefield. I wouldn't advise you to try it, either. The river's too whipped up. It's not safe."

That seemed reasonable to Saul. He tried to get a wind block next to the hut while the two preachers rode to the edge of the bank to more closely consider the water. They all looked up at the sound of hooves coming along Bridge and Water, from the uplands and the meadows on the wet road. Ministers from towns up and down the river approached with water dripping from their hats, coming to join the Grand Itinerant, Mr. Whitefield, in his travels. Across the swollen river, Saul could see more figures on horseback gathering to wait for them on the far shore.

Before the newcomers arrived, Mr. Whitefield reached into a pouch and pulled out a coin. He squinted at the ferryman in something close to a wink, and said, "Heads we go, tails we stay here."

Saul knew that Mr. Edwards had a weak stomach for rough water and didn't approve of games of chance, but there was no missing the excitement in his eyes when Mr. Whitefield slapped the coin down on his wet sleeve.

"Heads!" Mr. Whitefield cried. "We go." He handed the coin to the ferryman. "Yours."

The group made it safely across the river thanks to the ferryman, who spoke of spending the night in his shack on the Hadley side. Then they rode south. At first they had to shout to be heard above the rain. When the weather relented, they drew their animals closer together. Saul dropped behind, but he listened. Clumping together on horseback seemed to open everything up for debate. They jostled and argued, riding their theology through ego and mystery while their horses engaged in snorting matches that led to the occasional bump. It was a kind of richness, to be in the presence of so many other minds and voices intent on the things of religion. Mr. Edwards raised up from his saddle and leaned into questions. The others kept answering. People came to their doorways to watch, then follow.

The rain stopped, and they were soon on dry roads, with Mr. Whitefield preaching at every town along the way. He sent messengers ahead to let people know that he would be preaching in Suffield on Tuesday afternoon. They crossed the river again so that he could do it.

As they approached the town, it was clear that word had spread. At the sight of them coming, farmers dropped their plows and ran for their horses. Old women left off harvesting dark greens from late gardens. Families came in on mules and donkeys, kicking up dust and spilling out of wagons. Many horses were heaving and lathered with sweat from being ridden so hard to get to town to hear the preaching. By the time they reached the common, the ministers were covering their faces with handkerchiefs to save their voices from the dust, and Saul was in the midst of the biggest crowd he had ever seen. He heard someone say that it numbered seven thousand.

He kept to the back once the preaching started, tending the animals since Mr. Whitefield wanted to be able to move on quickly once the sermon was done. The famous voice carried as Mr. Whitefield railed against ministers who might, unconverted, be trying to teach the word of God without having experienced grace in their own hearts.

Saul watched as the man crouched and acted out being struck by the light of God as if he himself were great Paul on the road to Damascus.

As the horses drank from a trough, Saul understood Mr. Whitefield to be saying that people had to fight through the tangles of words to find their own sense of God and reject the guidance of anyone who didn't show clear evidence of having been saved themselves. That people had the right to judge those above them.

Saul had not heard anything like this in Mr. Edwards's church or anywhere else. As he stood on the edge of the hard-praying throng on a trampled, muddy field, he put his hand on the back of his favorite roan, which Mr. Edwards had been riding, and thought that the things Mr. Whitefield was saying sounded right to him. A God who stood ready to take down those falsely laying claim to his authority was a God Saul wanted to know.

The roan backed up closer, wanting to be scratched. Saul brushed through sweat-stiff hair with his fingers and let himself become one with the crowd panting after the presence of God. He felt as if a board between him and an unspoken world had been slid away. His thoughts were inexact, but the experience had precision. It was not partial. It was not abrupt, but had a slow sweep. He felt as if the most difficult parts of his life were being offered up, beautifully rendered, for his own witnessing. He could see so much. As he listened to the preacher's magnificent voice, he measured the performance in it and set that aside as nothing he needed. But something there, something else, left him with his head knocked back, neck arched, open, opened, overcome.

He added to the noise by beating on the side of the water trough until he had gathered himself enough to think of the skittish horses and lead them farther away.

When he and Mr. Edwards left to return to Northampton, leading the spent horses of other ministers behind them, Saul said, "If you'll have me, I've made up my mind to join the church."

Mr. Edwards, shaken by all he had received in his own soul, sat -up straight on his horse and looked Saul in the eye, forgoing his usual questions. "Yes."

When Saul told Leah in the Edwardses' kitchen, she slapped the table and kissed his neck.

That afternoon, Mr. Edwards took himself out to the barn to try to embody Jonah cast overboard by heathen sailors in a storm and swallowed by a whale. He noted that, much like the sporting Mr. Whitefield flipping his coins, the sailors had decided who to throw overboard by casting lots. He shouted loud enough to set rats scurrying in the rafters, kicked up straw, and disturbed the horses. Saul passed by the door and looked in to see Mr. Edwards thrashing in the ocean of hay, but he kept right on going. He was halfway to the chicken coop before he started to laugh. Mr. Edwards ended with a coughing fit. He splashed his face with murky water from a bucket and resolved to try no more acting. He didn't speak of it, not even to Sarah, but as she picked straw from his wig, she knew something had changed.

Mr. Whitefield gave ninety-seven sermons in forty-five days. By the time he was done, some people were praying so much that dry sticks accused them of neglecting their chores. Ministers would jump on a horse and ride away from their own quarrelsome congregations to fan a conflagration of spirit down the road. They preached in barnyards if they weren't welcome at the local church. Lay people, with no training, stood up to testify in the meadows. Old Light ministers—who thought God gave people religion through the brain, not through any organs involving sweat, moans, and tears—were against it, but they couldn't stop it. Too many people were in the grip of a great awakening, bigger and wilder than any outpouring of religion that Christians living in the colonies had ever seen.

Chapter 9
July 1741
Enfield

Mr. Edwards, shocked to find himself so hungry, took two helpings of ginger beans at the midday meal at the parsonage in Enfield. He was dining on viands and fervor with the local preacher, one Mr. Reynolds, and a group of ministers who had been riding throughout the region. Mr. Edwards was relieved to be among the others, yet, as so often happened, felt himself holding back from the company. He wanted to be in the work with them so badly that, everywhere but the pulpit (and the occasional heated theological discussion on a horse), he became afraid of joining in, unsure of his welcome. It was like his student days in the buttery at Yale all over again. He bit into a tender bean, spraying juice onto his chin. He saw Mr. Reynolds glance at him and then away. Mr. Edwards took a moment of refuge behind his napkin.

He knew that Mr. Reynolds had invited Mr. Eleazar Wheelock of the Crank to preach the sermon that afternoon. Mr. Wheelock had brought people to screeching in the streets across the river in Suffield the night before. Mr. Edwards himself had given communion to five hundred there three days ago. There had been more conversions than he could count, although, no doubt, someone would count them, and multitudes had joined the church. The next day he had preached at a private house to a crowd of two hundred, preached for three hours while people came unbraced as if they had no bones, and he himself had nearly fainted. He had had two days to rest, but little time to reflect on what it meant that people he didn't know were sucking at his sermons like leeches at a vein, while his own congregation seemed more open to others than they were to him. Perhaps, if he found the right moment with young Mr. Wheelock, they might speak of it. He wished for Sarah, who would know how to frame the question in a way that drew other people to answer back, and not act as if he expected them to say nothing but "Amen."

The Reynolds women, who had put aside gay and worldly white aprons for more solemn blues and greens, kept bringing more food to the table: salmon in cream sauce fresh from the great July run at Shelburne Falls, with clabboard beans, parsnips, and summer pears, which were particularly good in Enfield that year, as was the spruce beer. They handed bowls to the children who were eating on trunks and boxes around the table.

Mr. Wheelock picked a fish bone from his teeth and said, "Did you hear how, this past winter, James Davenport of Long Island waded waist deep through snow impassable for horses to preach at a church that was not his own?"

Most of the men gave admiring laughs. Mr. Edwards smiled, and thought, "That's an opening, I could say something, but not about Davenport." Mr. Davenport was one of the wildest of the itinerant preachers. The moment passed quickly, as between mouthfuls of beans and salmon, they started quoting scripture, thick and fast. Mr. Edwards spoke up then, his voice carrying strongly over the clattering dishes. Leaning forward with his cuff in the butter, he called out Psalm eighty-four, "My soul longeth, yea, even fainteth for the courts of the Lord: my heart and my flesh crieth out for the living God."

The women murmured at the force and beauty of the verse, flicking flies away from the table by switching their fans. People kept coming to the door to ask the itinerants about family in Northampton, Hebron, Longmeadow, or the Crank, and the ministers accepted letters and packets to bring back to their towns. Mr. Wheelock, returning to the table with a handful of letters, said, "I tried to make it clear to the man that I didn't know when I might next be going home. I'll keep traveling as long as the Lord keeps blessing my preaching."

As he spoke, Mr. Wheelock's voice, already hoarse, failed him altogether. He had been preaching past midnight the night before, and again that morning. Mrs. Reynolds hurried to bring rum for his throat, and, as he sipped it, he turned to her husband and croaked, "Mr. Edwards seems much strengthened today. Perhaps he could preach this afternoon."

Mr. Reynolds took a bite of pear to mask his disappointment. He had very much wished to hear a sermon from Mr. Wheelock. But he nodded graciously at his Hampshire County colleague, Mr. Edwards, who, with a great wave of relief and excitement, immediately left off eating and went to his satchel to look over the notes he had brought to find a sermon fitting for the occasion. It was for this that he had been made.

It was a sweltering day, a Wednesday, and they had already had a sermon on Tuesday, but people were waiting in the packed meeting house. The heat rising from so many gathered bodies was enough to make anyone light-headed. Women mopped sweaty brows with handkerchiefs pulled from their sleeves; men refrained from chewing tobacco or getting out their pipes, but, instead, swapped stories they had heard about religious excitement in the surrounding towns, with frequent mentions of the Suffield woman suspected of fornication who had been allowed to own the covenant, and the deaf man found kneeling for prayer in his chamber, sweat rolling down his chest in streams, who had been making such a strange noise that it drew the whole neighborhood.

The congregation was wasting daylight, and it wasn't even their usual lecture day, which came on Thursday. They knew that they had been called to the meeting house because Suffield was in a fever of religion just across the river, and the divines were hoping for contagion. The people gathered that afternoon in Enfield were hoping for it, too. Most of them had heard George Whitefield the year before, and it was hard to imagine that a handful of New England ministers could top that. Getting to watch them try was both a chance for salvation and an experience to be threshed like wheat for inspiration, edification, and gossip long after the itinerants were gone. People from other towns were crowding the pews next to acquaintances and family connections, stuffing the gallery and clogging up the aisles.

Joseph and Elisha Hawley slipped in the back with Mr. Edwards's slave Saul. Joseph was home from his studies at Yale for the summer, and Elisha was only ten days from his fifteenth birthday. Their mother had charged them with bringing a cartload of deer skins from Northampton to Enfield to give to a local merchant, who would travel to Boston and New Haven, hawking them for a good price. Elisha had extracted a promise from her that she would bring scraps to his cat in the attic while he was gone.

Rebekah had not been sure that she had liked Elisha's eagerness to go to the children's meeting in Northampton over the past few months. She had not liked what she could hear walking by, which sounded to her like animals grunting and yelping, but which Elisha assured her was most moving and fitting prayer. She wasn't sure that he would be any better off worshipping with a congregation of strangers, but she counted on Joseph to enforce all proprieties. Besides, the skins needed to be moved. She had hired the Edwardses' Saul, known to be trustworthy—and now, she had heard, even pious—to go with them and help with the loading. Saul had the expectation of keeping some of the money from his hire.

A tithing man spoke to the Hawleys; then Joseph and Elisha were given a spot on a bench in the back, while Saul sat with slaves and indentured men on the stairs to the galley, just below a very dark-skinned man in a brown coat with a striped waistcoat and unbleached breeches.

Saul leaned back against the stairs, just a little, and the man sitting above moved his knees to make room. One of the man's pinchbeck buckles grazed the back of Saul's head. He looked up, and saw the stranger glance around at everyone who was nearby. Then the man murmured, "Where are you from?"

Tilting his head just a little more, Saul could see that the man's breeches were the roughest fustian, and that he had a pattern of scars marked with gunpowder just visible under the cuff of his coat. Reminding himself that he was the true stranger in this place, Saul turned to look him in the face and said, softly and politely, "Northampton."

The other man leaned down farther, cocking his head toward Joseph and Elisha. "With them?"

Saul nodded. Joseph was peering over his shoulder at them, trying to look stern. Elisha was distracted by a young lady across the aisle, who had dropped her fan and, perhaps unwittingly, kicked it so it slid against his boot. Elisha trapped it between his feet, then picked it up to return to her. Once he did that, Joseph glared at him instead of Saul.

The stranger, who gave his name as Pompey, was speaking with a lilt that made Saul think he might have spent time as a sailor. "I heard Whitefield when he was in these parts. He's the best of these preachers."

"I know," Saul said. "I heard him, too."

Pompey leaned down until his face was as close as his knee was to Saul's ear. "What I hear is, he's got a big charity orphanage down in Georgia, where it's against the law to own slaves. He's one of those who wants to change the law so that he can bring in slaves to do the work of running the orphanage."

Saul let out a breath. "Huh," he said. "Huh." It was not surprising to hear that one more white preacher owned slaves or was looking to own them. At least half of them did, as far as Saul could tell. But he had felt God move in his heart when that squinty-eyed Englishman had taken on the liars who preached but didn't live as they said others had to do.

Pompey stopped his whispering as the pack of reverends came striding in the door. Mr. Edwards was so tall and thin that he always seemed just a little unhealthy, but he was straight as a cross and unhesitating as he made his way up the aisle to the front of the church.

Mr. Reynolds beckoned to the singing master, a fierce old man, to start up a hymn. The master clasped his hands behind his back and strained his neck to throw out the *fa do so do* of the tune, which the people took up in an old-fashioned raucous caterwauling that made Mr. Edwards wish for the more restrained harmonies which his own congregation had mastered. Still, the hymn made a tremendous noise, and while people left off their murmuring to raise it up to God, Mr. Edwards regarded the shivering mass of the singing master's wide-bottomed wig, which even he knew was a style thirty years out of date.

He slipped his hand into his waistcoat where it was unbuttoned over his belly, the old familiar pattern for a sermon pounding in his brain like a pulse. Text. Doctrine. Application. He had been experimenting with preaching more from notes and the fresh inspirations of God, rather than working methodically to build arguments for experiences which superseded logic. Still, he loved the old forms. The singing master let one hand rise as he sang bass. Mr. Edwards listened as the people carried the song. Were they spoiled by so much awakening? Would they accept light and truth from him as they had from the expressive, charming, famous, and *English* Mr. Whitefield? Mr. Edwards brought his shoulder blades together and then let them drop as he felt himself begin to go dull beneath the grip of envy, then realized that in succumbing to his baser nature this way, he was as corrupt as the worst of the churchgoing sinners whom he was about to portray being trampled by God. He had to face this almost every time he preached, and he hated it in himself every time. The sermon. He held his mind on the sermon. He had preached a version of it earlier in the summer in Northampton, throwing it out like one more stone skipping across those familiar souls, leaving barely a ripple, although some were plenty stirred up already, he knew, particularly the young people. Now he glanced at Elisha, who was looking across the room to the back benches of young women, some of whom, flushed with song, were looking back. His brother, Joseph, though, was gazing at Mr. Edwards with the eyes of true belief, as earnest a young man as he had been as a three-year-old. Mr. Edwards was moved by the sight of the Hawleys, with their family faces and vulnerable souls, fatherless sons that they were. The thought of their father and how he died scraped an old wound. Steadying himself, Mr. Edwards rose to take the pulpit as the hymn finished, palmed his sermon, put one hand on the Bible, and—speaking in his soft, certain voice—began.

Their foot shall slide in due time.

Saul's hip started aching as soon he sat down on the stairs after the hymn. At the opening verse about the slipping foot, his ankle, where a mule had once kicked him, joined the throbbing in his hip. He had heard this sermon in Northampton, and recently, too. He tried to be open, tried to truly listen, but all he felt was that ache, ankle to hip.

Mr. Edwards was going at it hard, looking into the faces of the people and preaching out:

That world of misery, that lake of burning brimstone is extended abroad under you. There is the dreadful pit of the glowing flames of the wrath of God; there is hell's wide gaping mouth open; and you have nothing to stand upon, nor anything to take hold of; there is nothing between you and hell but air; 'tis only the power and mere pleasure of God that holds you up.

Elisha had heard the sermon before, while his brother had not. He watched Joseph's hands grip the bench beside him as if he feared that he might slip off. Women began screaming, "What must I do?" The young woman who had dropped her fan was on her feet, calling out over and over, "Help me, oh God, help me." Men were standing as well, shouting out to God to save them, and some reached for the timbers of the church, any seam or joint in the walls to hold on to. Some fell to the ground and rolled on the floor, coat tails splayed and flying, calling out for God.

Joseph made himself see the lake, feel its molten heat beneath him, let the cries all around him separate into the voices of angels and the hellish screams of the damned. He thought he heard his father's voice among them, never risen, never resting, never quenched, and he felt his own soul spilling blood under the gnashing of his sins. He shook, sunk, and felt himself horribly alone, unreachable to his brother beside him or to anyone except the devils come to bind him and drag him into the pit that his father, in his sloppy dying, dug for him. He dropped from the bench to his knees, holding his head in his hands as he shook it back and forth. His only contact with the warmth of life was the good, known voice of Mr. Edwards telling him what he was and what he must do.

You probably are not sensible of this; you find you are kept out of hell, but don't see the hand of God in it, but look at other things, as the good state of your bodily constitution, your care of your own life, and the means you use for your own preservation. But indeed these things are nothing; if God should withdraw his hand, they would avail no more to keep you from falling, than the thin air to hold up a person that is suspended in it.

Mr. Edwards could feel God alive within him, lighting his words. Every dram of jealousy and worldly ambition had drained from him, and he felt dry and light as a husk. His throat was parched, but he did not stumble or cough. His voice was his body. He let it go harsher and louder, leaned forward over the pulpit, and kept preaching:

Your wickedness makes you as it were heavy as lead, and to tend downwards with great weight and pressure toward hell; and if God should let you go, you would immediately sink and swiftly descend and plunge into the bottomless gulf, and your healthy constitution, and your own care and prudence, and best contrivance, and all your righteousness, would have no more influence to uphold you and keep you out of hell, than a spider's web would have to stop a falling rock.

Men dropped from front seats one after another to crawl and stagger toward the pulpit. They rose to their knees or stayed on their bellies to reach up and hold on to it, begging for help from God.

Were it not that so is the sovereign pleasure of God, the earth would not bear you one moment; for you are a burden to it; the creation groans with you; the creature is made subject to the bondage of your corruption, not willingly; the sun don't willingly shine upon you to give you light to serve sin and Satan; the earth don't willingly yield her increase to satisfy your lusts; nor is it willingly a stage for your wickedness to be acted upon; the air don't willingly serve you for breath to maintain the flame of life in your vitals, while you spend your life in the service of God's enemies. God's creatures are good, and were made for men to serve God with, and don't willingly subserve to any other purpose, and groan when they are abused to purposes so directly contrary to their nature and end. And the world would spew you out, were it not for the sovereign hand of him who hath subjected it in hope.

Mr. Edwards could see that the men at his feet were sobbing. One was grabbing at his stockings. He shifted his legs and shouted, "Quiet!" The yelling and crying didn't subside. He took a breath and, ignoring the tugging at his ankles, went on, raising his voice to give the name of God its full weight every time he said it, feeling strangely unsurprised by the screaming and clutching below him.

The God that holds you over the pit of hell, much as one holds a spider, or some loathsome insect, over the fire, abhors you, and is dreadfully provoked: his wrath towards you burns like fire; he looks upon you as worthy of nothing else, but to be cast into the fire; he is of purer eyes than to bear to have you in his sight; you are ten thousand times so abominable in his eyes as the most hateful venomous serpent is in ours.

Pray, prey, Joseph thought. Is the sinner the spider? He was still on the floor on his knees. If he held a spider over the fire, couldn't it fly? Couldn't it retract the web, propel itself back up until it reached his hand, sank fangs and filled his blood with poisons and demons, making him into a spider self? Couldn't that be the danger, dangling the spider at all? And fire, so dangerous. Babies, old people, and drunkards fell into it. If the fire went out, a boy would be sent to ask for a coal from the neighbors, and terrible things could happen to a little boy carrying fire home who, starting to fall, seized the coals.

Oh, Mr. Edwards, Joseph thought, preach hard to me. I want—still, again—to be saved.

Saul wanted to be taken with spirit again, himself, wanted to howl out for shelter, for safety, for the fountain of love at the center of heaven to rise and pour forth over him, but felt instead as if he had just watched the gallery in Northampton fall again, as if he should be bruising his fingers and straining his back to throw timbers off of the people groaning and crying all around him. He had been left cold by Pompey's whispers about Mr. Whitefield and slaves. As predictable as it was, Saul had failed to account for it. He felt himself shaking off his new faith even as he watched Pompey slide past him to the bottom of the stairs and lie belly up, shivering on the slats of the meeting house floor. The cuff of his coat rode up his arm so that Saul could see that the gunpowder picture on his wrist was a tree.

And there is no other reason to be given why you have not dropped into hell since you arose in the morning, but that God's hand has held you up; there is no other reason to be given why you han't gone to hell since you have sat here in the house of God, provoking his pure eyes by your sinful wicked manner of attending his solemn worship; yea, there is nothing else that is to be given as a reason why you don't this very moment drop down into hell.

Saul looked past Elisha putting his arms around the trembling shoulders of his brother to gaze intently at Mr. Edwards. Saul watched his master's face as the screaming became so frantic that no one could hear the sermon. He saw what he always saw: a man who thought others owed him work, who didn't tend to bodies because he was busy with God's law, who, just then, stopped in the middle of a sentence and seemed a little bit lost.

The noise was so loud that Mr. Edwards could not continue. This had happened to him before when the meeting house itself was breaking apart. His heart was pounding, but his belly, for once, was calm. He stood at the pulpit above the men who, still sobbing, had all gone limp, and looked out across the congregation at a young woman whom he had noticed earlier because her skin had flushed so beautifully as he read the scripture. Now she turned to the women on each side of her, seizing their hands and calling out. The din was much too loud for him to hear her. The women bent to her, blocking her face with their leghorn hats, so that he could not see her mouth as she spoke, and he thought that God was telling him to let the words go, let the text go, let the elegant shape of the sermon with its heartfelt assurances of love at the end go uncompleted, only half preached. People were reaching toward God, whether he shouted above them or not.

Mr. Reynolds, who had been praying over the singing master as he writhed on the floor, stood up as he saw his aunt fall into a faint, tended to by her children. He climbed to the pulpit, stepping carefully around the huddled men, and put his hand on Mr. Edwards's shoulder. Mr. Edwards looked into the sweating face of his colleague, at Mr. Wheelock behind him, then down at his notes. His hands were trembling.

Mr. Reynolds, leaning toward him, shouted in his ear. "God has sanctified your words. Now, let Mr. Wheelock pray with the people, then let us minister personally to those souls in distress."

"I am ready, sir," said Mr. Wheelock, his voice hoarse but strong.

"Of course," said Mr. Edwards, standing aside. He felt emptied and, for a moment, almost alone, but sank to his knees next to the base of the pulpit, bending close to listen to the cries of the men fallen there and guide them if he could.

Mr. Reynolds didn't take the pulpit, but cupped his mouth and hooted over the din, sounding like a boy calling in dry cattle, until he had the attention of enough of those gathered that Mr. Wheelock could lead a prayer.

Saul slipped out the door while Mr. Reynolds was hollering. He half expected the steps of the meeting house to be strewn with sinners overcome by the prospect of hell, but instead he walked out into a still, hot summer afternoon empty of prayers and lamentations, although he could hear the desperate voices calling from within.

He walked toward the horse shed, where he and the boys had left the emptied wagon. When he got there, he wanted nothing more than to take a blanket and go to sleep on the shaded ground beside the wheels. Instead, he slapped the oxen on their shoulders and led them down to a shallow spot in the river to drink their fill before the people of Enfield pulled themselves together and brought their own animals down to muddy the water.

While the oxen stretched their thick-muscled necks to drink, Saul squatted down to wet his hands and face. He had done no shouting or writhing, but felt as tired as if he'd been hauling water from the river to try to drench the fire Mr. Edwards had raised up in that church. He dug up a little dirt from the bank and drizzled it into his pouch, in case he might need it, thinking of a holy man he had known who carried dried fish scales that he would rattle in his pocket with an eerie, unworldly sound. Saul had seen too much to be easily scared, but always walked away from—not toward—such rustlings.

He braced his palms on the bank to help support his aching hip as he stood, then turned away from the river and started back up the hill to the horse shed. It was a small climb, but he was very tired. As he and the oxen crested the hill, he saw that the doors of the meeting house were open, with some people spilling out, although the noise had not subsided within. He spied one of his young overseers, Elisha, holding the ankles of the girl who had dropped her fan as he helped carry her to rest on a lady's shawl spread out in the shade of a tree.

Saul rolled his eyes and caught a grasshopper in mid-leap, which he fed to the right-hand ox, who ate it as calmly as if it were a palmful of grain before they settled down to wait.

People groaned and cried long into the night.

Chapter 10
July 1741

Saul went to find Leah as soon as he and the boys had returned the wagon. Rebekah had paid him with a chit for store credit for the Edwardses, with a portion for him. Before they got into town, Saul and Joseph had rousted out Elisha, who had spent the greater part of the journey curled up against a bolt of canvas in the back of the wagon, sweating in his sleep. He had been upright and driving, although still a little puffy around the eyes, when they pulled up the team before the store and greeted Rebekah, who looked him up and down, but said nothing.

Leah was walking home from the well, hauling water in two heavy buckets that left ridges in her hands and stiffness in her neck. Moving swiftly in the heat, Saul caught up with her and gave her a slight bow before he took the buckets.

Leah, who limped herself, said, "Don't argue with me," and took back the bucket Saul was holding on the side with his stiff hip.

They walked together for a while in silence, Saul looking down at the cracks in his fingers where they curled around the handle of the bucket. Before they were in view of the house, he said, "Come on with me."

Leah nodded, and they stepped off the road and walked to the shelter of a field of high-grown wheat and rye, sure to be Saul's next work.

He took off his coat and spread it on the ground for her to sit, then dipped his hand in a bucket and drank before he sat down beside her. "I brought you something," he said, opening his pocket and pulling out a brown pear from Enfield.

He put it in her hand and said, "Eat it now, Leah."

She reached up and stripped a seed head, averting her gaze. "You've told me nothing about your journey."

He stretched his legs and propped himself up on one elbow. "I brought you a pear. And many souls were saved."

She looked at him sharply, but he put his hand around hers and raised the fruit to her mouth before she could tell him not to speak lightly of the great things of religion. He drew a breath and said it himself. "I am not speaking lightly. Eat."

She lowered her eyes and bit. The crisp flesh gave a crack as it came away. The taste was sweet. Juice welled up in the hollow, wetting both their fingers as she took another bite. She ate it down to the stringy stem and sucked the seeds, which she dropped carefully into her pouch when she was done.

He brushed the juice on her face with his lips, then spoke softly into her cheek. "With just a pear for a bride price, will you still be my bride?"

She sucked the last piece of skin from between her teeth with slow aplomb, and said, "You honor me." Then she kissed him.

He wept like a convert, tasting pear.

When Mr. Edwards got home, he told Sarah that he never should have eaten the salmon. He had suffered on his horse and was taken with the heaves all night. Despite his physical discomfort, he was so excited that she thought he might be feverish, weak and exhausted as he was, but as she listened it was clear that he had spent himself on another mighty work of God. She applied burdock leaves to his stomach and kept the bed curtains closed in the morning to keep him from waking at first light. As if anything could.

———

On the day before Saul and Leah's marriage, Sarah, humming, dipped into the portion of flour she had set aside to give to the widows who came begging food at her kitchen door. She gave it instead to Jerusha, who wanted to bake a cake for the couple. The girls had been berry-picking all week, so Jerusha crushed a few raspberries and tied them inside a whisk to flavor a bowlful of cream for a topping while the cake was baking. It was a ginger cake, because Jerusha knew how much Leah hated allspice.

Leah was out in the yard, where it was cooler than in the kitchen, gutting a barrel of shad to be pickled for winter. Sarah had wanted to salt it, but they were low on salt, although Rebekah Hawley had said that a shipment was due any day. While they had been discussing how to preserve the fish, Leah had felt Sarah's desire to send Saul with the wagon to haul a few hogsheads of salt from Hadley, but Sarah had not said it, and so the wedding would not be delayed. Leah supposed she should be grateful, but she had to wonder if her own thoughts could possibly be as visible to the English as theirs were to her. She was of the opinion that when they looked at her, most of the time they were thinking of what they needed from her next, so that her thoughts about anything else would be beside the point. Still, the wedding was on for the next morning, and Jerusha, who had been hanging on her shoulder to tease her about Saul, was busy baking gingerbread, and so was giving her these moments of peace.

Leah's fingers were stinging with many tiny cuts. The cool bodies of fish in her hands—living when she seized each in one barrel, stilled and emptied when she slipped it into the other—made her think of her mother, who had taught her to grasp a fish by the gills, but who had not given her the secrets of marriage. Leah had been too young, and then she had been gone. There was no knowing if anything her mother might have said or if any of the women's teachings—the mask, the dancing, the secrets and whispers of knives that were suddenly flooding back to her as she slit the belly of another fish—would have helped her at all once she had been taken, tied, and trapped in the sea with other cargo ('allspice'), surrounded by people sick and dying in many languages, nearly stacked against them as she sloshed with slow inner waves like the barrels of molasses, whose stink, perhaps strangely, now caused her no offense. Gutting fish, turning life into food, Leah missed her mother, who had beautiful long hair and, even when she had been irritated, looked at Leah with a density of feeling that came back to her daughter now like a smell of palm oil strong enough to rise over a bucket of guts, over barrels full of fish, brine, and river water, and blessed her on the eve of her marriage in New England with a strong sense of certainty in love.

She was just beginning to think of her father, how tall he had been and how gently he had knelt down beside the twin kids just born of the nanny goat. He had told her to watch as the nanny licked them clean because the smaller one with the shaky legs would be hers. She was remembering how he would listen in the morning to what she had dreamed the night before when Mr. Edwards rode into the yard.

Leah rose from her seat on the stump between the two barrels. Mr. Edwards glanced at her and motioned with both hands that she should be seated, as if she were a congregation. His sleeves and the whole front of his coat were covered with scraps of paper that rustled as he moved. He looked as if he had been rubbing up against pine trees sticky with tar, and then standing much too close to a chicken being plucked, but Leah knew that he had chosen to put himself into this bizarre state. She had seen it before. He stopped under the elm, twisting to pull the coat off one shoulder, trying to read what he had pinned to the seam. Leah reached into the barrel for another fish, shaking her head.

Sarah, following Esther and Mary out the door with an exhalation of heat and gingerbread, shook her head, too. She was very aware that her appearance was under constant scrutiny in the town—the gift of a locket and chain from Mr. Edwards could provoke sly comments about extravagance instead of household economy for months—but her husband treated himself like a living hornbook with no thought to how he looked. "Your humours must be starting to be back in balance, Mr. Edwards," she said, taking the reins and handing them to Esther. "You've been gone all day." There was a note of reprimand in her tone. Leah heard it from across the yard, but Mr. Edwards did not. He dismounted with care, holding one arm across his chest to keep from dislodging the notes pinned there, then opened his arms wide and presented himself to her. "I've been working," he said, handing the reins to Mary, who was elbowing her sister to keep her from giggling. "I'm finally getting somewhere with that Northfield business."

"Girls, take the horse to the barn." Sarah looked over her shoulder at Leah, who was slitting another shad, then turned back to her husband. "May I accompany you into your study? I'd hate for you to lose any of your notes to the wind." She put her hand on his sleeve, willing him to notice her unspoken suggestion of discretion, this once.

Mr. Edwards followed his wife's glance to their slave's face, and said no more about Northfield. Instead, he patted her hand, paper crackling at his elbow. As they walked toward the house, he called out to Leah, "Fish!" It was all he could think of to say.

Leah, who knew full well what Northfield meant, said, "Yes, sir." There was little that happened in the households and congregations of Hampshire County clergy that Leah didn't know. Mr. Edwards had accepted an assignment from his association of ministers to write a defense for the Reverend Mr. Doolittle against a charge from some of Mr. Doolittle's Northfield parishioners that his ownership of slaves was a sin. Leah released the cleaned fish and kept her eyes down. "Shad for dinner."

He nodded and said, "I smell gingerbread."

"Are you hungry?" asked Sarah, letting go of his arm to unlatch the door.

He shook his head and looked back at Leah. "Come to my study when you have finished your work, and I will give you counsel before your wedding day."

Leah imagined walking over to him and ruffling the bits of paper on his chest with her sour, messy fingers. Instead, she thrust her hands among the live fish again and said, "Yes, sir. I will come."

Jerusha was keeping an eye on her baking as she scalded neat's foot and chopped apples to make a minced pie. She got up from her chair as her parents passed through the kitchen, suppressing a grin at the sight of her father's coat. She, who her sisters claimed was his favorite, risked making a joke. "Father, you are bristling with ideas."

Sarah gave her a quelling glance, but her father reached for a slice of apple and, chewing it, assumed a beatific expression, as if it were the best thing he had ever eaten. "Your labors are bearing fruit as well, Jerusha."

She laughed in delight. Any effort at levity from her father was rare enough to be funny in itself. Also, he looked so silly. She sucked cinnamon from her finger to keep from laughing again.

Her parents went into the study and closed the door. Sarah—reminding herself to pray later about worrying too much about what people thought of Mr. Edwards, and so, of her—rummaged in her pocket and found a nearly empty paper of pins. "May I assist you?"

He stood happily before her. "Start with the left shoulder and work across the coat, leaving the sleeves to the last. They've got to stay in order." He loved it when she unpinned notes from his coat. It was the best of all worlds. He looked down to correct the path of her hands, already amending arguments in his head before he even had a chance to copy them to a whole piece of fool's cap. They didn't speak about the letter he was working on, but she read bits of the fragments as she fell into the rhythm of her work, carefully sticking each pin into her paper as she freed it. Despite her worries about what people must think of him, she loved unpinning his thoughts, too.

If they ben't partakers of the slaves, they are of their slavery, wherein the injustice, if there be any, consists.

Sarah smoothed the cloth over his chest, noting the tiny holes the pins left in the worsted serge of his coat. She would like for him to get fabric for her to make him a new linsey-woolsey coat the next time he traveled to Hartford or Boston, but knew that he was reluctant to be seen spending his salary on clothes.

*Either let them answer them, or let 'em own the matter is well proved,
and not go on pretending that those arguments are of no force which they
can't or at least don't see cause to answer, only to make disturbances
and raise uneasiness among people against their minister to the great
wounding of religion.*

Sarah had felt the brush of their own congregation's judgments
about her beauty mark and the cut of her dresses, but no one had
questioned their need for slaves. She was a little surprised to find Mr.
Edwards being so incisive in defense of Mr. Doolittle, whose repression
of revivals which Mr. Edwards saw as surprising acts of God, was what
was causing some of his flock to speak out against him. She knew that
her husband had prayed mightily about this, but he was doing his duty
in support of the authority of another minister.

*The practice that prevails in the world of eating and drinking tends to
sin, and a world of iniquity is the consequence of it, but we are not
therefore to abstain from sin.*

She saved another pin, listening to Jerusha clanking pans in the
kitchen. Despite his display for their daughter with the apple, her
husband was indifferent when it came to eating and drinking, more
willing to abstain than anyone else she had ever encountered, but it was
true that the work of Leah and Saul was as common and helpful as salt.
The family could have done without it if slavery were truly an affront
to God, but many of his gifts that could have been otherwise well-used
would then have to be left to rot.

*It supposes that God gave a law that did tend greatly to encourage
iniquity in all the nations round about Canaan by his own pleasure. So
that instead of their being a light to the earth, a blessing in the midst, it
was dangerous for other nations to live near God's people, which would
be a blasphemous way of talking.*

Slavery. The whole subject made Sarah uncomfortable, even more than such a grave offense as blasphemy. Thank goodness it rarely came up.

"Finished," she said, gracefully setting the unwieldy pile of notes on the desk with his inkpot on top of it to keep them from scattering. And, then, because she knew that he had felt her eyes on his writing, and was awaiting comment, she added, "Strong arguments."

"Thank you, dear one," he said, rubbing a pricked place on his wrist. "The scripture is very clear."

She fetched a yarrow leaf to clean the tiny cut, and then took his coat, slipping the paper of pins up one sleeve so that he would have them the next time he got inspired on horseback. She kissed his forehead and left him at his desk, already lifting the inkpot to get at the notes.

When Leah came in from the yard and wiped her hands on a rag bound for the wash pot, Sarah sent her to the study with a piece of warm gingerbread and a cup of hot chocolate for Mr. Edwards. There was plenty of cake left for the wedding party, and the sight of Leah with her straight back carrying the treats made an allegorical illustration of Mr. Edwards's point about eating and drinking and slavery that Sarah found piquant as she watched her servant knock on the study door. Beneath her satisfaction, there was a stirring of questions, but she did not allow herself to approach them.

When he looked up and saw Leah, Mr. Edwards, who was unaware of the depth of his own uneasiness, wished that he had suggested that they speak at another time. He could tell her to go, of course, but his concentration had already been disrupted. He drew a vertical line through a paragraph, and set down his quill.

Leah set the cake and the cup of chocolate gently on the desk, then stood back to await his word.

He gestured at the cherry wood chair that was the place of seekers, church committee men, and Sarah late at night. He hadn't bothered to locate his cap, but had taken off his wig, so his scalp shone through his sparse bristle of hair.

"Sit down, Leah," he said. "You know, I see you and Saul as a couple of the beloved children of God, soon to be joined in happy bands."

She gave no sign of nerves, but inclined her head. "You are kind, sir, to agree to so unite us in the sight of God."

Spreading his hands over the papers on his desk, he spoke to her then of her precious soul and the light and gifts of God's love. She had, he knew, a sweet and lively sense of spiritual things. This, he warned her, could grow cold, flat, and dark, which would pierce her with many sorrows unless she could increase and abound in love toward all others in the church. If she could do that, her path would shine more and more until it was bright as perfect day.

Leah watched the chocolate in the cup grow cold and form a skin as he spoke of dark and light, but she wanted some of what he gave her, wanted words for being pierced with sorrows and letting wounds become openings that filled with sun, with joy, with Christ. She was never indifferent to God, and even though she was angry at Mr. Edwards and his defense of his right to own others—to own her—she did nothing to stoke a fury that she could ill afford. She wanted him to be an instrument of God at the next noon as he wed her and Saul, so she worked to hear grace in him there in the study.

He was leaning back in his chair and finally picked up his chocolate, long past his initial uneasiness. He was feeling warm with the honor of having saved Leah's soul for God, and confident that she was well-settled in his household as he asked, "Leah, is there anything else that you would want before you marry Saul?"

He expected an expression of contentment, perhaps even gratitude, or maybe a request for a bit of bright cloth for her head or an extra gallon of rum for the wedding. She had been lulled by his voice, but now she snapped her shoulders back as if this were another Bible history question in his usual catechism, and, surprising herself, told him the truth. "Sir, I only wish I could see my mother."

He sat very still, taken aback, then set down his cup. "Would you tell her of God's word?"

She was by no means sure that this was an opening, but believed that she would never get the possibility of another. They hardly spoke of such matters every day. "Mostly, I would want to listen to her voice and look at her face. I would like to tell her about all I now know and understand, tell her about my religion, but I fear that the fact that her children were ripped from her by men of a Christian nation might leave her unready to seek salvation." Her voice was full of palpable, complicated grief. She let him hear it.

Mr. Edwards felt a heat in his skin very much like a blush. It seemed to start in his palms, which were still touching his notes. He felt not anger at her forwardness, no sense of danger or any chance that Leah might be susceptible to the depravity that had led to mass hangings of slaves in New York City after, according to the papers, they had recently conspired to burn everything down. He felt, not doubt in his convictions about slavery, but a slight shift in his arguments, with this idea that the seizing of slaves in Africa might make that continent slower to come to true religion as it must in order for the last seal to break and the glorious thousand year reign of Christ on earth to begin.

"We must be your family, Leah," he said, already making notes in his head. When she rose to take the dishes, he insisted that she eat the gingerbread.

The ceremony was simple. It was held under the arch in the parlor with just the family. The only exception was Bathsheba, let off from her work by the Pomeroys, whom Sarah had also invited for cake and sack-possett since their servant was coming, but they had other guests, and had sent Bathsheba the day before with a pint of good honey from their hives, to sweeten the need to decline.

After she delivered the message to Sarah, Bathsheba had found Leah alone in the kitchen and given her some basswood to make a poultice for her knee, where the meeting house injury had lately swelled. Sarah had come upon the two of them talking just as Leah, holding her belly, had said that she was worried that she was about to get her moons. Sarah had winced in sympathy and offered to send the girls to gather balm flowers to hold it off. Bathsheba and Sarah had agreed that Leah should touch her feet and then sniff her fingers as a way to relieve any cramps, although Sarah had hastened to advise that this should happen only at night, never during the preparation of meals.

Leah wore a gown of red and green that she had dyed herself, which was usually saved for Sundays. Bathsheba had braided her hair the day before and bound it up in a cloth that matched both the gown and Saul's red waistcoat. The girls had brought the balm flowers and a bunch of marigolds tied together with an embroidered ribbon long enough so that when they looped it around her neck, the flowers hung over her heart in a way that made Jerusha sigh happily.

Bathsheba stood alone behind the gathered family as Saul stepped forward from his place beside the parlor door to stand with Leah before Mr. Edwards, who faced them through the arch. He had put on his good wig, and a damp mist of sweat rose on his forehead beneath it.

He spoke to them about their duties and obligations as husband and wife with, Leah thought, at least half a mind toward his other listeners. Timothy, in his mother's lap, was too young to be much improved by a sermon, but Mr. Edwards warmed to his subject as he gazed at his daughters; their earnest, pious, beautiful faces; the bit of ash on Lucy's chin. Jerusha most reminded him of Sarah when he had first admired her, and he resolved to take the girls out to climb Mount Tom so that they could roam a bit, praying or singing alone under the sky, as their mother had once done.

He brought his mind back to his servants, standing so close before him. Looking straight into Saul's eyes, he said, "Remember that pride is the worst viper that is in the heart, the greatest disturber of the soul's peace and sweet communion with Christ; it was the first sin that ever was, and lies lowest in the foundation of Satan's whole building, and is the most difficultly rooted out, and is the most hidden, secret, and deceitful of all lusts, and often creeps in, insensibly, into the midst of religion and sometimes under the disguise of humility."

Saul gazed steadily back, only moving his toes a bit to feel the crackle of the pages from one of Mr. Edwards's published lectures that Leah had lifted from a pile of duplicates in the scrap paper on the desk and tucked into Saul's shoes as well as her own that morning. She said that ghosts would have to read every word before they could haunt, so would be too busy and distracted to trouble the wedding day.

The gingerbread and cream were delicious. Sarah gave the couple the rest of the pan to share with their other friends at night after work when they might gather in the woods. She warned them not to have a fire, since people roundabout were highly suspicious of parties of Negroes and fire after a night frolic in Boston had burned a warehouse down, and the stories of arson planned in New York City and Charlestown were well known.

It was a beautiful summer night, although buggy near the river. Leah used the sharp edge of the broken shell she carried in her pocket to cut the marigolds loose from their ribbon. When she tossed them at Sam, he laughed at her. People gathered, and Joab brought his drum. They danced to his rhythms with shaking gourds and a fiddle made out of pine shingles and lumber scraps, drinking rum with their cake in the dark. Looking at the sky, Leah remembered that a new moon purged a young woman, and wondered if that was still what she was, but the basswood and balm flowers had worked, and she moved happily, a bride. Afterwards, Saul dragged his chaff bed down from the loft, but left the bundling board up the ladder. They drew their bodies together and let the lantern burn all night.

Chapter 11
September 1741
New Haven

A few Yale trustees in town for commencement were at a sermon in the church on the New Haven green the night before, sitting stiffly in front pews as James Davenport screamed about hell and grace. Joseph, squeezed into a bench with friends from the college, felt uneasy watching the trustees, ministers all, who listened stonily as behind them those seized with the conviction of sins stammered, jerked, and fell. Joseph, who found himself feeling furtive rather than improved, hoped that the trustees didn't see him. At least Mr. Davenport didn't stand in the middle of the women's pews shouting until they fainted, as he had been known to do. Nor did he, this time, call the local minister an unconverted hypocrite and the devil incarnate.

Joseph kept upright in his seat with as much dignity as he could muster, willing his friends Brainerd, Buell, and Hopkins to do the same. Mr. Edwards was coming in the morning to preach the commencement sermon. Joseph wanted a good report of his conduct to go back to Rebekah. He knew that Mr. Edwards embraced the presence of strong emotion in religion—Joseph had intense memories of watching his father shiver at meeting and of his own body falling amidst the screams in Enfield—but it was difficult to imagine that he would approve of Mr. Davenport, who believed in the simple life so deeply that he never washed his clothes. Perhaps Mr. Davenport had such doubts himself, because at the end of the sermon, he announced that he was leaving town that night. Brainerd groaned, but Joseph found himself a little relieved.

The college was too close for Joseph and his friends to go directly back after such a powerful, saving exercise, so they walked to the harbor, singing psalms in the dark. They made sure that they were far enough across the green so as not to disturb those in Rector Clap's house, but did not take much care for the sleep of the other inhabitants of the town. Joseph felt freed and visited by mystery, passing still houses as the sea breeze stirred on his skin. It reminded him of going to the river to hunt eels with Elisha back home. Up ahead, David Brainerd, so pale that he was practically luminous and as zealous as they came, started a new hymn:

> *Alas, and did my savior bleed?*
> *And did my sovereign die?*
> *Would he devote his sacred head*
> *For such a worm as I?*

Joseph, who sometimes wondered why anyone did anything for him, oaf that he was, felt the release in giving voice to this question. Once they reached the water, Buell unleashed his baritone, more like a choirmaster than a worm. Hopkins was singing off-key. Joseph threw back his head and half-tripped on a piece of driftwood. Hopkins reached out to steady him on his feet.

Brainerd and Buell had been knocking on the doors of all of the other students to talk with them about religion. Hopkins, who at first had been annoyed, was Brainerd's first convert. Joseph thought it might be because his own father had died in agony over the state of his soul that he found himself reluctant to confront the unconverted. His tutor, Phineas Lyman, studied law, and sometimes Joseph felt drawn to the worldliness of that vocation, but it could not compare to the glories of being a minister. Still, he hoped that their singing would not wake any seamen on their ships. They tended to curse and to make a corporal response to any annoyance.

Joseph let himself lean against Hopkins for a moment, taking comfort in their common undisputable ignorance, in Hopkins's bad singing voice and his willingness to belt out a hymn without regard to that. He would, no doubt, grow out of it, but, more sure in his footing with his arm around Hopkins's shoulder, Joseph was glad that he hadn't yet.

The next morning as he was buckling his shoes in the chamber he shared in the hall, Joseph heard a knock on his door. He was expecting Hopkins, but when he opened the door, he saw Mr. Edwards holding a very large cheese. "Mr. Hawley. This is from your mother."

"Thank you, sir." Joseph bowed and took the cheese, which he put into the chest at the foot of his bed, thinking of mice. He said, "I didn't expect to see you until the ceremony."

"The cheese." Mr. Edwards said, as if that explained everything.

He had to stoop as he stood there in the doorway, assuming a proprietary air that both flattered and troubled Joseph. Mr. Edwards seemed to be expecting something, but Joseph had no idea what. "Would you like to come in, sir?"

Mr. Edwards stepped back and straightened his neck. "I need air before my lecture. Would you like to accompany me for a stroll around the green?"

As Joseph set out with Mr. Edwards, he glanced back and saw his classmates sticking their heads out of the many windows of the hall to stare at him proceeding in such a familiar way with the commencement-day lecturer. Mr. Edwards had become quite well known since his *Faithful Narrative* had been published in London. Buell gave a salute. Hopkins faked applause. Joseph mouthed, "Stop."

Mr. Edwards strode briskly along, oblivious. Turning firmly away from the sight of Hopkins flicking his own nose as if putting airs, Joseph looked sideways at Mr. Edwards's gaunt face. He wondered if he should seize the chance to ask whether, upon the whole, Mr. Edwards considered him suitable to enter into the work of the ministry.

He didn't speak until they had almost completed their circumambulation of the green. Then Mr. Edwards reached out to pat one of two trees known to have been planted in the early 1600s as they passed them.

"I used to serve meals when I was an underclassman," he said. "Did I ever tell you that? A gang of seniors once hauled me off to the upper garret and fined me five shillings for carrying myself in an unbecoming way. Can you imagine?"

Joseph, who had had his share of hazing, sadly, could. "Yes, sir," he said, with feeling.

Mr. Edwards looked at him sharply and was about to speak when they were suddenly surrounded by Rector Clap and what seemed to Joseph to be the entire board of trustees. They clumped around Mr. Edwards, murmuring intimately and urgently, while Joseph took himself away to a discreet distance. Watching out of the corner of his eye, he saw Mr. Edwards stiffen up as the rector threw an arm around his thin shoulders, and wondered if his cousin was always so awkward among his peers. Joseph thought that perhaps he was nervous away from home. He saw Rector Clap unfold a sheet of paper and give it to Mr. Edwards, who read and returned it, his expression inscrutable.

Joseph, who had lapsed into staring, became aware that both Mr. Edwards and Rector Clap were looking directly at him. They leaned together as they did so, suddenly in league, and as he watched them whispering, Joseph was struck with certainty that the secret benefactor who had paid for his education was Mr. Edwards. Thinking of his cousin's proprietary air as he had handed over Rebekah's cheese, Joseph felt faintly sick. The last thing he wanted was to be beholden to Jonathan Edwards.

Mr. Edwards beckoned to him, and Joseph hurried to join him and the leaders of the college with his manners firmly in place, already admonishing himself to remember, in his confusion, to be grateful.

Joseph took his assigned place in the Hall, next to Hopkins, who whistled softly in admiration as he sat down. Brainerd glared at the irreverence from across the aisle.

Rector Clap opened by reading a new decision from the trustees aloud.

Voted that if any student of this College shall directly or indirectly say that the Rector, either of the Trustees or Tutors are Hypocrites, carnall or unconverted men, he shall for the first offense make a publick confession in the Hall, and for the second offence be expell'd.

The sudden depths to the silence in the Hall helped Joseph quiet his mind enough to think about what this might mean. Beside him, Hopkins had started wheezing. They had both heard Brainerd, for one, say such things, and Joseph had no certainty that he would desist. Mr. Davenport, securely long graduated, surely would not. Brainerd, staring straight ahead, did not turn to meet Joseph's eye, but, from the next row up, Buell threw him a sideways glance. There was trouble ahead.

Joseph watched as Mr. Edwards stood up and began his lecture with scripture.

Beloved, believe not every spirit, but try the spirits whether they are of God; because many false prophets are gone out into the world.

Here it comes, thought Joseph, who, like his father before him, trembled every night in fear for his soul, here comes the wrestling match between propriety and true religion, with Mr. Davenport condemned as a false prophet and Mr. Edwards currying favor with the trustees. He didn't question why he was so ready to attribute unclean motives to Mr. Edwards. As he half listened, Mr. Edwards presented an elegant double twist of thought: a careful list of things that were *not* evidence that a thing was *not* a work of God. Joseph's indignation was deflated before it had a chance to take hold, while, in the front rows, the trustees and the rector began to fidget and slump.

Using logic and scripture, Mr. Edwards showed that neither effects on the bodies of men, such as tears, trembling, groans, loud outcries, agonies of the body or the failing of bodily strength; nor great noise about religion; nor that some had been in a kind of ecstasy, wherein they had been carried beyond themselves; nor the power of examples; nor even that many involved in it were guilty of great imprudences and irregularities in conduct proved that a work was not of God.

Joseph was trying to reconcile what he knew of Mr. Edwards's rigid and stringent morality with having just heard him say that even great imprudences of conduct did not prove that something was not of God when his cousin, preaching out, said that lukewarmness in religion was abominable. Zeal, he went on, was an excellent grace.

Hopkins, whose breathing had quieted, was murmuring yes. Brainerd was gripping the bench, and Buell was listening with an intensity that brought his entire row to lean forward with him. All around them, young scholars were nodding, while the ministers in the front exchanged wary looks. Mr. Edwards was not backing up their proclamation against criticizing ministers.

Mr. Edwards said much more about the distinguishing marks of a work of God: how such a work raised esteem in the people for Jesus, operated against Satan's kingdom, caused in men a greater regard to the holy scriptures, and spoke as a spirit of love to God and man.

Joseph, melted, was rapt, taken by familiar power, for this was the voice he had grown up with, and he had knowledge of Mr. Edwards far beyond what he could ever hope to know of someone like Mr. Davenport. His mind closed over the arguments like the teeth of a mule on a bit. He filled with surprising love for Mr. Edwards, who had acted in both material and spiritual ways with deep concern for him. Joseph's father's ghost was not forgotten, but neither was it heard to speak.

At the lectern, Mr. Edwards was describing the folly of gathering in a field to pray for a rain, then finding it to be a confusion or an unhappy interruption to have to break off because of a shower. He spoke of ministers who doubt or clog the work of God's spirit. By the time he said that silent ministers stood in the way of the work of God, Joseph was gasping at Mr. Edwards's nerve before Rector Clap and the silent trustees.

Mr. Edwards said that those who waited to see a work of God without difficulties were like fools at the riverside waiting to cross until all the water ran by. He raised his voice to declare that the great Jehovah had been in New England.

Later, Joseph realized that he had listened least to the section of the sermon intended most for him and other friends of the awakening. Mr. Edwards spoke against pride and praised the influences of ordinary grace. He warned the young scholars against following impulses or despising human learning, and urged them to more fully consider how far, and upon what grounds, the rules of the holy scriptures would truly justify passing censure on other professing Christians.

I once did not imagine that the heart of man had been so unsearchable as it is. I am less charitable and less uncharitable than I once was.

As he spoke these words, Mr. Edwards looked directly at Joseph, whose ability to concentrate was lost for a few moments. Mr. Edwards kept speaking.

The longer I live, the less I wonder that God challenges it as his prerogative to try the hearts of the children of men, and directs that this business should be let alone till harvest.

Joseph held his preacher's gaze with dry eyes, feeling as if he and his family were receiving an apology. Well-trained in the practice of testing his own heart, he was seized with terror as he realized that he was not at all sure whether or not he would accept it.

Chapter 12
January 1742

It was a hard winter in Northampton. The girls had trampled a path in the snow to the woodshed and the barn, but it had steep sides. Walking in it, Leah slid and hit her sore knee on an edge of ice. The pain was so sharp that she dropped the chamber pot she was carrying. The contents were half frozen and too sluggish to spill more than a dog would leave to mark its ground. Leah, wincing, kicked a bit of snow over the stain, picked up the pot, and went on.

Making her way over the uneven ice ratcheted up the pain in her knee, but she was glad to be out of the house, where Mr. Edwards was shut up in his study and Sarah had been sharp-edged and bitter for weeks. Everyone who was interested, which included most of the women and all of the gossips in town, could see that Sarah wasn't pregnant even though it had been a full eighteen months since Sukey had been born.

Earlier in the week, Leah had found herself slipping out to the barn carrying a coal from the kitchen in a warming pan so that Saul might have some source of heat as he tended the livestock. She had set the pan on a bit of bare earth safely away from hooves and straw, then leaned against the warm belly of an ox—which leaned gently back, as if she were one of the herd—and watched Saul pour a bucket of icy, rotten turnips into the trough for the hogs before he raked out their pen. Finished, he had come toward her with that uneven walk of his complicating his grace. Drawing warmth from the ox and none from the pan, she had let herself be drenched with the details of him—the elegant hang of his old coat, his deceptively mild eyes, buckwheat in his hair—then had drawn his cold, cracked hands to the waist of her apron and said, "A child."

He had tucked his fingers around the waistband and looked at her face, his mouth opening into a half-grin she had wanted to drink like cider. The worries and talk about dangerous labor and being born owned came later, in the dark, but in the cold, sheltered barn amidst the quick stock, Saul's eyes had been alight, and what he had said was, "My dear one. My sweet."

Leah, who figured herself to be three months along, had told no one else. She wished that Mr. Edwards, who listed her and Saul on his will as quick stock themselves, might never know.

Now, carrying the chamber pot, she slipped again on the way back to the house, but the narrowness of the path kept her on her feet like a child tied with a bolster around her middle. There was very little room to fall.

The house was cold in corners, cold everywhere away from the hearth, where the large tea kettle had been hung on its hook in the center of the fire to boil. The Reverend Mr. Chester Williams was visiting with Sarah in the parlor, and he had tramped in thick gray slush from the road. Leah dried the floor with a mop made of strips of old shifts, then gave Mary a hand carrying the china tea cups into the parlor. At the clinking of the cups, Mr. Edwards came out of the study to join the company, just in time to hear Mr. Williams, who considered himself a friend of the revivals, say, "Well, but people on their knees braying like donkeys hardly constitutes prayer."

Sarah took a cup from Leah, then, with a delicate rise at one side of her mouth, took a sip. Leah, who could see that she was furious, was impressed. Sarah, who had a temper, could paste her beauty mark to her cheek and hold the posture of serenity under almost every public circumstance. Leah, who had to know when to steer clear, could always see the force of other feelings underneath. She knew for sure that some could not, but suspected that others could, too. Now she watched Sarah give another tiny flinch as Mr. Williams, who was definitely one of the unobservant, took the tongs from the sugar dish, used them to stir his tea, then put them back in the dish.

At that moment, Mr. Edwards stepped into the parlor from the hall, but Sarah did not glance at her husband, whose entrance could have been a graceful way to redirect the conversation while Leah, who had her own skills at serviceable neutrality, saw to the sugar. Instead, gazing at Mr. Williams, Sarah said, "I am of course not qualified to judge such matters as you are, sir, but if you are wrong, to have compared a soul in an intimate state of contact with God with a dumb animal bawling out its lusts will perhaps come to be a source of regret."

Leah stepped between her mistress and the visitor to retrieve the dish and the sugar-caked tongs. Mr. Edwards, hoping to prevent a reply, called out, "Mr. Williams! What a pleasure to see you, sir."

Mr. Williams peered around Leah to murmur, "Quite, Madame." Leah, moving slowly, spared Sarah the sight of him bowing over his cup before he turned to Mr. Edwards and pointed with his elbow toward the study. "Another masterwork in the making?" It was Mr. Edwards, after all, that he had come to see. The gentlemen withdrew.

Leah put a log on the fire in a show of sympathy while Sarah seethed over her cup. When Mr. Williams emerged from the study an hour later, she was flawlessly polite, and he left smiling, but she was uneasy all evening. That night, while Mr. Edwards snored with most of the coverlet tucked under his long legs, she lay within the bed curtains wrestling with herself for submission, quietness of spirit, and the willingness to wait upon God.

At the moment sleep finally came to Sarah, Leah was awake on her pallet with her hand on Saul's thigh, thinking about whether or not she believed that her first child would complete her marriage, as her mother had taught. She had left a palmful of flour and a few walnuts as an offering under a red maple in the corner of the meadow lot and, now in her bed, prayed to God to keep her body and the baby from harm, but she had no way to return to her mother's house, as she should, and she was scared. Soon she would tell Bathsheba, who would grind up herbs into a paste and promise to attend her labor, as surely Sarah would do, as well, but Leah felt tugged from inside, pulled beyond promises into a kind of forced patience that felt both crudely familiar and against her nature. She wondered if anyone would make groaning cake for her.

The next morning, Sarah slipped out of the curtains and raised her shift to squat with knees stiff with cold over the chamber pot. She would have preferred to dress and walk to the outhouse, but her body, dross that it was, would not wait. She covered the pot and pushed it back under the bed, then returned through the silk fringe of the curtains, letting in cold air, and slid beneath the coverlet to lie next to her husband, who was almost awake.

It was good to let her hands drift over the curve of his hipbone beneath his long shirt, to draw close and pull her hands easily over his belly, a smooth, delicate pathway beneath the linen. Her touch was not insistent. Her husband, more awake now, held her near, bending his bare leg over a knee to stretch. Light was beginning to sift in through the edges of the curtains, and he was reaching across her to find, she thought, his flannel vest where it was tucked in beside the coverlet, when he arrived on top of her as if she were another place to sleep, and she felt that she was, that she could hold him. Desire was simple and predictable, both burden and gift. She lifted her hips beneath him. Her breasts were tender that morning and his weight was keen, like the cold coming in under the blankets and the squalls of the heifers wanting to be fed.

They dressed within the scant warmth of the bed before rising to go into the parlor for morning prayers. Leah had already laid a fire, and the girls were still dressing or out tending the animals when Mr. Edwards pulled his chair a bit closer to Sarah's (she caught the scent of cedar soap), and said, "I felt that you failed in some measure of prudence when you were speaking with Mr. Williams yesterday."

Sarah bit her lip, losing her hard-won calm. As she flinched from his criticism, she also felt the disposition to fight it. Not the criticism, which she knew to be justified even as she felt it like a slap, but how much it made her reel to be confronted with her imperfections by her husband. His good opinion meant too much to her. She shot a look at him before she lowered her head. He patted the back of her neck. She said, "I'm not a plow horse."

Now he was shocked. "Of course you're not. Sarah . . ."

She interrupted, "I will do better." She wouldn't look at him again, but reached up, took his hand from her neck, and clasped it in her lap as the children, slaves, and visiting ministers came into the drafty parlor.

Mr. Reynolds, visiting from Enfield, led the morning prayers. Sarah sat in the midst of her children, unable to sort out what she was feeling, but very sure that she was longing to hear Mr. Reynolds say *Father* as he prayed. If she were going to fuss like a tired child, she wanted Father God to put her right. God, not her husband. She was neither accustomed to nor willing to be childlike with him.

Jerusha's chair was next to hers, and the sound of her daughter's breath helped her control her own. Then she could hear nothing, not the prayer, not Jerusha's breath or her own as all of her sins started hammering loudly inside her skull. Her knees hung slack against her skirt and her hands dropped from her lap as God laid aside his displeasure and smiled at her.

When she could manage her limbs, she rose from her chair and went to her chamber to be alone with God. She was weeping, the presence of God so near that she was scarcely conscious of anything else. She lay on the coverlet with the bed curtains open wide, seemingly lifted above earth and hell, out of the reach of everything she knew, so that she could look on the enmity of men and devils with holy indifference. The same words came to her mind over and over. "My God, my all; my God, my all."

She thought of the ministers in the house, not just Mr. Edwards, but Mr. Reynolds and young Samuel Hopkins, who was lodging with them as a student. She thought of their worst habits: her husband's condescension, Mr. Reynolds's pompousness, and poor Hopkins looking covetously at her daughters. She saw all that, and still felt willing to undergo any labor if they would but come to the help of the Lord.

Sarah felt more perfectly weaned of the world than ever before, but, stretched out on the bed with her shoes leaving smudges of dirt on the coverlet, she tested herself further. She let herself imagine the worst: that the hostility she felt from a few in the congregation would heighten into hatred and spread throughout the town. If they ever chose, the people of Northampton could strip her and her family of their home and livelihood and leave them disgraced and naked to the world. She imagined being driven from her house into the snow, chased from town with the utmost contempt and malice and left to perish in the cold. She could feel how the dogs would snarl at her heels and tear at her skirt, and how boys would throw rotten eggs and balls of ice packed around rocks at the back of her head as she fled. There on the bed fully dressed, she was shivering, but alone in the woods, she would have a burning, deadened feeling in her skin. Her hands and feet would stiffen and swell until she could not even manage to knock branches away from her face as she stumbled along. There would be a constant ache in the back of her throat and pain in her chest as she coughed. She could feel herself desperate, lost and shaking, simplified by snow to knowing only the need for protection, but, in her bed-bound trance, she was safer than she had ever been, full of compassion and in deep abasement of the soul, able to see herself in a life of hard ice without the least disturbance in her inexpressible happiness and peace, thinking only, "Amen, Lord Jesus!" as the instinctive language of her soul.

She saw a small bug with a black body standing on splayed legs at the half-folded edge of the coverlet. She wasn't sure if its back were shell or wings until it flew. Remaining in a sweet and lively exercise of yielding to God, Sarah got up, brought a bushel of potatoes and turnips down from the attic, scalded the meat from a hambone, and started a soup. She felt inspired but distracted. After she nearly cut off the tip of her finger, she called her daughter Mary over to finish the chopping. She didn't tell her husband about the state that had gripped her body and dimmed the world. It was not his, but hers.

Mr. Edwards was called away to preach. He left on Monday. By Wednesday, young Mr. Buell had come to try his voice in the Northampton pulpit. He was scant months out of Yale, but already his reputation as a preacher came ahead of him. Sarah noticed that their boarding scholar, Hopkins, who had been a classmate of Mr. Buell's at Yale, was accompanying his private prayers in his chamber with sounds that were suspiciously suggestive of a fist (or head) banging against the wall. She thought Mr. Hopkins might be battling envy of Mr. Buell's spiritual success, and made sure to seek him out in conversation and offer him extra helpings of the pudding when they dined.

She was relieved to find in herself neither envy nor anxiety at Mr. Buell's instant popularity amongst her husband's congregation. The young divine had an open manner which Mr. Edwards could never match. He stepped closer to people as they approached him, looking into their eyes, ready to listen to their struggles. Sarah, who knew so many ministers, admired his discipline and found it easy—young as he was—to open herself to his instruction.

As Mr. Buell preached in Mr. Edwards's pulpit on Wednesday afternoon, his white horsehair wig fell about his collar and framed his rawboned face in a way that heightened the light in his eyes. Looking out over the congregation, Sarah saw Mrs. Clapp shaking, Mrs. Hutchinson rocking, and the oldest Bartlett boy in tears. She felt God returning to Northampton again, strong as in the fiercest days of earlier revival. These were her husband's people: his criers, his singers, his unruly crowd calling to God as with one voice.

After the sermon ended and the people went out, she felt drained of bodily strength. She couldn't stir from her pew, but remained, slumped and talking excitedly about her raptures to anyone who would listen long after the meeting was done. Her children stayed with their mother, Jerusha and Esther tending the younger ones, praying, listening, and keeping a protective distance between Sarah and any who might look upon her agitation with critical eyes.

Leah, carrying baby Sukey wrapped in a beaver skin, had left the meeting house with Bathsheba in a snow squall, before the sermon was over. The oldest Edwards daughter, Sally, was sick in her bed. Leah had to tend the fire, put on water for tea, and lay out cold beef and pickled cabbage before the family and their guests arrived, famished from their spiritual exertions. It was best, after a sermon, to have the meal on the table with no visible effort to remind the company of the distractions of the carnal world.

Bathsheba came with her along King Street instead of heading directly up Main toward Sheriff Pomeroy's. She stopped in the hall of

SPIDER IN A TREE

the parsonage to shake the snow off her shawl and warm up a moment before she hurried home to enact her own version of the miracle of the loaves and fishes.

Leah listened for any stirrings upstairs before she motioned Bathsheba into the kitchen, lay the baby on her fur near the hearth, then took up the chopping knife and sliced a well-peppered sliver of cold roast, which she folded into a piece of bread and handed to Bathsheba. She cut a piece for herself and took a big bite. All meat, no bread.

Bathsheba said, "Feeding the stranger?"

Leah, who had not yet spoken of her circumstances, looked at her and swallowed.

Bathsheba laughed, "Oh, now, don't worry. It isn't everyone who keeps such a sharp eye as I do on a happy wife."

Leah took another bite and started bringing plates to the table. "Will you help me when it's my time?"

Bathsheba swatted at her sleeve with her beef and bread. "Starting now, Leah. Keep those arms down. You want your whole womb up around the poor thing's ears?"

Leah made a face, but she drew a stool from a corner and climbed up to reach the rest of the plates in the sideboard, handing them down to Bathsheba. "He's off to preach in another town, and she's forgetting where her feet are every time she hears a hymn. Who do you think will be doing the work?"

Bathsheba set the dishes on the table, then put the food half eaten into her big pocket and shook out her shawl before she tied it around her shoulders and pulled it up over her head. "I figure that it's been fifteen years since Sarah Edwards has gone this long without starting a new child herself. She's probably in distraction from drying up."

"Shush," said Leah. The stairs were creaking. It had to be the oldest daughter, up from her sick bed. Bathsheba gave Leah a hug, flicked a bit of beef fat away from the corner of her mouth, then unlatched the kitchen door and disappeared into the snow.

Jerusha stayed with Sarah at the meeting house, but the other girls returned home and helped Leah serve tea to those who were flocking there in hopes of a private meeting. Esther, in her mother's absence, was effective in engaging Mr. Buell in suitable conversation, offering him her father's study if he wished time to reflect after his exertions.

He bowed slightly as he accepted her offer. When she opened the door, however, they disturbed Samuel Hopkins, who was slumped in a straight chair in a corner as if too cowed to sit near the great man's desk, reading and picking idly at a hole in his stocking, through which protruded a pale, hairy toe. He flushed quite scarlet as they entered, tripping on his empty shoes as he leapt to his feet, but Mr. Buell laughed and said, "Oh, sit down, Hopkins," while Esther, with only the slightest smirk, graciously withdrew.

When Sarah finally came back from meeting, they all prayed and sang again. Mr. Buell held forth in the parlor, but Sarah felt it her duty to see to the house before she stopped to listen. Finally, looking for her cloak, she stepped into the parlor and heard him say, "Oh, that we, who are the children of God, should be cold and lifeless in religion!"

Sarah had paused just inside the door when her legs began to tremble, and she fell to the ground, knocked over by a gut sense of the ingratitude of the children of God. She felt formal and calm, oblivious to the others in the room, but her belly started jerking and her breath came in sharp pants. She felt protected, encompassed, and utterly known. She was making small noises. "Uh huh. Huh. Huh."

The grit in the floorboards was rough against her cheek. She opened her eyes and saw crystals like salt, soot from the fire, little scratches in the wood, and a single black hair, longer than her own, that she knew as her daughter Jerusha's. The sight of it gave her a tiny twitch of her old desires, of a sense of propriety, but she lay there and let it go, willing to be the messiest soul in the colony if that was the will of God.

Gradually, she became aware of the uncomfortable way her clothes were bunched beneath her ribcage. She thought of the seeds of everything inside her, including, at the core of her immaculate ovum, old Adam himself. She cleared her throat, coughed a little in the dust, then leaned her face against her palm, holding her forehead. A strand of her own hair threatened to scratch her eyeball, and she brushed it away so that it dragged the floor as she raised her head, picking up bits of dirt.

There were people on the floor beside her, trying to lift her. Young Mr. Hopkins. Mrs. Clapp. She was returning to her body again, as if she hadn't left it. God was with her as she brought her hands to the floor, let her weight rest on her knees, then pushed up to stand. Those who had come to her aid quickly settled her back into a chair.

Sarah started talking. Her younger daughters came running to hear, standing clumped in the doorway, except, of course, for the infants in their obliviousness. Jerusha had her hand on the arm of her mother's chair as Sarah spoke from the fullness of her heart. "God has saved me from hell. My happiness runs parallel to eternity. There is such peace and joy in giving up all to God, in an entire dependence on his mercy and grace."

Mr. Buell began to hum beneath her words, and then to read, almost chant, a hymn by Dr. Watts. Jerusha pressed closer to Sarah as she leaned forward to listen, and felt the rush of skirts as her mother leaped from her chair, drawn upwards.

Mr. Buell kept reading hymns and another minister prayed while Sarah danced out the glories of the upper world on her parlor floor.

Leah was close behind the little girls in the hallway with a pain in her belly. She couldn't see her mistress's feet in her satin slippers, which Sarah had put on that morning as if it were not winter, missed the half pliés and the elegant sliding capers, the pointing of the toes and the placement of the heel. She couldn't tell if Sarah was rising onto the ball of her foot or rising into the air. Her shoulders were symmetrical, still and controlled as she sprang among the parlor chairs. People sang the hymns as Sarah sank into a half coupé and bounded again, sweating, red-faced, and exultant, giving honors to the company and to her partner, who was clearly God.

Leah was one of the women who carried her mistress to her chamber when she collapsed again, her strength gone. She saw the heeled slippers; then, as they laid Sarah on the bed, Leah removed them carefully, thinking what a hard time Sarah would have had making her way to the barn in the snow wearing those. The Pomeroy ladies, Mrs. Hutchinson, Mrs. Clapp, and other women of the town, along with the eldest Edwards daughters, were all milling about the room, discussing whether to offer Sarah an infusion or a decoction in the way of herbal tea, except for elegant Mrs. Stoddard, who advocated Madeira, and Esther, who, with her mother indisposed, once again assumed the duties of hostess in the parlor. They seemed flustered and excited, but also genuinely kind, all of the small animosities that could accumulate between a minister's wife and the congregants in a small town dissolved in their generosity and her need. As the sudden terrible pain struck her, Leah saw Mrs. Hutchinson move a strand of hair from Sarah's face as gently as if she were her own child.

Leah stumbled away, feeling a hard cramping and a wetness where her shift was tied between her legs, thinking, strangely, still of slippers: ladyslippers in the woods in early summer with their swollen, veiny pinkness, shoes buried under houses, beneath hearths and doorframes, sacrificed from the rough feet of people stubbing their toes and scrabbling through muck to keep the spirits from walking through openings in any habitation, blocked by their soles curling in the dirt.

Leah knew her thoughts were scattered, but the pain was bad, and the house was overcrowded with the pious and the hungry. She was sure that she couldn't cook or fetch anything. Saul was gone with the sleigh to the woodlot. She opened the back door and started down the path to the outhouse, but saw Mr. Buell ahead of her, his wig whiter than the snow.

She cut out off the path into the deep snow, sinking past midcalf when she broke through the crust, and scrabbled her way to her dark cabin. There, she squatted over a pail, snow dripping from her stockings, while she passed clots of blood and tried to think of a name for the baby before everything was lost.

When it was over, she was exhausted, and slept through the mid-day meal, but the chaos in the house was such that she wasn't called to task. She was back there in time to mind the babies while the people went to meeting again to hear Mr. Buell.

At the end of the day, Saul came to her with a weariness almost as deep as her own. He didn't weep when she told him, but sat up nights until January was out, soaking and bending wood to make a new bucket. He had taken the old one deep into the woods, almost to the base of Mount Tom, and hung it, unemptied, in a tree.

Mrs. Clapp ran from her house, hallooing at Mr. Edwards as he rode down King Street on his return from the preaching tour. He sighed, taking a deep breath of tannery air, when he saw her coming. He was eager to be home, and she was an exuberant gossip. She scared him, though, by clutching his stirrup and saying, "We've been frightened that we might lose your wife, with all of her leaping and swooning, before you finally got back."

He stared for a moment at Mrs. Clapp's face, shaped as it was by concern and minor malice, and remembered the same face during the first awakening, covered with tears, looking at him and past him to God.

She offered him a corked bottle. "Syrup of mullein. Good for women's troubles."

He accepted the bottle and thanked her without any questions, but took the rest of King Street at a run, prodding his tired horse, reckless of people and carts.

Sarah, who kissed him on the chin and pinched him at the waist to make sure he hadn't lost more weight, seemed fine. Mr. Buell had moved on, but she was still riding herd on a houseful of children and ministers. Mr. Edwards left her to it and stayed in his study until late that night, when even Leah, who seemed sluggish and sad, had gone to bed. He had noticed Saul hauling water to the kitchen, though that was usually Leah's job. When the house was finally still, he persuaded Sarah to go out of it with him. She gave him a look to let him know that she was being indulgent, but put on an extra pair of stockings, borrowed his flannel vest, and walked with him as he carried a stool and a lantern across the snow-rutted yard.

He leveled the stool carefully, holding it steady as he helped her step onto it. When her footing was solid, he set the lantern down on the hardened snow and tried to hoist her into the crotch of the elm. The stool wobbled, and Mr. Edwards stumbled back under his wife's weight, but she grabbed the lowest branch and scrabbled up the slippery trunk with her skirts trailing and him heaving from below. She heard the back of the waistband rip as she swung into a seated position with both of her legs dangling over one side of the branch. It was slick with ice, but she inched farther out and held on as, leaving the lantern melting a hollow in the snow, he clambered up to join her.

"Tell me what happened," he said, hugging the trunk with one arm as he wrapped the other around her waist. "All of it."

Sarah, who had been talking with unstoppable fervor to everyone she encountered, suddenly felt shy. She stalled as if they were chatting at dinner instead of perched in the yard. "Did they feed you anything interesting while you were gone?"

He kicked against the trunk, and their thick branch swayed. "Pickled lobster," he said. "Pepper cake."

She reached past him to the trunk, steadying the branch, aware of both his impatience and the cold dampness soaking through her skirts, feeling chilled and foolish, but also very much at home. Then she began.

She described her recent spiritual experiences, which it grieved him so much to have missed. She did not refrain from references to his ill will or to the bliss of her release from it. Speaking calmly, she changed nothing to please him. He so loved that in her. She said that God in his mercy had given her a willingness to die and also a willingness to live. One thing she offered as evidence of the depths of her new humility was that she would rejoice to follow behind the negro servants into heaven. He didn't wince at that, but thought again of the look he had seen on Leah's face as she banked the fire. Could it have been grief?

For a moment, listening in the cold tree, he heard pridefulness twining in with Sarah's ecstasy. The blunt shove of recognition pushed him up against his own failings. He held on to her tighter and let it pass, obscuring his questions about Leah's feelings with the urgency of his wife's and his own. Even as he—like a sleeper in church—gave way to human corruption enough to skew his response, the grace in the rest of Sarah's story rang true.

When she finished telling him everything, he let go of the trunk and turned to her. She reached for him, too, and they fell off the branch. He knocked over the stool, and Sarah landed so close to the lantern that, raising his face from the snow, he feared her skirts would burn.

Chapter 13
July – December 1742

One late afternoon in high summer, Joseph was annoyed to run into
Samuel Hopkins not far from his mother's house. What was the point
of graduating from Yale if he was going to keep running into Hopkins
on Pudding Lane? He pulled off his hat without waiting for his friend
to go first, even though he felt that Hopkins's degree of distinction did
not require it.

Hopkins, gawky and friendly as ever, responded in kind, adding
a bow that, in Joseph's view, risked affectation and the loss of his wig.
Joseph was fleeing the house to walk off irritation with his mother—
who seemed to talk of nothing but the virtues of her dairy cows and the
failings of their neighbors—and was in an ungenerous mood. He wiped
sweat from his neck with a handkerchief, then flicked it at Hopkins, who
jumped. "You've got oatmeal on your cravat," Joseph said. "I thought
you were preaching on supply somewhere."

Hopkins brushed his thin hands over the front of his coat
ineffectually, leaving the oatmeal gummed in place, then came closer to
Joseph, oblivious to his irritation. "Mrs. Edwards sent me with these
for your mother." He held up a string bag half full of balls of chocolate
wrapped in linen. That Hopkins was carrying evidence that he had been
boarding with the Edwards family increased Joseph's irritation. "Wait
a moment while I give them to her, then I'll walk with you and tell you
where I've been."

Joseph reached out and knocked the damp oats from his old
friend's collar, then waved him inside. He waited in front of the house,
although he wasn't sure that he wanted to. He already knew exactly where

Hopkins had been: West Suffield, where, last summer, Mr. Edwards had brought a houseful of people to shrieking just before—Joseph would never forget it—he crossed the river to preach "Sinners in the Hands of an Angry God." Now the sermon was famous, and the people who had been baptized in raucous crowds last year were impatient with what they had started calling the Suffield church's Old Light preacher, and so had split off and were looking to hire a New Light for their congregation. Joseph and Hopkins were both studying with Mr. Edwards (in fact, Joseph should have been inside reading *Body of Divinitie* by Bishop Usher instead of grinding a lump of oatmeal into the dirt with his shoe), but Hopkins had been licensed to preach in May. Mr. Edwards had urged him to consider applying for the position at West Suffield, so Hopkins had turned itinerant to take the measure of that congregation and let them get a look at him.

When Hopkins came out of the house carrying a round of cheese in his string bag, Joseph, who had been hoping to pursue the West Suffield position himself, now felt forced to choose a destination or be exposed as an idler, so he jerked his head toward town, and the two of them fell in stride.

Hopkins, kicking up dust as he shuffled along, launched into the story of the blessings that had been showered on his preaching in West Suffield. Joseph watched Hopkins's face get redder as he spoke of how strengthened by spirit he had felt when he heard people calling for salvation in screams fierce enough to pierce the most sin-hardened soul. Hopkins had come near to fainting himself, but God had held him up before them and his words poured out like sweat in the steaming meeting house.

Many were affected, but some, it emerged, were not pleased. He had preached again that evening at a private house, and had felt the Lord moving all night in his dreams, then had walked back to the meeting house at daybreak, ready to preach again. Joseph could picture Hopkins, who would have forgone breakfast, marching through town alone, jittery with excitement, praying as he went and swinging his long, skinny arms. As he passed, people tending their animals called out to him, praising

God with high feeling, but as he climbed the hill to the meeting house, the houses were still. He saw men converging silently toward the meeting house. There were five of them, all of them larger and older than he was, and one, who had a neck like a bull, said to the others, "Shut up the meeting house door."

They swung it closed with a defiant thud, then lined up before it as Hopkins, feeling a strong sense of menace, continued to climb. He stopped a good ways away from them, suddenly weighted down with exhaustion, as the bull-necked one called out, "You will not preach here today." Joseph suspected Hopkins of embellishment, although, in their time together at Yale, he had not been prone to it. The two of them came to the end of Pudding Lane and stopped at the middle of the Bridge Street bridge. Hopkins put his hand on the railing, as if to hold himself steady. He had clearly told the story before, more than once, but he was shaking as he spoke, and Joseph, whose blood was up, was stripped free of doubt by the bewildered intensity in his friend's eyes.

He asked, "Did you fight them?"

Hopkins shook his head. "It was the house of God. And they had thick staffs. I tried to pray, but they were unmoving. People, some hot-headed, gathered behind me, and some, too, with the men before the door. They held the meeting house for seven hours, while I went out of Suffield proper back to West Suffield, where I preached in a regenerate man's outyard. Despite the gobbling turkeys and sudden flurries of distraction when everyone looked over their shoulders in case of attackers, the people who gathered there were much moved."

A yoke of oxen pulling a cart was approaching. They moved off the bridge in order to give it room to cross. Joseph had a strange mix of feelings, much like those that had swept him when he had heard that David Brainerd had been expelled from Yale for saying that his tutor had no more grace than the chair he was leaning on. Brainerd, it was true, had been overheard through a window in a private conversation, but, still, he had presumed to judge the heart of one who ranked above him, then had refused to stand up in the Hall before the whole student body for the humiliation of a public apology. Yet now Brainerd had other ministers, Hopkins and Mr. Edwards among them, pleading his case. Hopkins had nearly caused a brawl at a meeting house: could this be a work of God? Nobody knew better than Joseph that Satan could start whispering and unleashing his hounds in the midst of a revival—that was what had done in his poor father—but he also remembered how strongly Mr. Edwards warned that equivocating could damn a religious man's soul.

They reached the well at the crossroads of Main, Pleasant and King, in front of the courthouse, which had been there for some years now, about as long as the spire had been up on the new meeting house just up the hill. Hopkins bent to try to get a drink of water, but his hands were shaking too much and he dropped the dipper. Joseph was unsettled in his feelings, but the dipper was muddy on the ground, so he reached into the well and raised his cupped hands to offer his friend a drink. Hopkins looked at him a moment before he bent to take it. Then he reached and drank again, using his own hands. They had steadied.

Joseph said, "May God guide us."

Hopkins took his leave and headed off down King Street to attend to his duties at the Edwards's house, while Joseph stayed to clean the dipper for the next person coming thirsty to the well. He stood for a moment, looking down King at boys from the brickyard hauling wheelbarrows of clay from the river, smelling the stench from the tanning yard that meant they were working the hides with dung, nodding up Main at the young Stoddard ladies coming out of Mr. Hunt's hat shop. It was all ordinary business. No people were crying out for their souls from a private house, or, if they were—unlike in the late summer and fall of the year before, or even as, as he had heard his mother say, as late as this winter, when Mr. Buell was preaching and Sarah Edwards had been practically swooning in the road—it was not now loud enough to hear.

He turned and walked purposefully back across the small bridge toward the ferry to Hadley, as if he suddenly were drawn by duty. He took off his hat and fanned his face, only half aware of where he was really going. It wasn't far.

Joseph tried to pray as he walked, but instead of scripture, his mind raised thoughts and feelings matted together like the feathers dipped in milk that he'd seen Sarah Edwards give a sick baby to suck on. He tried to smooth them into order, or, at least, draw sustenance.

He was, he knew, consumed with desire to have done what Hopkins had, to have preached with such power as to fill the people with spirit like pipes fill a tavern with smoke. He wanted to have faced defenders of dry religion at a meeting house door. He thought he might have struck a blow, staffs or no, and he might have been struck himself, knocked to the ground, kicked and cursed or prayed over in an insulting way, with the worst of intentions. Joseph could imagine himself huddled on the ground, admonished for pride and blasphemy, and he could see the men raise their cudgels, but then stop them in midair and help him to his feet, as with bruised lips and broken teeth, he spoke the words that were needed to make them follow behind him with changed souls as he limped to the meeting house and pushed open the doors. Then, again, he admitted to himself, he might not be brave at all. He wished never to be persuaded by the forceful will of others to act against what he knew to be right, but he felt it was possible that he might have just slipped out of town in fear of the cudgels. He wished to know the quality of his own courage. He wanted, like Hopkins, to be tested.

It was hard to know that people were doing battle about the things of religion so close by, while, in Northampton, once again, Joseph was noticing the intensity of religious feeling start to fade. He himself was pious as ever, but he wondered about Elisha, who had been so taken with crying out at young people's meeting with his fellows such a short time ago. Now Joseph, sitting next to his brother at meeting, could feel his attention wandering. It did no more good than it ever had to elbow him in the ribs.

Joseph reached the graveyard just past the Parsons's place, laid out between the meeting house and the river (and the tavern near the ferry dock) so that the people of Northampton would feel the possibility of their own deaths and think of God every time they passed. Joseph couldn't say that this truly seemed to do much to alter most people he knew, who passed by so often that the graves seemed like pails or fence posts, ordinary artifacts of lives full of feeding pigs and fetching scythes from inconvenient fields, nothing to slow the mule for, unless there were particular graves that drew the mind, or if the passersby in question felt vulnerable to spirits and the day were cutting too quickly toward dark.

The sun was still hot, though, as Joseph, a habitual ambler who could uncoil in sudden impulses of speed, entered the graveyard. He felt the slight dip in the ground that marked part of the fence line of the old palisade that had forted in the whole town when the settlers first arrived. His head itched under his wig, but his stubbled scalp would burn should he be so rash as to take it off. A catbird made mad ribbons of the songs of other birds. Joseph, following the pious habit of inner probing, felt how jealous he was of Hopkins over the scholarly attentions of Mr. Edwards, and he felt himself both longing for those attentions and—he was in fear for his soul as he realized this—resenting them as well. He had never decided whether his father had died because he listened too much to Mr. Edwards or because he didn't listen to him enough. Joseph knew that the question was unholy and unfair. Men didn't control the fate of other men's souls, or even that of their own; as everyone knew, this was a power that was sovereign to God. If God had visited Joseph's father with something of grace, then the man would not have listened when Satan came whispering in his ear.

Joseph came to his father's grave, with its deathhead angel carved into rough pink stone, leaning a little away from the stone of Lydia, his father's mother, whose body was laid between that of Joseph's father and the body of his father's father, Captain Joseph Hawley, Esquire. Joseph crouched, thinking of the ox that gored his grandfather, thinking of the stain in the parlor from his own father's blood. Then he let his knees, sweltering in his stockings, dent the grass with their blunt, blind weight, so that, almost without volition, he had taken up a posture of prayer.

Sweat was dribbling down his neck, so he lifted his wig to let a bit of air cool his head. He settled it back against his skull, then closed his eyes. His shoulders clenched, as they often did, beneath his coat, so that someone who loved him could have picked him out from the road by the tilt of them alone.

What he heard inside himself above the churn of his jealousies and desires was the voice that had been promising momentous, terrible things since he first had the power to discern meaning. Mr. Edwards. He had tried to ignore it, but it had a pull like the beat of the sun, hot with truth and error, made even louder by family and familiarity.

Joseph, in his meditation, was given, at last, a verse of scripture, Isaiah 60:9. "Surely the isles shall wait for me, and the ships of Tarshish first, to bring my sons from far."

Just the evening before, Mr. Edwards had leaned forward in his chair toward Joseph and Hopkins within the outer circle of listening daughters, and said, "That verse is one of many things that make it clear that the millennium will dawn in America. 'Tis signified that it shall begin in some very remote part of the world, that the rest of the world have no communication with but by navigation. It is exceedingly manifest that this chapter is a prophecy of the prosperity of the church, in its most glorious state on earth in the latter days, and I can't think that anything else be here intended but America by 'the isles far off.'"

The idea of America, much less Northampton, as having the honor of communicating religion in its most glorious state to great Europe had been strange and compelling as Mr. Edwards made his case there before the fire (Joseph had not heard such things from his minister at any other time), but what was catching in Joseph's blood in the hot graveyard was the phrase "to bring my sons from far." Near to home as he was, he felt far. He felt toward Mr. Edwards such son-like feelings, things that he had felt for his father, and, at his best, also for God—so sinful to let the human, the dead, and the everlasting blur in this way, so difficult to make them hold their edges. He wanted a legacy from Mr. Edwards or his father (he knew better than to demand such things from God) and couldn't bring himself to feel that it mattered much which. He opened his eyes and, staring at his father's stone, felt a crackling flurry in his chest. He was insanely angry, just for long enough to think *our father*, as if starting a prayer. The wave of it knocked him out of his kneeling stance, so that he sat back full hard on the ground and saw some kind of beetle coming toward him across his father's grave.

It was large, with an abdomen so swollen that it could barely walk, but it kept struggling on. It tried to climb a blade of grass, but was too heavy, and bent it awkwardly with flailing, sticky limbs. It looked sticky all over. Its shell was striped copper and iridescent green, and it kept trying to flick it open, but then would fall over and have to struggle back to its feet to go on, clear inner wings slipped out from beneath the shell and dragging in the dirt.

It stopped near Joseph's left hand, close enough to make him uncomfortable, although he held still. It had big pinchers and seemed to see him. Watching it, Joseph felt on the verge of remembering something important and insistent, stoked by indefatigable insect energy. He wanted to be seeing God burning the bush, but knew that if this beetle was beyond nature, it was more likely to be of the devil. Sun of righteousness, he thought, sweating, keep me on your paths.

The beetle sat up almost on his cuff, and began stroking a back leg across its shell as a dog might scratch for mange. It seemed to ride the rhythms of the blood pulsing in Joseph's wrist. It rubbed its head with two more legs, and still had legs to hold its crouch as it bent forward, the light behind it hitting a tight horizontal joint of the wing shell and making it spark green.

It had begun, terribly, to rub sticky whiteness off its belly, which had a dark red blotch on its high center, when Joseph was distracted by the sound of human voices reaching him softly from much closer than the road. Before he could make out the words, he heard a passionate undertone that made him think, for a moment, that he had stumbled across Northampton people overtaken by prayer, after all. They seemed to be moving toward him, though.

Feeling pointlessly embarrassed to be discovered at his father's grave, he dropped flat to the ground and saw the bug scuttle off through the thickets of grass. If anything, he felt more embarrassed to be lying in the grass than he had sitting in it, a sense of mortification that was a bit relieved when he recognized the voice of his brother Elisha saying, "Here, I brought this for you."

Joseph had nothing to fear from being discovered by Elisha, so he sat up, frankly brushing dirt from his coat. He didn't see anyone, but heard a woman's voice answering, or perhaps a girl. It could have been any of a number that Elisha had been idly courting that summer, Joseph thought, probably a Bartlett or maybe a Root. Her voice was soft, held to a murmur, but Joseph heard his brother say clearly, "Here, let me thread that for you."

Joseph stood up, thinking that the graveyard was a strange place for a girl to do her sewing, but the thought of his brother, who had just turned sixteen, leaning over anyone's mending seemed like a sight to see. Before he could move to find them, though, he heard her laugh, and say, louder and in a state of some agitation, "Oh, I keep them half-laced to let me work in the fields. Thank you kindly for the bodkin, but I can manage my own stays, if you don't mind, sir."

Joseph froze when he should have gone running. Elisha, who had lowered his voice, was speaking, but Joseph could no longer make out what was said. He knew that he had a duty to himself, his mother, and to God to catch the sinners and reprove them at once, but he didn't think he could bear putting his brother through the consequences of his conduct. If David Brainerd had lost everything rather than face a public confession, how much more stubborn might Elisha be about renouncing a dalliance that, from the rills and hesitations in their receding voices, had brought nothing but a bit of a frolic in a graveyard. Why graves, Elisha? Joseph had to wonder. Why not the woods?

He was standing there, boiling hot, unsanctified, letting his brother wander away having offered to use the blunt needle of a bodkin which he must have brought from the family store to thread a woman's garment, when, once again, he saw the beetle, big enough to be visible from a distance, still backlit and catching sun, raised upright while a crow cawed in a tree above it, but, for as long as Joseph stood watching, did not swoop.

———

Rebekah was waiting for him in the kitchen when he got home. Elisha, of course, was nowhere to be found. She stood up from the table when he walked in and handed him a slice of bread spread with some of her new white cheese. "I'm not asking you questions," she said as he bit into the bread. "I suppose I can do the milking by myself. I did it most nights all those years you were gone to Yale College."

He sat down at the table, and said, "Mother, do you ever fear for our souls? Elisha's and mine?"

She pulled her spine a little straighter like the Stoddard she was, and said, "Joseph, the soul resides in the stomach, and fear is a great cause of indigestion. Ask me again when you're done chewing if you really haven't had enough of such talk today."

So he ate good bread and soft cheese, making plans with his vigorous mother for a trip to net eels. Sister the cat was yowling in the attic. When Elisha came home, not late enough to cause a scandal, he helped himself to more of the loaf than the two of them combined.

Winter again. Nearly a year had gone by since Leah's miscarriage. She was restless with the memory, made sharper by the return of the cold. She had spoken of it only with Saul and Bathsheba, but not much, and not for months. She was surprised at how keenly she felt the loss of her baby, whom she had known as a presence inside her, a tightness, a gurgle that might have been her own guts. She had had the certainty of danger, so many dangers, and still she had wanted this life, this one baby coming, to come further, to be with Saul and her. Eleven months later, her gut ached when she thought of it. The baby would have been five months old now, speaking sweet babble and raising its arms for her like any of the Edwards babies, if the birth had come at its time. She did not know what the Edwardses might have done, had she told them, but she thought that she might have been left to do her work and raise her child with Saul. What was one more mouth, soon to be useful, in a household so peopled with children and visiting divines? Who in this house would sell a soul that could be led to God?

She prayed in secret, in the woods, whenever she could. She got down on her knees on the fallen, frozen leaves and prayed to God that her baby's death be sanctified, that it become a holy thing in her instead of this nauseous weight of loss that seeped in and spread like the ice and rot melting into her skirt. She found little relief; giving up all desire for that was her hope.

When the days came that snow stayed on the ground to pile up with each storm, she prayed inside while Saul carved. One night, she wrote a prayer bid on the back of a curled scrap of paper scavenged from Sally and Jerusha's lacemaking:

Saul & Leah Negro Desire the prayers of this Congregation that God sanktifie his Holy & aflicting hand To them in the Taking a way of thire unborn child by Death.

She dropped it in the fire without reading it to Saul. She couldn't call on the congregation to pray with her over a death she did not let them know. It did not matter whether or not they would. They could not.

Her knee ached more in cold weather, so Bathsheba made her a poultice of basswood to bring the swelling down, muttering that she'd do better if she could bathe it in turpentine, but basswood was all she had. If Leah couldn't stand the pain of kneeling, she would lie prostrate on the rough planks of the floor. Saul's hip ached more than Leah's knee, or, at least, by his bearing, she thought it must. He slept with snow packed in lint held against it at night. The snow, as it melted, drenched the bed, so that Leah would wake with the hem of her shift wet and her knee throbbing. One bad night, she slung the lint at his chest as he slept. He let out a frightened cry and threw the lint out of the loft before his eyes were even opened.

Leah said, "It's nothing. All is well."

He stared at her, then went back to sleep. She was full of regret in the morning when she found the mess of lint hanging like an abandoned mouse's nest on the bottom rung of the ladder to the loft.

She took to keeping a bowl next to the pallet, so that she could move the lint there to drain when the melted snow did Saul no more good. Sometimes the room was so cold that, away from the warmth of their bodies, it froze again in its bowl. If Leah noticed, she'd pry it out, wrap it in a dry stocking, and put the bundle of cold against his hip to balance its hot choler; then she would draw up her knee to press against it, too.

Restless, she would be visited by thoughts that were not the stuff of day. She did not wish to be with child again. She was wordless and practical about it, bringing a cupful of hog's grease to the loft. Saul didn't push her, but let her draw his fingers between her legs. He watched her face as intently as when they had first learned the nuances of each other's responses with the bundling board between them. Now he limned her breasts with grease until they slipped and shone. She knelt across one thigh and bent to let her breasts fall around his yard as she held it tightly between them. He thrust and rested on the rustling bed, and she rubbed hard against his thigh. They were both subject to sudden moods of shyness, and sometimes had to stop abruptly and turn away from each other, estranged, but even at these moments, Leah would reach behind her to hold onto his leg, and Saul would touch his mouth to Leah's neck and breathe there, letting the smell of her mix with his troubled humours like smoke from burnt camphor, which was said to heal.

They had heard religious talk of sodomy and abominations— although in the past months Leah had noticed less religious talk of every kind in Northampton—but she felt stubborn in her wishes and correct in her attentions to her husband, which were as reverent as she could make them. Saul had shame and thwarted desires, but what could he love more than he loved her?

One night she brought him black currant jelly instead of grease. What they stained, she cleaned. What couldn't be cleaned, she threw into the fire or picked into threads to use to make something new. Often as he held the plow, the palms of his hands remembered themselves, sticky with currants, cleaving to her hips.

———

The snow was too thin on the ground for sleighs and the ice was too treacherous for horses, so the children walked to the ruin of the Lymans' burnt house. Mr. Edwards, wearing his old great coat and a beaver hat that was shedding fur, was at the head of the group, with the procession of children coming silently behind him. He hated to bring the children to this place, which he could barely bring himself to look at, but even as he helped the people in the community grieve their great losses, he did not flinch from his terrible duty to the little ones. He did not notice how unusual he was in this regard, but others did.

Joseph followed miserably at the back, trying not to think of the snowball fight he knew that Elisha, Oliver Warner, and the Root boys were having in the frozen meadows. Someone was sure to be hurt, and it was a foolish, raucous way to mourn. But he wanted the thuds and cries of hurling snow at his brother and his red-faced friends, so crude. So full of life. He bent to pick up a red mitten that one of the children had dropped.

The fire that burned down the Lymans' house had happened at night and so quickly that no one had time to run to the meeting house to ring for help before it was too late. It had started in the chimney and burned through the kitchen. Mrs. Lyman had grabbed the baby from the trundle and fled the house while her husband had smothered the fire in his middle daughter's hair, then seized a shovel to beat back flames in the hall, but he had not been able to reach Anne and Hannah where they had succumbed to the smoke on the floor beside their bed.

The house had been gone by morning, a pile of ash smoking in the sparse snow. Mrs. Lyman's sister and her husband had taken in the family, wracked with loss.

Now, as Mr. Edwards was gathering the other children of the town, Sarah sat with Mrs. Lyman in her sister's parlor while the grieving mother pounded her fist into a piece of cake that someone had put in her lap. Sarah took the plate, murmuring, "The Lord their God shall save them." It was what she had in answer to Mrs. Lyman's unburned stupor, that and pulling her chair closer and waiting with an air of witness until Mrs. Lyman finally ripped off two buttons of the borrowed dress that was cutting so tightly into her waist (all her own clothes were lost—everything was) and said, "The hand of the Lord."

Sarah touched her then, wiped crumbs from her clenched fingers and placed a torn stocking, thread, and needle on the empty chair beside her, offering the consolations of useful occupation. That, and witness. Sarah was more than willing to sit with her as long as she possibly could.

The two women pretended for some barren, endless time to sew together, then put the work aside as Mrs. Lyman's surviving daughter came into the room, smelling of the poultice (rum, onion, and Indian meal) which Sarah had used to dress the little girl's burns. Sarah and the mother went with her to the table and sat on either side of her to help her write a prayer bid for Mr. Edwards to read in God's house on the Sabbath.

"Mention your sisters," said Mrs. Lyman, her voice oddly mild, as if she were reminding her daughter to share a boiled egg. The child rubbed her-heat blistered neck through the bandage, then carefully took up the posture of a scholar to write to thank God

> *for his goodness to her when she was in so grat dangior of being burnt up in her fathers hous in that She was presarvd and held of the burn She met with thare and deziers prayers that the dath of her two Sisters and the murcy may be Sanctified unto her and her parants desier the Same.*

At the ruin, most of the children stood very still. Martha Root, an older girl slumping near a doorframe, kicked at the corner of it with her damp boot. Mr. Edwards, grieving in heart and gut, was saying what he had brought them there to hear. "If you live and die insensible of your misery, you will come to feel it in hell."

He went on with his warnings. The children who cried did so without moving. Joseph, flooded by their feelings, could barely identify his own. He was a little boy again, winded on a stump, his father newly dead, with Mr. Edwards murmuring about his own soul in his ear. He brought himself back to the present with a lungful of air cut with cold smoke. The ragged half circle of children were sniffling before their minister and the burned house, but not one of them dared to cough.

Mr. Edwards was still speaking, but Joseph, sweating in the cold, could not listen. This had been a conflagration of a house and of children, not of the spirit. Standing there at these new ruins, he found himself unable to wish that such a thing might come of this. He had been taught that all children were, by nature, heirs of hell, exposed every moment to destruction, unless they were in Christ. In theological discussions with his scholars, Mr. Edwards allowed that children could be saved if their parents were subjects of grace, but he had not brought them to the ashes of the Lyman house to speak of that. Joseph noticed Lucy Edwards standing too near the heap of ashes with a still face and a twitching mouth. Her father loved her, Joseph was sure of it. He loved all of these children and was fighting with everything he had for them. His voice was trembling.

Joseph toyed with the mitten, twisting and pulling wet wool. Next to Lucy, a Bartlett boy with one mitten was crying hard. Watching the boy's nose start to drip, Joseph saw that he himself might not be cut out to be a minister. Or maybe just not his cousin's kind of minister. He wasn't sure, though, what other kinds there might be, although he had heard that Harvard produced some very different men.

He did know that he did not have the stomach to put a child through facing the remains of a fire where other little ones had died, not even to save a soul. Wiping his mouth with the back of his hand, he decided that it was time for his studies with his cousin to end.

He edged over so that he was between Lucy and the ruin. Even though Mr. Edwards was still talking, Joseph squatted down to the Bartlett boy, who reminded him of Elisha. He held out his handkerchief, and, feeling like his own mother, whispered, gently, "I've got your mitten."

Chapter 14
March 1743
New London

One day in early March, Rebekah Hawley and her son Elisha traveled by wagon to New London in pursuit of trade. Rebekah had heard that a large shipment of indigo had come in from the south, and she wanted to do business with a merchant whose home on the waterfront gave him a first look at everything that came into New London. She was fond of this merchant, who had known her late husband, so she had chosen to combine some sociable trading with keeping an eye on Elisha, whom she feared was too distractible to be trusted alone in a seaport full of sailors and strangers.

Besides, Rebekah and her youngest enjoyed each other's company, perhaps even more since Joseph had left Northampton to study theology in Cambridge. She had to admit to herself that the chance to talk with him alone was part of why she preferred to go overland rather than by river or sea. They spent hours of the slow trip with their empty wagon talking about the gaits, markings, and humours of their small herd of dairy cattle, arguing about which calves most resembled their mothers, and whether they might sell more cheese if they planted a field of sweet timothy and grazed them only on that to flavor the milk.

Elisha found the idea fussy and impractical. "Why not feed them roses? Why not rebuild the chimney with gold bricks, while we're about it?"

Rebekah, who knew she would plant what she pleased, had clucked the oxen and said only her son's name, enjoying his firm opinions. She suffered him to call her "Rosy" and "Rosemilk" for the rest of the trip.

They were delayed in their travels by the spring snow, which swirled around the ankles of the oxen and caked the wagon wheels. They spent the Sabbath crowded on the back benches of a freezing little meeting house, cheek and jowl with what seemed to be a population of onion eaters. It was already Monday evening as they approached New London. Elisha, who had a scarf Rebekah had made him wrapped high around his cheeks, watched his mother's face, bare under the hood of her cloak as she drove. Flecks of snow caught in the dark hollows under her eyes, and in the wattles just starting to crease the sides of her cheeks. She was a handsome woman for all that, and he was just unwinding his scarf to offer it to her when she pointed through the blowing, fitful snow to a denser place of white, and said, "Is that smoke?"

Elisha wasn't sure, but as they drew closer, they could make out puffs of gray and black within the white column, and soon began to smell burning over the tang in the air from the sea.

The town, as they entered, seemed empty of life. They had planned to drive straight to the wharf, but the usually placid oxen got balky in the smoke and noise rising from that direction. Rebekah managed to find a boy who agreed to tend the animals and watch the wagons for a shilling. He directed them into a stable where he was employed.

Elisha jumped from the wagon and leaned against the stable door, looking out at the hazy, empty street. "What's happening here?"

The boy fidgeted with the buttons of his checked waistcoat. "Mr. Davenport and them. My master said he'd whip me if I went anywhere near them. Their fire burned all Sabbath and through the night."

Rebekah and Elisha looked at each other. Things had been quiet lately in Northampton, but they were not frightened by the effusions of the Holy Spirit. Elisha took his mother's arm and said, "Steady, Rosy." Then they set off to do their business by the wharf.

"You should stay here," Elisha said as they passed a tavern. "Just in case there are ruffians or any sort of excesses." The outcry was increasing, and now the streets were crowded with people headed toward the docks. They saw a woman running with her arms full of what looked like fine crewelwork bed hangings, and a group of young men with their cropped heads bare, waving wigs in their fists. Others were trudging grimly toward the flame, which could now be seen flickering in the street. Some carried staffs over their shoulders like clubs, as if prepared to defend their town and its peace from all comers. Rebekah, beginning to feel rattled, held onto the sleeve of her son's surtout. She didn't speak as they walked in the midst of the thickening crowd.

When they reached the waterfront, they were stopped short by the density of townspeople who were refusing to budge as strangers and neighbors attempted to jostle past them with arms full of clothes. There were something approaching a hundred people near the fire, singing single lines from hymns over and over and throwing velvet capes, fine shirts, and petticoats into the blaze.

"Indigo," said Rebekah as a pile of gowns smoldered over the thick timbers that must have been hauled from a prime wood lot miles away from the coast. It took a few moments, but she soon recognized her husband's old friend, the merchant, face smudged with ash, casting bolts of raw cloth on the fire, which, she realized, had been set directly in front of his house on the wharf. They would do no business in New London that day.

Beside her, a young woman said, "I could do with a new dress. Yesterday, it was books."

Rebekah turned to look at the speaker, who raised her eyebrows and pushed back her cap with a dramatic gesture of her arm, narrowly missing a child's head with her elbow. "We came out of Mr. Adams's sermon at the meeting house, saw smoke, heard this great noise, and came running, not knowing if the town were on fire or if the papist pirates had come marauding into the harbor, ready to kill us as we prayed." She gave a snort. "Instead, we got here to find Mr. Davenport and those Shepherd's Tent people."

She pointed through the smoke and snow to the disheveled young man with rather plush breeches and clerical bands, seated in a chair that someone must have brought into the street for him, head back and howling, "The hand of the Lord is upon me! The hand of the Lord is upon me!" as the crowd around him sang, too, dancing and feeding clothes to the flames.

Rebekah, transfixed by the screams of Mr. Davenport, barely noted that she had lost hold of her son. The woman beside her edged closer, full of the story, seeming to want to tell it rather than be too much a part of what was happening. She kept her plain cloak clutched tightly over her collar and whispered to Rebekah, "I left my best hood safe at home."

Rebekah was staring at the great light of the fire, her nostrils full of the stink of burning wool, watching as better goods than she could get for the shelves of her store were burned by their owners under the sing-song chant of "the hand of the Lord is upon me," which ebbed and peaked as more people hugging garments approached the flames. The woman beside her was murmuring on about Mr. Davenport, how she had gone to see him two summers ago when he had preached through a thundershower until two in the morning under an oak tree near the old meeting house. He had preached for days out on the rocks and under trees to great crowds of people who had haying to do.

She said, "I myself was much affected. I had felt stirrings in my heart until Mr. Davenport was so severe in condemning our own good minister that I went back inside the meeting house to hear him preach instead."

A stately lady in visible distress threw a pearl necklace into the fire. Boys who looked like brothers were burning their nightgowns, setting them alight but not quite letting go, until a young man with an authoritative look took hold of their wrists and shook the gowns loose, the white stuff of them fluttering and caught on the edge of the fire, but the boys safe from setting their stocking on fire while still on their legs.

"Books, yesterday," the young woman said again, her face red, snowflakes melting in her hair. Rebekah was relieved to see Elisha, not disappeared in the crowd but hovering on the other side of the young woman to listen. The crowd was getting even thicker, pressing in behind them, pushing them closer to the flames. "They burned the work of great divines. Mr. Henry, Mr. Sibbes, Increase Mather, Benjamin Colman." Rebekah was startled to hear the name of Mr.

Edwards's publisher, a staunch friend of the revival. Her informant was still talking. "Mr. Chauncy's pamphlets against the revival, of course. People were rushing down here with great stacks of books by our own pastor, who has tended our souls with such care. All into the fire, while people sang Hallelujahs as if they were hard at prayer."

Now Mr. Davenport was struggling to stand. Young men stepped forward to help him upright, and he rested his hands on the back of his chair, seeming not to care about the heat or his unsteadiness near the flame. The seminarians from Shepherd's Tent were stomping around the fire—coatless, most of them, without wigs and some without waistcoats—faint with heat and hunger, swallowed up in God—or something else.

Rebekah, close enough now to get heat from the fire, could feel their conviction and the possibility that the whole world was consumed with change. She stopped listening to the woman beside her, who was talking about all the radical strangers pouring into their town, the split in her church, trials and arrests. Rebekah was watching the faces of the rampaging worshippers, young, most of them, as they burned the things they loved too much. Mr. Davenport had left off chanting to shout, "Root out Heresy! Pull down Idolatry!"

A slave woman threw her head cloth onto the fire, then a well-turned out young man ripped the velvet collar from his neck and tossed it into the flames.

Rebekah was too warm in her thick scarlet cloak. She was not young, and not usually an excitable woman, but strong-willed and stubborn, a divine's daughter and the relict of Mr. Hawley, whom she remembered with clear-eyed love as a soul too troubled by Satan and God. Rebekah had done a rare thing in that she never remarried, but had raised two sons to pray and prosper, equipped with good posture—although she had noticed that Elisha was starting to slouch and spit into the hearth when he thought she wouldn't notice—and fed with plenty of her good cheese.

But now she was hot, even as the night grew darker. It stopped snowing, and she unfastened the fine lace that tied her cape at the throat, tempted by the flames. The burners, divested of every piece of clothing that had more than one color, were praying together as Mr. Davenport called out for a full discovery of the Mind. The divine Mind. God. Rebekah wanted this, too, wanted to be known in the place of every knowledge, wanted to loose the strings that held her so hard to the ledger book, wanted to feel scripture sew through her like needles of light and bind her to the fires of the Lord. She was a visiting merchant with nothing to buy on such a disrupted, violent night, but she was also a Christian with a soul to ignite. She looked up at the sky and saw wells of indigo where the clouds were beginning to clear, and hot crackling stars too far away to drop into cinders, but burning, she was sure. Smoke crossed them as it blew hard out to sea.

When she looked down, still holding her loosened cloak at her neck, she gasped at what she saw. Mr. Davenport had dropped back into his chair and was struggling out of his plush pair of breeches, already unbuckled at the knee as he pulled them off over his stockings and shoes. He was covered by his long, crumpled shirt as he wadded his breeches into a clumsy ball and hurled them into the mound of burning clothes, shouting, "Go you with the rest."

The woman who had been talking to Rebekah gave an outraged scream and darted forward. She thrust her hands into the fire, dragged out the breeches, already burning, and threw them at the preacher's feet, shouting, "Put these on, sir. You put these on. We will not have nakedness in our streets."

Mr. Davenport stood there in his long shirt, one of his knees swollen and both blotchy, his mouth open to call on God, but a new flush of something else in his cheeks. Rebekah was holding tight to her cloak, trying to make sense of the scene before her, when she saw her son rush to stand beside the incensed young woman, very near the fire. Elisha shouted, with obvious insincerity, "I'll burn you, Mr. Davenport! I've made you too much an idol, as you have done with your breeches, and must thrust you right into the flames."

The people hanging back on the edge of the crowd let out a great laugh, but Rebekah gasped at the impertinence. She was relieved to see him move quickly away from the fire as some of the men standing close to Mr. Davenport began to advance on him. Another gentleman stepped forward as Mr. Davenport, silenced for once, awkwardly picked up his singed breeches and pulled them back on again. This man yelled out in a stentorian voice, "You, Mr. Davenport, have made a golden calf of this fire!"

Mr. Davenport was backing painfully away from the flames, face full of confusion, surrounded by his followers, one of whom grabbed the chair.

Rebekah, who had come fully back to herself, was circling, searching for her son, when she caught a glimpse of him striding away from the wharf in the company of the young woman who had been so bold in grabbing the preacher's breeches from the bonfire. Rebekah drew in a great lungful of smoke and bellowed out his name. "Elisha!"

If he heard, he did not look back.

She walked the streets of that unsettled town calling him for more than an hour by the town crier, until he finally turned up at the stables, full of apologies, his only explanation that he had feared that the woman was at risk for attack and so had seen her home. Rebekah was on him like a burning cloak while he gave the tired boy another coin to lead them to a safe, warm tavern room. It would have been a quiet room as well, but she shouted at him long after she was hoarse, until strangers were brought in to sleep on the floor.

Mr. Edwards walked into a New London parlor filled with ministers, some of them kin to him. He was sick and travel weary from a long preaching trip, but they had persuaded him to come to New London to admonish Mr. Davenport for his behavior on the wharf. Mr. Edwards felt Mr. Davenport's excesses as a personal insult and a great wounding of religion, but he had not wanted to do this. He had agreed to this meeting only on the condition that a large group of other divines would come, too. And, so, here they all were.

Underneath the ague and the weariness, he was seething with anger. He considered that Mr. Davenport might have been seized by the devil or by physical maladies as he suffered from gonorrhea contracted in his youth (sin for which he had fully repented, or so Mr. Edwards understood), but what seemed most likely was that he had fallen into spiritual pride. It was a constant danger for ministers, as Mr. Edwards well knew.

Work had piled onto work, as it always did, so that once Mr. Edwards had agreed to meet with Mr. Davenport, he had also ended up preaching after the trial of others who had participated in the bonfire. He had taken it up as doctrine: the sin of spiritual pride. The magistrate himself had commended his sermon as very suitable for restoring order. Three of the men who escorted and protected Mr. Davenport on his travels and three from the Shepherd's Tent seminary had been convicted, with fines of six shillings, plus court costs, each.

This morning, Mr. Edwards had stood on the scorched wharf in the sea wind, thinking of the ashes of little girls at the Lymans' ruined house. His throat ached. He squeezed his handkerchief in his fist, furious at the arrogance of Mr. Davenport, who had taken it on himself to destroy by fire.

As he turned and walked back up the hill to the house where Mr. Davenport was staying, he had thought of Sarah. He could have been sitting at the table at home with his head under a towel, breathing steam from herbs and boiling water which Sarah would have poured into a sauce boat for him to use to clear his head. If his throat were bad enough, she would have sent one of the girls to card some black wool for him to wear, wet with vinegar and salt, from ear to ear. It would be a comfort, despite the stink.

He worried about Sarah, who had suffered bodily pangs and weakness all winter. Dr. Mather had sent to Boston for Myrnischtu's Emplastrum Matricale, used to treat hysterical cases caused by an unbalanced womb, and had advised her to take Jovial Bezorardick and a decoction of mugwort and apply them as a poultice to her navel and forehead with a damp cloth until the supply ran out. Mr. Edwards missed her sharply, but, as he stood now in the parlor door, he became impatient with himself for grinding out pharmaceutical thoughts as if his mind were a mortar in which to mix salves and clisters rather than a bowl to be filled by God.

He looked around the room. These were men he had preached and prayed with; men who had felt God moving through Enfield with him as the people in the meeting house held on to keep from sliding into hell; men who had brought a rush of spirit to his contentious congregation; men who had listened to him at Yale as young scholars, then had taken to the highways and byways with his sermons as atlas and the scripture as light.

Men who now made people ready for the heat of revival all across the colonies, which brought Mr. Edwards hope now when there were dead times again in Northampton.

There were nearly a dozen them, sitting formally about the room as if each were prepared to preach to the others, some with scraps of notes in their laps, some looking nearly as travel worn as Mr. Edwards felt. Every chair was full. Young Samuel Buell, whose preaching had so moved Sarah in Northampton, was there. He stood and bowed to Mr. Edwards, who nodded his head. Mr. Buell gestured to his empty chair.

A middle-aged slave woman was bending in one corner, offering someone a cup, and when she stepped aside, Mr. Edwards saw Mr. Davenport, still wearing scorched plush breeches, the bandages on one leg visible under his stockings, looking ill, shrunken, and so withdrawn as to be unreadable. Still, he made the effort to stand and call out, "Welcome," in a rotund voice when Mr. Edwards came into the room.

Mr. Edwards took the chair that Mr. Buell vacated for him, stared at Mr. Davenport, and said "Let us pray."

Mr. Edwards barely spoke for the rest of the meeting, but his eyebrows rose and settled like troubled crows. Mr. Buell, who was the youngest man there, stood quietly against the wall. Everyone else took turns reproaching Mr. Davenport and invoking God's word. Mr. Davenport was uncharacteristically quiet, listening to men he was known to admire chastise and condemn him. Now and then, he rubbed his leg.

The room was chilly, and they didn't open the door to draw heat from the rest of the house. When the slave came in and offered more tea to Mr. Davenport, Mr. Edwards heard her whisper, "I burned my head cloth in your fire."

Mr. Davenport lowered his eyes and shook his head. She nodded back, affirming what she had said, then left the room without pouring any more tea. She shut the door, so that they were, once again, closed in and cold. Mr. Davenport gazed at the faces of the men who encircled him in parlor chairs, and then at the floor as he gathered himself to speak.

He said, "Brothers in Christ, I would be naked to you, naked in spirit. I have been blessed by God's presence and ask for your prayers that I do no more to mar or dishonor it. If by encouraging lay preachers and relying on impulses, I have unloosed disorder in the country, I renounce them. I will go back to the towns I have visited and try to undo the damage I have done."

At this, there was some uneasy shifting in the chairs, especially among the ministers from Connecticut, none of whom were eager to have Davenport back in their towns.

"If I have been distracted by pride, I repent. But I cannot step away from the flames. God appeared to the apostles in cloven tongues of fire. I have felt myself feverish from illness, and I have felt myself alight with the Holy Ghost. With my fellow divines here to stoke my powers of discernment, I can see the truth that is in you, and see the difference between sickness and God's light in myself. I repent my sins."

Mr. Buell murmured, "Amen," and stirred to go to Mr. Davenport, who began to weep, but Mr. Edwards motioned him to stop. Mr. Buell sank to his knees on the floor. Humbleness was rife.

Mr. Davenport closed his eyes and threw back his head. He left his eyes closed, his face upturned, his sun-reddened neck arched and vulnerable. His hands rose slightly, open at his sides, and he neither sighed nor spoke, but, giving off heat they could all feel, surrendered himself.

Mr. Edwards had a terrible urge to spring from his chair and knock the much smaller man to the floor. He was still angry, but he knew a soul in need when he saw one. He stood and crossed the room in two strides. Taking Mr. Davenport's head in both hands, he said, with a welling of tenderness, "May God forgive you, Mr. Davenport. May God forgive us all."

Chapter 15
October 1743 – June 1744

Bathsheba was laughing in a Northampton barn. She had been hired out to help with the preparations for Noah Baker's marriage, which was to happen as soon as Mr. Edwards returned from a preaching trip. Ever since he had brought people to crawling and screaming in Enfield, he had been much away from home. It seemed that every New Light church in New England wanted him to preach the same sermon to them.

Bathsheba was done with her day of beating linens and baking with the bride, who now had gone to her sister's house to have supper with her family. Naomi Judd, a hired girl herself, had coaxed Bathsheba into a night walk and a frolic in the barn to keep Naomi, saucy as she was, from being the only young woman there with Noah Baker, Timothy Root, and Oliver Warner.

The boys were all in their twenties, plenty old enough to be men, but without land or, except for Noah, the husband-to-be, a wife. Timothy Root threw a deer hide down on a stack of hay and invited Naomi and Bathsheba to sit. Bathsheba, who carried a piece of broken glass sharp enough to cut in the pocket tied around her waist, was alert but relaxed. She knew these men, had tended to Timothy Root when a half-sawn tree had fallen on his leg, and had given Naomi hysterick powder when she had troubles with her courses. Now Timothy and Oliver were making sport of Noah, threatening him with the pitchfork if he should try to flee his wedding day. They knocked each other over and flopped down on the hay like a row of scarecrows with their sticks pulled away. Bathsheba laughed, feeling the glow of being performed for. Oliver got up to light the lantern, and Noah Baker reached into the lining of his coat to draw out a book.

"Oh no," said Naomi, who had clearly seen it before. "Not that unclean thing."

Bathsheba stood up, sure of danger, but Timothy Root got up, too, talking in a gentle voice, standing between her and the door. All three of the men were standing, their manner still joking and easy, while Naomi sat up a little straighter on the hide, and Bathsheba put her hand on her piece of glass.

"Well, fellows," said Noah, crossing over to Timothy, "I have learned plenty of what a man needs to know on his wedding night. I reckon I know more about my wife than she does herself."

The men all laughed, and Naomi called out, "Stop," in a voice like the bawling of a calf penned away from its mother before slaughter. Timothy held the book up for Bathsheba to see the title. She could not read, but did not have to, since Timothy was telling her all about it. "You know this book, don't you, Bathsheba, a midwife like you? It's *Aristotle's Master-Piece: or, the Secrets of Generation Displayed in all the Parts thereof*. Here, come here, look at it with me, maybe you can explain some matters that puzzle me."

He took a step closer to her, and she stood her ground. Noah Baker sat back down on the hay, and Oliver Warner leaned against a plow. Timothy Root flipped the book to a page that fell open, as it had been visited many times before, to an illustration titled *the form of a Child in the Womb, disrobed of its Tunicles, Proper and Common*.

Bathsheba stared at the picture: the strange cut-away of the child sitting cross-legged and wide-eyed in the belly of a woman who has been opened in four flaps of veiny, petal-like flesh. Her torso ended at the upper thighs, with the birth furrow represented as a line. The cord was tucked under the babe's knees. Breasts marked the uppermost limit of what could be seen.

As Bathsheba looked, feeling less degraded than mystified, Timothy was reading in a soft, pleasant voice, with suggestions of trembles underneath: "The stones of a woman contain several eggs. . . . The clytoris is like a Yard in scituation, substance, composition and Erection. . . . The preparatory or Spermatick Vessels in women do not differ from those in a man but only in their largeness and manner of insertion."

Naomi stood up. "Stop that nastiness about womankind."

Oliver Warner suddenly ran at her, grabbed her shoulders, and shook her. He was laughing, his face very close to hers. Naomi didn't scream or laugh, but thrust her elbow to his gut and broke away. Oliver doubled over, and Noah Baker rose from the hay. Timothy said to Bathsheba, so softly that no one else could hear, "I'm ready to kiss you."

Bathsheba, who had seen this man helpless in pain, pinned beneath a tree, said, "As you love God, you will not."

Naomi grabbed the pitchfork, thrusting it in front of her. Oliver stared at her, angry, while Noah, the husband-to-be, tried to calm him. "Don't mar my happiness. We were reading *Aristotle*. That is all."

Timothy turned to them. "Don't catch hold of her again." He shut the book and walked over to hand it back to Noah. "It's the young folks' Bible. You'll be a preacher of it, soon enough."

Oliver backed off with an eye on Timothy. Naomi was still jabbing air with her pitchfork. Bathsheba let go of her edge of glass and groaned like every woman she had ever tended giving birth. The people in the dim barn all looked at her. No one made a joke about what might be cross-legged in her belly or cut open above her heart. She shoved back the board that served as a latch, threw open the heavy doors, then took the pitchfork from Naomi, unmolested, and walked her out into the scratched-over yard past the edge of lantern light.

Leah tied her shawl around her waist and took the left-hand path beyond Wilton's Meadow Brook to begin to climb the hill on the way to the cranberry bog.

Sweating from her exertions, she found the round spot like a mark to shoot at that someone had made on a pine tree by beating the bark off with a rock. She stopped and traced it with her fingers before she followed the line of stones from the root of the tree toward a tall spruce near the bottom of the descent from Mount Tom. From there, she checked the sun and walked northeast, picking her way across the swamp until she reached a dry stump, where Bathsheba sat waiting for her, plucking a chicken and stuffing the feathers in a sack so that she would have work to show Madame Pomeroy on her return.

Leah sat next to her on the stump and said, "Saul told me that you wanted to see me. I hope you and that chicken didn't leave a trail of blood in the woods. As it is, you'll be attracting beasts."

She expected her friend to laugh and make a joke about how much like a moose she had sounded thrashing up the hill, but instead Bathsheba stretched up the skin of the carcass to pull another feather, and said, "I've been to see Hannah Clark. She said you should go to Miss Jerusha."

Leah sighed and pulled her shawl up over her arms. She never thought of Jerusha, who was fourteen, as calling for a title like Miss or being anything but the small girl who used to try to order her about from below knee level and who had been the most passionate among her sisters about teaching Leah to read and write.

Leah knew that Bathsheba had been listening at the well, at meeting and in kitchens, gathering stories of the young men in town and their secret books. Some young women wouldn't tell such stories in front of a slave, but others couldn't imagine how it would matter if they did; still others simply wanted to talk and to hear what everyone else had said, and what had been said to them.

Leah sat on the stump with Bathsheba and listened to extractions from the list she already knew: Naomi Judd. Hannah Clark. Rebekah Strong. Rachel Clapp. Timothy Root. His cousin Simeon Root. Oliver Warner. Ebenezer Bartlett. Noah Baker. Eben Pomeroy, who was the grandson of Bathsheba's owner and the son of a church deacon. Eben's sister Betty Pomeroy had found a different book, *The Midwife Rightly Instructed*, which she assured Bathsheba was not her mother's, hidden in the chimney.

Leah watched her friend's face as she stripped the chicken and said the names. Her own impulse had always been to hold the most important things close and secret, away from the ugliest assumptions of the English. She never would have dreamed of trying to gather testimony. "Bathsheba, can't you forget all this?"

Bathsheba tied shut the bag of feathers. "I wanted to. You know that. Naomi Judd won't say a word. But they are sputtering on about what they call 'guts and garbages' every time they see me, saying unclean, lascivious things: 'We know what nasty creatures girls are.' The same men, and different ones, too. They've all been talking. I don't have a husband like you do, no family to protect me. Hannah Clark says she will speak if I do."

Leah was not sure if it was because of Saul, Mr. Edwards, or just dumb luck, but she had never been read to from a midwife's book at any time by anyone, not even when she was with child. The loss of her baby, always with her, cut more sharply as she listened. The child would have been fifteen months old now, walking, following her from room to room as she worked, hard to keep away from the hearth. No one had ever come up to her on the street as Oliver Warner had come up to Bathsheba and Hannah. He had stood much too close to them, muttering, "When does the moon change, girls? Come, I'll look at your face and see whether there be a blue circle around your eyes. I believe it runs."

The rudeness, to speak to women about their monthly courses in an insinuating, sniggering way, even though all Oliver Warner had managed to communicate was his own oafishness. Leah gazed at the base of Mount Tom and said, "Bathsheba, I've been meaning to ask. Have you ever heard anything about blue circles around a woman's eyes when she's bleeding?"

Bathsheba put her hands on her hips. "No."

Leah took her friend's arm. She didn't ask again to leave things be, even though she thought that the next step would be dangerous for both of them. And even though she believed most of the men involved to be dolts, she was mindful of her own encounters with Satan's temptations in regards to wantonness and concupiscence. Some part of her believed that insults of this nature, and far worse, were bound to come to any woman living as a slave. The taunting of English women who were not indentured changed that, but she could not parse exactly how. For love of Bathsheba, who felt besieged and pestered to the point of giving up her vocation of healing, Leah said, "I'll speak with them."

Bathsheba, tucking the chicken and the sack of feathers under her arms, took her leave. When her friend was out of sight, Leah turned her back to Mount Tom, resisting a strong desire to climb it, for she had been gone from her work too long already. She had never been up the mountain, although she knew that Mr. Edwards and Sarah rode there almost every afternoon. She was usually much more drawn to the river than the heights. Saul had been to the top and told her of how steep the highest part of the path was, how full of small, loose stones, and how beautiful it was to see the prospect from the summit: to see the valleys round about and the great number of mountains heaving up one beyond another—and here, he had looked at her—some supposed to be sixty or seventy miles off. She knew that he dreamed of the mountains, of a cave, perhaps at first, then a small, plain house, enclosed in a fence like the houses of their separate childhoods. He dreamed of their own children tending chickens and chewing tamarind seeds in the yard; in a place like that, she would be willing, again, to risk becoming a mother. Saul spoke, too, of the company of others whose names had been crossed from account books or the rolls of church membership, or whose names had never appeared there; people who lived by stories and sometimes danced in British clothes made into something different by their wearers. Leah had once seen a woman in a man's tri-cornered hat dipping a net in the river.

This was not the day to go to the top of the mountain, which had been mapped, prayed over, and eaten upon by Mr. Edwards, visiting scholars, and ministers, the ground serving these formal of men as table, no one but themselves to clear it. As she looked at it, Leah wasn't sensing God's presence. She felt pulled too far into the affairs of men.

Leah found Jerusha breaking ground for an early garden. She fetched another hoe, and they talked as they chopped at dirt still hard with frost.

Jerusha was the object of deeply respectful attention from pious boys like David Brainerd. Samuel Hopkins had made her a gift of a Bible. Sally, the eldest, had not been the recipient of such gifts, and Jerusha sometimes forgot to be scrupulous in deferring to her older sister, but the loyalty between the Edwards girls was not subject to doubt.

Jerusha brushed wisps of hair behind her ears and listened very seriously to Leah's account of a midwife's book being compared to the Bible. She had heard bits of gossip about the bad behavior of certain boys, and everyone knew that Timothy Root had trouble governing his tongue, but to speak profanely of the Bible was not something that the spiritually gifted daughter of a rigorous father and an inspired mother was inclined to overlook.

Jerusha's hoe hit a rock. "I'll speak to mother. She'll know what to do."

Mr. Edwards had not declared the morning of the hearing on the matter of the midwives' books to be an official fast day, but as the women got ready to feed the church elders and witnesses who were coming to the house, he forswore breakfast. Sitting at his desk while the others ate, he studied Colossians 3:8. "Put away all filthy communication out of your mouth."

The scripture was clear enough. The young men involved were church members, most of them, come to religion through Mr. Edwards as part of the surprising work of God in Northampton. Through the early revival, and through waves of the second one, the great one, which now felt very far from Northampton, although it was still sweeping across the colonies. The degeneracy of these young men was a slap in the face. They had indulged in it together, in public, corrupting others in the process. He had been, perhaps, too trusting when accounting for conversions and letting young people join the church. He felt the importance of the revivals pulsing in him, sure as his own blood, but he had let false awakenings and hypocrisy take root in the congregation. He could not be sure how deep the trouble went.

His quill was sharp, but he picked up his penknife, rolling the handle in his palm a few times before he started scraping at the hole in the surface of his desk. In testing himself and his own weakness, trying to find the fault which had allowed such widespread lust and talk of lust to pollute the young people of Northampton, what he found did not please him. It was the question of profession. Of speaking, out loud, in public, before the church, not of corruption but of personal experiences of grace.

He had long followed his grandfather Stoddard's policy of allowing people to join the church without having to make a public profession of faith. In East Windsor, though, his father required such professions, in detail. It might startle and alarm his people were he to require a profession in order to join the church. But it was the only solution he could see that might prevent such corruption as he had been told that so many young men under his care had wallowed in. He resolved to search out the writings of other ministers on this subject, and to pray about it.

He would be the only minister among those sitting in judgment. Colonel John Stoddard was on the committee. His presence always bolstered Mr. Edwards with powerful backing and family love, and that pocket watch of his could come in handy for timing breaks in the deliberations as well. Captain Roger Clapp would be there, and as would Deacon Pomeroy, whose son was suspected of hiding a book in the chimney.

He put down his penknife, closed the Bible, and muttered a prayer that none of the Northampton youth, unlike the Reverend Mr. James Davenport, had been reckless enough to contract gonorrhea. He hurried down the hall, seizing his last chance before the hearing to get out of the house. He heard Sarah and Saul in the parlor, arranging the best chairs for the committee. They had carried plain chairs upstairs for the women waiting to testify. Mr. Edwards banged his shin against one of the hard benches crammed in the hall, which had been fetched from the meeting house for the accused young men. "Blast," he shouted, the pain in his leg heightening the anger he wanted to walk off. He had to be able to preside over the hearing in a judicious manner, without longing to kick the legs off the furniture. He didn't feel judicious. He felt nauseous. Those young men had been coming to his church, signing on to his covenants, and, all the while, carrying on with the vilest coarseness, whole groups of them. It was disgusting.

He went to the front door, but cut back toward the pasture rather than face the people already loitering on King Street, hoping for news. Ever since Mr. Edwards had read the list of suspects and witnesses to the brethren of the church, the town had been in an uproar, with parents first condemning then defending their wayward sons and compromised daughters by invoking the rule of the eighteenth of Matthew, which held that private offenses should be first addressed in private, not by names read from the pulpit before most every man in town.

Mr. Edwards was clear that this case was widespread and well known enough to be considered public. He also felt very sure—as he always did—of his scriptural backing and of church law, but, still, as he tromped across his back lot, his anger faded, and he was sore at heart. The children of his first Northampton revival, which had reached so many and changed so much, had been committing gross sins in barns like beasts. And there was something else that was bothering him, something he was not at all sure of how to classify. It had, perhaps, to do with the fact that he was the father of seven daughters.

Yesterday, on his ride with Sarah, he had said, "Did I ever tell you of the moment of extraordinary grace my sister Hannah once had while she was walking in our father's orchard?"

She had shaken her head, slowing her horse to ride beside him. "Tell me now."

They had ridden along Hulbert's Pond almost all the way to Hog's Bladder. He had looked out at the marsh and the river. "She told me that she had been walking, working to offer herself to God. When she leaned against the back fence, she saw a huge Bible rising in the sky above the trees."

Sarah gasped loudly enough that it spooked her horse, but kept a firm hold on the reins. They both gave such acts of God, mind, and grace their gravest attention.

Mr. Edwards had waited until the animal settled, then continued. "This was twenty years ago. She and my sisters were employing themselves by boning corsets to aid the household economy. When she looked up in the orchard, she said that the pages of the Bible were open, and she wanted to read it, but a corset stay lay across the pages, keeping her from the words."

He had looked at Sarah, thinking of her beautiful voice reading scripture, of all their daughters, and of his sisters, as well. If anything were to keep any of them from the words of the Bible, it would be a terrible thing.

She had been silent for a moment, then asked, "How did Hannah interpret it?"

He had shaken his head. "The world. The corset stay was her work, and she was letting too much of the world come between her and God." That answer seemed right to him, but somehow, also, at this moment when bad words, bad images, and bad books had been spreading by young men to young women in ways that had made some of the women very unhappy, he felt that there might be something else to see there, too. It was not a question of virtue. It seemed to him that it might be a kind of blocking, a stay across a page, or some kind of dangerous lack.

Sarah, eyes down, had patted the neck of her horse. "The world. That must be correct," she said. She had scratched the horse's long jaw; then she had looked at him and touched his face as well. "Glory to God."

Now Mr. Edwards gave frustrated praise with the clomp of his shoes on the grass, free for a moment from trying to negotiate the shallows of human society. He went into the barn, which his people had built for him during an illness a few years back. Exhorting himself to remember their kindness as well as their sins, he reached into a burlap bag nailed to a post and fed handfuls of last year's acorns to the horses in their stalls. Then he opened the stalls and slapped the horses on their rumps, letting them out to graze for the first time since fall. He waved his hat to hie them into the pasture, then, feeling the nervous twinges in his belly that always came before he entered a group, hied himself back to the house.

Sarah told their girls to go about their duties in the upper chambers, where the little ones spent the day underfoot of the group of women, all of whom were sewing while they exchanged family news, staying away from talk of the case under Sarah's watchful eye.

Bathsheba and Leah snapped a final withered heap of last year's beans, sitting on trunks that Saul had dragged into the kitchen to replace the chairs. Bathsheba had brought a hambone from Mrs. Pomeroy to help with the provisions, so Leah was working on an enormous pot of soup to go with the bread. They were too tense to speak much, but as they reached for beans from the basket between them, each felt that she was working for herself and for the other, with enough beans to spare for everyone else who assumed that they would be fed.

The committee called witnesses in for testimony one by one, starting with the women and preceding slowly down the list of accused.

As the tithing men escorted English women down the stairs one by one, and finally, after the midday meal, brought Bathsheba in from the kitchen, the young men were very restless on their benches in the hall. They had been talking defiantly, not only in barns or behind them, but in taverns and around their own family's fires, garnering both condemnation and support.

They sat in the dark hall while the sun shone, a group of stiff-necked, unruly young men, waiting for hours with no acknowledgment except ugly looks from the tithing men, who mostly left them to their own devices, and a cold shoulder from the slave who had shown them to their seats so many hours ago. None of them had brought anything to eat, nor had they been offered food.

It was while the first of the two town doctors were testifying that Timothy Root said to Oliver Warner, "Stop complaining about being thirsty and go in to ask leave of the committee for us to get some refreshment."

Oliver, who had a squinched face, blushed beet red, neck to scalp. "Why should I do what *you* say, Timothy Root?"

Timothy's cousin Simeon gave Oliver a shove with one of his boots, which were propped on the seat of the bench. "Because you are thirsty, haven't we all heard?"

Oliver fell to the floor and got up with his face even more red than before. "I shall say that you sent me. Do not think that I would not."

"Say what you please," answered Timothy. "I won't worship a wig." It was loud enough to bring Sarah into the hall upstairs.

Eben Pomeroy gasped, and said, "Respect is due to our elders."

Timothy, who had heard about the burning of finery in New London, said it again. "I won't worship a wig. Wig!" he yelled. "A wig!"

"I am going. I'll ask them," said Oliver. "Just be still."

He straightened the buckles on his good breeches and marched to the parlor door to knock. As soon as he was admitted, the young men heard a shout of disapproval go up from inside the room, much louder than the ruckus they had been making. Oliver, more scarlet than a judge's robes, was summarily pushed back into the hall. He swallowed hard, and looked at his friends standing among the benches. "They were very much displeased."

Simeon jumped up and pounded toward him. "Displeased, were they?" He was speaking in what Colonel Stoddard and Captain Clapp would characterize in later testimony as a loud and earnest manner, very near the parlor door. "What do we here? We won't stay here all day long."

Timothy slapped Oliver on the back, "Good fellow. Come, we'll go away. Do you think I'll be kept here for nothing? They are nothing but men molded up of a little dirt. I don't care a turd or a fart for any of them."

Eben Pomeroy was appalled. "Timothy! The ladies!" They could, it was true, hear skirts rustling on the landing. Timothy said, "I need some air," and marched out, not through the front door past the staircase, but out the back, through the kitchen. Simeon was close behind, dragging Oliver with him by his collar. Others followed, too, although Eben Pomeroy (thinking of his father, the deacon, sitting with the rest of the committee within the parlor) stayed put.

Leah and Bathsheba waited out the unruly rush through the kitchen by chopping onions and stirring soup with their backs to the men, but left the kitchen door open to keep an eye on them as they charged around the Edwards back lot like spring colts. Simeon danced a wild jig in the grass. Timothy was still yelling, with half an eye toward Bathsheba beyond the kitchen door. He didn't spare a glance for the upstairs room where a dozen women's faces were pressed against the window.

"I will go away, and if you were not devilish cowards, you would have gone some time ago. If they have any business with me, they may come to me; I ben't obliged to wait any longer on their arses, as I have done."

He was heard by John Birge, going along in the street, who later testified, as did Joseph Lyman and his wife, who saw Timothy Root and Simeon Root come to the tavern among a company that called for a mug of flip, and drank it.

After they had their flip, the young men some were calling boys returned to the Edwards back lot. Passing by on his way to the woods, Elisha Hawley saw them. Before they were caught, Oliver Warner had offered him a chance to read *Aristotle's Master-piece* for the outrageous price of ten shillings, but Elisha, who had laughed in his face, would not have spent two pennies for that book. On the day of the trial, he watched them flinging themselves over each other's huddled backs in a wild game of leap frog, but, up to new wickedness of his own, he never came forward to testify.

Timothy Root's father took to turning around in the meeting during hymns to stand with his back to the pulpit, because, he told Mr. Edwards, he considered it very wrong that the church had set aside the singing of psalms in favor of hymns by Isaac Watts, with the music firmly written out, taught by a singing master, not called and led. Mr. Root sometimes went so far as to walk out during a hymn.

Mr. Edwards, gritting his teeth, let the rudeness slide. Although he found the congregation to be in very bad voice, he did not let them give up singing hymns.

In June, Mr. Edwards called for a fast day when he learned that France, with troops so close to the north and allies among the Indians as near as Albany (or—terrible thought—even nearer), had joined in war against England.

He gazed hard at the town's young men as he preached. "Sin above all things weakens a people at war."

Oliver Warner, Timothy Root, and Simeon Root stood at the front of the meeting house to make public confession of their sins before the church. Timothy and Simeon, mumbling, admitted to "scandalously contemptuous behavior toward the authority of the church." Timothy's father made a noise that sounded suspiciously like a snort when his son resolved to behave himself "more humbly, meekly, and decently." Simeon stared at the ceiling as he vowed to treat his betters "with due honor and respect."

Only Oliver Warner, who moved away soon after, confessed to using unclean and lascivious expressions. As he read his confession, his voice shook. He said that he did not remember using those expressions. He was confessing because of the two witness rule in Matthew eighteen, since two witnesses "so positively and constantly declare that I did utter those expressions."

As he spoke, he gazed at the floor, but one of those two witnesses, Bathsheba, who while walking down the street with Hannah Clark had been asked if her eyes were encircled with blue, sat very straight next to Leah with her hands clasped in her lap, watching him tremble before her.

Chapter 16
August – December 1746

Elisha lay flat on his belly on the platform of the watchtower at the end of Pleasant Street, near the pen for stray livestock, calling down the ladder to Simeon Root's sister. "Come up," he said, "it's safer."

Martha Root looked up at him, eyes glinting in the dark, then raised her skirt and stepped onto the bottom rung. "Keep your voice down."

Elisha held the top of the ladder to steady it, then reached around her shoulders as she came to the top, so that as she clambered off the ladder onto her knees, he clasped her to him and rolled with her to the center of the platform, which had a roof but no sides. They might have been in danger of falling seven feet to the ground, but he had helped build the tower and knew its edges well. He was meant to be guarding the people of the town from attack by night from this quarter. Fort Massachusetts had been burned, its residents taken to Montreal. Joseph—gone again now to study in Suffield—had been to battle at Louisburg on Cape Breton as chaplain to the general. They were at war, and Elisha was resolved to protect his mother and the town.

At the moment, though, he was opening Martha's cape and his own great coat. They kissed, long and deep, held together by a rush of feeling. They might have been seen, but the night watch had already passed by, and there were two stray cows in the pen that would bawl if anyone came near. They were white-faced red heifers, and Martha knew they could be counted on to raise a fuss, since they were her excuse to be out in the night. Her brother Simeon had been careless with the gate.

She had seen them in the town stock pen before dark and was hoping that Elisha might help her get them out without paying the fine for stray livestock. He had not come to her house for dinner and bundling for weeks, not since his mother had followed him there and stood in the road hollering for him to come home.

Now, though, he was stroking her bodice and teasing her, saying, "You have so many bows on this gown, anyone would think you were Madame Pompadour."

She drew apart from him, dark hair falling in her face.

He said, "Of course, you are the enemy. I should have known."

She didn't care for that, but he had a laughing kind of smile on his face and she could see that he was taking the most exuberant pleasure in her. They were still holding hands, and she kept near him, away from the edge, as he stroked her gently, touching her face, running his hands beneath her shift. She pulled him to her, and soon they had no thought of protecting the town, which, despite everything, did not burn.

It was very late when Elisha scaled the fence and unfastened the latch on the paddock while Martha plied the heifers with oats and salt, which she had brought to keep them quiet. He kissed her and climbed back up the ladder with agile nonchalance. Martha had a switch to drive the cows, but she walked all of the way home up Pleasant and onto King Street past the minister's house with her arms around their necks, which were dusty, but so warm in the dark.

Within a fortnight, two houses abandoned by people who had fled the outlying settlement of Southampton were attacked. A bed was torn to pieces. Cattle were killed. Only eight miles from Northampton.

The government of Massachusetts made it known that the scalp of a Frenchman or an enemy Abenaki would be worth thirty-eight pounds. A living male prisoner was worth forty. The bounty for women and boys under twelve was twenty pounds for prisoners and nineteen for scalps.

———

In his study on a September afternoon, Mr. Edwards was writing urgently about how to tell which affections were truly spiritual and gracious, arising from those influences and operations on the heart which were supernatural and divine. He explicitly rejected arrogance by stating that he had no signs that could enable saints to certainly discern who was very low in grace, or who had departed from God and fallen into a dead, carnal, and unchristian frame.

He rubbed his hand over his face and took a sip of water from a white stone teacup to calm the painful spasms of his belly, which were always with him.

He had been writing about Christ's tears and moving through his Bible to find references to God's feelings, to holy joy and brokenness of heart. The scriptures, he could see, did everywhere place religion very much in the affections, such as fear, hope, hatred, desire, gratitude, and zeal. Most of all, though, they represented true religion as being summarily comprehended in love, the chief of the affections and the foundation of all others.

Mr. Edwards was calming his fears by lingering over scripture in order to make more plain the ways and will of the Lord, so far as the human mind could apprehend it. This was, of course, a labor he loved. He was responding to attacks on the awakenings as miasmas of emotional excess, and to the wildness he had seen in scorch marks on the New London wharf. He was wondering, too, if he could allude to his new ways of thinking about public profession as a requirement for joining the visible church. He wasn't sure if this was the place to do it, for reasons of inner logic and coherence of his arguments of the book as a whole, as well as for pastoral reasons.

In his way, he was responding to the war with his writing, as well. There were soldiers staying with them, stationed in the parsonage. Mr. Edwards had been keeping track of their meals, for reimbursement from the government in Boston. He had pumped Joseph Hawley and Seth Pomeroy for news on their return from the expedition to Louisburg. He had the same anxieties as everyone else, but he was also looking for signs of the coming salvation of the world. He believed that God wanted the British to defeat the French, but the English government was itself a problem, worldly and corrupt. Every skirmish or attack by the Abenaki was a sign of God's wrath because the colonists had not done more to bring scripture to the heathens. He thanked God for missionaries like David Brainerd, and for the mission to the Mahicans at Stockbridge. The thought of young Brainerd, who was, no doubt, diligently laying up stores and firewood for a meager winter camp, made Mr. Edwards restless. He put down his cup and pen to go outside. Sarah had had to write to the church committee several times, but their parishioners had finally delivered two wagonloads of good birch, which Saul and Timothy had been stacking in the woodshed. Sarah told him that she thought the delay in delivering their wood was deliberate, that people had been punishing their family ever since the humiliation of so many of the town's youth over the midwives' books. He could not waste thought on activities as petty as that.

He went through the gate in the pickets, put up by order of Colonel Stoddard and the militia, to fortify the house. Sarah had sent Saul to the sawmill to get pickets. They were nine and a half feet long and sharpened on the top, as she had heard was required. The whole town had been divided into garrisons, each with a large home that had been surrounded by palisades in case of a raid. The parsonage was an official shelter for their garrison, so, if they were attacked, most of those who lived along King Street would rush within the pickets. He had heard Sarah suggesting in the churchyard that families might keep an extra bucket of beans at the ready and near the door of each household, for who knew, if the people of King Street were forced to flee to the parsonage, how long they might have to stay.

Sarah had been careful to make sure that the elm tree came within the pickets. Mr. Edwards had seen Jerusha climb to the very top of the elm to read and look out over the palisades. None of the family cared for the loss of light, or for having their house filled with soldiers instead of preachers, but they had heard of one Mr. Phipps, up in Putney, who had been killed while hoeing corn alone in his field.

Mr. Edwards started to move hunks of wood from the messy pile where the loads had been dumped to the half-finished stack. He had formed a difficult resolution and needed the physical work. He fitted the pieces of wood carefully together, tight enough to be stable, but with gaps for air to discourage rot. He had learned how to stack wood as a boy in East Windsor, right along with Hebrew and Greek, and now began to go at it with swift efficiency, thinking that it might be wise to start a new pile within the pickets, so that they would have enough fuel, should they have to withstand a siege. He thought that Sarah might already have a plan for the wood supply if they were to come under attack. He would ask her. He was eager to talk to her about his new decision, too. She read the mood of the town so much better than he did.

He was reaching for another hunk of wood when he saw a small, pale spider drop out of the stack, then crouch on the end of a rough-hewn log. Strangely, it began to turn in a circle.

Mr. Edwards stopped to watch, feeling the old itch to find meaning, motive, or mechanism in the spider's actions, an impulse which was far stronger than his desire to get the wood stacked.

The spider took up a pugnacious stance, jointed legs waving in air while the shorter legs on each side of the body rubbed together. Mr. Edwards was bending closer to examine its fangs when another spider suddenly leapt off the top of the stack and hung in midair, not far from his shoulder. As he turned to watch, it flipped upside down and made some kind of knot in its strand of web, then began to climb the web again, curled around the knot, carrying it higher, then dropping away from it to hang far below, completely still. It swayed a bit in the slight stirring of air, then bunched together again to make another knot.

Mr. Edwards was thinking that the knot might be an egg sac when he looked up to see Sarah coming out of the house into the yard. She walked toward him, holding up a small earthenware pot. "I'm going to put salve on the lead ox. His hide is rubbing under the yoke."

Mr. Edwards rested his hand on the end of a log, reckless of spiders, and said, "Sarah, do you remember, when we were young, how

I wrote to you about how soon lovers see all that is to be seen in each other?"

She blushed like she was still thirteen. He could see that she was taking pleasure in being reminded of their long knowledge of each other, but she gave him a very solemn look and said, "What I'm seeing right now is that your wig could use a dressing with pomatum and a little time in the oven to tighten its curls. Perhaps it would help if you refrained from wearing it while chopping wood."

Sarah was the only person in the world to tease him to his face. He didn't laugh, but he appreciated the spirit of it. Scraping a bit of bark with his thumbnail, he broke his news. "I can't in good conscience continue to let people join the church who cannot make a profession of their experiences of godliness. Outward appearances are not enough."

Sarah, taken aback, fumbled for her pocket to stow the salve. In many New England churches, people gave public accounts, often highly repetitive and stylized, of their spiritual history before they joined as members. But no one had been asked to submit themselves to this requirement in the church in Northampton—or in most of Hampshire County, for that matter—in decades. "They now must make a profession? And what of your grandfather? Sixty years of his influence here, and all these years of following him yourself?" She was shocked. The people would take this very badly.

Mr. Edwards glanced at the road and saw Martha Root driving the family's cows and heifers home from grazing in the meadows. The Roots lived a little farther up King. He lowered his voice as she passed by. "I have no wish to disrespect Mr. Stoddard or to enter into the arrogance of those who claim to be able to discern by their own sense whether or not another is converted, but it would be better for one or two good Christians be turned away from the church than for it to be filled with hypocrites."

The wood beneath her fingers had a fresh smell. Her heart was pounding with worry. "So many in the congregation have become backsliders and returned to their sins. We are all jittery about the war. Is now the best time to introduce them to something new?"

Mr. Edwards tried his skin against the point of a splinter. "I am their shepherd. I must act on their behalf as led by scripture and conscience." He looked at her face and sought to reassure her. "I will try not to startle them, but will wait until the next person asks to join the church before I speak of this in public."

She sighed. "You have noticed, have you not, that not one person has asked to join the church since the trial about the midwives' books?"

He looked down to see another spider hanging off the corner of a log and launching itself straight at him, coming at his throat along a tendril that he hadn't known had been attached to his wig. Mr. Edwards threw up his hand and batted the web aside. The spider dropped to the ground and escaped from sight.

It was only a spider. He was not distracted from her question. "Of course, I've noticed. It has been more than two years."

"They are angry at you. At us. There will be trouble."

A little disturbed, he said to her, "I will wait until one of them comes to me, ready, and asks to join. I am very loathe to contradict my grandfather. But the mood of the people cannot dictate who becomes part of the visible church."

She flecked a stray strand of web from his wig. "They will be even more reluctant to listen than you are to speak." She took his arm. "Come walk with me to the pasture. Give me time to reflect on this."

Before they turned away from their house, now also a fort, he paused to look for more spiders, but saw only the shine of new filaments threading over the wood he had stacked.

October was mild. Standing in her family's henhouse, Martha Root cracked an egg still warm from the hen. She tilted the yolk from one half of the shell to the other and collected the whites that dripped off in a wide-mouthed vial—already half-filled with water—which she held below. She dropped the yolk in the dirt and buried it with the shells by digging a hole in the dirt with her foot, then swirled the vial and watched the way the egg whites floated and curled, whispering and counting off with her fingers against the glass. "Farmer, weaver, merchant, miller, preacher, tinker, tanner, soldier."

Her sister had told her that this was a way to predict her future husband's occupation, but she wasn't sure how it worked. She was careful not to give the option of "none." The twist of the egg white seemed to point to the finger for "miller," or maybe it was "preacher," which would disqualify the whole attempt for sheer unlikeliness, but neither of those choices could in any way be thought to point to Elisha.

She was sick again as she stood (and then bent) there, but she buried the vomit next to the yolk and covered the spot with clean straw before she left the henhouse.

On a cold day in December, Elisha had gone to the uplands to cut wood with several families of Pomeroys, who used more wood than was common in order to fuel their smithing. They wanted to chop as much as they could while limbs were bare, the snow was deep, and sleighs were easier to pull.

Mrs. Pomeroy sent Bathsheba to tell Rebekah Hawley that the men had made a camp in the woods, the better to get to work early next morning, and, Bathsheba was sure, knock back plenty of rum. She hurried down Main Street, looking up at the clock in the steeple as she passed the church, then looking again at the sky. She wanted to make it to the Hawleys before dark, and found it easier to slide along on the icy crust on the side of the road than to try to fit her steps to the frozen ridges in the trampled snow in the road itself. She wished for snowshoes. Moving swiftly, she approached a figure standing on the little bridge over the freshet where Main turned into Bridge Street at the corner of Pudding Lane. It was a tall woman with dark hair under the hood of her cloak. It took Bathsheba a moment to recognize Martha Root.

"It's a cold day to be out," Bathsheba observed as she stepped carefully onto the bridge, which was slick. She had known Martha since she was a child, so spoke with some freedom. "And nearly night at that."

Martha was a weaver, and her cloak was blue and thick. She shook snow off it, enough to make Bathsheba think that she must have been standing there for quite a long time, and said, "Oh, Bathsheba. Where are you going?"

"I've got a message for Rebekah Hawley that might interest you. Elisha made camp with the Pomeroys cutting wood tonight and won't be home for a day, perhaps two." Bathsheba reached out to dislodge a patch of snow that had settled on the front of Martha's cloak. As her hand glanced across Martha's belly, the other woman took a quick step backwards and would have fallen if Bathsheba hadn't caught her arm.

Once she regained her balance, Martha brushed the snow off herself. "A crossroads is the worst place to linger," she said, as if that explained her skittishness. "I was on my way to the Hawleys myself to see if Rebekah might let me have a cheese. I can give her the message, if you wish.

Bathsheba nodded slowly. "That would be kind of you," she said formally. "I'm going on to the Edwardses, since their Saul is out with the woodcutters, too."

Although Martha would be going home to King Street, she did not offer to take the messages, too. Bathsheba was as happy that she did not, because she welcomed the chance to spend some time with Saul and Leah. The women parted ways. Bathsheba turned back toward King Street, and Martha finally crossed the bridge and turned onto Pudding Lane. Her face was protected by her hood, which she had dyed with berries that past summer. She was warm with the resolution to speak to the mother, since she could get no satisfaction from conversation with the son.

After the hearing about the midwives' books, Sarah Edwards had presented Bathsheba with the copy of *Aristotle's Master-Piece: or, the Secrets of Generation Displayed in all the Parts thereof* that she had first encountered in Noah Baker's barn. Bathsheba had been confused when Sarah called her into the Edwardses' kitchen. Sarah had gestured at the book on the table as if introducing Bathsheba to a guest. "I have been entrusted with employing this book for the medical purposes for which it was intended. I know that the servant population sometimes makes use of your services as a midwife and trust that you would benefit from the instruction of learned men in those matters."

Bathsheba had hesitated, looking at Sarah's face. Neither of them were slow to broach the subject of the female anatomy in the course of their midwifery, but she had not been sure of Sarah's intentions. The book was the last thing she wanted. It brought back ugly memories, and she was not sure if she would be safe with it in her possession. She had gone unmolested since the trial, and, since those troubles had been made so public, thought that she might be able to go to the sheriff should she have trouble. Still, Sheriff Pomeroy had not been happy to have his grandson Eben among those called in to testify, and he was, Bathsheba knew, unhappy with Mr. Edwards about that yet.

Sarah had been pouring mustard seed into her mortar when Bathsheba came in, and she went back to grinding as Bathsheba thought. Bathsheba watched the minister's wife, who, for a moment, had reminded her of her own mother grinding spices for a meal. It was strange that Sarah Edwards should think that a slave might be suited to decide the fate of a valuable book, one that she might have made use of herself. Bathsheba sensed that she was trying to right an injury, or perhaps more than one. It would take a terrible delicacy to refuse the gift. Bathsheba had wished that Leah were there, but the two of them were alone. She decided to risk accepting the gift instead of risking to refuse it. She had said, "That's good of you, Madame."

"There are illustrations. You could study the pictures." Sarah had handed Bathsheba the book, then her voice became uncertain, as if she hadn't quite anticipated the sight of her with it in her hands. "That is, if you are confident in your ability to keep it from further misuse by youth."

Bathsheba, who had seen the pictures, rested the book lightly against her hip, and said, "Oh yes, Madame. I know how to do that."

She had left the book with Saul and Leah. She herself had no place to keep anything safe, and neither of them were afraid. Leah wrapped it in a shawl and put it in a book box that Saul had built for her, carved with twining leaves and her name. She kept her Bible in there, as well. Sarah, who had seen the box in the making, had given Saul winter work of making another bookcase for the house, since Mr. Edwards kept scavenging for books.

Bathsheba came to Leah when she could. They would tell each other everything that they had heard and seen in the two households, and Saul, if he was there, would give his news from the fields. They would drink cider and work out the most likely meaning of events to their own interests as best they could. Then, from time to time, Saul might carve a little, and Leah would read to Bathsheba and Saul from the Bible or *Aristotle's Master-piece*. Over time, Bathsheba found that, in Leah's voice, it had lost its sting. The Bible had better stories, but also more devils and death. *Aristotle*, they knew, was improper except for use in travail, but it promised that by describing the parts of a woman's body it would open "a cabinet of many rare secrets." Also, some passages were funny. Saul usually went to the loft early if this was the choice, and, as he snored above them, Leah and Bathsheba would try to discover if there was information in *Aristotle* of any practical use.

And so, on this particular cold December evening, already fully dark by the time Bathsheba got to the cabin, Leah went to the house and informed Sarah of Saul's camp with the Pomeroys in the woods. She came back with a bowl of roasted pumpkin seeds. She and Bathsheba chewed seeds and sipped cider while Leah read that a man was different from a woman in nothing else than having his genital members without his body rather than within. It seemed that "once nature hath made a female child, and it has so remained in the belly of the mother for a month or two," then a rush of heat made the genital member push out ("like an overcooked turkey leg" added Leah) and convert a baby girl to a baby boy.

Bathsheba split a pumpkin seed with her fingernail to get at the kernel, and said, "Well, then, cold as Martha Root is keeping by wandering out in the snow, she's bound to have a girl."

Leah—who had been trying to remember if she had felt a rush of heat in the last month of her lost pregnancy, years ago now—wasn't particularly surprised, but she said, "What! That girl is with child? With no husband?"

Bathsheba handed her the shelled seed. "She was out on the bridge, just now, on her way to the Hawleys. Said that she was out in the snow at dark to buy cheese."

"Oh. Elisha Hawley." Leah felt tired of this topic, tired of babies and bodies, and tired of *Aristotle*. Her little one would have been four and a half now, old enough to wade with Leah into the river if they held hands. She didn't want to read any more, and she didn't want to talk.

Madame Edwards was with child again, too, but Leah didn't bring it up. She closed the book, heaped the shawl around it, put it back in the carved box, then sat silently with her friend eating pumpkin seeds in the lantern light. After a while, they sang a little, a psalm about a vine brought out of Egypt land and planted here, but every line about the heathen became lists of fava beans, lima beans, scarlet runners, acorn squash, cucumbers, and every other thing that might drop off a vine.

On his return, Rebekah asked her son, "Do you wish to wed Martha Root?"

Elisha took the heavy pail of milk from her. "No."

"Then you shall not."

Chapter 17
January – June 1747

Seizing a few moments alone in the parlor after the noon meal, Sarah sat in a straight chair and read *Religious Affections,* her husband's new book.

> *Sometimes the change made in a Saint, at first work, is like "a confused chaos;" so that the saints "know not what to make of it." The manner of the Spirit's proceeding in them that are born of the Spirit, is very often exceeding mysterious and unsearchable . . .*
>
> *Ecclesiastes 11:5: "Thou knowest not what is the way of the Spirit, or how the bones do grow in the womb of her that is with child: even so thou knowest not the works of God, that worketh all."*

Sarah would never claim to know the way of the Spirit, but she knew a lot about being with child. The swelling in her ankles and the ache in her back from her current condition had urged her to the chair in the midst of her duties. Uncomfortable and restless, she decided to pay a call on Rebekah Hawley.

As she rode over the snowy roads and across the bridge to the Hawley place on Pudding Lane, she found bits of her husband's writing drifting through her mind along with idle speculations about whether or not she could get Hannah Root to make over her green silk gown with sleeve flounces that were short inside the arm and long over the elbow in what she had heard from Prudence Stoddard was the new style in London. With all of Colonel Stoddard's traffic with governors and generals, Prudence heard news of Europe fresh from the harbor. She said that shoe buckles were getting bigger, with pointed toes and lower heels, but there was no call to waste perfectly good brass buckles, so there was nothing Sarah could do about that.

Between considering these problems of dress and the chastising mysteries of the way the bones do grow, Sarah didn't think seriously about what she might say to Rebekah until she was tying her horse in the shelter of the barn. Then it occurred to her that she might suggest to Mrs. Hawley, who was the head of a household which was resisting the duty to heal the sin of fornication with marriage, that she consider how the generation of a principle of grace in the soul was similar to the conception of a child in a womb.

When Rebekah came to the door, though, all Sarah said was, "Mrs. Hawley! I've come to enquire whether I might purchase some cheese."

Rebekah, who was used to dealing with Leah or one of the girls on such an errand, barely stifled a snort, but she said, "Of course, Mrs. Edwards, please do come in."

Sarah, shaking snow from her skirts, observed that Rebekah's face looked puffy and the shadows under her eyes were darker than ever. "I hope you don't mind, I've already put my horse in a stall."

"Of course, that's fine. As you know, neither of my boys are here to see to it."

Sarah thought that they would go to the parlor, since that was where she was used to being received, even when she was on a humble errand like the acquisition of a cheese. But Rebekah, who as her husband's aunt was entitled to familiarities, led Sarah through the hallway past the empty rooms to the kitchen. She pulled out a chair and said, "Sit down, my dear," with unexpected warmth.

Sarah, who had been unsure of her welcome, took a seat while Rebekah moved between the table and the stove. She set out a plate for Sarah and one for herself. "I'm delighted that you could join me. I invited Mary Pomeroy, but she had her children to feed."

Sarah had not been expecting a meal, and thought that the food smelled better than anything she had ever tasted in her life. She had been trying to stay out of the kitchen as much as she could in the early months of her pregnancy at home, turning the meals over to Jerusha and Leah and settling her own belly with endless bowls of boiled oats. But now she prayed with Rebekah—"Ye shall know them by their fruits"—over this strange, sparsely-peopled meal with a God-given hunger that moved her to take and eat. Even though the soldiers who had been garrisoned at Sarah's house were gone now to their new base at the Fort Massachusetts, her table was always crowded. She could not remember the last time she had sat down with only another grown woman for a meal. Had she ever? Rebekah was giving her a feast worthy of the Sabbath, heaping her plate with corned beef, biscuits, and mashed turnips. There was roasted squash, too, its hollow filled with ginger, nutmeg, and maple syrup, making a dark, sweet crust that crackled under her fork (a rare utensil which Rebekah had inherited from Widow Stoddard). Rebekah didn't say much, but her stern face softened as she watched Sarah eat. Rebekah had closed the family store to concentrate on cheese and butter, and seemed a bit strapped for company.

Warmed by the food and the cider, Sarah found herself talking about her children, her Mary's fear of thunderstorms, so like her father, although, of course, God had reformed his terror into proper awe. How Nabby and Sukey had gotten lost in the woods, and Timothy had been the one to find them, and how it worried her that the baby, named Jonathan for his father, seemed to have an affliction that gummed up his eyes. She didn't bring up the fact that her eldest daughters were beginning to attract admirers or complain of the many small humiliations her family had been facing since the trial about the midwives' books. Not in this household, which was suffering from the licentious courtship of a son.

Rebekah was taking slow bites, chewing carefully, occasionally closing her eyes to savor her own cooking in a way that gave Sarah an impulse to tease her, and if she hadn't come expecting to find Rebekah in shock or raging or in some kind of mourning, she might have tried. Mostly, though, the older woman was watching her face with a kind of tender intensity, which Sarah, sopping up juice from the beef with her biscuit, received as an ambiguous blessing.

When Rebekah brought out the whortleberry pudding, Sarah exclaimed, "Berries in January! You're wasting your treasures on me."

Rebekah served her a wedge and said, "I was about to squander them on myself alone. I am glad that you came along."

Such a big empty house, Sarah thought, could make a woman strange. She tasted the berries, then said, "You must miss your boys."

Rebekah blinked, then sucked her spoon. She took another bite and wiped her mouth. "When Joseph came home from the siege of Louisburg, he wept at the table. Elisha found it terribly embarrassing. Joseph followed me that night when I carried a gourd full of whey to the attic to feed Elisha's old cat Sister and told me that he was going to Suffield to stay with his old tutor from Yale and study law." Someone else might have amended her comments for Sarah Edwards, but Rebekah took a sip of cider and pushed on. "I don't care much about whether Joseph becomes a lawyer or a minister, but Elisha was so disappointed that his brother had come back from capturing a fort with sixty-foot-high stone walls from the papist French with nothing to say except that the flux was a bloody mess of a disease and Seth Pomeroy was handy at unstopping a plugged up cannon." She looked at Sarah over her cup. "That was when I knew that Elisha was bound to be a soldier."

"Mmm," said Sarah, who had her own opinions on this matter.

Rebekah put down her spoon and folded her hands in her lap. "Joseph is coming back from Suffield to set up here as a lawyer. Phineas Lyman thinks he's ready to be licensed. I won't have to live alone."

Sarah had heard this. "You must be pleased."

"I am, of course." Rebekah was recovering her usual distance. "Finish your pudding."

Sarah felt a little rattled and aware of the sin of gluttony. Still, the berries were tart and the cream was light, and each bite she took brought her a wave of pleasure, heightened, she knew, by her condition. This was her tenth pregnancy. She had had such carnal interludes before.

Rebekah licked her finger and waggled it at Sarah, who had to struggle to control a fit of giggles. Rebekah said, "Elisha ate this. This meal."

Knowing that the family was prone to melancholia and other mental and spiritual distempers, Sarah stopped laughing. "Did he?" she enquired delicately, wondering if Rebekah was feeding the ghost of her husband, along with the spirit of her younger boy in his peril. "You mean that he is here?"

Rebekah's tone was brusque. "You know that he is not. He's at Fort Massachusetts, poor child, the fort they threw together again, and shoddily, too, no doubt, after the papists and heathens burned it to the ground."

Sarah had come hoping to speak to Rebekah about this, about Elisha's sudden enlistment at the very moment when Martha Root's condition began to be visible, and how the safety of his soul demanded that he return to his church to confess his sins and marry the girl. The situation was terrible for Martha and her coming child, wrong for Elisha, and this open disregard for Christian duty by a member of the church (and a kinsman) was an awful blow to Mr. Edwards. Sarah could not believe that Elisha would have joined the military campaign without his mother's blessing, so she had come to see for herself how things stood with Rebekah.

"Did you hear about that court case?" Rebekah leaned back in her chair. "Joseph told me the details when he was here the last time court was in session. The unexpurgated details. I insisted. It seems that what Mr. Adams actually said of my brother, Colonel Stoddard, was that he is—do excuse the coarseness of expression; it's hard to believe that the fine was only five shillings—'a cussed lazy devil; he sits there on his cussed arse.' He also said that it was my brother's devilish, cursed doings that those forts were built and that those at Fort Massachusetts were taken."

Sarah had risen to her feet. "Madame, I know that you are in distress, and have no doubt about the affection in which you hold your brother, whom I honor and love as well, but surely such language is best not repeated."

Rebekah gestured for Sarah to resume her seat. "You must have heard some version of the incident before this. Yes, I do love my brother, and I trust him with my own life, which is what I did when I called on him to give Elisha a commission and send him into the fighting rather than stay here and fall into the hands of that Root woman."

Rebekah began to cry, but as Sarah came around the table, ready to comfort her, she raised her voice sharply. "Mrs. Edwards, please sit down and eat."

Sarah murmured, "I am quite full," and returned to her chair.

Rebekah scraped her plate with a fork. "Seth Pomeroy sees him, you know. He was in Louisburg with Joseph, too. God knows, I worried about Joseph, but he was on the campaign as a preacher, not a soldier. Mr. Pomeroy writes home more than Elisha does, and his wife told me that he sent her a letter about having this meal in Deerfield. Biscake, suet, whortleberry pudding, corned beef, squashes, and turnips. Far better than what they usually get, although he said they had no cider." She looked at Sarah. "I've been eating this same meal for a week, ever since Mrs. Pomeroy read me the letter. I'm out of beef and berries now, but I have been trying to taste some of what Elisha might be having to swallow, the very daintiest part, I'm sure. And, still, I would rather he be out fighting than for our homes to be lost to the heathens, or for him to be trapped by this woman."

Sarah reached across the table. Rebekah let her take her hands. "What could it possibly be that has set you so hard against Martha Root, to the point of grave risk to Elisha's soul?"

Rebekah pulled her hands away, placed them in her lap, and sat up straighter. "He was entrapped, and has no wish to wed her. Besides, she is not of our station. Your own husband, so bent on forcing a marriage, has taught us that an archangel must be supposed to have more existence, and to be in every way farther removed from nonentity, than a worm or a flea. Elisha is not to be wasted on lesser lives."

Sarah shook her head, but pressed the matter no further. They said a prayer for Elisha's safety. Sarah left with cheese and the rest of the pudding.

"Sustenance," said Rebekah.

"Mrs. Clapp has tethered her horse in the road," Joseph, uneasy in his militia uniform, complained to his mother as he led a donkey loaded with a sack of cabbages and potatoes down Pudding Lane.

"Mrs. Clapp has been tethering her horse there since before you were born." Rebekah negotiated a mud patch, holding her skirt above her ankles. "You used to carry old apples tucked in your gown to feed it as we passed by. Remember?"

Joseph, who did remember, paused to scratch the old nag under its chin. If his mother had not been there, he might have broken off a hunk of cabbage and let the mare split it with the donkey for old times' sake. Despite his complaints, he was very glad to be back in Northampton. He raised his chin and said, in a tone that reminded himself of her, "It is a violation of town ordinances."

Rebekah patted his arm as if he were a small boy instead of a new lawyer. She was sixty, which astonished him every time he thought of it. They walked along, listening for the drums.

When they reached the bridge at the end of Pudding Lane, the donkey stopped cold at the noise. Much of the town had turned out to Main Street to watch a company of Mahicans from Stockbridge being mustered to send to Fort Massachusetts. Joseph, who secretly shared the donkey's wariness, clucked to her, and they went on into the crowd.

The sound of drums took Joseph back to Louisburg, to washing blood and vomit off his hands with reddish swamp water after tending the sick and injured, and then stumbling back to his dank pit of a turf house to sleep on a mud floor with worms falling from the dirt ceiling. He had been sick on the ship from Boston to Cape Breton, sick in the dug-out, then sick again in a bed after they had seized the fort and the families who had lived in the houses had been put on a ship back to France. When he was well enough to stand, he had given up the bed to Seth Pomeroy. They were both lucky not to have been among the many who died of the flux. He shuddered.

When Rebekah stopped to chat with Mrs. Hutchinson in front of the courthouse, Joseph approached Colonel Stoddard with the donkey. "Cabbages and potatoes for the troops, sir."

The load was generous. At Louisburg, Joseph had seen hungry Northampton men butchering stolen horses for food. He wanted to spare his brother from the stealing and the hunger, both.

The colonel nodded in the direction of a supply wagon. "They will be glad to have it, if we can get it there over the hog trails that pass for roads. Any message for Sergeant Hawley?"

Joseph handed his uncle a packet of letters. He wrote often, advising Elisha against being too familiar with the men, trying not to remember seeing a youth's leg blown off by the very cannon he was lighting. He said, "My mother and I appreciate everything you have done in the interests of our family."

Colonel Stoddard gave a slight bow. "No thanks are due me, Mr. Hawley. Your brother makes a good soldier."

Joseph had a hard time picturing Elisha at war, but he stood a little straighter under his uncle's level regard. Fatherless as he was, he found the respect of the older men of the town irresistible. He clasped the colonel's hand.

After he unloaded the supplies, he joined Rebekah in front of the courthouse to watch and cheer the new troop. He gave a brisk wave to Saul, who, dapper in his own militia uniform, was regarding the soldiers intently. In the course of his work as a lawyer, Joseph had been reading land deeds. He knew that the ministers who had formed the mission to the Mahicans at Stockbridge, Mr. Edwards among them, had traded these same people 280 acres of good bottom land for 4,000 acres on the edge of Stockbridge. He couldn't help but wonder if all of the soldiers, who had been issued government hatchets, were happy with the terms of that deal and others like it.

Rebekah spoke suddenly in his ear. "I'm thinking of Eunice."

Confused, Joseph looked at her. The Edwardses had a daughter by that name. She watched the troop. "My sister."

Joseph put a hand on her back. His mother's sister had been killed by Abenaki years ago in the raid on Deerfield. He said, "Don't worry about Elisha, mother. He can take care of himself."

She sighed. "I'm thinking of her daughter, too, the one who was taken and married into the Kanienkehaka. I heard she became a papist."

Joseph didn't know what to say. His mother never spoke of her niece, the captive who had stayed in Canada. As boys, Joseph and Elisha used to sneak out to eat roasted green corn at fires in the orchard with visiting Abenaki who had, years before, captured Mary Clapp in the Deerfield raid. Long returned and settled in Northampton, Mary had welcomed her visitors and their children with a fondness that had always confused him. His grandfather, the Reverend Mr. Solomon Stoddard, had, he knew, proposed to the legislature that dogs be used to hunt Indians, as they were to hunt wolves. "But these men are Christians."

Rebekah looked at him with more rage and sorrow than he could stand to see. He looked away, and saw, across the road in the doorway of Pomeroy's store, Martha Root with her enormous belly, big as sin. He did not meet her eyes, but turned back to Rebekah. "Wouldn't you like to move a little more up the hill toward the meeting house? The smell from the tannery is worse than it usually is in winter."

She glanced at Martha Root and planted her feet. "We're fine right here."

Martha Root went into her travail the first week in May. Bathsheba had been with her all day before they sent for her women, but now Martha was upright on her sister Hannah's lap, screaming. Another sister had taken the first baby, but before Bathsheba could call for a basin for the afterbirth, it was clear, as she had suspected, that another baby was coming. Martha's mother was beside her, talking to her softly and helping to hold her on the chair.

Bathsheba was kneeling to wipe Martha's thighs with a dry cloth, warm from the irons. Martha, exhausted, was crying, then screaming again. One of the sisters said to Mrs. Root, "It is time to ask."

The older woman took her daughter's hand and spoke close to her face as Martha shrieked and struggled. The height of travail was known to be a time when much good could be done for a frightened woman's soul, but her mother didn't ask Martha about her spiritual estate. Instead, just as she had as the first little girl was being born, she said, "Daughter, who is the true father of this child?"

Martha stopped biting her lip, and, in a voice coarsened by pain, said, "Elisha Hawley."

He could not be convicted of fornication without witnesses, but her testimony in travail was enough to make him the reputed father, responsible for support of the children. Everyone knew that a woman in midst of giving birth could not lie.

Her mother held her around the waist and her sister hugged her across the chest until Bathsheba had received Martha's second daughter and closed off the new mother's loins with cloths over her belly, between her legs, and bound loosely over her thighs.

The women lifted Martha into the parlor bed and wrapped the babies tight. They were Anne and Esther. Their mother said their names. She was soon asleep, and the women had cake with the men and children in the kitchen, arguing about whether or not it was good luck to give birth to twins. Bathsheba said that Anne, who was born second, was the eldest because she had the good sense to send Esther out first to see what the dangers were, but the Roots made no note of that in records in the family Bible.

Sarah Edwards had her tenth baby, Elizabeth, the next day.

Leah left Sarah to her daughters and the cake to the neighbors after the birth and went to sit outside on the chopping stump. Her own breasts were aching. While she had been thinning gruel for Sarah, she had heard Madame Pomeroy remark that barren women often made excellent nurses. Leah hadn't turned her head. She was not barren. Her own child would have been nearly five years old.

Sitting on the stump watching flicker-tailed squirrels shake the tree limbs, she caught a glint from a single strand of web bent in a long arc from the bark near her hip. She followed it with her eyes, trying to see if it were attached to the big-budded limbs of the tree above her or just going nowhere, blown by the wind. She lost track of it against the sky. She wished that she had a cup of rum to warm her, but there would be no chance for her to go back inside and leave with a tonic for herself with so many birth attendants and visitors to serve. She felt like talking to Saul, who listened even in his sleep, but was too exhausted to search him out in the fields.

Leah had stopped reading much, but she had opened *Religious Affections* by Mr. Edwards a few months before when she had found it in the study. Now she thought of the verse of scripture he had used to begin part one: *Whom having not seen, ye love.*

That was, of course, Jesus. Leah did love him. She didn't see him, but she felt him, strongly. Feelings, it seemed, were what *Religious Affections* was about. She had been working her way through the pages when she could. She had not gotten very far, but far enough to find brokenness of heart counted as a great part of true religion, along with fear, zeal, hope, hatred, and holy joy, with love, a source of all the other affections, at its very core. Now, on the stump, she drifted for a moment, and started to tell herself a story about a spider with nothing to trap with except strands of light, but her mind trailed off as she watched a crow dart at a scuttling bug and eat it quickly in the grass. She felt a sob rise in her, then fall back, dry.

Her mind was on her child, never born: another whom, having not seen, she loved. She had walked away from Sarah's groaning cake to groan alone in her soul, but the sun was like honey on the budding limbs, and she did not feel alone. This was prayer, secret prayer. She kept her open eyes on the tree limbs, which moved, then fell still.

The affections, Mr. Edwards had taught her, resided not in the body or in the animal spirits, but in the soul. An unbodied spirit could feel love. True religion was known in love. Her love for her child, the child whom she had never seen, never raised, never risked in a world where even a baby could have been sold or ground down in the service of owners, was unbodied.

Still, it was a specific surge in the great waters. Her heart knew its current by feel. She gave it up to God, raised her head as she sat on the stump as if the strand of web had wound round her hair and was gently pulling her skull upward, her neck straight, and her spine more upright. She stretched her body, raised her arms, and accepted absence, presence, and consolation, then turned away from the trees to watch the open sky. She could find no language within her, not even private words from home, for the way the sky filled with birds that were so soon gone on by.

Elisha, in his fort, was smoking a pipe with Major Seth Pomeroy, who was there in command of the Northampton-based company that had been formed in anticipation of another invasion of Canada. At the moment, though, all they had done was march to the Dutch settlement at Hoosack. Elisha and Seth had just eaten soup made from the last of the cabbages that Joseph had sent. Although he knew that, come winter, he might long for cabbages, Elisha was not sorry to see them go.

Seth tamped down his bowl, and said, "I hear from my Mary that Martha Root has twins."

Elisha, who had not heard, breathed in the news with his smoke. He had spent a long day supervising the troops as they worked on the road to Deerfield, which was rocky, narrow, and nearly impossible to negotiate with wagons full of supplies. He loved being in charge, even if just of a road crew. It felt as if parts of himself that he had not known to exist were being harnessed and used. When he thought of Martha, it was like thinking of swimming in the river in the middle of the night as a boy: deep sensations, clouded by loss. He was someone else now, very far from Martha. He couldn't even imagine the babies—her babies, their babies—and didn't try. He wished her every happiness, but not hard enough to wed her. He wasn't even sure that she wanted that, although he knew that Mr. Edwards did. Elisha wished that he could go see Martha and get a look at the babies when he went home, but Rebekah would never tolerate it, and he doubted that Martha would, either.

Seth was still regarding him over the bowl of his pipe with stern but not unsympathetic eyes. Elisha said, "I know that she names me, sir, and that I am many times a sinner. My brother advises me to speak no further of this matter until there is a judgment in the courts."

Seth drew in smoke, and said, "What does your conscience tell you?"

Elisha dumped his ashes, though they were still hot. "My duty is here."

Chapter 18
September 1747 – January 1748

Martha Root held her four-month-old daughter, Anne, who was, at that moment, a gape-mouthed, lumpy-headed sleeper, with dark hair like her father and blue veins where her eyebrows would be. Careful not to wake her, Martha put her living daughter into the cradle and turned to her Esther. Same dark hair and in a pose close to sleep. Martha, crying in a utilitarian way, washed the body of her child, then dressed her in a small shroud that Martha's own mother had made from the baby's nightgown while Martha had lain gasping with grief in her bed the night before.

Martha had long since confessed before the congregation to the sin of fornication. With Elisha so quickly gone to the fort, sparing her no word—although his mother and brother spared her plenty of looks—she had been truly sorry for her sin. Truly. Sorry. But she loved her girls.

Now, as she finished stitching her baby into burial clothes, her mother came into the chamber, touched the small body and then Martha's hair. Martha swayed a little. Her mother steadied her with a hand on her shoulder, then picked up the cradle and carried Anne, still asleep, into the parlor. Martha knew she should follow, but stood in a stupor, holding the needle, until her mother came back and led her by hand to the parlor.

She sat numbly on a trunk while her mother made a fire, although it was a warm September day. There was a sound as her brother Simeon, who usually stomped, came quietly into the house. Martha turned her head and found herself looking into the face of her minister, Mr.

Edwards. He was stooping in the doorway with bright leaves fluttering behind him.

Mrs. Root was on her feet to welcome the minister, who had never before been to the house, although he lived but two home lots away on King Street. He kept his eyes on Martha. She was slumped on the chest, fingering the needle with no sewing in her lap. As he approached her, she sat up straighter, but didn't stand.

"Martha." Her mother spoke sharply. "Don't forget yourself in grief."

Martha stuck the needle neatly into her skirt and regarded Mr. Edwards. He looked back at her, sadly. She spoke no word, but got up and walked out the front door, leaving Anne to her mother and Esther to God as she ran for the woods to find a leafy canopy thick as suffering above her.

Leah washed David Brainerd's feet in vinegar while Jerusha held the basin. Jerusha, very poised at seventeen, gazed discreetly away from the young missionary as he hacked and gasped, but Leah saw her watching out of the corner of her eye to make sure that he didn't need the basin at his mouth instead of at his feet. Patting the oozing soles dry, Leah smiled in approval. Over months of nursing Mr. Brainerd, she and Jerusha had built a rhythm together.

He had come, coughing and sweating, at the end of May from his mission in New Jersey, where he had been preaching to twelve-house towns of Delaware people in the howling wilderness between the Susquehanna and Delaware rivers. Boiling his bedsheets in the yard, Jerusha had told Leah that she could not decide whether Mr. Brainerd's life as a missionary was penance or prize for the excessive zeal which had gotten him kicked out of Yale.

"Luckily," she had said, stirring the sheets with a stick, "no one asks me."

Leah, who had just asked Jerusha what she thought of Mr. Brainerd, tucked up the hem of her own skirt to keep it out of the fire. "Huh."

Not long after he had arrived in Northampton, the town had been violently stirred when a man in Southampton was killed threshing grain in his barn. The Abenaki had left sixteen poles in his yard, which people said meant that there had been sixteen members of the war party. David Brainerd had told Leah that the praying Delaware at his mission, with kindness he attributed to Christianity, had brought him food and made fires on mornings when he had been too oppressed with illness to rise, just as Leah and Jerusha had been nursing him since he had come to town. Sarah, her own hands full with a three-week-old baby, had set them to it.

Now he fell back, half propped up in bed, and closed his eyes against the afternoon light, murmuring, "Faces like men and tails like scorpions. Locusts."

"Are you quoting Revelations?" asked Jerusha, emptying the basin into a bucket.

He was already asleep. Leah covered his feet lightly with a sheet, and Jerusha sat down in one of the good parlor chairs, which was covered with a checked cotton towel to protect it in the sickroom. Sarah had moved Timothy to a cot in the kitchen and let Eunice share the trundle with Johnny so that she could give Brainerd a bed in the parlor. He could no longer climb the stairs. Jerusha looked at Leah, who was draping towels on the windowsill, and said, "There's a bump breaking out on my chin."

She flashed a grin, and Leah laughed. She could see that the girl was indulging in triviality with an eye to amuse her, which it did. It was something Leah loved about Jerusha: that she knew herself well enough to attempt self-parody. Leah started to reply, but then Brainerd groaned. In a heartbeat, Jerusha was out of her chair, leaning over him to learn what he needed. Unsurprisingly, it was the basin again.

Leah stayed near the window, watching Jerusha. The girl had embraced the messy work of tending to Brainerd's illness with a passion which Leah suspected had less to do with him than with the relief of expending some of her pent-up energy. When the doctor had recommended a trip to Boston on the theory that horseback riding might break up the congestion in Brainerd's consumptive lungs, Jerusha had traveled with him, caring for him and sending detailed reports on the state of his health back to her father in Northampton. Brainerd had almost died in Boston, but Jerusha had managed to get him home with her.

When he was able to look up from the basin, Brainerd gazed at Jerusha. Damp hair was falling into his face; it was time to shave his head again. He settled into a strangling hiccough, but seemed determined to speak. Jerusha stayed close, nodding at his gurgles as if she already understood anything he might say.

Whispering to Leah one night in the hallway, Jerusha had said, "He speaks so beautifully about giving all to God that it makes my skin seem to melt away." She had leaned on the wall. "Listening to him, I seem to rise like a cloud of dust in a ray of sunlight."

Leah had paused to make sure that they both were hearing the slow rasps of breath from the sickroom and the sounds of other breathing coming from everywhere in the house. Then she said, "The last time I saw you in a cloud of dust was when you spilled that sack of flour. We were picking broom straws out of the biscuits for a month."

Alone in the dark hallway, they had laughed. Leah was pretty sure that Jerusha's heart was in no danger except from the brutalities of death, which no one could escape. It occurred to her that the girl, with both parents and all of her brothers and sisters living, had never really known loss. Leah, whose life had been otherwise, could not imagine what that might be like.

She did not have a poetic response to young Mr. Brainerd, but, like Jerusha, she knew both his talk and his illness intimately. She had never been more tired than she felt now as she brought Jerusha another towel to wipe the blood from the corners of his mouth. She had been coughing in the night, herself. The previous night, it had been so persistent as to cause her to sleep on the floor of the cabin instead of up the ladder, where she had feared that she would wake her husband. She had lain on her old pallet worrying about Saul, who had started taking shifts with the militia, patrolling the outlying fields with a musket so that Southampton men would not be too afraid to work their crops.

Leah was resting her elbows on the back of a chair as she wrung out another towel when, with evident effort, David Brainerd stopped coughing, raised up in bed, and said to Jerusha, "I am quite willing to part with you."

Jerusha was used to feverish talk of scorpions, but she was taken aback at the rudeness. She stepped away from the head of the bed, but allowed the faintest suggestion of flirtation into her voice as she moved to wipe new ooze from the places where the skin of his heels had ripped. "Mr. Brainerd, I thank you for not encouraging me in any sin of vanity."

Leah was startled as Mr. Edwards walked into the room. He waited out a spasm of the young man's cough, then said, "No doubt Mr. Brainerd means that he is ready to leave every person he loves in the natural world, even his brothers, even you, since he has assurances that we will spend eternity together."

Brainerd stopped struggling to speak. Jerusha summoned her most formal voice to say, "Of course, Father."

She gave one more pat to Brainerd's swollen feet, set the basin with its dark stains on the table beside the bed, and swiftly left the room. At a glance from Mr. Edwards, Leah followed her, wet towel in hand.

Mr. Edwards watched them go before he sat in a chair and drew it close to the bed. "How are you today, sir?"

Brainerd attempted a brisk nod. "Fine, sir. And you?"

Mr. Edwards spoke lightly about the donations of money and Bibles which had been pouring in from Boston in the dying missionary's honor, thinking as he did so how composed Mr. Brainerd was for a young man with fresh blood on his pillowcase. Mr. Edwards had been urging men—Joseph Hawley, Timothy and Simeon Root, Bernard Bartlett, all the Pomeroys, and every other Northampton man who had become careless or defiant—to visit. He wanted the men to think of their own bodies filled with putrefaction until their skin was tight, their lungs drowned, and their feet too watery to give them purchase on the ground. He wanted their arrogance to burst like so many blisters. So far, only Joseph, who had known Brainerd at Yale, had come.

Brainerd, who had been overtaken by hiccoughs, steadied himself and said, suddenly, "You have never heard me preach."

Mr. Edwards offered him a sip of water. "Have I not?"

Brainerd waved the cup away. "If I were ever to take the pulpit again, I would wish to share it with you."

Mr. Edwards leaned toward Brainerd, who sat up and looked at him earnestly. Sick as he was, the young man was clearly smitten by his elder's fame as a preacher. Mr. Edwards knew that he should draw Brainerd's attention to his own many flaws, his profound unworthiness, and send the young man's dreams back to their deeply grooved channel flowing toward heaven and God, but it was such a simple desire, so nearly able to be achieved. In fact, they could have preached together if Brainerd had aired the ambition before his illness had reached this point.

Mr. Edwards said, "It would be my honor." He meant it.

He felt strangely shy, and fell silent, holding his breath with Brainerd's coughs. Finally, he said, "Would you like to go out?"

Brainerd wiped his mouth with the back of his hand. "Yes."

Mr. Edwards stepped into the hall, calling for Leah and Jerusha. They sent Lucy to find Saul. They carried Brainerd, with his blanket and basin, out to the yard. They set him down under the elm tree, and Mr. Edwards sat on a corner of the blanket beside him, so that, together, they might take in some air.

Eight ministers, seventeen gentlemen of liberal education, and a great concourse of people came to David Brainerd's funeral in October. Mr. Edwards had sent word as quickly as he could by way of an excellent rider with a fast horse. As he stood before them, he was both stricken and comforted. Brainerd was, surely, reaping the promises. His illness had been grueling, especially for Jerusha, who, at the funeral, was so closely surrounded by her sisters that it looked as if they were wearing one great cloak. Leah stayed home to make a meal for the mourners.

Mr. Edwards closed his eyes and breathed on his own hands to warm them before he began to preach. "True saints, when absent from the body, are present with the Lord."

Joseph tarried near the crossroads of Market and North on a bright January day. He kept a bit back from the road, but thought that if anyone should hail him, he could say that he was doing some sort of surveying as part of his work for the select board on a matter concerning the roads and the schools. They just had the one school building, of course, but they had every intention of passing a resolution to build more. He thought that here near the burying grounds and the minister's sequestered land would be a good site, so anything he might say about it would be true. At twenty-four, Joseph had developed great confidence in the power of his tone and station to lead most conversations in the direction he wished them to go.

He stomped his feet in the grass, which was stiff with frost, and tucked his hands under his arms inside his cloak to keep them warm. He imagined smoke coming from the chimney of the proposed school. This gave him satisfaction, since heat had been an ongoing problem in the little school building in front of the courthouse until he had helped Colonel Stoddard push through an edict that families had to provide a cord of wood for every scholar they enrolled.

One afternoon last month, Joseph's mother had put a pound of butter into one of her best bowls, covered it with a cloth, and handed it to Colonel Stoddard, her brother, who had been pulling on his great coat and protesting, "Surely just the cloth would do, Rebekah. I would not rob you of your china."

Rebekah, who wanted to keep in close touch with military news and gossip such as might affect Elisha, had said, "Take it. Prudence can bring it back to me for more butter when you're finished with that." She had reached out and jiggled the chain of his fancy gold watch with familiarity only a sister was allowed. "Joseph tells me that he'd been wanting to talk with you about our Elisha. I trust that everything has been worked out in a way that seems satisfactory."

Colonel Stoddard had tucked the butter bowl into his satchel. "The government has ordered forty men to the Fort, some of whom are already on their way. Ephraim Williams will command them, I think, but he is not yet back from Boston."

"So I heard," Rebekah had said.

Colonel Stoddard had continued on to something else that Rebekah would have heard. "Joseph thinks that Elisha might like to be our cousin Ephraim's second-in-command. I am satisfied with that if Captain Williams agrees."

Rebekah had been satisfied, too, but she had pressed again. "And supplies? For all of those new men? He writes of shortages."

"Snow shoes and moccasins," Colonel Stoddard had said. "The recruits will replace the men currently there, who can come home."

Joseph had been lingering in the study to give his mother time to grill her brother. He hurried to join her when she called him to the table a few minutes after Colonel Stoddard was gone.

Rebekah, who disapproved of the drinking of tea, with its sugar tongs and fancy cups, had taken a good gulp of hot cider. "It's an honor for Elisha, Joseph, but do you think he should take it? He does seem hungry and miserable, and there's no doubt of the danger."

Joseph had halved an apple to show the star of seeds in the middle, just as she had taught them to do when they were boys. He had not mentioned to Colonel Stoddard that it would be of benefit to the family to keep Elisha in honorable service far from Northampton while his role in the lives of Martha Root and her surviving child was in dispute, but both men had been aware that this was true. He handed her the big half of the apple. "He would not be free of danger at home."

Rebekah had taken a bite, thinking of the babies, her grandchildren; the one who had died and the one still living, whose name was Anne, and who, she had heard, was sickly. She had not let them linger in her mind. She never did, if she could help it. She didn't want to risk Elisha, who had not yet proved himself to be tempered with her toughness, seeing the child—and her mother—at meeting every Sabbath day. "I suppose he's better off at the fort."

Now, out at the crossroads, the wind made Joseph hunch his shoulders. An image came into his mind of doing sums as boy while his younger brother had slipped him pumpkin seeds under the desk and spit the shells in a high arc over his head; how irritated, envious, indebted, and fed his brother could make him feel.

Lately, Elisha had written in a letter that he had been thinking of their father running the family shop as he himself meted out rations of bread and rum by the ounce to the men under him. He said he felt like a shopkeeper, a stingy one with his thumb on the scales. The amount of food each man got was set by printed order of the General Court in Boston, which was very far from his men and their hunger. Sometimes they had a little tea, sugar, or tobacco, but he was constantly on the verge of running out of stores.

When Joseph had finally decided to tell Elisha that one of Martha Root's babies had died, he had not written a letter but sent word with a newly conscripted soldier along with a bundle of shirts and stockings from Rebekah. He was furious whenever he saw the child in her mother's arms, and beneath the anger, confused and disturbed. In the course of protecting his brother, Joseph had been fighting to keep his babies from having a father. In way, with the child who had died, he had already won. The thought made him miserable. He didn't trust himself to write to Elisha about it in a professional way.

He was staring across the burying ground at the bare trees, thinking that they looked like letters in an alphabet written upside down to make browsing easier for God, when he saw Martha Root coming up North Street. He had hoped that he might be able to intercept her as she returned from taking milk to the dock on the Connecticut. She sold a bucket to the ferryman every week. He had been watching her. She had the empty bucket in her hand. He stepped into the road and walked a little way toward her. As he approached, he saw her stiffen. When he was near enough to speak, he said, "Mrs. Root, may I have a word?" He spoke cordially and used the title to indicate respectful intent, but Martha flinched and would have hurried on if he hadn't raised his hand in front of her. "A word?" he asked again, still mildly, as if he were sipping frivolous tea in a parlor rather than accosting the mother of his brother's unclaimed child by the side of the road.

Martha, who was not easily shamed, recovered and stood erect, resting the bucket on the ground. "What do you have to say to me, sir, that cannot be said at my parents' house, with others present?"

Joseph, who had a feeling that the setting she had just described might have been best for this conversation, after all, held on to his cloak, which was as blue as hers, to keep it from flapping. "I've seen you where paths meet so often that I felt that that the crossroads would be the best place to find you. Clearly, I was not wrong."

Ghosts of criminals who had been hung there haunted crossroads, as did prostitutes and strangers whose birth and place were not known. Martha picked up the bucket and hung the handle across her arm. "I won't wait in the cold for your insults. The court will be in session soon enough."

She started walking quickly, and he fell into stride beside her.

"That is just it. You know that I am trained in the law and will have every advantage in the courtroom. My brother is protecting the people of this colony at great risk to himself. He is willing to offer a substantial consideration for the upkeep of your child, but the one hundred and fifty pounds that your family is asking is too much. I thought you might prefer to spare us all further misery and make a settlement for a more reasonable amount."

"I won't be bullied out of a good life for my daughter. We're asking one hundred and fifty pounds, and you will find me no less adamant than my father in that regard." She stopped at the gate to the minister's sequestered land. "And I won't be seen walking through town with you, sir, but will traipse through pastures all day if I must."

Flushed with cold and frustration, Joseph watched her walk in amongst the Edwardses' cattle, which came toward her with her bucket as if they were her own white-faced herd.

Chapter 19
February 1748

Timothy went instead of Leah (who was tired enough that her slowness had been noticed in the family) the first time that Sarah sent for a doctor for Jerusha. After that, the doctors came of their own accord, alone and in consultation with each other. They agreed that the illness was a pleuretic disorder. They tried leeches and plasters to raise blisters on her chest, which stung Sarah's hands as she applied them. Her other daughters cooked and cared for the younger ones. Everybody prayed.

On the second afternoon of Jerusha's illness, Mr. Edwards thought to scrape coals from the fire and fill a warming pan to try to abate the cold that Sarah had told him was consuming their daughter's extremities, despite the fever. He filled the long-handled pan in the kitchen, where Leah wrapped the handle in a towel so that he could carry it upstairs. She worried, as she did it, that he might trip and burn the stairs or his hands, but what Mr. Edwards lacked in physical grace, he made up for in clarity of purpose. She did not offer warnings or to carry it herself.

He climbed the stairs slowly, shoulders hunched. The doctors were gone, for now, but the whole family was gathered in the chamber. They couldn't all stay in there all day, but Jerusha was so suddenly so sick. It drew them to her. The children stood when he came into the room, as they always did. Sally, older than her mother had been when she herself had been born, made soothing noises to the baby. Esther clutched a paper fan. Mary had been sharing a chair with her arm around Lucy, and Johnny slid off their combined laps. Sukey and Eunice stood very close together. Timothy, who was a favorite with Jerusha, let go of Sarah's chair and stepped back among his sisters.

Sarah had not eaten supper or come to bed the night before, but had slept in the chair where she sat beside the bed. Mr. Edwards had awoken in the middle of the night to the sound drifting through the house of his wife singing softly to their daughter. Now Sarah rose and took the warming pan from him, nodding to the children that they could sit, since he had forgotten. She wrapped the heater in another towel, then tucked it carefully under the coverlet near Jerusha's feet, saying to him, "It's dangerous, but we'll watch it."

His eyes were on Jerusha's face. She was conscious, gasping for breath. He was relieved that she seemed to recognize him. His quick Jerusha, much distracted with pain, had spent the morning vaporous and confused. If it were up to him, and he well knew that it wasn't, even one hour would be too long for her to be suffering this way. He stood close by Sarah, bending toward the bed with her as she wiped the blood and spit that funneled down the side of Jerusha's mouth. He wanted to pray, but felt a terrible dryness.

Esther, who was turning sixteen in two days, brought her chair next Sarah's so that her father could sit down. For a moment, she fluttered the fan in the air above her sister. Jerusha, burning even as her feet froze, shifted in the bed.

Esther offered the fan to her father, but, just then, Jerusha tried to speak. He brought his face close to hers, thinking, as he did it, of the patience with which she had hovered over Brainerd. His eyes took up hers as they had all her life, but his chin was shaking.

She slid her tongue over her lips; then, trying again, managed a whole sentence. "I don't desire to live longer for the sake of any other good but living to God and doing what might be for his glory."

It was so exactly what he would wish her to say. Her mouth fell slack after the effort, which, he could see, had exhausted her. Beside him, Esther started to cry. Mr. Edwards felt overcome, unable to reach for either daughter. Often when he prayed with the ill, they could do little more than grunt or complain. He was not so perfect as his daughter in turning everything over to God's will as he watched her chew her dry lips with the late afternoon light making patterns on her face. He took her hand. Esther made a breeze for them both.

Sarah saw Jerusha wince against the light. She made her way to the window, letting her hands brush the shoulders of her other children as she went. She did not, for a moment, close the shutters, but instead shut her own eyes. She found the light still there, coming through her lids as red, with threads and blots floating through it, or as a flash then a hive of brightness, red-gray ponds and deeper marshes, something different every time she opened and closed her eyes. When she kept both eyes open and looked out over the yard, she saw pickets and the highest limbs of the elm bare against a strip of cloud drenched with light.

Deeper in the room with his back to his wife, Mr. Edwards watched her shadow shelter Jerusha, who was straining to breathe again. Then he caught the smell of burning cloth.

He lunged for the warming pan. Esther, beginning to cough, fanned smoke away with great swoops of her arms. The rest of his children jumped to their feet, all talking at once. Sally backed toward the door with the wailing baby. Sarah called out from the window. "Mind the coals!"

He shook the warming pan free of the blackened bedding. The handle was still cool enough to touch.

Esther dropped her fan and took the smoking pan from him. "The bed's not on fire."

Now, Sarah was beside them. She pushed aside the scorched quilt and said, "She's unharmed. No burns."

He heard her tell Esther to take the pan to the hearth. Sarah said something to him, too, a question about butter for his hands, but he did not answer. All he could do was stare at Jerusha as she drew a harsh breath and otherwise did not stir.

It was only five days from the onset of the fever until she was dead.

The family's grief was structured by submission to God, but trying to contain it was like trying to fence in smoke. On Saturday, Sarah left the family prayers with Timothy, who had fallen into ragged sobs that sounded like Jerusha's struggles with breath. Hearing that from him was awful. She took him outside, and they sat, shivering, on overturned buckets near the henhouse until he could control himself. Finally, he spoke in a whisper, gasping after every sentence. "I'm scared to pray. What if I do it wrong? I'm not as good as Jerusha. What if I die?"

Sarah drew him close to her, wrapping them both in her cloak. He threw his arms around her waist and huddled against her. She thought that by leaving the house she risked bringing them both closer to the beasts, but she had to tend to Timothy, whose face contorted and strained as he tried to stop weeping. A flock of crows set down to peck and hunt like chickens in the icy yard.

Sarah couldn't promise Timothy that he was saved. She rubbed his back and held him, crying herself. They rocked together. She did not question God, but, for a few moments on a bucket in the cold with her oldest boy, she howled.

Saul came up behind Leah as she heated the irons to press Sarah's mourning dress and whispered, "Mr. Edwards was crying in the barn."

She spoke without turning around. "He's heartbroken."

Saul stayed close. "When I walked in, he was oiling the scythes, with his eyes red and great streaks of bear grease on his breeches."

Leah thought of Mr. Edwards in the parlor that morning, leading the prayer after Timothy and Sarah had left. His voice had been steady while his hands trembled.

She leaned back against Saul, grateful that she had him with her. "I'll read you the story tonight about Jonah and the whale."

The story would be for Saul and for her. Who didn't like a story about a man who could survive being thrown off a ship in a storm and swallowed by a great, hollow beast? In some ways, this story was their lives, Saul's and hers. She could tell it in a voice that made their loft shiver, planks groaning beneath them like storm-hurt waves or like the combs of baleen in a whale's mouth. In her version, Leah and Saul swam in swallowed water, snatching tiny creatures with shells or gills that the whale had sucked in for its own. They made a dwelling place together where no one could actually dwell. Still, they did, or that was the way Leah told it, backed up by the Bible and, just now, by the fact that Saul's hand was pressing the muscles in her shoulders, loosening pain.

This night, though, she would not tell the story, but read it. She would read for Jerusha, who had been one of her charges and also one of her teachers. Leah had loved her and was mourning her in the held-back way in which knowledge is love—but not only love—when one person studies and serves another without being much studied but is still (somewhat) known in return.

"That will be good," said Saul, into her hair.

Once he was gone, Leah put the cold iron back into its holder in the fire and warmed her hands on the skirt.

Before he left, though, he made her sore chest ache with a stifled laugh as he kissed her neck and murmured, "It's a sign of divine grace that he found where the bear grease was."

Joseph folded a letter for Elisha, sealed it with wax, and brought it to the hall, where a sergeant was pacing impatiently, anxious to begin the dangerous journey back to the fort as early in the day as he could. Joseph thanked the man, listened to him march out the door, then went to the kitchen in search of Rebekah and breakfast.

She gave him porridge with cream. As she dished it up, he said, "I've just written Elisha that Jerusha Edwards is dead."

She clanged the ladle against the side of the pot, which rang like a bell. "If it's true what they say about consumptives being vampires, perhaps David Brainerd is rising at night to drink the blood of that family one by one." She set the bowl on the table in front of him and handed him a spoon.

"Mother." He was shocked.

"Eat." She pointed sharply at his mouth.

He obeyed.

The porridge was delicious. As he worked his way to the bottom of the bowl, he considered that he had never before seen how much fury his mother had at Mr. Edwards and his family. As he swallowed, he felt the weight in his gut of long-buried fury of his own.

Mr. Edwards dug through his records to find the sermon he had preached after a youth named Billy Sheldon had died suddenly seven years ago. That had been the winter when Sarah was in ecstasy and the young people were on fire. He took comfort in touching the old sermons, sewn neatly into booklets. It was the first Sabbath after his daughter's death, and he could not bear to start from nothing.

He read the scriptural text for Billy Sheldon's sermon. It had been haunting him:

> *Job 14:2. He cometh forth like a flower and is cut down: he fleeth also as a shadow, and continueth not.*

He felt, with Job, that his stay in this world was not clean and not long. The bitterness of his grief choked him. He opened his blank Bible and reread the chapter in Job, the ghost of younger selves taunting him with scribbled references to *Use and Intent of Prophecy* in the margins. That man, with his scholarly notes, had not known this loss. He came to the end of the chapter.

> *But his flesh upon him shall have pain, and his soul within him shall mourn.*

He cried with his fist in his mouth. His hands had not, after all, been burned by Jerusha's warming pan.

When he took it out, he said her name. "Jerusha."

He gathered thin scraps of paper that his daughters used to make fans. It was paper she had touched. He piled it on his desk with the sermon for Billy and an old marriage notice, which he flipped over so that the blank side was up. Then he picked up his pen.

Sarah and her children wore mourning to the meeting house, crapes and hatbands that Jerusha had brought home with Mr. Brainerd from Boston. Her mind shattered and wandering, Sarah found herself thinking that she was glad that Jerusha had taken the chance to go to the dry goods shop at Cornhill. Just the week before, she and the girls had spoken of the flowered velvet and capuch silks that Jerusha had seen there. Last Sabbath day, Jerusha had been at meeting, seated between Sally and Esther. Facing that empty place on the bench before the entire congregation was the hardest thing that Sarah had ever done.

He cometh forth like a flower and is cut.

Mr. Edwards was preaching.

There was in this case, after she was first taken ill, speedy advice of physicians, like means speedily used, and physicians were consulted from day to day while she lived, the means used that they jointly agreed upon, yet nothing prevailed.

God's appointed time was come and no care or tendence of friends or means or consultation of physicians could avail to prevent death from doing its work.

It was awful for Sarah to hear her husband recite the events of the previous week. His voice was stiff and jerky, like a frozen pump. Her mind flicked away.

Which may be a warning to you not to flatter yourself in a dependence on anything for the preservation of your lives.

If there had been time while she was in Boston, Sarah was sure, Jerusha would have brought home striped brocades and poplins for her sisters to make into dresses for winter.

Her pains and bodily distress from day to day were so great that if she had not taken care beforehand she would have had but a poor opportunity.

They had no need for kid lamb and satin gloves, but Sarah had wished for some English stays. Mrs. Hutchinson—mother of Abigail, long-dead—met her eye, then looked away.

What will you do when your extreme parts grow cold and death begins to get hold? What will you do with death? Where will you look for comfort? What will you do for your poor soul that is going to leave the body?

Martha Root, as she listened, thought of her Esther cold in the grave. Anne, still unclaimed by her father, was wriggling in her lap. If Martha died today, she would, she knew, appear tired before God.

I would take occasion from this instance of that blooming flower that was lately cut down by death more particularly to exhort the young people here present to the following things:

Avoid a light and vain conversation. Don't let any filthy communication come out of your mouth contrary to that rule, Colossians 3:8. Come, don't delight in lascivious talking and jesting and lewd and filthy songs contrary to those rules, Ephesians 5:3-4.

Simeon and Timothy Root did not look at each other because Simeon knew that there was nothing like a condemnation of mirth, even in the most solemn of circumstances, to tempt Timothy to laugh.

Avoid those customs used by young people and those liberties they are wont to take in company that by sufficient experience are found to be of an evil and corrupt tendency. As, for instance, not only the gross acts of lasciviousness, but such liberties as naturally tend to stir up lust. That shameful, lascivious custom of handling women's breasts, and the different sexes lying in beds together. However light you may any of you make of these and may perhaps be involved. The custom of frolicking as it is called.

He was burning with grief, but through its heat, he felt the unease of the people as they sat before him, thinking their own thoughts about bundling and the lascivious custom of handling women's breasts. He had been blunt, but, lingering tensions from the midwives' books trial or not, at this moment, he would do anything to reach them. Bringing more people to God would sanctify Jerusha's death and relieve his grief. It was the only thing that could.

Mr. Edwards spoke to the young women, urging them not to allow liberties. Joseph could not look at his mother. The Edwards girls sat very straight, numb with loss. Timothy sat straight, too, still afraid to pray. Bathsheba took up her own prayers, which skewed off from the sermon, as did those of Martha and all of the other women present.

Even Sarah, who held this unspeakable loss with Mr. Edwards, let her mind drift to bone lace.

Voice rising, he spoke of Jerusha. In the continuous present, he saw his daughter *manifesting a relish appetite as her supreme good.* She had *also ever found the most strong and lively hungerings and thirstings after grace and holiness.* Finally, he said, *O that this instance of death might be a means of awakening the young people.*

Sarah was with him, now, seeing Jerusha's thirsts and appetites, too. Oh, she had been such a healthy baby, eager for the milk. In the pain in her husband's voice, Sarah could hear traces of Jerusha's curiosity and the small flashes of vanity that reminded her so much of herself. She caught strains of her daughter in all of her beauty, and felt slammed again with the loss. Awaken, she thought. Awakenings. The souls of the valley coming back to life would keep her daughter close.

Leah and Saul did not mark any passages in the sermon, because Leah was too ill to come to meeting. Saul stayed with her. By morning, she, too, was dead.

Elisha read Joseph's letter at the fort:

> *Mrs. Jerusha Edwards died last Sabbath morning of a pluretek disorder of about 5 days continuance. A very sudden death and a most awakening and admonitory providence, is to be interred this day.*

Elisha was twenty-one to Jerusha's nearly eighteen. Reading of her death, he got a very clear picture of her six years earlier, prostrate and wailing in her family's parlor during a prayer meeting, then recovering enough to help her sisters pass out doughnuts and cider with trembling hands. Jerusha had been cordial and sweet, but what he remembered best from that day was standing in the corner of the room, stuffing his mouth with a doughnut to make his cheeks bulge out like a chipmunk's, chittering at Martha Root, who had neither laughed nor scorned him, but had pushed on her nose with her thumb and snorted like a pig.

Reminding himself never to tell that story to Joseph (although, of course, he wanted to), Elisha wished rest to Jerusha's soul, then turned back to the letter. After some business about a money-making venture they were attempting by trading in deer skins, Joseph went on:

> *As to yr affair I was to manage, I tried for an agreement before the court. They insisted on 150 pounds which I thought was too much, considering what risk there is of*

(here there was a word so shaky and jumbled that Elisha couldn't make it out, but he thought it must say something like *short*)

> *life. I therefore thought better to tarry a while longer before I concluded the affair, and till I could have some account of your mind, nor doubting but I could obtain a continuance of your recognizance, which accordingly I did—though with some difficulty. I hope before next session I shall accommodate the affair upon easier terms than they seem at present to insist upon; if not I should think it best to abide by the order of the Court but hope I shall have opportunity to inform you further of the affair ere long.*

Elisha swore, freshly angered as if he were reading it for the first time instead of the fourth. It was, he thought, the worst possible news. He could not believe that Joseph would need a new account of his mind to know that what he wanted above all other things was to conclude the affair. "Tarry a while longer?" How lightly Joseph put it. Elisha half suspected his brother of enjoying both his own precarious position and the way in which being his advocate allowed Joseph to display his skills before the court. One hundred and fifty pounds made up a very tidy sum, but if the settlement would silence Martha and put the matter behind him, how could Joseph doubt for one moment the urgency of his need for it to end?

Apart from the sad news about Jerusha Edwards, God rest her soul, the remainder of the letter was no improvement in tone. After writing that the sergeant waiting for the letter was in a considerable hurry, Joseph took the time to deliver a substantial amount of advice. There was the usual—

Pray let your conversation and belief be religious towards God, steady and manly towards men

—which Elisha read as a familiar mixture of judgment and love. He had no need to be urged to be manly, and the terms of the rest had changed for him since he had left home, although he was not inclined to parse out just how. He did not care at all for the tone of the last sentence:

Take heed you be not surprised through carelessness which is a very ignoble cause of mischief.
yr. Brother and hub. ser., Joseph Hawley

Ah, Joseph, Elisha thought, you do a poor imitation of being my humble servant.

He felt uneasy with the implication that they should try to get a bargain rate for the settlement because the baby might die like her twin. He knew that this was a matter of practical concern, but surely it was also a matter of the famous conscience to which his brother so constantly referred him to provide support for a child he had fathered, even one born of sin. Elisha was in no position to say so, but he felt that Joseph might be well advised to mind the danger to his own soul.

Saul had not wanted to leave Leah's body, so he and Bathsheba had worked together to wash her and lay her out. The family, wrung out with grief as they were, had given her a Christian burial at the edge of the graveyard, which Saul, who had made sure that she had her head to the west, thought was fit and right. Devils might have business with the unrepentant slave owners buried in these graves, and it would be no rest to lie in the midst of all that.

No sooner had Saul returned to this thought at morning prayers with the family than he spared a prayer of his own for Jerusha, who had been decent and was gone, now, so young. He imagined that Jerusha was content with her spot beside Mr. Brainerd. Leah knew how to be any place she found herself. Great God, he missed her.

The family prayed for Leah morning and night as they prayed for Jerusha. The girls had taken up most of her duties. Work was the wheel that kept Saul grinding out his time. The first night after Leah was buried, he had tried to sleep in the barn with the blameless cattle breathing cold smoke for company and no smell of Leah such as was found in the loft. The barn proved too cold, so he had stumbled back to the cabin in the dark to climb the ladder with half-frozen feet.

Over the next few nights, he sat up carving himself a bowl from a piece of ash which, last fall, he had found in the woods, dragged home, and saved from the fire to make a Bible stand for Leah. Her fingers had been starting to tingle and lose their grip, and he had thought that she might like to go back to reading more if she could let her hands rest. Mr. Edwards had a book table, of course, but Saul had thought that he might make Leah's stand be a place to hold two books, instead of just one or Mr. Edwards's six, so that two people could, if circumstances ever brought this to pass, sit across from each other and read two different books, or one could watch the face of the other full on as she read. There was enough ash for two bowls, but he left it at one.

Now it was Saturday night, almost a week since she had died, burning hot and strangled, it had seemed, by her coughs, and choking on every infusion Bathsheba had tried to get down her. He had sat behind her all that night, keeping her propped against his chest as might bring her ease. This had helped a bit, but not nearly enough.

Late as it was now, Bathsheba came to his door and entered without knocking, softly saying his name. "Saul. People are coming."

She showed him a sack of bottles and a package of food. He took up his own sack and walked with her toward the woods along the Mill River, where the ground was firm, not swamp.

Saul paused at the edge of the trees, and Bathsheba stopped with him. He closed his eyes and thought of his unborn child, his and Leah's, buried in these woods. He asked their baby if he might enter, as he never thought to do during the day. He wanted to ask her now, though, and to ask his mother and father, and Leah's mother and father, and their aunts and uncles, all those he knew to be dead and all who might be, to give him leave to enter. He didn't go in until he felt that he could. Bathsheba waited quietly beside him, eyes open in the dark.

Joab was already at the clearing close to the water with its islands of ice, beating his drum. Anyone coming through the woods could follow the sound, the same way that people were called to meeting by the bell. There were four or five people in the clearing, talking quietly, and more came in behind Saul and Bathsheba. The men grasped his shoulder and murmured in sympathy. They were servants and slaves, come to pay private respects.

Bathsheba walked to the center of the clearing, and the drumming stopped. She threw back her head and recited the Twenty-third psalm, as Leah had taught her. "Yea though I walk through the valley of the shadow of death, I fear no evil, for thou art with me. Thy rod and thy staff, they comfort me."

Saul remembered the words, found them easy to remember. He heard Bathsheba saying them, and Leah's voice was there, too, on the edge of exasperated as it might have been if, as often happened, he had been falling asleep as she read to him. He had loved the comfort and company of drifting off to the sound of her voice, and she had been so irritated at him almost every time for wasting her effort and not listening to the words.

Bathsheba was beside him again, not touching, but very near. The people had formed a rough circle, lit by lanterns hung on the tree and pine-tar torches stuck in the snow. No one was speaking, but they had started a song. Saul, stamping his feet for warmth and release, felt the slap of the drum in his body, but he wasn't listening. He was trying to remember the first time he had seen Leah, what she had been doing and whether she had spoken or just cut him a glance in that way she had that scared him as much as it drew him closer. He couldn't get there, couldn't remember anything but the way she had bent down away from him to lift a pail, the strength in her hips, and the way that, already, young as she had been, she had held herself unevenly, as if in pain. It was the thought of the ache in her joints all those years ago that made him start to cry and yell, "No. Oh, no," over a song he couldn't really hear, but which didn't stop.

Other people were sobbing. When he opened his eyes, he saw the tears on Bathsheba's face. She glanced back at him, shook her head, and then looked down at the ground, which they had stomped and kicked clean of snow. Saul waited for the worst of his confusion, waited for anger. When it came, it hit so hard that he was knocked to his knees on the cold dirt. He wasn't repentant, wasn't begging to be saved, but felt the weight of Leah's spirit slamming him chest down on the ground. He stayed there, chin to a small ridge of mud and ice, breath pressed out of him as if she still needed it, needed his. He was crying and holding her on his shuddering back as if he could keep her low, soiled, and wet with him if he became a snake who could part the snow.

He was kicking the ground like no snake ever could, and Bathsheba crouched down to him, holding open his sack. He sat up and pulled it between his legs, hugging it to him. Someone had brought out a fiddle and was sawing away. He waited a long time on the ground with his arms around the rough sack. Then he reached in and pulled out a plate, which he placed carefully on the ground. He found the cups with the chips on the rim that Sarah had given Leah on their wedding day. He wrapped his hands around them in the familiar way, then stood, turned, and flung them one after another against a tree with a lantern hung from a branch.

His friends surged around him, throwing plates and saucers which shattered against the trunk. Saul broke all their bowls and wished he had brought the new one to throw, too, but he didn't touch the plate on the ground. Bathsheba was heaving stoppered bottles, precious things she used and loved, yelling Leah's name, telling illness and devils to go on. There was no music now, just the sound of things breaking against a living tree which wasn't a church or a grave. Some of the things that missed the tree hit the river, skidding and shattering on the ice. Saul threw everything he had, then moved close to the tree to gather shards and throw them again. He picked up fallen chunks of bark soft with algae and threw them, too. He was hit a few times before everyone else saw to stop.

Then they brought out food, sitting on logs, stumps, and empty sacks to eat and talk. Bathsheba unwrapped the packet she had brought and held it out to him. He looked at it, then reached in and took a greasy piece of smoked shad, which he put on Leah's plate with cold mashed turnips and left on a rock beside the tree for her.

Chapter 20
May – October 1748

No new awakening came to the valley. Instead, Martha Root put on her best dress, borrowed her mother's lace cuffs, and walked toward the courthouse. Her mother and brother offered to come with her, but she chose to go alone. The cherry trees along King Street scattered the yards and pastures with white flowers.

The rest of Northampton was caught up in war fever. A young farmer had been killed in Southampton, walking home in the morning from the pasture where he had just driven his cows. The entire town had fled the eight miles to Northampton, where they were now crowded in with their relatives, and a party of men were out scouring the countryside for enemies. Still the walk to the center of town, not away from it toward the pasture, seemed safe enough, even for a young woman on her own. The worst thing Martha could imagine would be Joseph Hawley lurking to try to speak with her again, and even that seemed highly unlikely, given the nature of her business with the court.

As she neared the courthouse, Martha smelled the newly opened pits at the tannery and spared a thought for Elisha in danger at his distant fort. She felt that he was too frightened to live his own life, and she didn't want him to be part of her own, but had no wish to hear that he were injured or dead. Take care, Elisha, she thought. Don't get killed because you can't face meeting me or my Anne on the street. Anne, home with Martha's mother, was already a year old, already so much her own. Elisha had fled his chance to ever see little Esther. That thought made Martha tug on her cuffs and step a bit more briskly as she walked through the courthouse door to swear out a statement:

Know all men by these present that I Martha Root of Northampton in the county of Hampshire, in the province of Massachusetts Bay in New England have received of Elisha Hawley of Northampton the sum of one hundred fifty-five pounds old tenor in full satisfaction for and toward the support and maintenance of a bastard child born of my body now living, which child with another some time since deceased which was a twin with the for mentioned child that I the for mentioned Martha charged upon the for mentioned Elisha as their father.

She kept her eyes down before the witnesses, but signed her name with harsh satisfaction. One hundred and fifty-five pounds. Five pounds more than what, months before, Joseph Hawley had declared was too much.

Sarah was called to Boston to tend Colonel Stoddard, who had suddenly taken ill. Mr. Edwards urged her to go. She had been quiet in the months after Jerusha's death, speaking with animation only to the children, and he hoped that the travel, even if to another sickbed, might do her good. In her absence, he threw himself into work. It was one of his ways of mourning, as easing bodily suffering was one of hers.

She rode much of the way in the company of Elisha Pomeroy, who had business in Boston involving the possibility of a large order for some of Seth Pomeroy's guns. Sarah was grateful to be accompanied on the path through so much unsettled country, although they were in much more danger of raids in the west. Still, after many hours, she found both silence and conversation with Mr. Pomeroy to have become a chore. Ever since Jerusha died, she had found herself easily exhausted, frequently muddy-headed, and much more limited in patience than she had been in the past. Now both travel and onerous company wore her down.

Finally, late in the day, shortly before they were to part for separate lodgings, she dropped her guard so much as to fall into a theological dispute with him. He had been speaking ill of churches in the towns they passed through in the east, whose pastors demanded professions and thought that they could take on the weighing of human souls as if they were fit to do the work of God. Every bone in Sarah's body told her to hold her silence on this delicate matter, but she had had time to study and pray about it since Mr. Edwards had first told her his inclination toward change in Northampton, and when she finally spoke, her words poured from her with more passion than she would have wished.

"Sir," she said, turning her face toward him. "I cannot agree. Mr. Edwards has been giving this matter much reflection, and he feels that it is suitable for only those to join the church who can give credible profession of Godliness."

Mr. Pomeroy was not a man in the habit of attending closely to the thoughts of women. Surprised to be contended with, he turned jocular. "Did he say such a thing? Perhaps, madam, you may have misunderstood."

She rode along silently for a long moment, trying to calculate the miles before they would reach Boston. She looked up at the sky, where the clouds seemed to be making a slow advance until it suddenly became an enormous white mass, the flank of a great whale filling the sky. Then she spoke again. "I have felt God speak in me, sir. I spoke to people of it as it happened, and I wrote it down. I spoke of its sweetness to my husband and our children, and to all those in our town who would listen." Wisps of darkness were mist from the spume of the cloud, and there were modulations in texture that became water, waves, ocean, then schools of dolphins swimming in smoke from a fire above them. Sarah looked at her companion. "Anyone who has come to God should be happy to speak of it."

Mr. Pomeroy gaped at her. She did not ask him if he thought this were true.

———

Back home in Northampton, Mr. Edwards had been soliciting letters and subscriptions for his edition of Mr. Brainerd's journal. (Hopkins, Brainerd's old classmate, had responded quite fondly.) Now he turned to the many letters that Jerusha had written about Brainerd from Boston. Smoothing the hole in his desk with his knife, he lingered over her intimate accounts of pain, nocturnal sweats, and vapory confusions. She, like her mother, had an unflinching eye for a body's worst mess. He felt close to her spirit as he drew on her words, tending to the record of the young man's life just as she had tended his body. As he marked passages and made clarifying comments, he felt as if he were inhabited by the voices of Brainerd and Jerusha as well as his own. He welcomed their company.

He missed Leah, too. The children spoke of her as often as they did of their sister. Saul was distant, inconsolable. Mr. Edwards saw it, but kept his counsel to a bare minimum. Saul was a man who spoke when he was ready, and Mr. Edwards, mourning himself, knew more than he used to about how to tend a grieving soul. He let Saul be.

Days without Sarah turned into weeks. The household was in upheaval. When both Sally and Esther came down sick, Mr. Edwards had to call Hannah Root in to help. He wrote to Sarah:

We have been without you almost as long as we know how to be.

A little awkwardly, he asked her to bring cheese from Boston, if she had money to spare. He preferred, at the moment, not to have commerce with Rebekah Hawley, who was still abetting Elisha as he refused to do his duty by the Root child and her mother. He knew that there had been a settlement for money, but money wasn't the half of it. Unrepentant sin like that had no place in his church, and without the church, Mr. Edwards considered Elisha to be without any hope for true life.

Colonel Stoddard died of apoplexy. It was another terrible blow.

When Sarah came home, still looking weary, she brought, not only new English stays and an excellent cheese, but also a slave, whose name was Rose. When they first rode into the yard, the younger children hung back, startled by the sight of the stranger on the back of their mother's horse. Sarah regarded Saul's drawn face as she handed him the reins, then sent Rose to an attic room instead of into the shed with him.

Rebekah went to the buttery to cry for her brother. She turned the big rounds of cheese and polished them with oil, mourning and wondering why John Stoddard had sent for Sarah and not for her. Sarah was better with tinctures and poultices, everyone knew that, but Rebekah would have wanted to see his face.

When he heard her crying, Joseph came and stood in the doorway of the buttery, as he had never done in all the years she had grieved for his father there. Then, he had known that she wanted to be alone, but now he walked in like the man he was. She found comfort in the wry way he offered her a handful of sage, torn to bits, ready to flavor new curds.

Rose was a young woman, Boston born and raised, who knew how to weave fine linens. She spoke with deference and a touch of city brusqueness. Saul half hated the sight of her in her checked petticoat and red skirt headed toward the henhouse on the path that Leah's feet had made. There was nothing to blame her for, but he avoided her as far as he was able. He stood beside her at family prayer, and they ate silent meals together, but he never asked what had brought her to be sold.

"Dead mistress." Bathsheba, who felt no compunction about talking to Rose, had him know. "Small pox, but Rose said that her mother had dosed her with it as a child, so she never got sick. She doesn't know what to think of us, especially you, but the selling is done with, and that's one thing. It wouldn't kill you to speak to her."

Saul took a sip of birch beer from his wooden cup and didn't answer. Leaning forward, elbow to knee, she answered herself. "And it wouldn't kill you to be quiet, Bathsheba." She took a drink, too, then got his knife from the peg where it hung in its sheath and offered it to him. "Carve me something if you won't talk."

He regarded it bleakly. "Might as well."

He went outside and broke off a branch of green wood. He carved her a cane with the crude head of a bird for a handle, not carefully and not well.

Bathsheba watched in silence. As she had loved Leah, she was determined to search out what might get Saul to do something except work when he had to and act civil on request. He didn't offer to make her anything else, and she didn't ask.

It was a dry, hot summer. The river was muddy and low. Peas never swelled, but turned brown and dried on the vine. Everyone washed less and moved more slowly, carrying buckets from the well to try to save their crops and gardens.

Mr. Edwards, deep in Brainerd's journals, tried to imagine what it would be like to be a missionary, sleeping alone under the trees (in his mind, he edited out the cold shack and the bloody coughing), far from any British town. He liked the idea of preaching to people who might have never before heard the word of God instead of to his hardened congregation, who—he thought of them at their worst—had been snoring and snickering under his sermons for two decades now. Escaping into missionary dreams was difficult because he could imagine neither hauling his family through the wilderness nor leaving them far away for months at a time. Also, he loved his study and the elm in his own yard. Still, he was so tired of the endless bickering among the people in Northampton.

He preached a sermon on the theme that select persons and not the mixed multitudes were fit to judge causes. God, he said, had proved with Moses that he knew judgment to be a difficult business, often attended with intricacy and need of great exactness to judge aright of persons and things. Moses himself had complained that it was very hard, difficult work, but he had not left it to the congregation in common, because he had known that such a company was not fit for it.

Listening from her bench among the sweaty congregation, Sarah saw Mr. Root, who had recently given up walking out during hymns, raise his eyebrows at Bernard Bartlett. With a pang of apprehension, she watched Mr. Bartlett lean over to whisper a comment in return. She rested her fan in her lap while a rivulet of sweat traced a vein in her neck and faces hardened all around her. Fit or not, she feared that the congregation seemed more than ready to judge.

Elisha began to spend time with one of the half-wild dogs that lived at the camp. He had first spotted her guarding a pile of entrails from a deer and was taken by the way that she turned and snarled at bigger dogs but came when he called her to drink the water he poured from a skin into his hand. They were both ready for something to trust. Elisha had Joseph and Rebekah, but Joseph was much distracted by Mercy Lyman, a young woman who lived in Brookfield. Rebekah wrote to Elisha that Mercy had a face like a toasting iron. She wrote, too, that his old barn cat, Sister, had wandered away one night and never came back.

The dog was small and black, with a white patch shaped like a bell on her low, broad chest. She had skinny legs and was quick to crouch, hackles raised, at the sight of a strange dog. The pack she ran with lived off the soldiers' leavings.

Elisha named the dog Delilah and kept a bowl of water for her outside his room. Every day, she followed him as best she could, staying clear of the hooves of the horses and the boots and moccasins of the men. She was quick and footsure even on hills, so he let her come with him on supply runs.

Elisha had been excommunicated by the Northampton church, but Joseph was hopeful about a reversal. Reading his letters with the rumblings of hunger in his belly, Elisha felt far from the world in which such things mattered. He had heard that a great army was fitting out in Canada to be directed against Albany, Schenectady, and possibly also Massachusetts. He got word from Stockbridge that not more than a bit of wheat could be transported until the roads were better, even that not in wagons, but on soldiers' backs (provided that they brought their own knapsacks). Pay for the soldiers was expected daily, but it was brutally slow to come.

Every day he sent two men to the top of the mountain called the Height of the Land, between the Deerfield river and the Dutch town of Hoosack. They had to set off in the morning and make a good camp on the mountain, then climb a tree at sunrise to search for smoke. If any were seen, one was to report to Deerfield, and the other to Fort Massachusetts. Smokes had been seen.

Elisha, Delilah, and about forty men were just back from a run to Deerfield on a parched day in early August. The stores had been scant, diminished by the drought, but he had hogs, flour, and salt, which would do them all good. Colonel Williams, his commander, was at the fort, which always made Elisha restless. After unpacking for half the afternoon in the relentless sun, he gave the men a respite and grinned when he saw Delilah crawling under the palisades. He needed to fill in that gap in the fence, but she was off to swim in the river, he was sure of it. Wishing he could join her, he climbed a watch tower, greeted the sentry, and sat down on the platform in hope of a breeze. None came, but he leaned back and looked over the high, sharp slats that protected the fort to search for Delilah's dark shape against the grasses.

He spotted her, but instead of loping toward the river, she was in a crouch, moving slowly toward an edge of woods halfway between the fort and the water. He expected her to flush out some quail or a possum surly with sleep, but instead she suddenly dodged to the right as a shot came from the woods.

Elisha jumped to his feet and sounded the alarm, as, to his horror, he saw a small group of his own men away from the fort with their guns out, firing at the woods. They had gone, without permission, to the river, and their fire was being returned. Shots were coming heavily now, and as Elisha pounded down the ladder, Colonel Williams came running out of his quarters.

"With me!" the colonel shouted. "Form your ranks!" To Elisha, he muttered, "They must have followed our scout."

Elisha joined the men who marched from the fort, but as soon as they were out of the gate, a crowd of Abenaki from Scaticook surged from the woods, firing and making an ungodly noise. The men from the fort were outnumbered, but reached the small group of men who had been caught outside. The group found themselves cut off from their right flank, and so fought their way back to the fort.

Elisha, who had seen Ezekiel Wells shot in the hips, was running numbly back toward the gates when he felt a burning pain in his calf. He went down, but two of his men stopped to drag him to the fort. He limped back to his room to staunch his wound with a sheet and found Delilah waiting by the door. She was unharmed, and sat shivering beside him as he listened to the cannon and tried to pick buckshot out of his leg for an hour and three quarters by the glass. Then the Abenaki fell back and the shooting stopped.

There were three casualties. Elisha, Ezekiel Wells, and Samuel Abbot, who had been shot below the navel and was not expected to live.

As soon as she heard that Elisha was wounded, Rebekah went to her garden and started picking herbs to grind for a salve. The plants were shriveled and close to the ground, but succulents, which were best for wounds, fared better than others in drought. She felt profoundly calm, as if there was only one thing to do in this moment, and she was doing it. The buckshot had missed the shin bone, and Elisha's life had been spared. If he were near her, she would have made him stay in the house, safe from all manner of miasmas and dangers until he was well-healed, but, as it was, she was grateful that his calf was all he had sacrificed to keep their people safe and restore his own good name.

Once Joseph saw that Rebekah was well-occupied, he went out and marched in the road, beating a drum, until he had gathered a group of twenty-nine men: Seth Pomeroy and his regulars along with others, like Joseph, who were hot to scour the frontier.

Saul heard the drumming while he was pouring water in the troughs for the Edwards cattle and came running to King Street, where he found himself standing in front of the house beside Mr. Edwards, who looked grim.

Saul put his bucket down and said, "Can I go and fight?"

Two young missionaries able to do chores were staying with the Edwardses that summer. Mr. Edwards, who saw the hand of God in every battle, also saw the spark of life back in Saul's eyes. He said, simply, "Yes."

Later, Saul came back to the house for food to carry with him. Ever since Leah died, he had worn her pocket around his neck, so he now had a place to stow his knife, knocking gently against her piece of shell. He gave Leah's carved box with the books to Bathsheba, who came running down the road to hold him close. For safekeeping, he said. He spoke gently to the children, respectfully to Sarah, and nodded to Rose, accepting prayers and blessings.

At that first moment on King Street, though, he fell in to march with nothing like a second glance.

Joseph wrote to Elisha from Deerfield with the troops:

> *I rejoice greatly and desire to praise God that your wound is in a healing way. I pray you to consider of special obligation upon you to live to him who thus preserved you and is saving and healing you. Mother is pretty much concerned about you but not so much as I feared she would have been. If things should so open that we should think we may be as serviceable in going to your fort as anywhere, I shall be set to see you, but don't expect it much. Mother has given me some salve to send you, which she thinks best to put above your wound to prevent the humours from falling into the wound as she imagines you will be inclined to stir a pretty deal.*

Joseph's troop was out for more than a week. Saul found that there were two other men from Deerfield, Cato and Cesar, who were also slaves sent to fight. They knew each other well and welcomed Saul into their company. He joined them by the fire at night, and they all shared food, but Cato and Cesar knew the country the troop was traveling through, so they scouted in front of the main group, while Saul was in back with the pack animals.

They did stop at Fort Massachusetts. Joseph embraced Elisha and examined the wound in his leg, as he had promised their mother he would do. It was healing well, and, along with less pleasant scents, smelled faintly of her garden. They had a meal together, then stayed up late, drinking rum and telling stories: first Elisha's recent experiences, then Joseph's Louisburg days, then gossip from home. They avoided some of Northampton's most heated rumors, which concerned Elisha himself.

Joseph slept that night on a pallet in Elisha's room. After they blew out the candles, Elisha lay awake in his cot as his calf throbbed. Finally, he spoke. "I'm sorry that my sins have caused so much trouble for Mother and you."

Joseph raised his head. It gave him great relief to hear the surge of remorse in his brother's voice, which bode well for his soul. He rested his chin on the pallet. "No need to speak of it."

Elisha said, "Thank you, brother." Then he muttered, "Although you could stand to be a little less arrogant, yourself."

Stung, Joseph whipped his blanket at him. Elisha caught it before it hit the floor, wadded it up, and threw it back, harder. One corner snapped across Joseph's cheek. They stared at each other's outlines in the darkness, then both of them started laughing as if they were boys bunking together in the attic again. When they were finally quiet, Joseph felt calmer than he had in months. He lay down, pulling the blanket over him, and said, "You know I'm right."

"About everything?" Elisha snorted.

Joseph's cheek burned and his eyelids were drooping. All he said was, "Mmm."

Then they both slept.

In the morning, Delilah licked Joseph's hand as gently and fervently as if it were a puppy. She barked after the horse when he rode off with his troop.

———

The militia headed home after ten days, having sighted no one to fight or subdue. Crops were sparse that summer, but it was time for harvest. They were needed at home and, most of them, ready to be there.

On the last night out of Deerfield, making camp near the river, Saul felt dry as the hambone he had already used for soup three times. He was unwrapping it to chew the last shred of gristle when Seth Pomeroy—who had a runner from Deerfield waiting on a written report to carry into town before they arrived—rode up beside Saul, dismounted, and said, "See to my horse."

Saul looked at the fine roan gelding, which was crusted with dried sweat and exhausted from the long days of travel. And so thirsty. Saul, tired himself, took hold of the reins and led the horse toward the river.

He had already taken care of the pack animals and, except for Major Pomeroy, who came and went as he pleased, had been traveling last, so he was setting out alone. Soon he and the horse were well out of the light thrown by the fires being lit by men leaning over them with tinderboxes. It was late, and night was coming hard. Saul tripped over a root, and then a rock.

"To blazes," he said, and, with some difficulty, mounted Major Pomeroy's horse. He didn't have a confident seat. The roan walked slowly, grazing in the dark, but when Saul pulled on the reins, it stopped for a moment, then went along faster. They could smell the river.

The air seemed heavier than it had been, saturated with heat, but Saul felt a little cooler riding than he had walking. He got out his bone to chew as he rode, and unfastened his waistcoat and shirt to bare his chest to any hint of breeze. He didn't feel that he was making a decision, but pulled on his long shirttails until they were flapping free of his britches. This annoyed the roan, which switched at them as if they were a swarm of biting flies. Thinking of flies, Saul shifted the reins to one hand and held the shirt together to cover his chest. He didn't button it.

There was a mild bank that led to a good place to water, but Saul let go of his shirt to guide the descent at a steep angle. The roan, eager to drink, took it too fast and stumbled a little as he reached the water. Saul threw up his arms and fell over the horse's neck into the river.

He went under, hitting something hard and sharp with both knees, but came up quickly, gasping. The water was colder than he had expected. Low as it was, the river had a strong current, and he had to move fast to strip his shirt from his arms, thinking of a story he had heard of a woman held underwater by the weight of her skirt. He tossed the shirt to catch on scrubby bushes on the bank, where, he hoped, it would mark the spot that he must have drowned. There would be no sign of him having stepped foot on the bank.

The roan had looked up and scrambled partway back up the bank as Saul fell, but it was cautiously approaching the water again, head lowered to drink. Saul was panicked and tempted to fight his way to the bank. Instead, he thought of Leah and her lessons, and began to stroke with his arms. He had once seen a strong current spin a sodden log. The other slaves, he thought, would not speak first, or track him down. The others might come looking for the horse, might search for him a little, but, he thought, not much. He could be, perhaps, a casualty of the war, taken by the river. He would go looking for those who might admit a stranger such as him to their fights, and, even, maybe, if he were lucky and patient, to any ways they had of living with hard losses. He never wanted to see Northampton again.

Saul said no prayers in the water, but as he swam, the drought broke. When he climbed out of the river and set out for the mountains, he was in a world of rain.

Mr. Edwards was chopping wood at the old stump when he saw Joseph riding up King Street. He stopped and watched as the solemn young man—built sturdily, like his father—dismounted with a soldier's briskness and held the reins rather than tying them to a post. Not staying long.

Mr. Edwards leaned on the axe handle and said, "Welcome back, Mr. Hawley. Are you ahead of the troop?"

Joseph, who had been putting on airs ever since he had come home to be a lawyer, seemed awkward this morning. He sighed before he spoke. "Bad news, sir. We lost your Saul."

Mr. Edwards felt it like a blow. He stood very straight. "Dead?"
Joseph nodded. "Drowned." He told the story: wandering horse,
river, Saul's shirt.

Mr. Edwards listened with twists of feeling he did not try to
understand. His heart had been wrenched dry by Jerusha's death,
Brainerd's, and, he knew, also Leah's. "May God sanctify this loss." He
hit the head of the axe on the side of the stump, feeling constrained in
grief by his duties. "Perhaps I should not have let him go. He wasn't
trained to be a soldier."

Joseph put a hand on his uncle's shoulder. "He was in the militia.
He was a good servant, skilled at his work."

Mr. Edwards wanted to sit down on the stump and weep, but he
couldn't, not in front of Joseph. He thought of the light in Saul's eye
the last time they had spoken, suddenly there after months of dullness.
It gave him hope that the man had died in an awakened state.

Joseph cleared his throat and spoke again. "I am sorry to say that
I do not think that there is any likelihood of compensation from the
government in Boston in these circumstances."

Mr. Edwards stared at him. He saw the little boy running out
of the woods to tell him about his own father's grievous, self-inflicted
wounds, and he saw the young man trying to act as if the rules of
human society were enough to guide him through the ravages of life.

Joseph looked at his boots. He had known Saul most of his life.
"Regarding the loss of property."

Mr. Edwards flinched under the obscene practicality of this
observation. Before the rain that had swollen the river which had washed
Saul away, Northampton had been in a drought of the land and was still
in a drought of the spirit. He had preached about how desperate starving
people could get in a drought, forced to feed on each other's carcasses,
sometimes even to devour their own flesh. The rain had brought some
respite from the drought of the land, but he felt the horror of spiritual
drought rising in him. When he spoke, it was to quote scripture to
sanctify Saul's death. "For I that is will pour water upon him thirsty and
floods upon the dry ground."

Joseph bowed his head, then rode away.

Mr. Edwards picked up his axe. He clove nearly half a cord of oak. He kept chopping—sweating and crying in full view of King Street— long after nature urged him to drink.

Chapter 21
December 1748 – July 1749

Rose knocked crisply, then led Simeon Root into the study. She shut the door on her way out. Mr. Edwards let Simeon stand there for a moment, crumpling the brim of his hat in his fist and shifting from foot to foot. Simeon, once a notorious rowdy, was now a respectable young man, formal at the moment in his coat and cuffs. He seemed to take the inspection in good spirits, bowing when Mr. Edwards motioned him into a chair. He took a deep breath and said, happily, "Sir, I wish to join the church."

Mr. Edwards lowered his eyes. Could the drought finally be ending? At the height of the great awakening, he had welcomed hundreds to the church in Suffield in a single day. Now, for four years in Northampton, not one soul. Not since the young man before him had played leapfrog while on trial for abusing midwives' books. He was almost afraid to believe it. He felt a buried tension begin to ease, then a rise of fear about what might come next.

He stayed silent long enough that Simeon sat forward in his chair, squashing his hat as it slipped sideways in his lap, and said, "I am to be married."

"Ah." Mr. Edwards wished that he didn't have to do this with Simeon, with his stubborn family and their public sins. Although everyone knew he considered it well past time for Simeon's sister Martha to be married, this was not about the Roots. Bracing himself, he said, "Simeon, I have come to believe that members of the visible church in complete standing should be, in profession and in the eyes of the church's Christian judgment, godly persons."

Simeon nodded as if this seemed obvious. "Godly persons. Right. Of course."

The young man was not getting the point. Mr. Edwards tried again. "All manner of persons may observe the Lord's day, worship, and pray that they might be led to give themselves over completely to Christ. But only those who have actually done so and," Mr. Edwards spoke slowly, "publicly professed to it with their mouths"—he paused—"should be full members of the church."

Simeon stopped nodding. "Publicly professed to it with their mouths. Sir, what does that mean?"

Mr. Edwards was tempted to catechize Simeon in the old way, prompting as needed, then go find Sarah and spend the rest of the afternoon rubbing his wife's feet with vinegar and rosewater while reading aloud from the Canticles. He had never idled away a day like that, but he was strongly tempted.

His conscience would not allow it.

"You'll need to make a profession," he said to Simeon. "A public profession of godliness."

Simeon turned red. "That's not how it's done."

Mr. Edwards kept his gaze steady on Simeon's face. "I am your minister, charged with seeing to the good of your soul. I have prayed and studied about this, searched scriptures and examined books that defend the admission of persons to sacrament without a profession of saving faith, but I no longer believe them to be correct."

Simeon muttered under his breath. "What about your dead grandfather? Did you happen to read him?"

Mr. Edwards ignored that. He knew he was asking something that no one in the town had been required to do within living memory. Even extreme states arrived at under the influence of an awakening had never required a declaration of faith before the whole congregation. He himself had followed his grandfather Stoddard's practice in the matter for more than twenty years. Until this day. "You only need say heartily, based on inward assent, that you wish to lead a life of true godliness. Can you say that, sir?"

Simeon stood up. He clutched his hat, as had most of the youth who had sought counsel or disgraced themselves before Mr. Edwards over the years. Mr. Edwards regarded Simeon as he stood there, jaw clenched tight, wanting to be churched and married, already thinking ahead, no doubt, to the baptism of his children. Simeon was miles ahead of Elisha Hawley, who might yet be brought by church discipline to become Simeon's brother by marriage. Still, it was not enough.

Simeon's lip trembled. "I can say that I wish to be godly, Mr. Edwards, and say it with the knowledge of my heart. I could say that, sir, but it seems to me that I should not have to make a profession to join the church. Nobody else has. My own father never did. It doesn't sit right."

He did not turn to go after he spoke, but stood there, shaking. Mr. Edwards, sensing an opening, stood as well. "I could write a model profession for you. You could amend it to suit your own experiences, as long as it kept the crucial elements."

"I need to think on that." Simeon took his leave.

Over the next several days Mr. Edwards wrote and refined four professions, all variations on:

> I hope, I do truly find a heart to give up myself wholly to God, according to the tenor of that covenant of grace which was sealed in my baptism, and to walk in a way of that obedience to all the commandments of God, which the covenant of grace requires, as long as I live.

When he read this to Simeon the following week, the young man barely listened. He stood like a rock before the desk with his hat still on and the study door wide open. After Mr. Edwards finished reading the profession, Simeon looked him dead in the eye, and said, "Sir, I've spoken to my family and examined my conscience. My answer is no."

Elisha, sitting at his portable desk at a small table in his room, unfolded a letter, then leaned to scratch Delilah's belly where she lay sprawled by the fire. He had relented and brought her inside at the first snow. There was a new shirt from a Northampton seamstress draped over the back of his chair and three pounds of Rebekah's butter, still frozen from the cold trip in a soldier's knapsack, gleaming in pale balls in a bowl on the table. Elisha scraped one of the balls with his fingernail and dangled his hand for Delilah to lick as he read what Joseph had to say about his upcoming church trial.

> *Were I in the case, I should have no regard at all to anything they pretended to do authoritatively in the particular of matrimony, nor would I attempt to labour to prove anything against her, since the burden of proof beyond all dispute lies wholly on either the woman or the church as they are respectively considered as acting.*

Joseph wrote that he was confident that the church couldn't enforce matrimony without proof of absolute virginity on the part of Martha Root prior to her liaison with Elisha. Enticement would have to be proven, and Joseph thought that there was a case that Elisha, not Martha, had been enticed. It was to their advantage that Martha, her father, and mother had now all declared themselves against marriage.

Delilah, who had sat up to address the butter on Elisha's finger, gave his knuckle a light nip, and looked up at him, wanting more.

"No," he said severely, pointing at the floor.

> *All therefore I at present would do (let the church take what course they would) should be to offer them a proper confession, and rest the matter. As to matrimony, I would do what I knew was right in conscience and before God, if there was anything that was particularly damning that nobody else knew of. I am, sir, your most affectionate brother.*
> *Joseph Hawley*

Delilah gave up on Elisha, and curled with her nose toward the fire. He tried to consider whether there was anything particularly damning between him and Martha Root which was unknown to others, but all he

came up with was the memory of laughing after meeting while she gave
herself a snout like a pig.

After the sermon one gray January morning, Sarah let the children go
back to the house to get the noon meal on the table. She thought to
have a few moments to herself in the woods. The ground was ridged
and frozen, but the snow was not yet deep enough to swallow her feet.
She craved the peace of it. As she crunched past the back of the meeting
house horse shed, she heard men talking inside.

"The great Stoddard never would have invited him here if he had
known."

"Of course not. He never thought his own grandson would betray
him."

"Betray us all. Who would?"

Sarah slowed, taken aback by the venom in the voices.

"He never would have dared if Colonel Stoddard were still alive."

"Knew what side his bread was buttered on. The Colonel was the
making of him."

She froze as the other men sniggered. The air smelled of pipe smoke.

"Kept it all a secret, his so-called change of heart. He despises us,
that's what it is. Wants to keep our babies from baptism."

"He's a radical. Next thing, he'll be building a bonfire and burning
our clothing."

"He almost ruined our young men. Everyone knows it. Shamed
them over those bad books in front of the whole congregation, instead
of talking to any of them as might have a problem in private, as would
have been decent."

"Thinks he can look into a man and see his soul. Only God can
do that."

Sarah's face was hot in cold air as the voices went on, getting
louder and talking over each other in their eagerness to spread poison
about her husband. They must be malcontents, she thought. Bartletts or
Roots, although one loud voice sounded a lot like Sheriff Pomeroy. She

could have opened a court case by walking around the shed to see whom she must accuse, but found that she had no stomach for it. The best it could bring would be more floggings. Besides, she didn't want to know who had sat through the morning sermon with such bitterness. Feeling sick, she turned away from the shed and the woods, toward home.

That night, she and Rose missed evening prayers to help a cow struggling with a breech calf. Once it was safely delivered, she sat, exhausted, on a bale of hay, watching the cow lick the mess of birth off the little one's trembling back. She tried to offer up her mind to be licked clean of the contempt in those men's voices. She missed Saul, who might have sat with her. Rose had already gone back to the house. Before the calf was half-clean, Sarah got up, washed her own hands in a bucket of rainwater she had set near the fire to fend off a skin of ice, then went inside to find Mr. Edwards.

He was writing at his desk next to a stub of candle, so that the shelves and cubbyholes filled with his papers looked like so many small dens rising before him in the flickering light. She approached quietly and drew up a chair. She didn't speak at first, but sat there noticing how much she still smelled of hay, muck, and blood. He nodded at her and kept writing, finishing a thought.

When he looked up, she said, "They are starting to talk as if they hate us."

His face crumpled as if he were a small boy. "Who?"

She thought for a moment. Elihu Parsons had been coming to the house to see Sally, and Timothy Dwight, whose whole family had stayed friendly, for Mary. Esther had a flock of admirers. But, still. "Almost everyone."

She drew her chair closer and told him all she had heard.

Mary Hulbert kept her head down when she came into the study, too shy to glance at Rose as she shut the door. Mr. Edwards was folding paper into the size he liked for writing and didn't stop as he gestured with his elbow toward the chair. She was the daughter of a man who owned a saw mill, a fat young woman wearing a new collar and her best gown. The whole town was more or less openly against him, and they had been bringing attacks to his study alone and in committees. He wasn't afraid of Mary Hulbert, or of any of them, but he wasn't looking forward to the conversation. "Miss Hulbert. What can I do for you?"

She almost tripped as she sat down, but, once she was settled in her chair, he was struck with the intensity of her silence. Finally, she said, "Sir, if you think it fitting, I would like to join the church."

He stopped folding and regarded her closely. This was unexpected, and it was brave. Simeon Root and Sarah King, having posted their banns and entered their intentions with the town clerk, had been duly married, but Simeon had not joined the church. People talked about what had happened between Mr. Edwards and Simeon as if it had been a hanging. Mary Hulbert fiddled with the strings of her cap. Mr. Edwards turned his chair all the way around to face her. "Do you wish to make a public profession?"

She folded her hands over her belly and said, "I will. I want to." The crackling of the fire was louder than her voice, so he had to strain to hear her. "If it won't make me the center of an uproar."

Mr. Edwards kept one hand on his desk to steady himself as he began to talk with Mary Hulbert about grace. It had been too long.

He brought Mary Hulbert's case to the church committee. They refused her.

"No," said Sheriff Pomeroy, color rising in his face. "We want no precedent of anyone having to stand up before you to be nakedly judged in order that they may join our church."

"Ah." Mr. Edwards spoke coolly, ignoring the bile rising in his throat. They were willing to risk a young woman's soul just to spite him. "Then perhaps you might wish to hear me preach about the nature and foundations of my position, since it is clearly being misunderstood."

"No preaching about this." The sheriff was eighty, but he bellowed like the son of a blacksmith. "Not one word."

Susan Stinson

"It's your pulpit." Sarah stopped stitching a tear in their counterpane to stare at him. "You choose what to preach." The counterpane covered her lap and spilled off onto the floor.

He picked up the new goose quill from the windowsill, where it had been hardening. He took up his penknife, cut it down to length, and removed most of the feathers without speaking. The silence tormented Sarah, but there was no way to make him speak before he was ready.

Finally, he said, "I am satisfied that it is best, at present, not to preach on the controversy. The people are in so great a ferment that there would be no opportunity to be heard with any degree of calmness."

She finished the mend and tied off her thread. This was her nightmare coming true. "If they expel us, where will we go?"

He had no answer. She cut her thread with a bite before he thought to offer the knife.

She watched him grit his teeth in the pulpit before he began to preach about the threshing, grinding, and baking of bread. It was a subject that she knew much more about than he did, but the point was that it was not—at least, not directly—about the controversy between him and the people sitting stone-faced before him. As she listened, she noticed Mary Hulbert crying on her bench. Sarah's eyes sought her own children. The older girls were composed, but it tore at her to see her young ones so miserable, sitting among people who would no longer greet their family on the street. Timothy was chewing his nails. He had, she knew, bitten them down to the quick. When she raised her eyebrows at him, he drew his hands away from his mouth with a clumsy alacrity that reminded her of his father. He sat on his hands. She pressed hers to her face, slapped by grief in front of the townspeople, who stared without mercy beneath the thrumming of her husband's persistent voice.

Bathsheba watched Rose coming up King Street as she sat on a bucket and sorted dried herbs on a rock near the town well. She had been

266

brutally lonely all winter, so, as the days began to warm, she found herself coming up with work she could do in public places where people might pass the time of day with her. The Pomeroys hadn't given her trouble about it. In fact, the Sheriff, always a bit of a gossip, had been listening with more than the usual eagerness to stories she brought back from the well. She knew he was keeping close watch on the mood of the town. She tried to slant anything she told him toward calm, but he always turned up the flame. "Rose!" she called. "How are your hands?"

"Much better." Rose carried her bucket with a piece of wool that Bathsheba had given her padding the handle. She was doing almost all of the errands in town for the Edwardses now, since Sarah and the girls preferred to stay home rather than face the hostile silence at Pomeroy's store. When Rose reached Bathsheba, she set her own empty bucket on the ground.

"Let me see." Bathsheba took one of her hands and turned it over to look at the cuts across her palms from where the handle of the bucket had been slicing in. They were scabbing up. "Good." Bathsheba liked Rose. She didn't have the energy to waste being mad at her for not being Leah. "Did you ever hear anything about that minister up in Northfield? Benjamin Doolittle?"

For somebody who worked at a house crammed with news and visitors, Rose missed a lot. Some people thought she was a snob because she didn't seem to bother to listen. "Who?"

Bathsheba shook some sage leaves free of webs, catching bits of herb as it crumbled in her skirt. "They say he freed his slave Abijah Prince because Abijah served in the militia during the war."

Rose twirled her bucket on its bottom on the muddy ground. Watching, Bathsheba was reminded of how young she was, making a bucket dance, barely attending to things she needed to know. "At one point, this same Reverend Mr. Doolittle was under attack from people in his church for all sorts of reasons. They even criticized his slave-owning as unchristian."

Rose stopped playing with her bucket and stared at Bathsheba. "They did?"

Bathsheba gave her the bad news, dusting sage from her fingers. "Mr. Edwards was ready to step up with scripture to defend him. Said slavery was in the Bible." She took a breath. "Leah told me."

Rose tilted her bucket so that it stuck on one edge in the mud. She shook her head. One of the things Bathsheba liked about Rose was that she didn't talk when there was nothing to say. There was an unsurprised silence long enough to let Bathsheba tie her cleaned sage into a square of linen and spread a gritty tangle of rosemary before her on the warm rock while Rose pushed the bottom of her bucket deeper into the mud.

When Rose finally spoke, she gave a sideways look at Bathsheba. "Do you think Mr. Edwards might have freed Saul, too, if he had made it back to Northampton?"

Bathsheba realized that she had been fishing to hear the girl say Saul's name. Saul and Leah. She missed them both so much. "Weren't you listening to what I just said? The evidence is against it."

Rose pulled her bucket loose from the ground. "What do you really think, Bathsheba? You knew him better than anybody. Did he drown, or did he go?"

Bathsheba, who had been wracking herself with this question, shook a few sprigs of rosemary clean of dirt and wrapped them into a tiny bundle. "Saul didn't say he was going, not to me. But I think he carved himself a cabin out of a single piece of pine and polished it so that it shines like honey in a dark part of the woods." She looked at Rose, who was just a little older than Leah had been when she had been hauled to Northampton on the back of the minister's horse, but Rose was listening with a skeptical squint that Leah never had. City girl. Bathsheba shook her head. "Can't know either way, so might as well believe."

"Uh-huh." Rose's gaze had drifted back to the road. Bathsheba turned around to see Joab coming in his checked vest. She had noticed him circling the well anytime Rose was drawing water. She pressed her bundle of rosemary into the girl's hand. "Crush it a little. It's named for you, after all."

Rose, who was no fool, broke a few leaves and cupped the crumbs in her palm. "Thank you."

Feeling old, Bathsheba murmured, "Let him smell your fingers." Rose smiled and strolled closer to the well.

Joseph walked into the wigmaker's shop for a shave and found Seth Pomeroy in the chair with the top of his head lathered up, waving a piece of paper at him and calling, "Hawley!"

The barber nicked his skin. "Please, Major. Stay still."

Seth rolled his eyes while blood trickled over his forehead. "Read this."

"All right, sir." Joseph took the paper and sat down to wait. "Your wig will never fit right if you don't let the man do his work."

Seth snorted, and Joseph started reading while his old comrade-in-arms watched him with most of his head swathed in a towel. It was yet another round in the war of the letters that had been shooting back and forth between Mr. Edwards and various committees ever since he had told Simeon Root that he had to make a profession if he wanted to join the church. Since Joseph was as much a grandson of Mr. Stoddard as Mr. Edwards was, he had been the object of a lot of attention from prominent persons in the town. He would have liked to think that the cordial way men twenty years his senior were tipping their hats had more to do with the fact that he had argued his first case before judges in their red robes at the court of common pleas than with an accident of birth, but he knew it wasn't true. If he chose to take a stand on the controversy, his words would carry weight. He knew what Seth wanted of him.

Mr. Baker started working his bristle brush on Seth's chin while Joseph read Mr. Edwards's letter:

> *I, the subscriber, do hereby signify and declare to such as it may concern, that if my people will wait until the book I am preparing relative to the admission of members into the church is published . . .*

"A book!" Joseph exclaimed. "A letter isn't enough anymore? Not even a pamphlet?"

"He's arrogant." Seth waved off the barber and glared from beneath the towel. "You know most of the ministers in the county oppose him. We've got good Stoddardians around here." He pulled away the towel and lowered his voice. "It won't do Elisha any harm when he has to go before the council if feeling against Mr. Edwards is running high." He beckoned the barber back to his work.

"Mmm," said Joseph. Elisha's case was coming up again in June. A council of ministers would decide once and for all whether Mr. Edwards and the Northampton church (in name, at least) could force Elisha to marry Martha Root and take up raising their two-year-old. Of course, Joseph wanted every advantage in Elisha's case. The problem was, he wasn't convinced that, in his position on making a profession of faith before joining the church, that Mr. Edwards was entirely wrong. He kept reading.

> . . . I will resign the ministry over this church, if the church desires it,
> after they have had the opportunity pretty generally to read my said
> book, and after they have first asked advice of a council mutually chosen,
> and followed their advice . . .

"Resign," whispered Joseph. He had no idea what he felt.

When the barber lifted his razor, Seth said, "We've got him where we want him."

When Joseph came into the house on Pudding Lane after his shave, Rebekah looked up from her candle molds and sniffed the air. "Lavender."

Joseph, who enjoyed the barber's scented soaps, nodded nervously. Rebekah had accused Joseph of playing the peacock last week when she had caught him checking the fit of his stockings before he had set out to Brookfield to see Mercy. Mercy was mild and yielding of manner, which Joseph found distinctly pleasant. It was traditional that if the eldest son in a household should marry, his widowed mother, if she had no plans to form a union with a new husband of her own, should quietly retreat to a spare corner and turn the running of the establishment over to the new bride. Joseph suspected that, in the case of his mother and the house she had ruled since she had married his father, such accommodation might not happen smoothly.

There was a knock at the kitchen door. Rebekah answered to find a soldier carrying a knapsack and dressed for the road. "My leave is up, Madame, and I'm heading back to the fort. You asked me to stop by for a letter?"

"Oh, yes." said Rebekah, leaving her candles to harden. They had not heard from Elisha for months. They had arranged for a local yeoman to plow his land, since he wasn't back in Northampton in time to do it. It was irritating to see soldiers home from the fort with no word from him. "Joseph here has one he is just finishing up. Have some grapes?"

Joseph hurried into the study. He found the letter and picked up his pen. Half listening to the talk from the kitchen, he filled Elisha in on the juicy details of the conflict between Mr. Edwards and the congregation. He realized that the soldier and Rebekah were pushing back their chairs and tromping out toward the buttery. Rebekah must have enlisted the man's help in turning some of the larger wheels of cheese, so he'd be tied up for a while.

Joseph sat very still for a moment, then began to write about something he'd been a little afraid to say:

True religion, my dear brother, and thorough religion, is of the pleasantest aspect of everything this side of heaven. It is the most reasonable of all things.

After he wrote that last sentence, Joseph flushed and gave a guilty glance over his shoulder. The religion Mr. Edwards had shown them was many things, but reasonable was not one of them. God's ways were not subject to being grasped by human beings.

What Joseph was writing tilted toward apostasy, except in the surprising schools of thought he had discovered in Cambridge. It made his heart race to commit such thoughts to paper. Elisha, he knew, would not condemn him, his own moral decisions being what they were. Joseph pushed on.

> *It don't consist in abstruse nice notions and speculations. But in that which, if unprejudiced, informed sense of humankind says is right . . .*

He wanted his brother to know that he could have the happiness of religion without submitting himself to the capricious dictates of an inscrutable God who would toy with lives as he pleased without any relationship to sense or reason as understood by the human mind. Mr. Edwards, in all his brilliance—and Joseph never doubted that— used logic and measured argument along with Bible-fueled poetry to draw from the scriptures a picture of an utterly sovereign God to whom all creation belonged, and to whom human beings were called and compelled to turn over every aspect of their lives.

Joseph took a deep breath and wrote:

> *We are thereby required to believe nothing but what is supported by good evidence, and in no other manner than the evidence will avail.*

Joseph was giddy with the idea of a world that made sense. All he and Elisha had to do was to examine the evidence and try hard enough. They did not have to be trapped, like their father, in torment and doubt.

The soldier was loaded down with butter when he left the house.

Parched and sweating from riding through a June drought, Mr. Edwards reached the meeting house in Portsmouth so late that he walked in on the Reverend Mr. Moody winging a sermon in his place. The journey had been very taxing. The man Mr. Edwards set off with had been so terrified by stories of drought conditions in the country they were entering that he had turned back, with Mr. Edwards trotting beside him, using all of his powers of oratory to persuade him to keep going. He was glad, now, to be traveling on alone.

He walked quietly to the pulpit and stood behind Mr. Moody, scanning the congregation for his daughter Mary's face as the old minister praised him to the skies without having noticed that he had arrived. Mary, who was visiting relatives in Portsmouth, seemed fervent as she prayed, but she gave him several discreet glances, full of affection, but perhaps a bit worldly, or even amused. He was resolving to speak with her about the state of her soul, when Mr. Moody finished, turned, and jumped like a squirrel at the sight of him.

"Brother Edwards," he said, recovering, "I didn't intend to flatter you to your face, but there's one thing I'll tell you: they say that your wife is going to heaven, by a shorter road than yourself."

Mr. Edwards stared at Mr. Moody, who lost his joviality to a cringe. He saw Mary shaking her head at him, and it crossed his mind that he might be acting a bit rude. Still, muzzled in his own pulpit, he did not have it in him to joke when it was time to preach. He had traveled too far, and, besides, Sarah would hate having her religious experiences remarked on in a smiling way. He bowed, stepped up to the pulpit, and did what he had come to do.

He was very glad to see old friends in Portsmouth and to have his talk with Mary, but he didn't linger many days before he went along to Boston to check with the printer regarding the progress of his book about the theology of the controversy in Northampton. He had written it in just two months, defining words like "saint" and "Christian" with exacting precision. When he had worked his arguments with great thoroughness, he articulated twenty objections to his own position, and answered every one. Still, something was missing. He thought it had to do more with the temper of the people than with theological arguments, but he could no more address that than he could bring back his grandfather to ask his advice. Some things were beyond him.

Meanwhile, Northampton people were trying to find another minister to answer his arguments. It would be, no doubt, an escalation of the letter war, with the material welfare of his family and the souls of his congregation at stake. He addressed the possibility at the end of the book:

> *If anyone opposes me from the press, I desire he would attend to the true state of the question, and endeavor fairly to take off the force of each argument, by answering them directly and distinctly, with calm and close reasoning: avoiding (as much as may be) both dogmatic assertion and passionate reflection.*

He doubted that this would happen, but a man could hope.

People in Northampton were getting more and more restless, so he was eager for them to have the book. He met in Boston with the Reverend Mr. Thomas Foxcroft, who had written an appendix, and was proofreading, collecting advance subscriptions to help cover the costs of printing, and taking pains to help. Mr. Edwards put his arm awkwardly around Mr. Foxcroft's shoulder and urged him to finish with all possible speed.

He set out for home on Thursday late afternoon, riding alone under a free and plentiful, drought-ending rain. He had promised his people when last he preached that he would return to them after two Sabbaths and was determined not to leave them to be made destitute or unruly by any further absence on his part. He had not been sorry, it was true, to be gone on other important business when the council of local ministers gathered at his meeting house for the last hearing in the matter of matrimony between Elisha Hawley and Martha Root. The wayward young father was to be absent, as well. The hearing would be over by now, and he knew that he needed to be in Northampton to face his detractors in the congregation for the sake of both his reputation and their souls.

The rain would not relent and the going was slow. He was riding a horse that he had exchanged with friends for his own on another trip months ago, when this horse had been fresh and his own horse had needed rest. Now the loaned horse was tired. He didn't reach the house of his friends until three in the morning, when he roused one of the sons to send for his horse. Mr. Edwards slept briefly while the boy got dressed and went out; then he drank rum and coffee to warm himself in the dark kitchen. The mother of the family gave him bread and cold sliced pork for the road.

The boy finally tromped back into the kitchen, shaking rain from his hair. As daylight later confirmed, the horse was skinny and dull-eyed from having been kept so long in pastures burnt with drought. As he mounted and waved to his friends (who stood in the kitchen door, lit from behind; it was raining too hard to keep a lantern burning in the open air), Mr. Edwards felt the discouragement of his horse to be even more profound than that of the travel-worn beast he had been relieved to return to his owners. They trudged along with rain plastering his already soaked great coat to his leather vest and breeches, which smelled so strongly of wet animal that he began to feel joined to his horse, both of them exhausted already with so many miles to go.

The day came on with a diffusion of gray light. The trees swayed back and forth like the tongues of bells beating to draw the people in to wait for God in his house. Mr. Edwards, urging the horse on with his heels as he pulled the collar of his great coat higher to try to shelter his face from the rain, remembered watching the bell from underneath when he was a child in his father's church. His thoughts covered more ground than his horse. He found them drifting to young Brainerd hacking and coughing his way across so much rough country. Brainerd had described dragging himself out of a near deathbed and barely managing to stand long enough to offer communion. Mr. Edwards, raising first one long arm and then the other over his head to try to stretch out his aching back, thought of Brainerd's brother at the mission now, and the hopeful reports he had sent of awakenings among the people there. Mr. Edwards had shipped the newly published volume of Brainerd's journals to his correspondents in Scotland and had heard back from them about awakenings in those lands, as well. Even in bedeviled Northampton, there were stirrings among the young people, and, now, not just the sawmill owner's daughter but even a few more were waiting to join the church, professions and all, when for so many years not one person had stepped forward. The fight between him and the congregation worked for the glory of God in this way. If only the church committee would allow it.

The thought of true Christians praying together across expanses of rocky, muddy land which took almost more than he and his horse had in them to cross, and, praying even farther, across the troubled oceans which he had never attempted to traverse, brought him comfort.

The rain which had been pooling in his collar spilled over and soaked the back of his neck. He pulled his great coat closer and went on.

He met with a party of strangers and was glad of the company. Their pace seemed to help forward his horse. They were heading to Worcester by way of Marlborough, and, encouraged by them, Mr. Edwards reached Worcester that night without being much exposed to the malignant influence of the evening air. He dreamed of groping through cold muck in the swamp in East Windsor with the young boy enslaved by his family who had explored with him there. His feeling as the dream receded upon waking was that he was pulling away from something both terribly troubled and dear to him.

The next day, again much hindered by rain, he pushed his horse so hard as to nearly ruin her but did not make it home for Sabbath, after all.

On Monday afternoon, his horse finally came limping down King Street with her head hanging low, so far gone that not even the close proximity of a known barn with its hay and shelter could quicken her pace. The sun was out and, as a bristly black bug hunkered down on the edge of the saddle, Mr. Edwards was surprised to be hard struck with love for Northampton.

The road was empty. Everyone must have left their work for a meeting. He was sick to death of endless, quarrelsome meetings. Now he spoke to the town itself in an intimate, formal way, as if preaching to the well, the courthouse, meeting house hill, and to all the people who used the tannery and the brickyard and whose horses scattered the road with manure. Tired and dirty from his days of hard travel, he slipped off his own suffering horse, and, walking beside her, he said aloud:

"How could I leave you whom I so love? How could I abandon you except in the grip of pure, clean fury? I am right, of course. I have been right. I must be right. You have turned against the clear instructions of the holy word. You are taking something clean and making it dirty, muddled, shabby, useless. Everything I've offered you, all my teaching, striving, and love, you squeeze, wrench, and twist until it drips like rain."

His voice was soft and shook with anger. He stopped speaking, but the voice became louder in his head as he walked in the rutted road, which did not answer him. He broke into wordless vision, which, he knew—always—was rising from the words and mind inside him and was not anything that he was seeing with his bodily eyes.

He remembered moments when the people of Northampton had risen, when he and they rose together, when they had been fainting, weeping, writhing, or lying still on the ground. They had filled with the spirit, the holy spirit, and it had been as if their bodies spoke without words, and maybe it had been their bodies speaking, the natural, the base, not the true heat and light rising in them as it rose in his own Sarah. Her body as much as broke the feeble laws of nature, expressed such great piety that it seemed that she could float over the rough wood floor in their hallway and levitate into the parlor—in a household full of children, servants, and visiting students of theology, mind, a house full of witnesses—rise and float into the formal room of greeting guests.

She had tasted the honey, dripped with honey. She knew the holy spirit, knew sweetness. She hadn't just read about it, touched the jar. Her whole soul was sticky with it, and her shoes fell from her feet, dropped to the floor. Her feet were bare and sticky, and there were crumbs, she was dabbled with crumbs. They looked like bread, remnants, crusts, ordinary leavings from an ordinary meal, but there was a light from them, and she was filled with sweetness, sweating honey, honey dripping from her pores, honey dabbing her forehead and capturing her hair, honey making her simple clothes darken from within. Her eyes were closed, but honey dripped down her cheeks like tears. He could look below her and see many slow viscous drops falling from her body as she floated waist high above the floor, reclining with the firm dignity of the righteous dead, but she, his wife, his consort, was, of course, alive.

The drops from her body fell slowly toward the floor, but as they fell, they spread and lightened and dissipated until they were no longer gold but took on the color of the air, thinning in slow curls of light so that there was nothing of them left to hit the floor. In vision, he slowly reached out and let his fingers pass beneath her to catch a drop before it was lost. He tested his fingers with his mind's tongue. The taste was there. Sarah knew honey. He might doubt himself, but she could bear anything. He was sure of it.

He was leaning heavily against his horse, but he had reached the forted-in house. He took one more step and fumbled with the gate as the horse breathed heavily into the back of his coat. He opened it to Timothy and Eunice chasing chickens while Esther gave instructions from the kitchen door. They ran to him, calling their mother. Refuge. He hugged both of the little ones at the same time, while they blinked in mild surprise, then kissed Esther before he led the horse to drink. The bristled bug dropped from the saddle and lit on the edge of the trough. He saw it fly before the rush of water spilled by a thrust of the horse's great-lipped mouth as Timothy and Eunice talked over each other to tell him that Northampton had finally gotten some rain.

Chapter 22
July – November 1749

When he walked into the kitchen, he said, "My horse is nearly dead of thirst. What happened at the hearing?"

Sarah cleared the children out of the kitchen and insisted on getting food in front of him before they talked. While he faced cold tripe and chopped greens alone at the table, she scoured the brass skillet, both feet very much on the ground. He found that strangely comforting. Ignoring the tripe, he said, "If you're trying to protect me from bad news, it's too late for that."

"Some days I wish that we'd never left New Haven." She set the skillet in the fire to dry and put the written findings next to his plate. "The council sent a runner with this. It's not good."

He read aloud.

> "On the question of whether it appeared to be the duty of Elisha Hawley to marry Martha Root with whom he had been guilty of fornication and who lay a child now living to him as the father, the council resolves in the negative."

He looked at her. "That's preposterous."

Sarah came over to the table and took a forkful of his greens. Her hands were red and chapped. "I know."

He continued to read.

> "However, we are far from determining that Lieutenant Hawley is not bound in conscience to marry Martha Root. Tho, it don't appear to

*us in so clear a light that we care to say that it is his duty. We therefore
hold it must be left for the determination of his own conscience, and
upon the whole we recommend it to the first Church of Northampton to
receive Mr. Hawley (upon his making a penitent confession of the sin of
fornication) to their Christian charity and fellowship again."*

Mr. Edwards threw the paper onto his plate. "Lukewarm squirming."

Sarah snatched it back, already stained brown and green. "There's no call to waste paper." He stared at his plate while she put the findings on a stool then sat down beside him. "Or food." She handed him the fork. "You're still married yourself, Mr. Edwards. Give thanks."

He ate.

The next day, Martha Root leaned into steam over the wash kettle in the yard while her two-year-old sat on the ground turning the pages of an old newspaper without ripping them. It was too hot to be making soap, but Martha wanted the smell of lye to clear her brain. She had been thinking of nothing but the hearing for too many days. She hoped that it was finally all over and hated that she couldn't be sure. She had been under the scrutiny of the town for so long. She looked down at Anne, who was delicately tasting a corner of the paper, newsprint smeared on her lips.

"Don't," Martha said, stirring the pot with a stick.

Anne nodded and offered her the paper with an encouraging air, as if the only sensible thing for her mother to do would be to sit in dirt, pretend to read year-old Boston news, and perhaps try to catch a grasshopper if one should come along. Martha was tempted.

"Martha!" They both looked up to see a figure coming across the pasture, lifting a fistful of skins. Simeon, Martha thought. She straightened up and gave him a wave. Still not a member of the church, her brother had built a small house on the far edge of the Root family woodlot for himself and his wife. He stopped by often to do chores for her mother or bring a treat for Anne.

As the man came toward them down the hill, though, she could see that he had a limp and a dog at his heels. And a uniform. It wasn't

Simeon. She knew who it was before he called again across the grass. "These are for you."

She stopped stirring the lye. Dear God, he couldn't suddenly be feeling bound in conscience to marry her, could he? She despised herself for knowing exactly how the findings had phrased it, but she did. Martha had wanted Elisha, once, but none of the rest of it: not marriage, not the trials and hearings, not even, at first, her lost Esther and her very present Anne, who jumped up and ran toward him and the dog with all her might. Anne was wild for dogs.

Loving her daughters fiercely, both the living and the dead, Martha shouted, "Anne! Stop!"

Anne paused and turned toward her. Elisha kept coming with his dog and his skins. Martha took a deep breath of hot lye until her eyes teared up and her chest burned. "Wait," she said to Anne, who sat down on the grass, staring with longing toward the little black dog. Martha put her stick beside the pot and put a stone down on the newspaper so it wouldn't blow all over the pasture. Then she walked slowly to stand beside Anne, watching Elisha come. The limp looked painful.

When he was close enough that she could see that his expression was both reckless and abashed, he said, "Rabbit. I do a little trapping at the fort, and thought that the little girl might need a winter coat." He must have been watching her face, too, because then he said the name. "Anne."

Anne got up when she heard it and held on to Martha's leg, looking shyly over her shoulder. Martha picked her up. She was in no mood to mince words. "I didn't see you at the hearing."

"No." He was next to them now, holding one of the skins out to Anne, who touched the fur with her finger. "Joseph advised me not to come, but I couldn't wait to hear the decision." He watched Anne petting the rabbit skin while Delilah sniffed around the fire. Martha felt acrid inside and out. Joseph had strutted at the hearing.

"Anne," Elisha said again, following her eyes. "That's Delilah." The dog glanced up and gave a brisk wag. The little girl blushed a little, her hand buried in fur.

Martha looked away toward the edge of the woods. "You're hurt."

"Not badly. I'm getting raisins and currants from Mother for a curative. There is nothing but shortages at the fort. No raisins, no peas, no rum. No pay for the men." Anne laid her cheek against the fur. They both let her. "Still, it suits me to be a soldier." He looked at her. "You can't have had an easy time, yourself."

Martha put Anne down, keeping a hand on her head. The little girl let go of the skin with no fuss, smiling a little as Delilah raised her leg on a stump. Martha shrugged at Elisha. "They insult me from carts and shun me in church," she said.

He looked pained. It would be like him to feel his conscience now that the hearings were done. Martha felt panicked. "My family treats me well. And the money helps." She didn't say the word *bastard*, never in front of Anne, but others did. "What is it that you want from us?"

Elisha put the rabbit skins on the ground. Delilah came and stood next to them, tail up, on alert. "Martha, I never meant you to come to harm."

She narrowed her eyes. "Well, harm's been done."

He nodded. He knew that. "And the baby. The one who is gone. I am sorry."

She had nothing to say to this. She could not stand it if she cried.

He looked at his feet, then at Anne, who was holding on to Martha's skirt. When he looked at Martha's face again, he said, "I am thinking of Elizabeth Pomeroy. One day, I hope, as a wife. I wanted to tell you myself."

A Pomeroy. Of course. Who else for a Hawley? Received by the church or not, perhaps it no longer mattered to a man like Elisha. He had bestirred himself to tell her this, after years of nothing but hearings and absence. Martha was glad that the hot lye was out of arm's reach. Spattering it in his face with a stick would do no one good. She said, "I make no more claims on you, Elisha. Wed who you will."

As Elisha and Martha stared at each other, Anne let go of her mother's skirt and reached for the dog. Delilah ducked her head and looked at Elisha as Anne grabbed a handful of her fur. Martha pulled her daughter back. Elisha whistled Delilah away.

"Keep the skins," he said, turning to follow as his dog sprang back up the hill.

One August night, Joseph sat down at his father's desk to finish reading Mr. Edwards's new book. A friend had brought twenty copies from Boston just as talk began to spread of acting against Mr. Edwards without waiting for anything else the man might have to say. There were those who felt that they had been listening to him too long as it was. Joseph, who suspected half the town of holding grudges against Mr. Edwards from that business with the midwives' books five years back, had been staying away from the acrimonious meetings, where respectable men were working themselves up into more and more bitterness against their minister. Joseph was all for just insurrection, but he had family loyalty, as well. He could hear Rebekah pulling irons in and out of the fire and smell the hot linen as she ironed his shirts in the kitchen.

He took off his wig and slipped a silk-tasseled cap over his shaved head. It was, perhaps, too hot for a cap, but sweet Mercy Lyman had made it for him, so the warmth radiated inward. He picked up the book, glancing at the title: *An Humble Inquiry into the Rules of the Word of God, concerning the Qualifications Requisite to a Compleat Standing and Full Communion in the Visible Christian Church.* Joseph, who heard it all in Mr. Edwards's dry voice, rolled his eyes, as he did every time he looked at it. The title page included a rather lengthy quotation in Latin, which was not inviting to many readers in the town, and a brief quote from the book of Job:

> *Behold now I have opened my mouth: my words shall be of the uprightness of my heart.*

Joseph was sure that most people would not read *An Humble Inquiry.* Not all of it, or most of it. They would, perhaps, be quieted for some months, though, as they tried to or intended to or thought about whether they would. He himself had been at it a week, drilling through Mr. Edwards's strict definitions and logic, thinking about how he would counter troublesome propositions and winning every argument in his head. He had beat Mr. Edwards at Elisha's hearing; in the man's absence, it was true, but still. It was exhilarating now to take issue with things he had received as sacred truths, and to apply reason to beliefs he had been taught to accept without expecting to understand. It was as if he had the chance to rebel and defend tradition, both, but more than anything else, he felt enormous pleasure at engaging his cousin's mind as an equal, rather than as a deferential boy, the recipient of charity, studying at the family hearth.

His face was sweating. He took off Mercy's cap, after all, then turned to the twenty objections Mr. Edwards had formulated to his own main argument, matched with the twenty answers he provided; each one, it seemed to Joseph, more impatient than the last. He read objection number ten:

> *Objection: The natural consequence of the doctrine which has been maintained, is the bringing multitudes of persons of a tender conscience and true piety into great perplexities; who being at a loss about the state of their souls, must needs be as much in suspense about their duty: and 'tis not reasonable, to suppose, that God would order things so in the revelations of his will, as to bring his own people into such perplexities.*

Joseph felt a sharp pain in his head that forced him to close his eyes and block the light from the candle for a moment, thinking of his father, who had killed himself in the midst of perplexities about the state of his soul. Trembling as if his father's body were still stretched out bleeding on floor behind him, Joseph returned to Mr. Edwards's answer:

> *Perplexity and distress of mind, not only on occasion of the Lord's Supper, but innumerable other occasions, is the natural and unavoidable consequence of true Christians doubting of their state. But shall we therefore say, that all these perplexities are owing to the Word of God? No, 'tis not owing to God, nor to any of his revelations, that true saints*

*ever doubt of their state; his revelations are plain and clear, and his
rules sufficient for men to determine their own condition by: but, for the
most part, 'tis owing to their own sloth, and giving way to their sinful
dispositions. Must God's institutions and revelations be answerable for
all the perplexities men bring on themselves, through their own negligence
and unwatchfulness? 'Tis wisely ordered it should be so, that the saints
should escape perplexity in no other way than that of great strictness,
diligence, and maintaining the lively, laborious and self-denying
exercises of religion.* ·

Joseph struggled to stay with the words on the page.

*Not but that doubting of their state sometimes arises from other causes,
besides want of watchfulness; it may arise from melancholy, and some
other peculiar disadvantages. But however, it is not owing to God's
revelations nor institutions, which, whatsoever we may suppose 'em to be,
will not prevent the perplexities of such persons.*

Sloth. Sin. Negligence. Unwatchfulness. Joseph made himself
note the disclaimer at the end about melancholy and other peculiar
disadvantages, but, for the most part, Mr. Edwards was blaming souls in
terror for their own fears. Joseph lifted his hands away from the book
open on his desk and, leaning back in his chair with his face slack, let
himself drop in mind down the dark chute that he had always known
was there waiting for him, down into the devil's cave where blacksmiths
forged pinchers to use hot to twist his fleshy soul. It was agony.

He didn't know how long he stayed there in torment, but he made
his way back. As he listened to the clanking sounds of Rebekah working
in the kitchen, he lifted his head and cooled the memory of his father's
suffering and the immediacy of his own with unsteady zeal.

He sharpened a pen and wrote to Elisha that he expected there to
be a separation between Mr. Edwards and the people of the town.

———

It was a warm afternoon when Bathsheba watched in the Edwardses' parlor as Rose married Joab Binney, he in a new brown jacket with pewter buttons and red cuffs. As Sarah gave the couple a trencher of apple pudding to share with those who stopped by the shed to congratulate them, Bathsheba felt a loneliness so familiar that she was coming to think of it as part of her nature. How she missed Saul and Leah. Breathing slowly, she did Rose's work in the kitchen while the younger woman walked out into the yard to bid Joab goodbye. Because he belonged to Mr. Hunt, they could not live together. He would be back in the evening, when his services were not required at the Hunts.

Once the pots were scoured, Bathsheba went to find Rose. She was in the shed, taking a taste of pudding. She offered a spoonful to Bathsheba. "He'll have to leave in the middle of the night to get to the Hunts by sunrise."

Bathsheba took the offered sweetness, both warm to Rose's happiness and alive to her own losses. She made a mild joke. "At least Mr. Hunt doesn't get up in the dark like Mr. Edwards."

Rose covered the pudding with a cloth to save for later. "Joab's working in Hunt's tannery, but he's been helping out at Seth Pomeroy's blacksmith shop, too. He's talking about buying his freedom, then mine."

Bathsheba was settled on a stump where she had sat many times with Saul and Leah. She didn't bring up the obvious fact that the struggle between Mr. Edwards and the rest of Northampton made Rose's future with Joab very uncertain, since Mr. Hunt was a leader in the fight against the minister. Instead, she touched Rose's forehead as if soothing a fever. "Happy day, Rose. I'll bring bread and cider tonight."

The summer passed full of hostile meetings and declamations. Fall brought more of the same. On a mild morning in late November, Sarah pasted her beauty mark to her cheek, put on her shawl, took up her basket, and walked to Pomeroy's store. She was happy to be out of the house and away from livestock and children, attending to the simple task of buying spices. Carrying a small quantity of allspice and cinnamon would not, she thought, trouble the babe in her womb. She was pregnant again, nearly five months along. No matter how things unfolded with the congregation, baptism would not be disrupted in any way that might keep her baby from receiving it; that was clear to her. That she even had to consider it was ridiculous, but the church had voted to suspend communion. It was a brutal refusal of trust that tore at her husband's deepest places. His belly ached every day. Sarah served him thick slices of warm bread even as she worried about how—and, dear Lord, where—they would eat if they lost their home. Not even her husband could live on air.

Her thoughts pounded to the hammering as she walked past men taking down some of the town's fortifications. Last month they had received word that negotiators for the colony had signed a treaty in Falmouth with the eastern tribes, so, since England and France had also ended hostilities, the town was no longer at war. There had been celebrations in Boston when the proclamation was read that the tribes had stopped fighting, but people in Northampton didn't celebrate. They were too much in the grip of their own struggle. Mr. Edwards preached a sermon with the doctrine that the joy of the soul was oftentimes like the joy of finding great spoils in war, but no one had seemed much moved.

Sarah liked the thumps and crashes from the forts coming down, but had taken to putting beeswax in her ears so that she didn't have to listen to the bell, which called people to meetings as well as to worship. Most of the meetings now involved the precinct, which consisted of every male taxpayer. Mr. Edwards did not moderate precinct meetings as he did church ones, so, over his objections, the precinct had evaded his control and taken up the questions before the church. It pained Sarah no end that Joseph Hawley had begun to add his name to their reports.

She passed a cluster of children who scattered at her approach, but paid them no mind. When she reached the store, she found the young Pomeroy boy with the cowlick behind the counter. She was relieved that it wasn't the sheriff.

The young Pomeroy was busy helping one of the Bartletts, who was too small to reach into the barrels to get what she needed. Mrs. Clapp was waiting patiently to make her purchases, and Sarah, stepping up behind her with the allspice (they had no cinnamon after all), said, "Good day to you, Mrs. Clapp."

Mrs. Clapp did not turn. She did not move, but stood holding her own basket with a placid expression on her weathered face. Sarah thought that she must be getting hard of hearing, so stepped closer and leaned toward her ear. "Good day."

Mrs. Clapp pretended that Sarah, whom she had known for more than twenty years, wasn't there. With her neck thrust forward and her shoulders hunched, she held her eyes steady on the same spot between the kettles and the sugar where she had been gazing when Sarah had joined her. She gave no sign of knowing she had been spoken to except for the smallest twitch of pleasure that Sarah, peering into her face, watched tighten her mouth.

Sarah stepped back, heart beating hard. She had thought that she was used to the hostility of people here, but she had never been shunned in such an intimate way that she could not help but know it. She felt humiliated, almost gone, as if the pointed hatred of a familiar old woman were enough to obliterate her. The Pomeroy boy finished with the Bartlett girl, and Mrs. Clapp stepped toward him. Sarah barely noticed. She wasn't noticing anything except waves of anger and obscure shame. Finished with her business, Mrs. Clapp walked around Sarah as if she were a stack of tea napkins and went calmly out the door.

The Pomeroy boy beckoned to Sarah and surprised her by calling her politely by name. This brought her back to herself, not the same self, but a consciousness blurred by Mrs. Clapp's tiny smile, and by the cumulative pressure of the thousands of small ways that most of the people around her for months, even years, had been letting her know that she was despised. She called on God. The boy was careful with the scales as he weighed her allspice, the scent hot like clove. Sarah expected to be cheated, but was not.

As she stepped out of the store, she looked at the brown grass, each blade distinct in the undemanding November light, and realized that she was willing. It had been almost seven years since she had dissolved in the presence of God, and in that time she had lost a daughter whose body was held in the earth of this town, but she found herself willing, still, at his sovereign pleasure, to stay or to go.

Near the well, she gave a polite nod to Martha Root, who, so often scorned herself, put aside her mixed feelings and called out, "Good day to you, Mrs. Edwards" in a strong, clear voice.

Chapter 23
December – August 1750

When Joseph got home from visiting Mercy on a December afternoon, Rebekah was waiting in the hallway. He stomped snow from his boots, exhausted from urging his horse down a narrow, uneven trail between great shoulders of half-frozen snow. His mother was never happy when he came home from Brookfield, because, he knew, she wished he wouldn't go at all.

She gestured him in the door and slipped a note in his hand as she helped him off with his coat. "From Sheriff Pomeroy," she said, sweeping snow from his clothes back outside. "Meetings spawning bigger meetings."

Joseph raised his eyebrows and said, "When it's all over, I should make sure that the man who rings the bell gets extra pay." She laughed. Griping about meetings had become like complaining about the weather. It was everyone's common ground. This time, though, it was different. There might be an end in sight. Standing in the hallway with Rebekah hovering, he unfolded the letter.

Five churches from other towns and their ministers were being asked to form a council to give advice and judgment to the church in Northampton on the conflict between them and Mr. Edwards. In the warrant to form the council, the Northampton church had formally supplicated the council to dismiss and release the church and Mr. Edwards from each other. The church had chosen three men to argue their case before the council. The note Joseph Hawley read with his mother in the hall let him know that he was one of them.

He sat down on a chest, put his satchel on the floor. In it was a doily that Mercy had made for Rebekah as a timorous gift. He said to his mother, "I would never stand a chance arguing against Mr. Edwards."

She sat down beside him. "Elisha won't be forced to marry. You won that."

Joseph half nodded, then shook his head. "Mr. Edwards wasn't at the hearing."

She looked into his face. "He was kind to you when you were a boy."

He wished, at that moment, that, after her period of mourning, his mother had married a Parsons or a Pomeroy. Somebody suitable. She could have had more children, other children who were not his brother and himself with their stumbles. The thought of taking the lead in opposing his cousin was very unseemly, but the thought of not doing it burned, too.

She had been gazing at him throughout his long silence, as if reading a psalm on his brow. "All the local ministers oppose him since he broke with my father's teachings. Many others do, too."

"I don't know what to do."

"You'll do what is right." She regarded him with a tenderness that was nothing short of beautiful, but her face tightened considerably as he bent down, unlatched the satchel, and brought forth the doily from Mercy as if presenting her with a crown.

Sarah rested one hand on her belly as she watched Joseph walk up King Street, picking his way over pits and ridges in the snow. He looked cold and miserable, making attempts at a dignified stride whenever he hit a patch of solid footing. Sarah loved being able to follow the comings and goings of people through the window in her kitchen since they had taken the palisades down, but she was not happy to see Joseph.

Still, as he used his walking stick to knock the top off a drift, she felt a rush of fondness. She remembered him at the age of her Johnny, when she and Mr. Edwards were newly married and living with his Stoddard grandparents. She thought of walking up the hill to their manse from the meeting house with John Stoddard (she couldn't remember if he had been a colonel then), who had taken a liking to her. He was dead now, like his parents. She and Col. Stoddard had Joseph with them because Rebekah had been home with a colicky Elisha. The boy had sung psalms all the way up the hill in such a serious way that Sarah had been surprised to notice that he had also managed to catch a frog.

She remembered watching Joseph ride back to his dying father with his arms wrapped around her husband's waist while Jerusha brought his little brother to her by the hand. Her girl had believed that her mother, then and always, would know the healing thing to do. Jerusha. If only it had been true.

Now Joseph, who was joining with those threatening to scatter every earthly thing she held dear, stood at her door, doffing his hat and knocking as if he were coming to bring them cheese and eggs. He had to be in pain or else so dry that he knew nothing at all of what he was feeling. "That Joseph," she thought. Then, "Poor Joseph."

She went to the door of the parlor and flicked her fingers. Esther and Mary rose to gather the younger children and take them upstairs. Sarah let her hands rest on her belly once more as she watched them go, then smoothed her gown and answered the door.

"Mr. Hawley," she said warmly. "Do come in. I expect that you are here to see Mr. Edwards. He is in his study. May I bring you some tea? And how is your mother?"

"No tea, thank you, Madame." She watched him hang his coat on one of the pegs he had been using since he was a boy. Then, as if he had suddenly become a ten-year-old running errands again, he did, in fact, offer her a small cheese.

"From Mother," he said.

Sarah took it gravely. She said, "We shall have it tomorrow with our bread."

He seemed to be lingering, looking at her as if he wanted something. "I've been away," he said. "Seeing Mercy."

She could not help but smile at the quaver in his voice. The preoccupations of the young were so unsurprising. "And how do you find Miss Lyman?"

He flushed with gratitude. She imagined that his mother did not smile at the sound of the young woman's name. He said, "She is very well."

Joseph followed her to the door of the study. The way he stared at his feet and knocked his wig askew as she knocked made her think of his father. Still, he bowed to her with an attentive delicacy all his own before he went inside to do whatever damage he had come to do. It broke Sarah's heart.

Mr. Edwards continued to write for a moment after he heard Sarah shut the door of the study. His whole self was bent over his sermon, taut with concentration and, within that, the release that came from engaging with scripture, language, and God. When he looked up, he saw Joseph Hawley standing there, staring at him with a tremendous look of wistfulness on his blunt young face. All of that human need, so insistently visible, came as a shock to Mr. Edwards as he wrenched himself from his work. What did Joseph, who had taken up such lax principles in religion, want from him? He sighed, not patiently, and put down his pen.

Joseph pulled up a chair and planted his feet. "I've just learned that the committee has asked me to be one of their representatives at the coming council."

"I know." Mr. Edwards looked at him, waiting.

Joseph sat up straight, suddenly vaguely affable like the lawyer he was. "True religion," he began. Mr. Edwards raised his eyebrows. Was he to listen to a layman's sermon? Joseph faltered, his mouth trembling. "Unprejudiced," he muttered, then stopped abruptly, clearly in distress.

Mr. Edwards tried to regard him calmly, as he had watched so many people thrash in that straight-backed chair, but he found himself writhing inwardly, too. Each of them barely moved. Joseph, his wig completely covering one ear, face contorted, staring down at hands clenched in his lap, looked so much like his father that Mr. Edwards felt a rush of the anguish he thought had been fully burned away in service to God. Joseph had come in service to other things, he was sure of it, at the bidding of a committee knotted together by their fibrous resentments, old Sheriff Pomeroy pulling the strings, and Joseph, unaware of his own vulnerability, flattered into eloquence, betrayal, and sin. Sitting across from him in his study, Mr. Edwards could see it so clearly.

Yet he was not resolved. He was not calm. He knew that he would very likely lose his congregation, his livelihood, this room. He knew it. The church wanted to turn him out. He had been writing letters to friends all over New England and Scotland, letting them know what he was facing in this wildly ungrateful town, trying to think through what a next step for him and his family could possibly be. He wasn't done fighting, but he was reconciled to the whole material world as he knew it being yanked away. Still, at this moment in the study, he was not ready to let go of Joseph, whom he had sheltered in every way he could think of for most of his life, and who, now, was reaching toward him, he thought—could he bear it?—about to take his hand. Instead, Joseph leaned across him to the desk. Mr. Edwards moved aside a little, shifting his chair to let Joseph brush a sleeve across his papers and pick up his penknife.

Will he kill me? Am I to be stabbed? Oh, Joseph son of Joseph, will he turn the blade on himself? Mr. Edwards stood, ready to grapple for the knife, but Joseph only bent over the desk like a scholar and slid the blade gently around the smooth pit in the wood that Mr. Edwards himself had dug over years of work and thought.

Joseph put down the knife and let his fingertip linger in the hollow. "I have always wanted to do that." He spoke plainly now, looking into the older man's face. "Ever since I was a boy."

Mr. Edwards sat down again, his own voice lost. He put both hands flat on the desk and lowered his head. Then he looked at the young man in front of him. "Please," he mouthed. "Please don't." No sound came out.

Joseph stared at his face as if in wonder. Mr. Edwards let him look. There was a pause. The young man raised his chin, folded his hands in his lap, and gave Mr. Edwards what he wanted. He said, "My judgments differ from yours in many things, but not all. Therefore, I cannot in good conscience plead for the church's position before the council."

Mr. Edwards took a breath and nodded slowly. He had no words.

The following Sabbath, Mr. Edwards let the women and children stream out into the bright afternoon after his sermon, but he stayed the men to make the announcement that Mr. Hawley would not be arguing the church's case. Sheriff Pomeroy, slowed by age as he was, stalked out in disgust, using both of his arms to wrest open the door. The full weight of it slammed behind him. Seth Pomeroy stood and bellowed that he would know why, but Mr. Edwards could not be goaded into further comment. Joseph, sparing himself the questions and anger, had slipped out the back after the prayers and before the news.

Seth Pomeroy, sitting at the table with Rebekah and Joseph, speared a hunk of parsnip as if he were hitting a wooden peg with an iron hammer. He swallowed it whole. Most of the town still ate only with spoons and knives, and Seth had never been one for European niceties, but Rebekah had inherited forks from Widow Stoddard, so he went ahead and stuck it in another chunk of parsnip before he said, "He's a tyrant, Mr. Hawley. And we've got him cornered. This is no time to back off."

"Mmm." Joseph, watching Seth manhandle the fork, thought about what he had seen at Louisburg, when Seth had led the men to unplug the touchholes of blocked cannons, drag them around to face the fortress, and fire cannonballs that had been aimed at them back at the French. He would never give up. Joseph, who had turned over his bed in the captured town to Seth when he was near dead with the flux, loved him for that. Testing his own heart as he chewed a piece of bread, Joseph did not find the same resolve.

Sheriff Pomeroy had been by the house earlier with a gift of pickled pork, which made Joseph think of funeral meats as Rebekah passed it around the table on her best platter. He took a sip of cider to clear out the smell of vinegar and tried to find a sticking place in himself. Seth and his mother ate their food, waiting for him to speak. He would despise himself if he went back on his word to Mr. Edwards, but if he won the case against him, it would be the making of him. He did not want to act from such a base motive, but he could not help but think it. He tried to draw on his newly acquired sense of true religion, so different from that he had received from Mr. Edwards. The good sense of humankind, wasn't that what he should be relying on? Not one rigid minister standing above all others like a king, but a whole town full of good people, his people. They knew what was right, and what they cared about mattered so much to him.

Oh, but Mr. Edwards had asked him not to do this. He had not commanded him as the instrument of God in this town, but asked him in a choked, vulnerable way. Joseph, on the verge of tears, pushed back his plate.

As if this was the signal he had been looking for, Seth stood up, towering over the table. "All right, then, man," he said. "Are we resolved?"

Joseph felt the force of Seth's certainty. He wanted very much to be on his side. Rebekah, who had been uncharacteristically silent, put down her mother's fork and smoothed the edge of the doily under the platter at the center of the table. He suddenly realized that she had given Mercy's gift a place of honor. Looking him in the eye, she said, "Perhaps Miss Lyman would come from Brookfield to hear you argue before the council." She pressed the tines of the fork so that the end of it lifted from the table, then let it drop. "I should be delighted if she came to dinner."

Joseph took a swig of cider. It would mean so much for Mercy to have a welcome in his mother's house. He could see what Rebekah wanted: an answer to old grief. Joseph had cracked open when Mr. Edwards showed raw need, but how could he deny his mother if she wanted the preacher gone from their town? He had said it himself more than once: true religion consisted in what the informed sense of humankind maintained was right.

Seth was still hovering beside his chair. Joseph stood up and punched him on the arm like a brother. "All right, Seth. We are resolved."

There was a moment in the meeting house that June which would haunt Joseph the rest of his life.

Sweating in his lawyer's robes, he was seated in the box where his father would have been sitting, if his father had lived, listening to the arguments. He himself had provided hours of vituperation toward Mr. Edwards, which (he could feel this deep in his belly and throat) had crossed the line from heated oratory into something feral, with the breathless approval of the crowds jamming the benches and packing the gallery so full that many Northampton folks had lost their seats to strangers who didn't want to miss the spectacle. He hated to think of Mercy among them, but she was.

One of the ministers who had traveled from outside of the valley to give judgment with the council stood up and said to the assembly, in his strongest preaching voice, "Let me remind you of the good things Mr. Edwards has brought you . . ."

Joseph leapt from his seat, yelling at the top of his lungs. "No! We want no such talk here!" The crowd raised a great din of shouting and catcalls as the dumbstruck minister closed his mouth and shook his head.

Mr. Edwards listened to the jeers with an air of injured calm. It was the sight of his face, as quiet and ominous as the empty pulpit high above them, that stuck like a splinter in Joseph as, with the voices of hundreds behind him, he shouted down any word of the blessings which had once rained upon the town.

The church won the case, and Mr. Edwards was dismissed.

One week after the church vote that decided the fate of her family, Sarah could not sleep. She put on a gown over her shift and found herself sitting in the parlor in the dark. Pierpont, the baby, two and a half months old, was down at last. She could have gone into the study and lit a candle, but she was too tired to read, and she didn't want to disturb her husband and the children by roaming about the house.

It was a warm night in late June, and her neck was sweating as she rested her head against the wall, the great nest of her hair unloosed from its combs to fall down her back. She might have expected to be sobbing—the council hearings, so terrible, had been haunting her—but, tonight, she found herself calm. She wondered if her Sally, just two weeks married to Elihu Parsons, was sleeping well. Soon, Mary, too, would be wed, to Timothy Dwight, and gone from the house. Soon, they must all of them be gone, herself and Mr. Edwards as well, to a place that would want them and could support them, although she could not imagine where that might be. Another town outside of this valley, Scotland, or a mission in the wilderness?

The vote of the church had been so greatly against them: two hundred to twenty, or maybe it was two hundred to twenty-three. Sarah was tired of counting their few friends over and over, and of numbering those among the women who would have supported them, if women had been given a vote. She closed her eyes, and as she did so, she heard a crackling sound like a falling twig. Opening her eyes and, looking down, she saw that a June bug had landed on her lap.

She was tired enough to stare at it with its hard, brassy back. Its rear leg flicked out as it squatted solidly on her thigh. Sarah watched, almost listening, as the June bug began to let its head protrude and pull back in a rhythmic way. She was pulsing in her own skin as the June bug stroked itself with its antennas, both of them vibrating with something like feeling, thought or sound, although, truly, it was none of these, not even a buzz. She breathed in time with the discourse of the June bug, impossible to comprehend with her rational mind, and impossible to ignore:

We shall endeavor to give an account of what it is like to be filled with dense exhalation that can reflect less flexible rays, which still appear a little reddish on the hard carapace of our back, or what it feels like to be drenched in fine drops of water dashed up by a stick from a puddle, but the thing that wants a solution is what should cause a reflection to be circular. The blue of mountains at a distance is not made by any rays reflected from the mountains, but from the air and vapors that are between us and them. The mountain occasions the blueness by intercepting all rays that would come from beyond to disturb the color by their mixture. Your beloved has observed this. But, enough science.

The bellows are burnt, the lead is consumed of fire, the founder melteth in vain, for the wicked are not plucked away.

Chewing under the floorboards, we have listened so long.

Sarah had been watching the June bug's abdomen quiver from within something close to the urgent and exhausted body of emotions with which she had watched Jerusha breathe in her sickbed. Now she sat up with a jolt. Nothing was dying here, except that which was born to die. All that must live would live. She raised a corner of her gown to keep the bug from falling to the floor as she stood, although it clung on tightly. She walked with it, barefoot, into the yard.

If we stayed, you would not love us, for all that you make love your work and then work to expel it as a small drop which extrudes into a great glistening trail you cast and follow into the air. We address you as a spider as you whisk us from the house. We can't help but drop here, in our generations. This is the season of our throbbing, flying and hunkering down, as it has been your time to use mind and limbs to imperfectly embody affections which otherwise might never cease grubbing in mold and roots. If you manage to leave us, we will sing after you.

Sarah didn't go near the elm tree, but stopped just outside the door of her dark house. The bug was bigger than a blueberry, and she had heard somewhere that, in the exigencies of drought or other famine, a body could roast a June bug in hot ashes, and then peel off the crisped legs, wings, and shell to eat the internal parts, which would be golden and taste like raw molasses.

Sarah, though, was far from starving. She was anxious and unsettled, haunted by sins that she never found words for, but—belly, life, and spirit—she was full. She shook her skirt and brushed against the insect three times with her fingers before she could get it to drop from her. Once it did, she could not distinguish the shape of it on the damp ground.

She could feel the dirt, though, cool and uneven under the soles of her feet. There was a breeze. She put a hand on the side of house (which was to be lost), then raised her toes and twisted both heels into the ground. It was hard packed, but when she looked in the morning, she saw two smeared, shallow dents among the purslane and wild mustard, not far from the trail of broken weeds that Rose's husband had made from the shed to the road as he left before dawn. There was no sign of the June bug, but Sarah's heel marks were still there.

After it was over, even years later—when he was married to Mercy, and Rebekah had put up the walls that divided the house in half (along with another addition to her buttery); after he had written his letters of apology—Joseph never accused himself of hypocrisy.

On a ravishing spring afternoon, when Mercy was out searching for fiddleheads and Rebekah was in the pasture checking on a new calf, he lit a fire in the dark of his study and read the copy he had made of his letter of apology to Mr. Edwards again. He had been, he wrote,

> *irreverent, immodest, derisive, magisterial and savoring of haughtiness and levity and such as very ill became me when arguing with you, sir, who was so much my superior in age, station and accomplishments, and who deserved from me great respect and deference for which I humbly and sincerely ask your forgiveness and am very sorry, not only for that it was disrespectful to you, sir, but also a very ill example to others and a tendency to abate the respect and reverence which the bystanders ought to have maintained and probably had an influence*

*upon the hearers toward prompting them to a disrespectful and
irreverent treatment of you afterwards.*

Joseph, sweating by the fire, meant every word. He felt profound
regret for the vehemence with which he had become the leading
spokesman for the case against Mr. Edwards. The years seemed to
sharpen his regret rather than dull it. He put down the letter and
picked up *An Humble Inquiry*, the despised book that Mr. Edwards had
written in the midst of the controversy. It fell open like a broken loaf
to the familiar spot where Joseph tried again to comfort himself with
a line that Mr. Edwards had written about their grandfather Solomon
Stoddard, whose rules for the church membership he had overturned to
such turmoil and dissension:

> *Certainly we are not obliged to think any man infallible, who himself
> utterly disclaims infallibility.*

Joseph felt this applied to Mr. Edwards himself. He may have
carried himself as if he were infallible, but he never claimed to be. Dry
down to his fingertips beside the spitting hearth, Joseph wished himself
capable of tears as he ran his eyes over the passage that Mr. Edwards
then quoted from their grandfather:

> *It may possibly be a fault (says Mr. Stoddard) to depart from the
> ways of our fathers: but it may also be a virtue, and an eminent act of
> obedience, to depart from them in some things.*

Some things, he thought. Which things? He had been so wrong
in acquiescing—or worse—to the derision and torment of the whole
Edwards family. Would he acquit himself better in any other rebellion
that arose over the course of his life? He turned to the fire, dangling
chilled fingers over the flame.

———

It was the second fall after Mr. Edwards was dismissed that the household moved to Stockbridge, where he had been given the position of minister to the small frontier community of colonists, Mahicans, and other Indian people. Mr. Hunt had been so glad to see Mr. Edwards go that he had released Joab Binney to be with his wife, Rose, who was pregnant. As soon as Bathsheba heard the news, she went to Sheriff Pomeroy's barn and fetched Leah's box, which she kept hidden under a half-splintered bucket behind a pile of hay. She felt bites of envy and knew that she was facing more loneliness, but, mostly, Bathsheba took up the warping, incomplete relief of Joab's manumission as her own. She swiped the box clean of hay and dust with an old rag before she opened it, carefully tracing carved vines and the letters of Leah's name. She left the Bible where it was, but took out the other book and carried it one night to the shed.

"Here," she said to Rose, who, spending the night alone, as Joab was needed early and late at the Hunt's for harvest, had welcomed her in with a cup of hot chicory. Bathsheba placed *Aristotle's Master-Piece* carefully on a stump. "Madame Edwards can help you with childbirth, but you might want to know about the secrets of generation, yourself."

Rose stared a bit blankly at the book, but said, "Thank you kindly."

Bathsheba touched the cover. "It's not that good. But there are pictures. If it's not useful, you can sell it." Bathsheba knew that she herself could never sell the book, not in Northampton. *Aristotle's Master-Piece* was still too notorious, although she did not doubt that young men had another copy, or something like it, circulating again in the barns and back fields. She was happy to be rid of it.

Rose took her hand. "I'll look at it and think of you."

Bathsheba made a wry face. "You sound like Timothy Root." They laughed. Everyone knew the story of the bad books, even a latecomer like Rose. Bathsheba let go of her hand. "I hear that there are all sorts of people where you're going. Mahicans, the Mohawk, and the Oneida, at least. Mary Stockbridge said so." She looked down at the stump where she had sat so often with Leah and Saul, feeling her losses. "If you should happen to catch sight of Saul, say hello."

Rose looked at her as if she were having delusions.

Bathsheba, who was nothing if not practical, added, "And make sure that the Edwardses do not."

Mr. Edwards, walking in the woods outside Northampton one afternoon the summer after his people so thoroughly and publicly rejected him, saw a crow flying from shadow to shadow beneath the trees. He stopped to watch it land on a high branch. Half hidden by leaves, it began to call with its whole body, tail lifting and falling as it cawed.

Another crow cawed in return, and, as Mr. Edwards seated himself beneath a maple, he saw a third jump from a rock to the grass. Crows were birds that had too much traffic with the earth, he thought, as he leaned back and watched a squirrel, summer fat, leaping heavily among the branches with a small clutch of maple leaves in its mouth. He looked up at the radiant mass of leaves, from which the crow on the limb began to sound anguished and, so, too human.

Mr. Edwards groaned in answer. He thought about his grandparents and daughter buried in this place; David Brainerd, too. He thought of Leah. All his children had been born here, and this was where his wife had come to be, if not fully, then deeply, known to him. He thought about the years of exceeding labor and difficulty in caring for the souls of these people, now so filled with spite, who were witnesses to how he had spent the prime of his life.

Shifting to try to ease the stiffness in his back, Mr. Edwards noticed a black feather on the ground. The tufts were matted in clumps. He observed the hollow in the white shaft from which the ink would flow if he were to use it as a quill, and, although there were bits of membrane flaking from the tip, it had broken off into a sharp point. Mr. Edwards couldn't recall that he had ever written with a feather from a crow, but he could see that the line it would make would be very fine.

He reached for the feather, feeling as if he might be taking something wicked in his hand, but the impression dissipated as the wind came up. The flock of crows was gone. He felt grass and sticks poking through his stockings. He didn't consciously notice the ants climbing his shoe, but used the feather to scratch his calf. Then he raised it toward the ruffling leaves above him to trace something not yet written into the air:

> *Therefore there is room left for no other conclusion than that the primary object of virtuous love is Being, simply considered; or that true virtue primarily consists, not in love to any particular Beings, because of their virtue or beauty, nor in gratitude, because they love us, but in a propensity and union of heart to Being simply considered; exciting absolute benevolence (if I may so call it) to Being in general.*

His legs were itching (later there would be rings of red bumps around his ankles), so he stood up, feeling, despite everything, true union of heart to being. He could not put it into words, but, finding that he did not have to, he dug his heel into a chunk of fallen bark as he blessed the place, along with some of its inhabitants and the whole length of its river valley stretching in peopled fields beneath the hills.

He kept the feather, which he never cut into a pen.

It was Martha Root who got the first letter of apology from Joseph, which he sent that summer, just a month after Mr. Edwards had given his farewell sermon at the Northampton meeting house, addressing the professors of godliness, the graceless, those under awakenings, the young people, the children, and also, without naming them, the aged and the bitter. He had taken as his doctrine "Ministers and the people that have been under their care, must meet one another, before Christ's tribunal, at the day of judgment." His opinion of who would be judged correct on that great day had not been in doubt. "A contentious people will be a miserable people," he had said before he ended the sermon, as he never did any other, with a simple, final word: "Amen."

Martha read over Joseph's painstaking recount of the number of times he had seen her on Pudding Lane before she was with child. He admitted that he could not have been certain of how many times he had seen her on their road, and that, on cool consideration, while it was true that he frequently saw her there within the space of that half a year, and more frequently than any other member of her father's family, yet as far as he represented this matter beyond the truth, he didn't suppose that he saw her more than once every week and twice every other week, which didn't add up to the forty several times he had declared to be his judgment before the council. And he had mentioned particular places where he had seen her, suggestive places such as the corner by the bridge or where the ways met, when he had no particular remembrance of any of those places. For that, so far as he had really injured her, and so far beyond what he had certain knowledge was truth, he was heartily sorry. In observance of the divine rule James 5:16, he confessed that to her, and did humbly and freely ask her pardon and forgiveness, and pledged himself always ready to own what he had written above.

Martha had never imagined that an apology could be that stingy. Elisha's had, at least, come with some rabbit skins. She set the letter on the table, took a deep breath, and laughed until her eyes ran and her daughter came trotting into the kitchen to find out the joke. Martha's mother, who came in from the garden, didn't have the heart to reprove her for levity.

The day after Joseph argued the church case against Mr. Edwards, as he prayed amongst the hogsheads of cider and barrels full of wheat and bailey on a warm afternoon in the attic, he heard a swarm of sluggish flies rise from the walls and sills. They filled the air with such buzzing that he left off praying to chase them into corners, slapping at their bodies with an ear of dry corn. For the rest of his life, Joseph prayed in that attic, and he fought the swarm often again.

Grateful acknowledgment is made for the use of the following materials:

Quotes from Edwards's MSS are courtesy of the Beinecke Rare Book and Manuscript Library, Yale University.

Quotes from Edwards material including "Of the Rainbow"; "Of Being"; May 30, 1735 letter to the Reverend Benjamin Colman; and the c. 1738 draft letter on slavery, as well as materials related to documents from the Bad Book Case, courtesy of Franklin Trask Library, Andover Newton Theology School.

September 11, 1749 letter from Jonathan Edwards to the Reverend Ebenezer Parkman from the Curwen Family Papers, American Antiquarian Society. Mss Boxes C, Box 3, Folder 2.

Joseph Hawley papers. Manuscripts and Archives Division. The New York Public Library. Astor, Lenox, and Tilden Foundations.

Leah thinks of a tavern song inspired by Richard Brown's "A Cat Catch" in Chapter One, and, in Chapter Two, sings two lines of Psalm 137 from *Whole book of Psalms 1627*, Thomas Ravenscroft. I heard both on www.1704.deerfield.history.museum, an outstanding resource on the raid on Deerfield and on the early eighteenth century cultures of the region. The alphabet verses that Elisha remembers in Chapter Three are from *The New England Primer*. In Chapter Eleven, the Yale scholars sing lines from "Alas! Did My Saviour Bleed?" by Isaac Watts, *Hymns and Spiritual Songs*, 1707. Also in that chapter, the trustee decision read by the rector is from *A Documentary History of Yale 1701-1745* (1916), by Franklin B. Dexter. *Aristotle's Master-Piece: or, the Secrets of Generation Displayed in all the Parts thereof*, first referred to in Chapter Fifteen, first appeared in various versions in the late seventeenth century. I learned of it, and found the passages quoted and image described in the novel in "The Immaculate Ovum: Jonathan Edwards and the Construction of the Female Body," Ava Chamberlain, *William and Mary Quarterly*, 3d ser., 57, no. 2 (April 2000). Other important articles by Chamberlain: "Bad Books and Bad Boys: The Transformation of Gender in Eighteenth-Century Northampton, Massachusetts," *New England Quarterly* 75 (June 2002) and "Jonathan Edwards and the Politics of Sex in Eighteenth-Century Northampton," in *Jonathan Edwards at 300: Essays on the Tercentenary of His Birth*, edited by Harry S. Stout, Kenneth P. Minkema, and Caleb J. D. Maskell.

I wish to acknowledge that I have infused the text with the words of Jonathan Edwards, his family, and contemporaries. Though it is based on these words and on the scholarship of many, *Spider in a Tree* is a work of fiction, and I have made frequent leaps of imagination. For instance, I couldn't find records for the birth of Martha Root's twins, so the nearness of the birth date to that of Jonathan and Sarah's daughter Elizabeth is conjecture.

I am indebted to Kenneth Minkema of the Works of Jonathan Edwards and of the Jonathan Edwards Center & Online Archive at Yale for his scholarship—especially for articles on Jonathan Edwards and slavery, and for his Edwards chronology—for critical readings of the whole of the novel, and for many acts of kindness during work on the novel. The Jonathan Edwards Center & Online Archive at Yale is a magnificent resource. It's where anyone interested in knowing more about Edwards should start: edwards.yale.edu.

I have used many of the books in the Works of Jonathan Edwards series published by Yale University Press and now available online at the Jonathan Edwards Center & Online Archive. The introductions make great reading, and they strongly influenced how I worked with the various subjects and periods. Two volumes I referred to over and over were *The Great Awakening (WJE Online Vol. 4)*, Ed. C. C. Goen, and *Letters and Personal Writings (WJE Online Vol. 16)*, Ed. George S. Claghorn. I also used *Religious Affections (WJE Online Vol. 2)*, Ed. Paul Ramsey; *Scientific and Philosophical Writings (WJE Online Vol. 6)*, Ed. Wallace E. Anderson; *The Life of David Brainerd (WJE Online Vol. 7)*, Ed. Norman Pettit; *Ethical Writings (WJE Online Vol. 8)*, Ed. Paul Ramsey; *Sermons and Discourses 1720-1723 (WJE Online Vol. 10)*, Ed. Wilson H. Kimnach; *Ecclesiastical Writings (WJE Online Vol. 12)*, Ed. David D. Hall (which particularly influenced my account of the communion controversy); *The "Miscellanies": (Entry Nos. a-z, aa-zz, 1-500) (WJE Online Vol. 13)*, Ed. Harry S. Stout; *Sermons and Discourses: 1723-1729 (WJE Online Vol. 14)*, Ed. Kenneth P. Minkema; *Sermons and Discourses, 1734-1738 (WJE Online Vol. 19)*, Ed. M. X. Lesser; *Sermons and Discourses, 1739-1742 (WJE Online Vol. 22)*, Ed. Harry S. Stout; *The "Blank Bible" (WJE Online Vol. 24)*, Ed. Stephen J. Stein; *Sermons and Discourses, 1743-1758 (WJE Online Vol. 25)*, Ed. Wilson H. Kimnach; and referred to others. I also read and used work available only in the archive. I particularly love *Typological Writings (WJE Online Vol. 11)*, Eds. Wallace E. Anderson, Mason I. Lowance, Jr. and David H. Watters, because it includes "Images of Divine Things."

Jonathan Edward: A Life by George M. Marsden is a fantastic biography, which has greatly influenced this book. Other fine biographies of Jonathan Edwards include, from the nineteenth century, *The Works of Jonathan Edwards* by his student Samuel Hopkins (who appears in this novel as a character), and "Memoirs of Jonathan Edwards" in *The Works of Jonathan Edwards, A.M.*, ed, Sereno Edwards Dwight. Also extremely helpful, from the twentieth century: *Jonathan Edwards, Pastor: Religion and Society in Eighteenth-Century Northampton* by Patricia Tracy. *Marriage to a Difficult*

Man: The Uncommon Union of Jonathan and Sarah Edwards by Elisabeth D. Dodds was interesting. Biographies by Ola E. Winslow and Perry Miller were enlightening. For an excellent introduction to the writing of Jonathan Edwards, see *A Jonathan Edwards Reader*, edited by John E. Smith, Harry S. Stout, and Kenneth P. Minkema. I also referred to *Jonathan Edward: Selections*, edited by Clarence Faust and Thomas H. Johnson.

History of Northampton, Massachusetts, from its settlement in 1654, by James Russell Trumbull (1898), has been an invaluable source of information on many aspects of Northampton history. The letter Rebekah Hawley based her meal on in Chapter 17 was sent by Seth Pomeroy to his wife and quoted in Trumbull. Trumbull is also how I know that the Hawley family lived on Pudding Lane, which people in Northampton now know as Hawley Street. The Map of the Homelots of the First Settlers of Northampton compiled from the earliest town records is also by James R. Trumbull. The map of Northampton in the County of Hampshire, 1831, by John G. Hales, was also a great source of specifics about place. Thanks to Elise Bernier-Feeley and Special Collections at Forbes Library for access to these maps (and much else). Elise also led me to a source of information on colonial tanning yards: www.nps.gov/jame/historyculture/tanning-in-the-seventeenth-century.htm (no longer available at this writing). The route that Leah takes to have a private conversation with Bathsheba in Chapter Fifteen draws from directions Jonathan Edwards wrote in his account book about how to find the cranberry bog. On the other hand, while I've heard that Sarah Edwards and a Mr. Pomeroy had a conversation about the communion controversy during a trip, I haven't read it, and my account here is fictional.

A Place Called Paradise: Culture and Community in Northampton, MA, 1654-2004, Kerry Buckley, editor, has been helpful as well, especially "Into the Maelstrom of Change," by Peter A. Thomas; and Margaret Bruchac, "Native Presence in Nonotuck and Northampton." Also in this anthology is "Hard Thoughts and Jealousies" from John Putnam Demos, *Entertaining Satan: Witchcraft and the Culture of Early New England*, which includes the story the Hawley boys are told at the flogging about Goody Parsons and Betty Negro. Kerry Buckley is Executive Director of Historic Northampton, whose website pointed me to many resources, including an article by Stephen Stein, "'For Their Spiritual Good': The Northampton, Massachusetts Prayer Bids of the 1730s and 1740s," *William and Mary Quarterly* 3d ser.37(1980):261-285, where I first found the prayer bids quoted in the novel (except for the one from Leah and Saul, which is fictional). *Northampton in the Days of Jonathan Edwards, 1727-50*, by Clifford Lyman (1937) was of particular interest in the Historic Northampton Collection. In addition to the Hawley Papers at the New York Public Library, *Joseph Hawley: Colonial Radical* by Francis Brown, is a fine resource on Joseph Hawley (and his family), whose pre-revolutionary war activities are fascinating, if beyond the scope of this novel.

Worlds of Wonder; Days of Judgment: Popular Religious Belief in Early New England, by David D. Hall, was a great source for considerations of portents, signs, and popular religion. The work of Douglas Winiarski is another must for those who want to understand religion of the period as experienced by ordinary people. His article "Jonathan Edwards, Enthusiast? Radical Revivalism and the Great Awakening in the Connecticut Valley," *Church History: Studies in Christianity and Culture* 74 (2005): 683-739, also greatly influenced my account of the preaching of "Sinners in the Hands of An Angry God" in Enfield and the story of Samuel Hopkins in Suffield. *How Early America Sounded,* by Richard Cullen Rath, is astonishing.

The best source for "The Narrative of Sarah Pierpont Edwards," which much of Chapter 12 is based on, is *Family Writings and Related Documents (WJE Online Vol. 41),* Ed. Jonathan Edwards Center. An edited version was printed in Sereno Edwards Dwight. I was also inspired, especially to think of dance, by a chapter in *Feminine Spirituality in America: From Sarah Edwards to Martha Graham,* by Amanda Porterfield.

There are many sources for information about the career of James Davenport. Some that I've found particularly valuable are CC Goen's introduction to *The Great Awakening* (*WJE Online Vol. 4*); "James Davenport and the Great Awakening in New London," Harry S. Stout and Peter Onuf, *The Journal of American History,* Vol 70, No. 3 (Dec 1983); and *History of New London, CT,* Frances Manwaring Caulkins (1852). The *Diary of Joshua Hempstead of New London, CT,* New London County Historical Society (1901), provides firsthand accounts of some of Davenport's preaching. *The Great Awakening: Documents on the Revival of Religion, 1740-1745,* by Richard Bushman, includes a letter about the bonfire from the *Boston Weekly Post-Boy,* March 28, 1743, and Davenport's *Confession and Retractions* (1744). Franklin Dexter's *Biographical Sketches of the Graduates of Yale College with Annals of the College* (1912) is also of interest.

For information on Native Peoples, in addition to those already mentioned, I found these materials useful: *The Mohicans of Stockbridge,* Patrick Frazier; *Native Peoples and Museums in the Connecticut River Valley: A Guide for Learning,* edited by Dorothy Schlotthauer Krass and Barry O'Connell; "'Poor Indians' and the 'Poor in Spirit': The Indian Impact on David Brainerd," Richard W. Pointer, in *New England Encounters: Indians & Euroamericans, ca. 1600-1850,* edited by Alden T. Vaughan. *Land of the Nonotucks,* C. Keith Wilber, Northampton Historical Society, and *In Search of New England's Native Past: Selected Essays by Gordon M. Day,* eds Michael Foster and William Cowan. Also, "Lessons from Stockbridge: Jonathan Edwards and the Stockbridge Indians," Rachel Wheeler, in *Jonathan Edwards at 300.*

The portrait of slavery in Jonathan Edwards's household in the novel draws extensively on Kennth Minkema's scholarship, particularly his article "Jonathan Edwards's Defense of Slavery," *The Massachusetts Historical Review* 2002, which includes a brilliantly detailed account of Edwards's purchase of his first slave, whose name was recorded on the receipt as "Venus." The article includes as an appendix "Conversion of an African Woman." This is "reportedly a description of the conversion of Jonathan Edwards's former Slave, Rose Binney Salter, written by Dr. Stephen West, Edwards's successor at Stockbridge, Massachusetts. The account is reprinted verbatim from the Jan.-Feb. 1797 issue of *The Theological Magazine, or Synopsis of Modern Religious Sentiment on a New Plan,* pp. 191-195." It strongly influenced my fictional account of Leah's experience in the barn. George Marsden also writes about slavery and Jonathan Edwards. Marsden credits Kristin Kobes DuMez with the idea that Edwards may have changed Venus's name to Leah, the name of the slave on record in his household during the Northampton revival. There is no historical basis for Jonathan Edwards using a catechism for Negroes (Pierson credits one to Cotton Mather), as I have him do in Chapter One.

Other important sources for information on slavery and African Americans in colonial times: "African American Engagements with Edwards in the Era of the Slave Trade," John Saillant, in *Jonathan Edwards at 300: Essays on the Tercentenary of His Birth,* edited by Harry S. Stout, Kenneth P. Minkema, and Caleb J. D. Maskell; *African Americans in Newport: An Introduction to the Heritage of African Americans in Newport, Rhode Island, 1700–1945,* Rhode Island Historical Preservation & Heritage Commission and Rhode Island Black Heritage Society; *African Americans Voices of Triumph: Perseverance,* foreword by Henry Louis Gates Jr., Editors of Time Life Books, Time-Life Books; *Black Yankees: the development of an Afro-American Subculture in Eighteenth-Century New England,*William D. Piersen; *Crossing the Danger Water: Three Hundred Years of African-American Writing,* edited by Deidre Mullane; "The Edwardsean Tradition and the Antislavery Debate, 1740–1865," Kenneth Minkema and Harry S. Stout, *The Journal of American History* Vol. 92, Issue 1; *The Gullah, Rice, Slavery and the Sierra Leone-American connection,* Joseph A. Opala. An online resource hosted by The Gilder Lehrman Center for the Study of Slavery, Resistance and Abolition www.yale.edu/glc/gullah/index.htm; *History of the Black Population of Amherst, Massachusetts, 1728-1870,* James Avery Smith.

Also "'Justise MustTake Plase': Three African Americans Speak of Religion in Eighteenth-Century New England," Erik R. Seeman, *William and Mary Quarterly,* vol. 56 (April 1999); *The Negro in Colonial New England, 1620–1776,* Lorenzo J. Greene; *Roll, Jordan, Roll: The World the Slaves Made,* Eugene D Genovese; "The Selling of Joseph: Bostonians, Antislavery, and the Protestant International, 1689–1733," Mark A. Peterson, *The Massachusetts Historical Review* 2002; "'Shining in Borrowed Plumage': Affirmation of Community in the Black Coronation Festivals of New England, ca.

1750-1850," Melvin Wade, in *Material Life in America 1600-1860*, Robert Blair St. George, editor; *Slavery in the Connecticut Valley of Massachusetts*, Robert H. Romer; "Visible Bodies: Power, Subordination and Identity in the Eighteenth-Century Atlantic World," Gwenda Morgan and Peter Rushton, *Journal of Social History* Fall 2005. I also drew on *Jamaica Anansi Stories*, by Martha Warren Beckwith (1924).

The following books and articles provided many essential details about daily life, medicine, childbirth, child-rearing, cooking, clothing, and the roles of women in earlier times: *The American Frugal Housewife: dedicated to those who are not ashamed of economy*, Lydia Maria Child. 1828; "Children of Wrath, Children of Grace: Jonathan Edwards and the Puritan Culture of Child Rearing," Catherine A. Brekus, *The Child in Christian Thought*, Marcia J. Bunge, editor; *Everyday Life in the Strong House: A Resource Guide*, Museum Education Project, School of Education, University of Massachusetts, Amherst; *Good Wives: Image and Reality in the Lives of Women in Northern New England, 1650–1750*, Laurel Thatcher Ulrich; "Hannah and her Sisters: Sisterhood, Courtship, and Marriage in the Edwards Family in the Early Eighteenth Century," Kenneth P. Minkema, *New England Historical and Genealogical Register* 146 (1992); *A History of Costume in the West*, New Enlarged Edition, Francois Boucher, translated from French by John Ross; *In Small Things Forgotten: The Archeology of Early American Life*, James Deetz; *The Journal of Esther Edwards Burr 1754–57*, Carol Karlsen and Laurie Crumpacker, eds; *A Midwife's Tale: The Life of Martha Ballard, Based on Her Diary, 1785-1812*, Laurel Thatcher Ulrich, especially the Appendix of Medicinal Ingredients; *Our Own Snug Fireside: Images of the New England Home: 1760–1860*. Jane C. Nylander; *The Protestant Temperament: Patterns of Child-Rearing, Religious Experience, and the Self in Early America*, Philip Greven; *Puritans at Play: Leisure and Recreation in Colonial New England*, Bruce C. Daniels.

I'd also like to recommend *The Black Veil*, Rick Moody; *Souls of the Labadie Tract*, Susan Howe; *River Gods*, Brian Kiteley, and *The Death of Adam*, Marilynne Robinson.

Many people have offered deep, gorgeous support for the writing of this book. If there are names I don't mention, please know that I've suffered a lapse of memory, but not of gratitude. The scholars listed above have been central, whether they know it or not. All errors are, of course, my own. I'd like to thank everyone who read and/or critiqued the work-in-progress: Sally Bellerose; Elise Bernier-Feeley; Mary Cappello; Carolyn Cushing; Valija Evalds; Judith Frank; Lynne Gerber; James Heintz; Rebecca Johnson; Mark Jordan; Elaine Keach; Paul Lisicky; David McCormick; Kenneth Minkema; my siblings, Karen, Mike, and Don Stinson; and Douglas Winiarski.

Thanks to Brian Kiteley; Elaine Crane; Kathryn Lofton, John Lardas Modern and Emily Floyd; and Jennifer Acker and John Hennessy for editing or inviting writing from me around the novel. Also, the staff of *The Daily Hampshire*

Gazette. I'm grateful to *Lambda Literary Journal*, *Lambda Literary Foundation*, and Bob Flaherty for, among other things, creating opportunities for me to speak and write about this work as my full self.

Money for Women/Barbara Deming Memorial Fund provided financial support for the writing of the novel, for which I am grateful. Jeep Wheat took great photos and was good company. I'd also like to thank Peter Ives, Kathryn Gabriel, and First Churches for hosting events and sharing historical material. Marie Panik from Historic Northampton has been very helpful. I've also benefitted from the Dublin Seminar for New England Folklife and the Jonathan Edwards in Europe conference in Budapest. The Jonathan Edwards Society has hosted conferences coordinated by Richard Hall in which I've participated. I thank, too, the Center for New Americans, where I tutored an impressive young man from Sierra Leone who gave me insight into being newly arrived in this country.

I currently am Writer in Residence at Forbes Library, the public library in Northampton, MA, which is a wellspring of resources, enthusiastic research support, love of books, and space to work. I'd like to especially thank Lisa Downing, who has been unstinting in her support; Janet Moulding; and Julie Barlett Nelson (who handled last minute requests with such grace) and Elise Bernier-Feeley. Elise, especially, is at the heart of local resources related to Jonathan Edwards, and has been very generous with her knowledge and friendship. I thank, too, the Friends of Forbes, the Trustees, and Diana Gordon. Participants in the Writing Room, the Local History/Local Novelists reading series, and the Writing Life discussion series have provided wonderful companionship, witness, and inspiration as I worked. I thank, especially, Cynthia Hinckley, Grace LeClair, Elli Meeropol, Naila Moreira, Jacqueline Sheehan, Mistinguette Smith, and lê thi diem thúy (who sent me square nails and gave me courage). Moving with Terre Parker has meant so much. I thank, too, the audiences for the readings and participants in the cemetery tours, who let me know that people are eager to passionately engage with this work. Barb Tobias has helped with the tours over the years, and is dear to me in many ways.

Thanks to Gavin J. Grant and Kelly Link of Small Beer Press.

Marci Riseman and Evan Sagerman have provided friendship and beautiful cottage time in which to work. I'd like to thank Vahram Elagoz, Lisa Nelson, Mary Newman Vazquez, Lesléa Vazquez Newman, Martha Richards, Alison Smith, Linda Stout, and Cynthia Suopis. Also, all of the folks from my livejournal and other online networks for every time they encouraged me to keep going, especially Max Airborne, Charlotte Cooper, Holly Hessinger, Deb Malkin, Bertha Pearl and Amanda Piasecki. My parents, Bill and Mollie Stinson, have offered so much love and help that it leaves me speechless. In addition to my sister and brothers, mentioned above, I'd like to thank Eva, Candace, and Parker Stinson; Barbara, Will, Marissa, and Emmett Stinson. Elaine Keach has been engaged, generous, present, and enormously patient over this long process: beloved.

About the Author

Susan Stinson is the author of the novels *Venus of Chalk*, *Fat Girl Dances with Rocks*, and *Martha Moody* and a collection of poetry and lyric essays, *Belly Songs*. Her work—which has appeared in the *Public Humanist*, *Kenyon Review*, *Seneca Review*, *Curve*, *Lambda Book Report*, and the *Women's Review of Books*—has received the Outstanding Mid-Career Novelist Award from the Lambda Literary Foundation as well as a number of fellowships. Born in Texas and raised in Colorado, she lives in Northampton, Massachusetts, where she is Writer in Residence at Forbes Library and also an editor and writing coach.

Short story collections and novels from Small Beer Press
for independently minded readers:

Georges-Olivier Châteaureynaud, *A Life on Paper: Stories*
"The celebrated Châteaureynaud."—*New York Times*

Karen Joy Fowler, *What I Didn't See and Other Stories*
"An exceptionally versatile author."—*St. Louis Post-Dispatch*

Greer Gilman, *Cry Murder! in a Small Voice*
Ben Jonson, playwright, poet, satirist . . . detective

Elizabeth Hand, *Errantry: Stories*
"Elegant nightmares, sensuously told."—*Publishers Weekly*

The Unreal and the Real: Selected Stories of Ursula K. Le Guin
Two volumes: *Where on Earth* & *Outer Space, Inner Land*
"No better spirit in all of American letters than that of Ursula K. Le Guin."—*Slate*

Karen Lord, *Redemption in Indigo*
Mythopoeic, Crawford, Carl Brandon Parallax, & Frank Collymore Award winner

Vincent McCaffrey, *Hound*
"McCaffrey, the owner of Boston's legendary Avenue Victor Hugo Bookshop, succeeds in
conveying his love of books in his intriguing debut."—*Publishers Weekly*

Maureen F. McHugh, *After the Apocalypse: Stories*
"Incisive, contemporary, and always surprising."—*Publishers Weekly* Top 10 Books of the Year

Naomi Mitchison, *Travel Light*
"The enchantments of *Travel Light* contain more truth, more straight talking, a grittier,
harder-edged view of the world than any of the mundane descriptions of daily life you will
find in the science fiction stories."—*SF Site*

Sofia Samatar, *A Stranger in Olondria*
"Samatar's sensual descriptions create a rich, strange landscape, allowing a lavish adventure to
unfold that is haunting and unforgettable."—*Library Journal* (starred review)

Our ebooks are available from our indie press ebooksite:

www.weightlessbooks.com

www.smallbeerpress.com